The Haunting of Marcasite

James A. Best

ISBN: 978-1-62217-864-3

Disclaimer:

This story is all fiction as it all came from deep inside my mind and soul. It does not reflect anyone living or dead. Nor does it represent any place anywhere.

Dedication

This book is for all those people who were unable to see into the crevasses of the darkest nights. Violent storms full of hail, pounding rains, extreme flashes lightning, the rolling thunder and then a complete pitch, absolute black again. Was something out there skulking around amid all this chaos?

Were there really ghoul and werewolf creatures hidden inside all that darkness? Dark trepidations built up due to these dark, sinister beings amid every storm. If, one has ever wet their pants in a surreal nightmare they will understand.

Table of Contents

Marcasite and *gem* according to the *Oxford Compact English Dictionary, Third Edition, Revised 2008*

Gem: a precious or semiprecious stone, especially one that has been cut and polished.

Marcasite: noun;

1. A semiprecious or precious stone consisting of iron pyrite

2. a piece of polished metal cut as a gem

Chapter One

The history of this story began long before Greg Braden was born. Many centuries before the Braden family would move into the town of Marcasite in Gopher County. Some kind of evil, heinous forces or beings that lived way back then came out only during the most severe storms every year. The First Nations Tribes believed that the star studded Milky Way allowed vile things a way into their world. When the thunder crashed, a slit opened allowing ghoul and werewolf creatures to rush out. As the noise overhead increased, more of these terrible, disgusting foreign assailants invaded their lands. This thunder roaring and rolling overhead was akin to the sound of a buffalo stampede taking place. Incredibility of ultimate death filled the souls of everyone living on the prairie landscape back in those times.

Continuing loud peals of thunder made the earth shake as these hideous things swallowed up people off the lands. Above them it sounded like huge war drums were beaten with such fury by the ghoul and werewolf creatures. The ominous, fierce noises carried on for many hours during those storms, never seeming to cease. Superstitions or reality were hard to distinguish among this clatter, noise, and din even during those times. Amid the flashes of lightning, shadows ran amok outside in the pouring rain and hailstones. The tornado winds began to howl and shriek with extreme noise, like a body being torn and ripped apart. A painful, horrific, terrorized screaming noise spread all through the native villages during those stormy nights. Lightning and thunder followed by torrential downpours of rain and large hailstones falling down upon them. In those deepest moments, it seemed like the earth was being swollen up whole. Maybe as the elders said, these unholy, inhuman, horrid aggressors were creating diversions in searching for victims to sneak away with?

Tribal medicine men did dances inside tepees during the vicious storms to no avail as the ferocity increased in the darkness of the night. Medicine men were the powerful members of their tribes, known for their healing powers and making evil vanish to the spirit world where it belonged. They called upon Mother Earth to assist in protecting her people from harm when called upon. Medicine men continued to dance through the nights, asking their gods to aid in getting rid of these horrible, terrible, devilish ghoul and werewolf creatures from another dimension. Members of their tribes seemed to vanish into the deep darkness amid the flashing bolts of lightning, deafening roar of the crashing thunder, the pouring rains, pelting hailstones and screeching, wailings of the tornado winds.

Missing bodies would reappear, sometimes days later, in dense woods or along streambeds. Bloody skeleton parts with deep incisor teeth marks on them and other bones wiped plane clear of all flesh just laid there. The chiefs of the First Nations knew ghastly, horrid creatures broke out of the cracks of the star studded galaxy the previous nights to attack and kill someone. Medicine men could only do so much to protect their tribes during those types of storms, which caused these brutal, horrid deaths to come around. Elders from all tribes passed down this tradition to the next generation. Pictographs were painted on most exterior walls of tepees to show the history behind their tribe. Some were to expose the devilish spirits as they could have been in an actual physical form. First Nations People had passed down tribal history by way of using these pictographs. These very colorful, vivid pictographs were understood by all tribes on the prairies in the west. First Nations told these stories through each generation of their lives.

Yet Mother Nature was not able to hold back the ghoul and werewolf creatures that attacked native people on the prairies. Being on the open land was not the safest place for anyone to exist. One of the worst locations for severe spring and summer storms to drop down on them was turning their lands into absolute turmoil. Suddenly the skies would go black, with thick, cumulus and nimbus clouds overhead. Rain poured down from high above as the white lightning cracked and the thunder roared and rolled high above them. Their gods were upset at them, they thought, for some unseen wrong so punishment was being given out. Winds stronger than anything ever experienced came at their village blowing, shrieking, hollering, and screaming. Voices seemed to come out of nowhere as if someone was being ripped apart. During these storms the legend said ghoul and werewolf creatures showed up as shadows on their tepee walls. The faraway, star studded Milky Way let these things escape through to attack them. Such dark, shadowy, vile beings could not be killed by bows and arrows, which scared them even more. Somehow people needed to survive the horrors from these storms every year through spring, summer, and into fall. Who survived was never known before the destructive, hellish creatures struck among the abhorrent storms plaguing the plains from spring to the fall times.

Every morning the tribes made sure their people were all accounted for, and as usual, some people were gone. Men rode horses to look for the ones who vanished and found nothing. Other times, these warriors came across the remains of their people ripped and torn apart. Bloody bones and body parts strewn around the ground as if a half-crazed wild animal did this damage. Many times it would be days later before a body showed up unexpectedly in the middle of nowhere. Sometimes no trace was ever found of the missing people, before moving on to the next traditional hunting sites. Tribal leaders believed those who were never located ended up in a worse place with the ghoul and werewolf creatures. Village sites moved according to the seasons as different types of food were found to assist in surviving throughout the year, especially after the long cold prairie winter months when food was scarce. Once reaching their sheltered wintering places among the ravines, they were safe from Mother Nature and her harm. Snug among the rolling hills dug out by the glaciers from long ago were caves, plus natural windbreaks. Here the native tribe was safe, snug, and well hidden from any of their enemies.

One of those settlers who came to Marcasite started a newspaper called the *Gazette* in the mid-eighteen hundreds. This owner, named Russell Pagan, was from somewhere on the east coast. Russell carried with him a big, old box camera that sat atop a tripod. Russell also brought with him an old printing machine for his newspaper, which he would print copies from. This would provide one-page copies of the newspaper to all who wanted one. Russell Pagan hoped one day to print more than one page per issue each time the *Gazette* came out. His paper carried stories of cattle rustlers being hung by the neck until dead when possible. Bank robbers who were making a slow getaway were usually shot on sight. Sometimes bank robbers shot people while carrying out their nasty deeds. Bank robbers and train robbers were actually hung once caught and going on trial in the local court according to the law. Gunfights on Main Street were really important, splashy news items. Russell usually stayed close to his office on Main Street, hoping never to miss out covering the events. Russell Pagan might be fortunate enough to get a scoop with a photo that would be really important. Russell felt enhancing the image of his newspaper among his readers in the dusty village of Marcasite was very important for circulation.

The *Gazette* carried stories in regards to the violent spring and summer storms of such surreal, dreadful force. Tornado-strength winds, black cumulus and nimbus clouds brimming with rain, huge hailstones, bright flashes of sheet lightning, rolling thunder hit across the entire area. Extreme screaming and howling wails from the winds helped to hide the morbid, hideous foreign beasts in their conquest of rustling up some victims. The sudden ruckus sounded as if the ground was being torn wide open. Russell knew then for sure the First Nations Tribes were telling the truth of these demons. Ghoul and werewolf creatures just stomped the ground with such fierce, rapid-fire fury sounding like huge bass drums being beaten during those storms. Dark shadows seemed to quickly appear in among the flashes of lightning on a canvas of black. Just as quick, they disappeared onto the jet-black dark area again. Were they really there, or was it just a reflection from the lightning bolts? Tales were passed down in this regard of diabolic, atrocious, destructive creatures appearing in fierce stormy periods from long ago.

Reports came in to the sheriff the next day after each storm that someone or, in other cases, more than one person had disappeared. The *Gazette* was full of stories every year before the storms stopped in the fall. Russell Pagan never found out why these eerie, chilling, deadly events kept coming back like clockwork again and again. Fierce storms shook the entire heavens and the whole earth below with tremors. The fears of being torn, ripped apart, and gnawed upon by some macabre, vicious, spine-chilling creatures during those times stirred cold fears inside them. Everyone was really scared beyond anything experienced in their lives up till this point in time. After all, they left their original homelands to cross an ocean and take up residence here in the western part of this country.

Russell knew, according to legend, these horrid, vicious, damning storms occurred every year, and each one was more severe. There was no record of how many First Nations People had been killed or how many white men were killed in those times. Russell Pagan truly had trouble believing ghoul and werewolf creatures attacked the prairies during any of these fierce storms from spring till fall. In time, he would come to accept as truth the First Nations Peoples view about all this. These fiendish, unhallowed, brutal creatures snuck in through cracks in the star studded galaxy high above the earth. Even without eyewitnesses seeing any barbaric, heinous alien attackers during these diabolical, atrocious storms, Russell would believe in them. What else could have caused the tearing, ripping, and deep gouging on the bones of the victims? No such devilish beast had ever existed in the wilds of the prairies in any time period, certainly not any Russell knew or was aware of.

As always, he stored his thoughts on notes and placed them away in crates and boxes in his back office of the newspaper. Russell figured he would have time to go through them all and put them all in order. He never did get the time to sort his files out before he died that one quiet night in his house. Could it have been the fear from the hideous, accursed, horrendous intruders causing his early demise? Russell was a real, live, tireless newspaperman who never gave up on a story. Russell may have been shocked and scared to death by sordid, ungodly ghoul and werewolf creatures revealing themselves amid the storms. Russell Pagan died in one whole piece as he should have, not like others who were torn, ripped apart, and gnawed to death and scattered in the dense bushes.

Russell Pagan died in a surprising manner, according to most residents who lived in Marcasite for many years. Russell passed away peacefully in bed one quiet, hot night in August that year. A lot of residents felt that ghastly, macabre creatures with the long, white, sharp teeth dripping with slime appeared to Russell, scaring him to death. For Mr. Pagan sought the truth behind the legend of their existence, the vile creatures took his life without leaving a mark. The only proof of why he died seemed to be he stopped breathing during the night. The undertaker did not seem to find any strange marks on Russell Pagan's body before his burial.

A new owner would now need to be found for the newspaper left behind by Russell Pagan's sudden and unexpected demise that night. As he did not have any living relatives to bequeath the business to, it would be put for sale by the village of Marcasite. A newspaper was very important for the village to maintain in operation. Notices of the intent to sell Russell Pagan's beloved newspaper, the *Gazette*, were being sent out in the next ten days. The village council felt it could sell the newspaper fairly fast. However, the *Gazette* would not be sold for another two years before another true newspaperman scooped it up. Once again the news would be circulating around their village.

A Mr. Richard Garry was the new owner of the *Gazette* in Marcasite now, which was still in the same office as before. Richard Garry was a stickler for making sure what he printed and sold was just as accurate, honest, and in all ways just like Russell Pagan carried his business out. The residents were really happy to have the *Gazette* back in operation and looked forward to the first new edition to come out in one week.

Richard Garry had little spare time once he started gathering news and information needed for his first issue next week. He had taken time to read a few old editions of the newspaper shortly after arriving in the newspaper office. The old office was exactly what was needed for many years, with great equipment in working order. However, Richard Garry had never experienced any of the wicked storms that still ravaged Marcasite and area. He had decided to buy a house to live in a few blocks from the *Gazette's* office. Now Richard felt like part of the community finally as a resident, businessman, and newspaperman. This was also his dream of building a legacy to leave behind to his future family. Time would tell what his dream could amount to.

Chapter Two

Teagan and Candy Welland bought the *Gazette* almost ninety-five years after the late Mr. Russell Pagan started it up. Owning the *Gazette* was a dream they had since both were teenagers when they started seeing each other. Their individual families moved to Marcasite almost thirty years before they took ownership. They both decided to follow all leads to find information about the history of Marcasite, including all strange storms and weird deaths. As the sole owners of the only local newspaper, the *Gazette* allowed them access to files no one else had. Their office was crammed full of files from many years ago as Russell Pagan never put them in any type of order. They found the backroom office was crammed full with boxes and crates of notes along with lots of old copies of the paper.

Digging up information in essence to help in these horrific, terrible, deaths and unnatural disasters fell upon them. Both of them enjoyed being in the reporting business as it was a natural fit with their instincts. Both were good at finding all creative clues and then gluing the puzzle pieces together, or at least trying to achieve that goal. Explaining all the unexplained facts was never an easy task when people died under some very mysterious circumstances. Teagan and Candy would one day start to wonder if buying newspaper was worth the aggravation, fears, troubles, and work getting each issue out on time. For the *Gazette* was the one true love the two of them shared, other than the love for each other.

These evil storms that lashed out brought dark shrouds of clouds, pounding sheets of rain, huge hailstones, bright flashes of lightning, loud rolls of thunder. Roaring tornado-strength winds tore at the very fabric of their souls, the buildings, and the earth. Such shrieks, loud howls, screaming voices, screeching wails, and awful, dreadful dying sounds as if the earth itself was being ripped open! The newspaper owners recalled how the local First Nations tribal chiefs told them all about their ancestors' legends. At that point, neither one was able to stop looking for more history and hand-me-down tales. Teagan and Candy were quite taken back by all this wanton, horrible, terrible evil that could exist side by side with humankind. As they agreed, going back to the very beginning may provide clues to what is doing such unimaginable evil. How did these ghoul and werewolf creatures get here from their place of origin at the precious moments of the storms? What allowed them to cross over so fast with the fierce veracity for tearing and ripping the bodies apart? How did they cause these deep gouges on the bones? Why did these unholy, accursed invading creatures leave some bodies behind to be found and others they just vanished into thin air? Many families were tormented by the terrible loss and deaths of their loved ones. Too many times families would never have a body to bury due to these ghoul and werewolf creatures stealing them away.

Teagan and Candy knew going back into the history of both the First Nations Peoples and the early white settlers was important. Researching took time; however, it was absolutely rewarding at the same time. Filling the cells of the mind with information and knowledge was their main aim in life. The *Gazette* was honest, focused, and diligent in all facets of reporting in their own rights to enthrall their readers. Yes, being operators of the only newspaper around was ideal for this young couple. However, they were ill prepared for the many hours of work and the long days of travel ahead, as neither thought of or even realized at that time. Both had often talked over such ideas when they had dated back in school. Still, this business was their dream that came true, just as they planned, even with the doubts at times such as this. Giving up was never an option, as both believed in hard work, due diligence, and integrity. Teagan and Candy said those words combined to create their motto of being the best, being on time, and being the most reliable little newspaper possible.

Teagan and Candy were still sifting through piles of papers from the earliest records of the *Gazette*. Some stories revealed how scared and terrified residents became back then, and why. Anyone who intently listened and took in what was said should have heard the truth and paid more attention to the details. Not all settlers did or felt they needed to, because belief in such things was beyond them. Not all people could fully fathom such dangers from evil beings from places like the Milky Way. Ghoul and werewolf creatures were just imaginary, or were they? That very first experience had approached too fast for them too fully understand the concept in reality. Exactly as the dread burned right into their inner souls, the storm clouds began to slowly envelop the countryside. Storms in the open, flat prairies were not like anything recalled from memory of being back in their former homelands. Not one memory could ever match the outcome and effect compared to these storms in their new homeland.

An extremely, dry, hot previous month had everything nearly burnt, everything brown as could be on the tips. Not one cloud had been seen during the entire month of May as the heat from the sun scorched the earth and beat down on them all day long. Suddenly, at the end of the month, the sky became covered in black cumulus and nimbus clouds completely from horizon to horizon. Rain poured out, the hailed pounded down, lightning flashed, and thunder roared and rolled. Were those ghoul and werewolf creature running around while the winds were ripping up the dirt into mud balls? Strong, tornado-force winds sounded familiar to the gale-force winds from coastal areas of back home, except the shrieks, howls and screams got louder as the earth itself was being torn and opened up by some unknown force. No one dared to move that night until well after the sun came up in the morning. The storm had receded a couple of hours before dawn as the sun rose in the eastern sky that morning. Still, no one moved till the golden orb of the sun shone high above the earth as noon arrived. Fear seared them right through during the very first devastating storm that year. Fear would do this time and again with no end in sight from their imaginations believing so. Everyone knew deep inside that pure evil existed from elsewhere to pounce on them in the mighty storms coming down. Their new land contained the worst things ever encountered anywhere in their previous lands.

Every place started out as a small village in the late-nineteenth century on the flatlands of the west. Marcasite had a more sinister history behind it than other places had or could imagine. At that time, everyone wanted a normal life, or one as normal as possible after the experience of the first storm with ghoul and werewolf creatures amid them. It was that very night that settlers started to take seriously the First Nations' words in regards to the wild storms and strange events.

Some disgusting, sickening, dark reasons brought storms like these back every year from spring until fall. Storms may have come back more as no one really kept track of them since no newspaper was around. Year after year, most people just gave up, thinking the storms would stay away for good, which was not about to happen. A joyous, blissful existence overcame the whole of the entire society in Marcasite. One day their very pleasant, happy existence would be blown up in devastation and death by horrible, fierce storms bringing back long-forgotten ghoul and werewolf creatures to this village of Marcasite. They were ready for the annual ritualistic feasts to begin once more among the residents, swooping down in amid the heavy storms, taking away whoever pleased their fancy for their ritualistic feasts on human flesh, ghastly, harrowing beings appearing as shadows in the flashes of lightning amid the deadly night storm when they pounced shocked the entire population.

In the late ninetieth century, the village of Marcasite was being established with law and order, dry goods stores, saloons, livery stables, and various other entities. People were happy to be able to go to town and get what they needed. Sometimes they had to take a long, hazardous trip to Goreville if what they needed was not available in Marcasite. Either by horseback, horse and buggy, or stagecoach, the lurching motions destroyed a number of horses, many wagon wheels, and lots of lives. Stagecoaches tended to get robbed more often out in the open, as it was simply a scary, dusty, and very bumpy ride. The prairie seemed full of tree-filled, rolling hilly areas in places between Goreville and Marcasite. Masked bandits were able to strike at will at those points, stealing any money, jewels, horses, handguns, and rifles of all types before killing those who resisted. Could this have been the source of some of the dark, evil spirits springing forth from other realms? Some thought of all the outlaws whose bad spirits were being stuck on this side because the Devil just did not want them downstairs. No one really knew for sure if this was the cause for the ghoul and werewolf creatures on those stormy nights.

Chapter Three

Now in the early twentieth century, Marcasite was a much older, emptier, dirty-looking town. These open prairies were struck with periods of long droughts where nothing grew except dusty, dry, brown, tumbleweeds blowing around the streets bouncing off half-dead trees and old, cracked fences. Homes were showing wear as the wood cracked and split under the hot, dry sun. Some people stuck around Marcasite during these very sad, rough times. Others left for greener pastures, as was their wisest thoughts and dreams far down the road. For some unknown reason, the drought always ended unexpectedly as rains wet the prairies, renewing everything. Many of those who left returned, hoping to find a better future at home once again. Many of the lost souls, burnt out from traveling, often after working at menial, low-paying jobs, again returned to Marcasite, looking for some type of tiny comfort and safety. Most people looked like scarecrows that were put up in garden plots to get rid of pesky birds. With absolutely no real emotion showing or any actual souls left inside of them, they returned. People just wanted to be home in Marcasite once again, hoping to feel relaxed, happy, and content.

Ghoul and werewolf creatures had plans in place since long ago, especially for the town of Marcasite. Throughout their entire history Marcasite was theirs to terrorize at will, to scare, to harass, and to kill victims for fun, for their enjoyment, and for feasts. Now all their evil wishes were indeed ready to come true once again. The time was approaching to call the brethren to a very special homecoming in a way. Yes, these repugnant, frightening creatures were actually sly, socially evil, shocking, surprising, nasty, cruel, and loved every moment of the fear they instilled in people. After all, they had centuries to practice their sick ritualistic objectives in order to inflict pain and suffering upon the residents of Marcasite again.

Many thought and felt that coming back meant leaving hell back down the road among the dusty, dry tumbleweed-strewn roads was right. Just as they returned a real, wrong dreadful feeling of dishonest intentions crept right into their souls. Everyone seemed to feel the same way toward whatever existed out there in their homes in Marcasite. An unnatural fear grew continuously over them with a weird sixth sense of being watched. Over time those, bad, ominous feelings continued to loom larger on all residents. Maybe with all those thoughts of leaving bad things behind, they had followed them along the road and train tracks deep in the shadows with them? Was it possible all the past hardships were about to release and fan the forthcoming fears of the unknown? Ten years of traveling and no one ever had anything at all except the bottles buried in little brown bags. Now the time to come home for rest was filled with such an ugly uneasiness, cold fear, and a terrible dread. Why, they did not know.

Ghoul and werewolf creatures knew exactly when they would return home, waiting very patiently. From the days when they left till the days of returning home, those intimidating, atrocious, vicious intruders were stuck in their faraway, star studded Milky Way, all waiting their pending release from that Milky Way prison again to feast pleasurably on the residents of Marcasite. This decade long drought kept the ghastly, frightening, decrepit creatures locked away in the star studded cells. Without being released from their faraway prison, there would be no ritualistic feast on human flesh.

Most old-timers told tales of strange beings that came from out of thin air at times to destroy the peaceful existence of the times. Their elder generations passed down stories from the local First Nations Tribes about surreal, disgusting, horrendous creatures suddenly appearing in the darkest of times. Whether they were from the star studded Milky Way or further away, who knew? The ghoul and werewolf creatures converged on Marcasite in the southeast corner of Gopher County during fierce storms with tornado-strength winds, pouring rains, pounding hailstones, sheets of flashing lightning and rolling thunder. Each successive storm was worse in its strength, violence, and intensity. In addition, the storms with those really strong winds might have attracted evil without any intention of doing so. Bad things brought it back full circle to within the boundaries of Marcasite. Residents seemed to have forgotten the storms with dreadful ghoul and werewolf creatures showing up every year for decades. Supposedly, for centuries through eternity, obnoxious, immortal, gruesome foreign offenders made this area home.

Teagan and Candy came across records of actual sites where glacial ice sheets really did bury dinosaurs and cave people. No one was aware of the ancient graveyards under the ground even after the first settlers arrived. None of the newcomers ever asked about any sacred places not to build and cultivate fields on. They believed the lands that belonged to them did not exist among sacred lands of the First Nations. Ignorance of not seeking this from the First Nations elders would come back to haunt them eventually. Young children became rattled from the tales told them by others who were just trying to scare the wits out of them. Yes, a life they were about to experience over and over through many decades ahead would scar them forever. Some of the worst spring and the summer storms were yet to arrive, maybe with less havoc and deaths. Evil lurched ahead in the skies and shadows being unseen until the time was right amid the storms. Dreadful horrid, spine-chilling, devastating creatures smacked their lips, rolled their eyes, and smirked, just waiting in anticipation. What an ideal feast laid in wait for those ancient ghoul and werewolf creatures!

The *Gazette* carried stories found among the messed-up records in their office. Also in the office hidden away in dark crevasses were stories of police officials who were said to be scared of whatever was out there. Teagan and Candy had to search for a long time to be able to locate information on other factual stories. Now they wished they had taken the time to straighten up the files when they first bought the *Gazette*. The newspaper owners needed many more hours and days to clean up all the records into some kind of order. After all, they sure needed to locate stuff that would provide their readers with the proper insight in every issue. Concrete information and, maybe with luck, actual names of any witnesses who could have seen something. Again, the publishing day for the next issue of the *Gazette* was fast approaching as they researched longer every day.

The paper was published four times a week with no problem, except wearing out the owners at times. With being publishers of the four-times-a-week newspaper caused them to burn the candle at both ends some days to get every issue out on time. As well, they needed to sell the paper on the same day it came out. The two of them had thought about setting collection boxes in stores to help sell the *Gazette*. However, there seemed little time to do so with all the research, story writing and printing, and selling the three-page newspaper.

Teagan and Candy found many stories in regards to Marcasite being a small village on the edge of nowhere for

a number of decades in the past. This small outpost was
at the end of a dusty trail for outlaws with the law chasing
them. History was always being told and rewritten from
one month to the next—in essence from one day to day, in
some cases as it actually happened. Marcasite had its share
of gunfights on Main Street with these outlaws shooting
each other. Trying to out quick draw each other became
a sport on the frontier on the wild western prairies. The
undertaker made easy money from the law when it showed
up. Dead bodies in coffins lined up for inspection by
a sheriff who came by roughly every month according
to information they found. The sheriff would allow the
undertaker to bury the dead bodies at once after he had
identified each one. Many unhappy, lost souls on display
in Marcasite could be responsible for all the appalling,
harrowing, pernicious beastly creatures that attacked in the
dark, stormy nights?

On top of this Marcasite was miles away from some
of the farmsteads and ranches. During those early
times, settlers were left undefended against whomever
or whatever came out from amid every storm. Rifles
and handguns could not kill these awful, deadly beings
according to any tales passed down. At least no one told
of trying to shoot at any time due to looking foolish
and crazy. Teagan and Candy were searching for any
information about stories from the First Nations Tribes
and how their medicine men got rid of ghoul and werewolf
creatures. Their dances banished them back to the star

studded Milky Way after the attacks in every storm. This was very important to the *Gazette's* owners as maybe a visit to the local band to find out how the petrifying, depraved, marauding raiders were driven away? Would their medicine men assist them in telling how they banished the ghoul and werewolf creatures back into the star studded Milky Way? A very intriguing question loomed large with the local tribe.

For under the curtain of fast-approaching dark nimbus and cumulus clouds filled, bursting with rain, flashing sheets of lightning, rolling thunder, and huge hailstones along with severe, tornado-strength funnel clouds that were starting to rip and tear the ground apart to increase the loud, tormenting screams and howls, ghoul and werewolf creatures got all ready to pounce on the residents to find someone to sneak away with. As always, the next day would be a sad one indeed for everyone within Marcasite. Some person or more than one person disappeared in the storm the previous night. So far, there was no sign of where they could possibly be found, just like in all other previous disappearances. One thing was for sure—the bodies would be strewn around, gnawed with incisor sharp teeth, leaving deep gouges in them. Bloody parts with pieces of clothing were scattered among the grass and bushes in this dump site. As in other multiple takings, only one body was found from this incident as well. Ghastly, obscene, malicious alien intruders sure enjoyed scaring people and obviously loved the killing, ripping, and tearing up of the bodies. Feasting on human bodies somewhere and dumping them in other places. Even more, so was putting other families through turmoil of not knowing where their loved ones ended up. Ferocious, formidable, brutal creations hid them in a secret location far away from prying human eyes.

All horrendous, diabolic, atrocious creatures knew when their feasts were ready for them to come get their victims. Hiding under the covering of the cumulus and nimbus clouds, pouring rains, huge hailstones, flashes of sheet lightning, and rolls of thunder pounded overhead, as the storm hit its stride. Great shadows showed up among the crevasses between the flashes of lightning every time a bolt shot out. Tornado-strength winds, with dark funnel clouds, appeared to assist the ghoul and werewolf creatures in finding victims once again amid the storm. Someone or more than one person was going to be missing in the morning as usual. Stories like these always got Teagan and Candy's attention, urging them to include them in the next issue of the *Gazette* for everyone to read for information about the past.

During trying times, some wondered why all stuff occurred only around Marcasite. Just then, out of the corner of someone's sharp eyes, shapes were seen in the sandy, dusty air on the gravel road. As drivers tried to maneuver down the road without swerving to avoid what was not there. As it was, the stories of the diabolic, hellish, antagonistic creatures rushed through the drivers scared, very irrational minds. Everything happens for a reason; how could residents blame these unseen forces for appearing in dust from the gravel roads? At times, crazy theories were thrown around, such as circumstances being out of their own control, or were they? Why had ghoul and werewolf creatures picked Marcasite to feed upon? Was theirs a method for madness aimed at the residents? What had they done to create such havoc, death, and destruction? Why had people disappeared from the population into thin air?

As the area population continually increased, the pressure to expand Marcasite from a small village into a larger commercial center increased. Traveling to Goreville took too much time away from their families, farms, ranches, and local activities. Farmers needed to be closer to their suppliers for fuel, seed, and getting other farm supplies. All beef, pork, geese, chickens, turkeys, eggs, and all grains had to reach far-flung markets as well. These costs of getting goods to markets for farmers were reaching a point of breaking these ranchers and farmers. Marcasite needed to ensure all the residents inside the town and area had access to markets to make money after a long-running recession due to the last drought. Nothing was ever easy, and making Marcasite in the southeast corner of Gopher County into a true residential and commercial gem was not going to be easy. This had to be done to make life easier and better for everyone in Marcasite. Their town was waiting to be built into a beautifully formed monument on the open prairie in the corner of Gopher County. All those residents wanted to raise a family in Marcasite and did all they could to ignore the stories.

Top agricultural representatives soon arrived in Marcasite to hold meetings to move plans ahead for everyone concerned. Anything asked about needed to be analyzed over and over, which became annoying. Their present system had been a sore point that festered for a long time. Now it seemed more cumbersome trying to build a central place for all places required. It would be six months before a formal agreement could be struck with all stakeholders in one building to hold a vote. Feedlots, stockyards and slaughter houses all were needed to be built as fast as possible due to the lengthy delay in getting the new agreement signed. Grain elevators needed to be erected along the siding for the trains to load grain cars to ship it all to markets.

Being an organized force made the government realize their part must be done immediately. To show and establish considerate action on the government's side, it needed to be implemented now! A cross-country railroad was already laying spur tracks to come here. Once rail tracks were laid down, this would enable Marcasite to achieve the elusive status that gem on the prairies. How right they were, except not in their way of thinking as a real gem, as all ghoul and werewolf creatures were still hidden away in the shadows, watching patiently as their feast grew. At the right moment, the awful, screaming, deadly rage would come down upon all these unsuspecting people as in centuries past where Marcasite now sat.

Hidden secret forces from the star studded Milky Way was ready to pounce and ruin life at their moment in time. However, no one understood or saw them coming down the road of storms that were due in the skies. With all the friction in society, something knew the time to strike was approaching slowly yet effectively. Especially with those ghoul and werewolf creatures history, it should have allowed everyone to keep both their eyes wide open. In addition, the cycle of disaster was not on anyone's radar as more daily important issues were in the forefront. Evil knew well ahead of time humans would pay a price for lapses in general thoughts and memories. Ordinary people could not be expected to keep aware of these nuances of abominable, macabre, repugnant foreign aggressors awaiting them. No one was able to really forecast when a storm would bring out these ghoul and werewolf creatures from the worst, darkest nights of the year. No one wanted to willingly recall when the last deadly storm had struck Marcasite.

Continuous, intensive, strongly applied pressure came upon the government as the next election was close at hand. No government wanted to be kicked out and be blamed for the mismanagement or incompetence of power, which could very well happen if these talks broke down before that deadline date. Bright minds, strong hands, and committed souls passed the final written agreement into law just days before the expiration date. A positive prospective of winning reelection just a couple of months away seemed to be a sure thing for this beleaguered, tired old government.

Fools would soon be dropped like rocks into a deep lake sinking to the bottom as the air bubbles rose to the surface. Beings from afar were approaching like laser beams to assist in those days ahead. Yet no one felt any of those cold, ugly, dreadful feelings in the air rushing, reaching out to all residents of Marcasite. One day, all the residents would awake with a certain, cold fear and guilt for not seeing with open eyes that real evil was among them sooner than expected.

That government was defeated even though the concerns that tested their mettle were passed. What the voters said stung them, hurt them, and that party never recovered after being rebuked. All those tired old politicians in those fancy pants knew what being ashamed was. Shame burnt into the soul and could not be compared to anything. Voters and any politics are strange bedfellows, even in good times. Something just made the voters across vast areas aware of that electoral power was theirs to wield. Banding together they could force any political party to bend and break like the trees caught in a massive class-five tornado, touching the ground from the force of the wind, snapping off at the ground as the strength increased hour by hour until no hope was left of surviving. One day the sun shines on a person, and the next the storms fall on that person.

Chapter Four

In addition, things from another dimension were with
them, doing all this for their own reasons, knowing
full well and understanding how a feeding frenzy
of young souls was coming their way. Cracks existed in
the Milky Way for them to slip back into the reality of
this place. Scary things were honing in on Marcasite in
Gopher County like a tractor beam aimed from a faraway
landmark. Around the rural area, there existed a lot of
abandoned, derelict houses from past times. In deep
retrospect, just maybe the ghoul and werewolf creatures
were in their hiding places already. The Milky Way may
have released these evil beings sooner than expected from
their prison in the stars. For these heinous, demonic,
nefarious conspirators could not have been more joyful
and sincere, being in this very great, imposing position.
Dark spirits were hidden away from the prying eyes of the
residents, who had no clue they had arrived. With many
shrieks, howls and loud hollering voices hidden behind the
rolling thunder overhead, they struck at will. Along with

extreme flashes of sheet lightning, the heavy pouring rains, hailstones pelting the ground, the dark shadows appeared amid all this. Hungry barbaric, murderous, gruesome invaders came to indulge on as many residents as they could that very night. Wicked, evil beings carried out their practices over many centuries, being self-taught through time. Ghoul and werewolf creatures knew exactly when to carry out this mission of fear, death, and destruction on human nerves.

As in the past, the following morning two sisters were gone from the safety of their very bedrooms, Olivia and Hannah Samuels. Olivia was eleven years old, and Hannah was nine years old. The police could not find any sign of a struggle in the bedrooms or inside the Samuels' house. Something invisible had gone through the windows and taken the girls, without any fuss or noise. What type of things could go through walls, windows, or doors and leave no trace of being present? Police Chief Harry Rook did not understand or really accept that beings capable of such terror existed. Yet everyone in the police department was aware they faced barbaric, grotesque, long-toothed beasts from another dimension. According to local legends passed down, deaths, disappearances, and twisted destruction was caused by those things. No trace was ever found, because they seemed to float and had to have invisibility to escape with their victims. No wonder everyone was scared out of their wits right now in Marcasite.

Search teams needed to be put in place to look for the two young girls. Lots of people showed up to aid in the search for the Samuels girls the next day. Once the teams were set up, the search grids were laid down for the day. Then they all drove out to their place along the highway to Goreville to begin from. As it would turn out, each day became more futile than the one before. Frustration often set in as the time slowly dragged on with no results. Most searches took tons of time and effort that people volunteered for and gave wholeheartedly.

It would be one week before either body was recovered outside of Marcasite, deep inside the dense trees off the highway going to Goreville. This site itself was not one any person wanted to see for sure as two small bodies were scattered about. No one was about to say what took them and attacked them or ate parts of them up. This was another extreme sign of sickness, an act of evil by these ghoul and werewolf creatures that showed Marcasite as their feeding grounds for now and in centuries past. Both girls were torn, ripped apart, and gnawed on with very deep, gouges of incisor teeth marks on their bones. Some of the bloody parts were left attached to some bits of clothing, just enough left behind to help form the identification for anyone who looked hard enough. Olivia and Hannah's parents would need to be told of their daughters remains being found by a search team. Officials were struggling with what exactly to tell them about the condition of their daughters' bodies. Just knowing their remains being located would provide enough relief for now, according to officials.

The Samuels would hold a funeral for Olivia and Hannah later in the week after things sunk in and the relatives could travel to Marcasite. Two small coffins, with only a very sparse amount of bones in each one, were to be buried beside each other as sisters should. Neither young girl deserved to die in this fashion or to be buried with less than a whole body. Everyone in Marcasite turned out to pay their respects for the Samuels' two girls and their family. Once again, this dark day came over Marcasite due to the ghoul and werewolf creatures who fed off of them all. Father Zach Watson presided over the funeral service for Olivia and Hannah Samuels, as he knew the family since they moved into town. Everyone was in a very somber mood, and there did not appear to be many dry eyes in the church. Father Watson gave one of his best services that morning to say good-bye to both Olivia and Hannah Samuels. Two young girls, lost well before their time, were taken away to a better place to rest and wait for their parents. All the people followed the hearse to the cemetery after to say a final good-bye to both of the young girls.

More of these deaths were yet to come as additional unhallowed, fiendish, foreign beings were slowly approaching from the star studded Milky Way. As these ghoul and werewolf creatures were only warming up toward their ten-year run once more, as if to say to the residents of this place, Be on guard. We can strike at any time and place. Certainly on any stormy evening or night beware! We are prowling around for more victims to feast upon or take away to our hiding place. No one felt safe inside their homes when those dark, eerie storms struck Marcasite with such fiery, down-pouring rains, hailstones dropping, sheets of flashing lightning, cracks of thunder roaring overhead. Tornado-strength winds tore at the earth, shrieking, howling, and screaming as if it was being opened up. Devilish, abominable, calamitous attackers were creating hiding places for other victims never to be found again. Such thoughts, at least, were in the minds of all residents at awful times during the storms.

Yes, life had gotten better for all concerned residents including the government officials who were trying to help. On top of that, the new government seemed poised to assist in any way possible. Maybe the landslide that brought them into office was massive enough to do the good everyone wanted. Yet no one gave up on their future in Marcasite as the city was growing more each year through these bad times. The outside world was not aware of the darkness that straddled Marcasite. Not one resident wanted the unwanted publicity of Marcasite being home to the known ghoul and werewolf creatures from the faraway, star studded Milky Way.

Another darker type of landslide waited in the wings for the town of Marcasite. The loathsome, detestable, hellish creatures from another dimension in the star studded Milky Way were even more powerful than any team of politicians. One blustery, stormy night the inhuman, brutal, depraved intruders were actually planning chaos beyond belief. More than the last time, they visited Marcasite during that last ugly, stormy night a year ago. People had to be reminded about who controlled the world around those parts of the prairies from time to time. Ghoul and werewolf creatures could show up at any time during any storm at their choosing, especially when it was dark, windy, rainy, and scary out. Creatures from the faraway stars were ready to frighten anyone who was not scared yet by those ugly, mean, nasty summer storms. This was their sole purpose—to scare, tear, rip and gnaw on all the bodies of their victims. Other unfortunate souls seemed to disappear into the twilight of the darkness of destructive, alarming summer storms.

The small local grocery store had lost money year in and year out due to unavailability of getting produce and food stuff anywhere else. With no competing stores causing these owners any problems, they provided credit to customers who were in need to feed their families. These original owners, Thomas and Alice McDougall, had opened it many years ago before the tough years hit, yet they survived. Being Irish people, they believed in the real good types of spirits, mostly from the bottle. In addition, they were hardworking, generous, kind, God-fearing people who saw all types of weird things over in their former homeland. Thomas and Alice never once gave one single idea or thought to their adopted country being home to some of these dark evil forces.

Sprites and other unworldly things existed for centuries over there in Ireland. Some old religions existed over in Ireland for centuries; people were killed and executed for no real reasons. Religious wars and wars against oppression left many bodies spread all over the grounds of the counties. After all, souls were said to have come back to haunt those still alive as devil demons. Yes, people of normal backgrounds never expected to see things come out of the mists of the darkest, scariest nights in shapes they be held. These very experiences of seeing ghoul and werewolf creatures with their own eyes stunned them beyond belief. All over the island of English rule, people were executed during wars over the past centuries. Many a ship also crashed into the extreme rocky coastlines in stormy weather. Had some of these lost souls or beings caught a ride over to this country aboard a ship?

Ghoul and werewolf creatures only existed in weak minds, was their very honest opinion. McDougall and his wife raised a family in Marcasite without any evil, scary, or real bad, troubling moments. About that time, he started to realize the hardships of the last ten years could be explained by some unknown force or forces. Their general store existed due to the local need for food stuff to the people. At times however getting supplies was really tough for even them. Old tales of swamp gases producing shapes was maybe not farfetched after being around for a while.

McDougall recalled how his grandparents told him of ghouls, dark shapes, ghosts, and spirits showing up in the dark of full moon. Their very own Emerald Isles seemed to be full of unworldly and unmentionable things coming out of the wild mists in the trees and shrubs. Hard times made even Thomas McDougall start to believe in spirits or evil beings causing trouble.

An inbred fear of the unknown always crept into every resident during the darkest of stormy nights on a continuous basis, especially as unexpected storms struck and people would vanish into the night only to be found days later, torn and ripped apart, totally ripped, bitten, mutilated bodies left to rot in the bush along the side of the highway to Goreville. Skies would become so dark black with cumulus and nimbus clouds full of rain, pounding hailstones, bright flashes of sheet lightning and loud rolling cracks of thunder opened up overhead. The torrential downpours came making it so no one could see a foot in front of their own vehicles. Was that an actual ghoul or werewolf creature running in front of them in the rain between those flashes of lightning? Maybe the simple thoughts of seeing loathsome, hideous, demonic creatures were burnt into their souls during the long, terrible trips in the tough, daunting spring, summer, and fall storms.

Extreme rates of accidents on the road to Goreville were unacceptable to all people and the authorities. A new road connecting Goreville with Marcasite needed to be built right now. A twin, two-lane highway with asphalt covering, not gravel, would be built as soon as possible. Time was now to cut or run, as the old-timers used to say in those early days. A new highway was required for people's safety and to cut the long travel time from Goreville to Marcasite. Dust as far as the eyes could see hampered drivers' visions as they went down these dry gravel roads in summer. Winter driving was just as complicated, with snowdrifts blown across the road, blocking traffic in both directions. People thought the ghoul and werewolf creatures were to blame for some of the deaths on that highway, evil beings who loved to play games with the souls of residents, wherever, at any time, except they only attacked from spring till fall. Sudden thunderstorms often appeared out of nothing, filling the roads with pouring rain, thunder, and lightning, and huge hailstones. Could these destructive, fiendish, heinous creatures be searching for a feast on this road today?

Any time at night, a sudden spring, summer, or fall storm could erupt, filling the sky with an eerie perpetual blackness. Images of hideous, horrid, ghastly creatures would appear in among the flashes of lightning similar to shadows on a drive-in movie screen. Screams of sheer emotional terror and ice-cold shivers ran through the souls of anyone caught out on the roads during storms. People's hearts raced, beating at a thousand of times a minute as their blood pressure shot up. All due to these freaky weather systems reaching out and coming through swiftly and dangerously damaging whatever was in their path. That Milky Way opened a tiny crack and beings crept out pounding the earth over the entire storm struck areas for six months every year. People died torn, ripped open and gnawed upon while others just disappeared into the vastness of the storm.

Deaths took place and howls from the winds allowed the dark to come alive even more so. Screams, and howls along with the shrieks really sounded like actual human bodies being ripped or torn apart. Tornado-force winds made the earth sound as if it was being pulled apart to assist these devilish, diabolic, horrid creatures to hide their victims. Noise from the rolling thunder overhead allowed ghoul and werewolf creatures to find people in the deadliest, darkest, scariest moments of all the storms, just to strike, kill, and take them away to feast on the bodies somewhere out there. No one had ever found that spot where bodies disappeared into the dark rage of the stormy nights. No protection existed for people from these evil, feral, impious creatures in Marcasite now or in the past or the future. Fear was going to be a fact of life with the residents of this town built in the southeast corner of Gopher County.

Each successive storm seemed worse than the one before as the storms became even more frequent every year. Abhorrent, murderous, malevolent adversaries took more victims each and every year within the darkest, most terrifying moments of these storms. Cemeteries seemed to have new graves almost every month as if the weird frequency of these storms increased. Marcasite was supposed to be an oasis on the open prairie and a real gem for all of the residents to reside in. Raising families to enjoy life had given them hope all through every year of their lives. Yet their strong spirits would not allow them to give up the dreams and hopes deep inside; they had come too far along. Nothing was going to deter the hope and happiness ahead in their Marcasite, if they had their way. Except the ghoul and werewolf creatures had their own agenda about how life would be for the residents of Marcasite for centuries to come as always.

People wanted a future place where they could possibly lead a very normal, happy, family-oriented existence. They had elected a town council to deal with all aspects of running the town. Lots of residents recalled those bitter, long, hotly and angrily debated meetings, passing motions, creating ways and means for a bigger town to exist. Everyone seemed happy to receive what they needed or wanted. At least it seemed so. After that, the next step was to build a wide, very glamorous town, an awesome location that would make all families, stores, dentists, doctors, and other businesses feel right at home. A brand-new community full of pride, with a sense of being neighborly, a real life, reflecting true values learned, handed down from past generations. Yes, a real town on the prairie was going to be a dream come true, right?

Many homes of all types will rise up soon on the edge of nowhere to form Marcasite into a prairie oasis.

A real true gem of a town that their elders told of, always dreamed of, fully envisioned, extremely desired was coming along. An awesome vision did sprout forth from the dirt of the prairies. Just whose vision it was remained to be seen as the time was really close for an evil feeding frenzy. A fresh meal being created for ghoul and werewolf creatures based on new families yet to be created by husbands and wives.

A thought of the unknown dread creeping around in their area sent a shock of fear within everyone. Also, why pick upon Marcasite? Could this sudden population increase become the sole reason for these sudden improbable surges in evil energy? Cold, dreadful ghoul and werewolf creatures knew no bounds or cared for any as Marcasite was theirs and theirs alone. Many of these eerie, scary types from the old country told stories of vampires or so-called werewolf creatures. Some others told tales of waifs and eerie ghosts haunting places around the English countryside. A small prairie town was far removed from there to believe any of those tales either. Years later, people would come full circle in believing in sinister beings from a faraway place. Did their elder generations know or feel that abandoned properties may hold and keep secrets hidden inside? Plus, the swamp gases bringing forth beings from the great beyond soared in their minds. Once the storms started, residents would need to grab their senses, open their souls, and realize evil indeed had arrived once more.

Chapter Five

After all, it never mattered as to the placement of this town to these inhuman, diabolic, malicious creatures. Just maybe, instead of being in a hurry, some research could have been carried out, just to relieve those certain feelings of uneasiness caused by the depth of the truth behind stories from the past. Fear breeds contempt for authority figures in any location. Marcasite was no different, which was very odd or even strange, considering the first-ever-mentioned known occurrence was only decades ago. Even after asking for information, none was forthcoming from any reliable source. All the grotesque, nefarious, accursed invaders knew nothing could stop their arrival time whenever they chose it. For centuries, the area of Marcasite was their feeding grounds for their ritual killings and feasts. Over time, these new arrivals and older residents would realize the torment they were capable of releasing at will. Ghoul and werewolf creatures hid among the blackest, cloudless, stormy nights filled with pouring rains, pounding hailstones, flashes of sheet lightning, rolling thunder and with raging tornado funnel clouds all night long. These ghastly, devilish, destructive beasts dined on human flesh amid these storms with a sense of utter glee, taking people from their homes to places in the woods, devouring, tearing, ripping scattering parts, and others disappearing without a trace.

The *Gazette* was unable to find the very first sighting of these old devilish, horrid, vicious creatures in either Marcasite or Gopher County. Russell Pagan had a few stories of people disappearing into thin air after severe storms struck the area. Of course, there were never any eyewitnesses as to what took place in the dark or among the flashes of lightning in those stormy times. Then again, no one dared to step forward and to say a word back then, let alone today. The Wellands felt it very strange people were too scared to say a word about odd sightings. No rational explanation could explain why concrete, clay, glass, and wood structures were more important to them, everyday residents who paid taxes, raised families, went to church, attended other community activities, and still kept silent about possible sightings of anything during those stormy nights.

The unknown fear and apprehension that gripped everyone was very apparent even in those days. A very large percentage of residents or would-be residents did not want any bad omens to come back on them. Building on some ancient gravesite from centuries or thousands of years ago still was wrong. No proof was presented or found to form any opinion on those ideas around these beastly, petrifying, morbid foreign beings. Unknown, unforeseen events from centuries ago caused shivers to run up and down the spines of people. No one ever wanted to disturb the final resting place of past lives without giving any forethought on their minds. If the residents and would be residents really knew the dangers waiting to attack from the far darkest corners of storms, maybe Marcasite would not exist at all as it actually did. All ghoul and werewolf creatures at their worst danced with glee, knowing they would again succeed in terrorizing Marcasite as always. All the pleasures of bygone eras played over and over in their simple minds. Terrorizing, scaring, ripping, tearing people to pieces was fun for those types of evil beings. Successfully disposing of dead bodies in wooded areas as they gladly scattered bloody body parts all over, monstrous, perpetual, inhuman creatures got rid of the somebodies that were never meant to be found as they were hidden in secret places in faraway places in the Milky Way.

Thoughts of what may have actually transpired in those days scared them to their very inner beings. Were there any ancient rituals performed or pagan religious sites located around the area? History of this area was sketchy at best, as only some was found in the one university in the province. As there were some town archives to search through, even at that, information was scarce. Where had all the information gone to? After all, it would not just up and disappear on its own without some trace left behind, or did it? Yes, those unseen beings only wanted a little bit here and there until their time to strike came around once more. Ghoul and werewolf creatures were very capable of doing many types of stuff—hiding or misplacing items like human bodies after feasting on them was just part of their evil plans, hiding their tracks from prying eyes and those who hunted for them yet could not see them at all, secrets these beastly, brutal, atrocious creatures had learned over time with care and precision to be at their best when they needed to. Some unseen forces apparently conspired to conceal evidence of some really, terrible, bad, awful, disgusting ordeals. In addition, Teagan and Candy were not able to disprove any theory of fiendish, unhallowed, gruesome creatures coming or going from Marcasite at all. Yet they both knew those evil creatures were responsible for the mayhem, deaths, and disappearances of people over the years. Finally, the searches for lost, unfound, or misplaced documentations were called off by the officials in charge of the situation. At this time everyone became very edgy, uneasy, and somewhat scared actually of what was being hidden from the public. People inside Marcasite and throughout all of Gopher County had been perturbed by these strange occurrences. In all of the history, this area was either very lacking or completely being ignored and left without assistance in solving the mysterious occurrences. How could all those many records go into thin air? Teagan and Candy knew this was the wrong approach in this area of abhorrent, obnoxious, frightening activities over the years. However, their concerns could not be eased let alone proven without some doubts existing. Except, they agreed with the cops, there was something roaming in Marcasite, inside the blackness of the wicked storms, taking residents away.

Searching behind the scenes may give them the elusive key to this old mystery of ghoul and werewolf creatures coming around. The publishers were at peace, hidden away in their back office, slowly, carefully sifting through all the boxes and crates full of papers. Russell Pagan, who started the *Gazette*, had simply stored all his records in crates and boxes as his filing system. Teagan and Candy were hoping to find a thread of some information among this mess to connect the violence of today's storms with the unreal violence of the past ones. If it was possible, maybe Russell Pagan's stuffed records from when he owned and operated the paper held the key. The *Gazette* records were the only ones they had to search openly and at their leisure. Local police would not open their records to them, seeing as they were reporters and owners of the only newspaper around. Police Chief Harry Rook was a reasonable man; however, even he had boundaries that were unreachable. The duo was left to their own devices in the search for information in locating results on how to connect the dots between times.

Marcasite needed to be home for thousands of people, companies, stores, including an industrial park. Engineers, architects and planners were drawing up blueprints for a marvelous place named Marcasite as they were hired to design, an oasis right on the plains amid the rolling hills covered in trees and green grass tucked away in the southeast corner of Gopher County.

Prairie winds silently, gently blowing across the land to relieve the very stifling heat in the summers. These same winds increased the wind chills in the dead of winters. Still, a picture of pleasure in the middle of the rolling hills of the prairies was the driving force behind their plans. Marcasite was to be their gem no longer hidden away, finally coming to life in their day and age. One day, this beautiful oasis would reveal the horrible, terrible ways of the evil ghoul and werewolf creatures waiting in the wings for their long-awaited new feast of young and old. Deadly creatures lurked from afar in the star studded Milky Way, light years away from Marcasite, yet close enough to attack in the blackest of nights as it stormed at its worst.

The world had just come out of a war; people wanted normal lives, to raise families, have homes and be happy. Everyone came to find a job if they could handle the extreme, cold, harsh winter weather out on the prairies. Not many thought seriously of any past sites here that could damage adults or kids. There was no jumping to an unknown probability that just might turn against them. Sites of possible sour gas seemed inevitable as there was indeed oil under the ground. Swamp gas that bubbled up in the sloughs and the dugouts, according to the old-timers, were where dark images came from. Of course, no such source was ever found in or around the city to back up those wild stories. Tales from ages ago were not believed by many of the workers who came into Marcasite. Though most of the men were veterans of the Second World War, they had seen and experienced all kinds of atrocities. Now all they wanted was to work and get their lives back together one more time. Working in Marcasite offered them a chance to make a go of life and build a future.

Greg Braden was the first one who eventually came to see these appalling, obnoxious, fiendish creatures. Ghoul and werewolf creatures did actually exist out in the star filled Milky Way. Years later, this phenomenon was readily recreated as these loathsome, hideous, accursed creatures from outer space arrived again. Marcasite was an actual gem that did come from the pressures of the earth, just not the gem everyone placed their hopes and dreams on after their great grandparents had arrived. Greg Braden was only six years old when he was attacked by the abominable, repulsive, malevolent creatures from the Milky Way. Marcasite would go through more twisted, evil, deathly times ahead as the years progressed. Greg Braden was going to have many bad nights in his lifetime.

The Wellands still kept sifting through all the records about strange events and weird happenings. They still had to produce four copies of the *Gazette* every week on top of their research. Teagan and Candy enjoyed life when they were knee-deep in old newspaper stories about actual facts and weird sightings. This is what drew them to the newspaper, wanting to be owners in teenage dream. The newspaper was a challenge with all of the facets involved in running and operating it. They both felt enthralled by how stories came to be and how the top ones were chosen for the front page. Both enjoyed listening to tales from their grandparents when they were growing up. Any tale told by older generations held them spellbound with every word as it came. This fascination drove them to own the *Gazette* after getting married, and it became available. Now carrying on Russell Pagan's tradition of storytelling and bold type setting on the front page to grab the reader's attention felt good.

No agreement was in place to cover the fear and death caused by these dreadful, obscene, raunchy brutes, ones that came from the deepest, darkest storms that struck at will in the beginning. With shrieking, howling winds, tall tornado funnel clouds, torrential rains, huge hailstones pounding down, sheet lightning was flashing across the skies, and loud cracks of rolling thunder came from every direction as if the winds were tearing the earth a new deep well to bury victims. However, the storms ravaging the areas sounded and acted so much more seriously each and every time. Shapes were seen amid the sheets of flashing lightning, and the rolling thunder that followed shook the ground. These silent destructive, revolting, lurid creatures seemed to stomp their feet on the ground extremely loud in unison with the thunder that made sounds like hitting a bass drum extremely hard in order to scare everyone. Could all this have been created by a number of unknown ghoul and werewolf creatures from the dark side of the Milky Way? No other explanation seemed to be available or feasible; something evil took people away late in the blackest and stormiest nights of the years.

As per all, negotiations with construction companies said they would need about three years to erect the buildings and things. Also, every agreement had in place a waiver to cover any late construction and costs over runs. Marcasite had never failed to secure anything in writing that may require legal fees in default against the town. All the main projects for Marcasite started close to each other. Maybe within about eight months of one another the timelines could be met. Time was of the essence in order to be able to achieve the lofty goals and high objectives laid out. A gem was rising from the dust of the prairie into a jewel of a town in the southeast corner of Gopher County.

Over time some, of the workers who went out at night said they had seen a lot of strange, weird-looking things. Shadowy images floating overhead in the storms filled them with dread, and cold shivers went running down their spines. In addition, to have these very tough, strong, hardy construction workers admit to being scared, maybe those tales of beings coming out of the stormy darkness were true after all? Others swore on the nights of the full moon well hidden behind that black nimbus and cumulus clouds a presence was felt that scared the whole crew.

Winds would come out of nowhere shaking their trailers as if to demand they leave. Just as fast as the winds swept against the trailers, images seemed to enter through the walls, similar in looks to ghoul and werewolf creatures. As they were known for heavy drinking, did this have something to do with these intense eerie, hideous feelings? As these workers knew, drinking always intensified their dreams every time when they were on the road away from home. Maybe the booze fueled the images and increased the effects of the storms while being in drunken stupors most nights inside the trailers, except for the fact all the workers would tell the same things the morning after each severe storm struck. Those tornado-strength winds howling and blowing all night long shrunk these iron-steeled men into shaking leaves from believing in diabolical, dreadful ghoul and werewolf creatures creeping toward them. As Marcasite was being erected these construction crews seemed to be mesmerized with the weird, hellish, malevolent occurrences.

Chapter Six

Another storm struck that very evening, with torrential rains, golf-ball-sized hailstones, sheets of lightning flashing across the black sky, followed by rolling thunder. Ghoul and werewolf creatures were seen running amok in this severest storm of the summer. Forces of evil had all the residents and construction crews scared to death at the same moment in time. Yes, one other person might disappear to be ripped, torn apart, and gnawed upon as the feast was being set up right now. Noxious, devilish, ghastly creatures returned to have fun and games at this exact moment due to their choice. Tonight was their time to fulfill a deep hunger in this worst storm to hit Marcasite this year. Enough past fears existed within the residents to keep them on guard to protect themselves and their families as the storm raged on in the blackness. As this storm grew in intensity, the deathly knowledge being one, two, three, or four could be gone by morning. These severe, tragic, seasonal storms struck with such fierce, destructive powers only came from the demonic, hell hound creations causing them.

The individual who went missing overnight was identified as Mr. Ryan Renton who moved into Marcasite with his family six months ago. Mr. Ryan Renton was young, yet a very good construction worker, moving wherever the work took him, along with his family of three. Ryan had a wife, one son, and one daughter who were going to be all alone after disappearing into the black of the night. Their families lived in another place far away from this deadly place of Marcasite; on the east side of the country was all the police were going to say for now. Police were providing all the help they could to Ryan's wife, Terri, their son, Mike, and their daughter, Carmen.

Ryan's body was not found after he disappeared into that scary, black, stormy night. Ryan's family held a small service for him with his fellow workers and all the residents of Marcasite. His wife could not send his body back home for burial to be close to their families. Ryan Renton was never ever found or seen again. They went back home a few days later after packing and hoping to ship all their belongings at the same time. The west had no more hold on them just a deep, sad gloom due to the sudden loss of a husband and father. Ryan Renton became a victim of an attack by the ghoul and werewolf creatures against the people of Marcasite.

Ghastly, monstrous, uncanny creatures were simply showing their natural haunting and killing skills for everyone to see. Residents of Marcasite were starting to get worried for their family's safety as this latest death and disappearance jolted them very hard. None of the others were right or just in anyones' minds. These horrid, beastly, morbid aggressors really existed as told by the First Nations elders many decades ago. Marcasite changed from their dream of a jewel on the prairies to a horrible, fearful, deadly, sickly haunting town. No one was willing to walk away from their homes in this oasis in the far southeast Corner of Gopher County.

A huge hospital named the Prairie General Hospital, the newest one for two hundred miles, now opened its doors. Insides the building were X-ray machines special ordered from way down south. Also, there was an emergency room, an operating room, nurses, doctors, lab techs, medical record staff, and other personnel, even complete with a psychiatric ward. Maybe someone knew about a future problem? Or was fate just planning ahead maybe? Who really knew the reason as long as it could and would function at one point in time? Whoever made this discreet decision about the psych ward knew about the ghoul and werewolf creatures waiting to unleash the worst, terrible, horrific damage ever on the residents of Marcasite. Images of many ghoul and werewolf creatures were going to suffer horrible problems on all the future generations of residents. One day, the new psych ward could reduce those feelings of fear and other disorders caused by the unseen evil beings.

Marcasite seemed to be on an upward or downward spiral, depending on how you looked at it. Construction seemed to be on target and everyone was working to ensure it was on time. Ideas of the dark forbidden past showing up with the ghoul and werewolf creatures seemed possible to many. Yet there were far too many reports coming in after each storm to ignore the chance of them coming back. Who would doubt their parents who explained the stories grandparents and their great grandparents told of these same frightful, callous, obscene attackers? Just like when the gunslingers roamed the prairie, no one believed those stories back then either in that regard. After people starting disappearing, the officials began to the check into strange events. Reactions of that nature were normal due to only having a few lawmen around in that empty prairie land. Yet Marcasite held a certain evil presence in its grasp that it could not release no matter what.

Now these days a very strange and different type of raider came sneaking around looking for victims. Crazy, wild spring and summer storms caused huge cumulus and nimbus clouds bursting with pouring rains; huge hailstones came down overhead. Sheets of lightning flashed across the skies; thunder rolled as giant bowling pins crashed into each other at the end of the lane. Shapes appeared in the dark below as the ghoul and werewolf creatures were roaming at will tonight. Seemingly searching for any victims among the residents, young or old, these things had no age preference. Ear-piercing screams, loud howls started up as the tornado-force winds tore and cranked up in intensity. The earth was being pulled and torn open to hide bodies in after they were done with them. All the ghastly, monstrous, brutal intruders created the sound effects as always to sound like mean, angry demons. At any point they could grab an unsuspecting person or persons and whisk them away to a secret hideaway to feast on them. No one knew where the secret hiding place for the ghoul and werewolf creatures was, except in the faraway, star studded Milky Way that could be seen from earth on clear evenings and nights all year long.

Sure enough, the next day, once the storm subsided, someone was gone. Another of those construction workers, a Mr. Paul Jameson, disappeared from his trailer sometime during the storm. Mr. Jameson apparently went out to the other trailer to use the bathroom and never returned. Marcasite police searched and could not find Mr. Paul Jameson's body or any of his remains that day or over the next few days. One local farmer got a hold of the police about a week later, as his dog found some bones and stuff by their barn. As it did turn out, the dead remains were similar to Mr. Paul Jameson's, according to skeletal bones, body size, with clothing similar to his and shoes matching the ones he wore. Mr. Paul Jameson was the second death to occur during a storm in Marcasite lately. These horrendous, long-toothed, murderous alien invaders ate part of his body tearing it, ripping it apart, and gnawing on it. Just leaving long, deep gouges on the bones as the only identifying marks to tell who did the damage.

Lots of fear and horror were being inflicted on the residents of Marcasite in every storm since spring up till that point. Police were unable to prevent deaths from occurring during the storms from spring till fall. None of them understood what allowed this or how such evil could exist only in Marcasite. Most people were aware of all the old tales of death and all the destruction that were wreaked on that area of the prairies from their elders. After experiencing the worst storm filled with sick, deadly ghoul and werewolf creatures, it was getting very intolerable on some residents. Moving out was not an option, no matter what did happen in Marcasite. No matter how desperate anyone may have felt at this point, giving up could not be good. Everyone felt that one day Marcasite might crawl out of this bad darkness and return as a gem for the town's residents.

The construction crews had a day off to hold a service for their colleague who passed away under some very eerie, deadly circumstances. As his remains were sent back to his family to bury, the service was in a large trailer on their site. Some of the men were not sure what actually transpired the night Paul Jameson died, except bad things happen to good men at times. A second construction worker was lost under the same very eerie, mysterious circumstances in a fierce prairie storm. A number of local residents showed up to provide support to the workers affected by the two sudden deaths this year.

When the land was surveyed, it literally was rolling hills as far as the eye could see. Heavy equipment leveled the town site way back in the beginning. Now the flat landscape would be filled in with green trees transforming the bleak emptiness into a glorious sight. Citizens would behold this reality and the awesome scenery then and in the future.

During all the digging for planting trees, not one ancient grave or any skeletons or bones crept out to be exposed. Plus, through all the construction and digging all over Marcasite, nothing was discovered by any crews. Yet that feeling of something eerie spying on their movements existed for all of the construction crews and residents. This new awesome town one day would awake to a real threat to the dangers from a faraway Milky Way. Or just from the swamp gas producing images of beings who came back from the dead? Mental health concerns of the citizens and their families would be dominant one day. Everyone was aware that no severe storms had struck Marcasite in a few years now. Being too complacent and relaxing about having no storms or deaths was going to come back to haunt them all.

Spring and summer storms lashed down with rain so thick one could not see through it. Hailstones the size of golf balls struck with such force they bounced off the house roof, the windows, and smashed car windows.

Winds of tornado strength hit the entire area fairly commonly. Loud, obnoxious screams and howls could be heard as the winds increased in power and ferocity. The ghoul and werewolf creatures came out from behind the curtain of true darkness. Rolling, roaring thunder made it sound like all these demon beings were actually stomping their feet in unison. Such noisy storms scared everyone who had recently moved into Marcasite, not knowing of the evil that penetrated the place. Even those who had been aware kept out of the windows so they could feel safe during storms. Those first few storms that year were an omen for the most evil seriousness yet to come. People that remembered the stories of the native elders who passed those stories on to their great grandparents were scared. Those residents recalled in fright the storms that brought evil down upon Marcasite long before it was settled. However, no deaths happened since the last construction worker died during the last deafening storm.

People were slowly moving into their new homes all year round in Marcasite. Once that occurred, they could plan how to lay their yards out in their own way. Of course, civic pride took over as the residents did try to outdo the others across town. Included were trees of every description plus flowers, sandboxes for the kids. Marcasite, moreover, was fast becoming what its name really suggested, a true gem on the flat prairie, a prairie oasis, a real true-blue paradise tucked away in the rolling hills of the southeast corner of Gopher County. Before nothing existed; now a major town had been born and raised out here on the rolling, green prairie landscape. A real dream had come true one day the residents would reflect and admire all that came about over these years. Marcasite was a hidden jewel, made by the pressures of the earth, built on past dead things under the dirt-covered surface.

However, diabolic, hellish, demon creatures looked down from the faraway Milky Way at their growing feasts below. One day they would unleash such unheard of terror, horror, and devastation on the residents of Marcasite as in times past. As they smacked their thin lips, rolled their eyes and drooled in anticipation of the homecoming ahead. Yes, ghoul and werewolf creatures loved to create panic, fear, and dread on civilizations as they had for many centuries through time. People were torn open, ripped apart, their bones gnawed on, and most of the bodies were eaten with a few hidden so no one would ever find the remains. Other times, the bones or what was left of them were in certain locations far away from their secret hiding places. These calamitous, dangerous, human flesh eaters had a few secret locations out in the star studded prisons to hide dead bodies for future ritualistic deeds. Some treasures needed to be kept close and admired at any time as a sign of their respect for them. Ghoul and werewolf creatures were sick, twisted, and greatly demented, according to all of the residents of Marcasite.

Families started to grow as baby booms occurred every year in Marcasite. Greg Braden was born in the second year of the baby boom as most of his future friends were. These doctors and the registered nurses in the new Prairie General's maternity ward were very busy for sure. I guess cuddling up during the very long cold winters did pay off for those couples. This was a standing joke at the hospital in every department in those early years after the boom started. The hospital was built for delivering babies as required to and other medical procedures. Lots of babies were born throughout those early years in Marcasite, which made the devilish ghoul and werewolf creatures very contented. If the parents and other residents had known ahead of time what was coming along, the fervor of having a family could have been slowed down.

In those early days after the schools opened for elementary classes, it was a source of pride for parents. Dropping off their kids to be on their own was exciting and thrilling to know their kids were growing up a little. Teachers were looking forward to using their educations and skills to help kids learn. As long as everyone was having fun, learning, and finding out how to get together, that was one lesson. No matter what, everyone knew these schools would be full with students every year. All dreams came true if one believed hard enough, strove hard enough, and never gave up. Greg was born the same year as his friends in the same area neighborhoods; it was obvious school activities would be important for all of them. Time will tell if all of them were going to excel or not.

Here are some of Greg's friends from the local neighborhoods: Lenny Farfeld, Janice Maribel, Caden McDougall, John Wallis, Teagan Sannerman, Abbey Brown, Bailey Hutton, Barbara Williams, Valerie Stockton, Bambi Payton, Adam Turo, just a few names. Greg would know more kids and lots of teens as he got older. Janice Maribel would one day become Greg's junior high school sweetheart. Marcasite's young population was going to have time to grow and mature as the new town grew around them.

The webs of life we weave sometimes become a real nightmare within our own minds and souls. Once filled with the awesomeness from our imaginations exploding into full Technicolor, the soul could succumb to dread. Filled with trepidations and fear along the way of growing up, Greg could not figure out, nor wanted to, about being haunted by horrifying, foul-smelling, accursed foreign beings. Even as he entered into the early years of being a teen, Greg grew unsure of his future. These dreadful, murderous, obnoxious creations took over his soul and mind when he was a young six-year-old boy in his closet during that one storm. Premonitions should always be paid attention to, even when we are young, he thought later on. Those scary, inner images can make the hair on our necks bristle and stand up—not fair for any one person, let alone a young boy of Greg's age back then, hiding in his closet. Such is life, because we have no control over bad things like ghoul and werewolf creatures. Children seem to have an overactive imaginations, or maybe they see things moving in the dark more than adults? Greg knew the souls of the young can see what all grownups could not grasp. Innocence can assist occurrences that do happen more than any other explanation available back then. Greg knew the vile ghoul and werewolf creatures were real life-like beings twisted creatures that haunted humans for fun. The creatures had long, bright white, sharp, incisor teeth with slime dripping from their mouths, disgusting grins, and huge, buggy eyes.

In addition, Greg's young life was compounded by some very unnerving, disturbing and unnatural thoughts potentially damaging to his brain. Could he survive these awful images scarring him at such a young age? Greg after all was only six years of age when these ugly sordid things appeared to him. Dark images of ghoul and werewolf creatures that entered from another dimension were right beside him. He tried to scream, but nothing, not a sound, came out of his mouth. He was petrified beyond his youthful understanding. Were those evil beings from the star studded Milky Way the same ones his parents and other people mentioned in talks? After these images left, Greg finally snuck back into his bed and never closed his eyes for the rest of that night. Greg thought about those few storms when his parents held him close to ward off any harm. He recalled the flashes of lightning, the loud, rolling thunder, the screaming sounds of the winds, the tearing, ripping of the earth as it fought against the wind.

Greg had hidden inside his closet due to the extreme, violent storm outside. Fear gripped his soul as he saw these ghoul and werewolf creatures smacking their lips, rolling their eyes, and with a huge grins spread across their faces. They showed Greg their very long, sharp incisor teeth to instill more fear in him. Slime seemed to drip from those sharp, gleaming white teeth in the dark of the closet that night. Greg was very petrified, unable to move as he wet his pajamas that evening while sitting in the closet. His fear of shadows he saw drove him in there; he was indeed aware of that much. He would always recall his mom saying stay in bed and crawl under the covers to be safe, and he hid in his closet of all places. Never again did Greg allow his fears to force him into the closet in any bad storm, no matter how fierce or violent it was.

He would never talk about seeing those devious, monstrous, spine-chilling creatures during that storm with his parents. Tom and Helen Braden had previously talked about the stories that were passed down from the one generation to the next and so forth. One day his parents were going to be shocked about his experience at six years of age when he explained that day a year later. Greg was a stronger boy than they could ever have imagined for his age. More experiences with ghoul and werewolf creatures lay ahead over the future years of his life. Exactly how many times had they invaded their son was never going to be known to them. Greg would keep that information secret for the rest of his life.

Whoever dreamed about these beings sure could seem to be crazy. Maybe Greg did have a problem deep inside from life before birth. Right then, he decided not to say anything or speak about these experiences, period! Being normal was all a six-year-old child desired or wanted. Fitting in was very important, so Greg would carry this fear and knowledge all his life. Why had these ghoul and werewolf creatures attacked him when no storm was still occurring? They found themselves a real live treat in Greg to play with now, unexpectedly though, for them. Not one of them planned this intrusion; however, they were happy indeed for this unexpected surprise. The nefarious, devilish, odious creatures knew children were more apt to see them than adults. Adults were not of the same level of innocence as small kids, so it was much easier to get inside their beings. Greg seemed to be the only one who saw them or heard these frightening, revolting, horrendous creatures. At least he never knew of anyone else as he kept things closed up inside him. How could he say anything to his friends about that night? Just thinking about the event made him shake with fear as ice-cold sweat ran down the curve of his spine.

Chapter Seven

All neighborhood parks soon filled with the noise from dozens and dozens of kids playing outside from one yard to the next all year around in the sandboxes building castles to making snowmen, snow forts, and climbing into tree huts. These young ones had it all thanks to their parents who built it all by hand. The pride really showed through each week on the nights when area barbeques occurred. Neighborhood parties were a festive feeling for all those, young and old. Afterward the kids would camp out in the backyards of the house closest to the block party. Parents became like teenagers again, partying up a storm, listening to music, and dancing in the fresh night air. Having their kids watch them drink never bothered them. After all, it was a fun activity. Later in life, this type of activity would come back on them in many ways.

Greg rather felt throughout his life something or someone from the other side was going to keep after him. He kept busy studying hard and doing lots of extracurricular stuff and exercising every day as he got older. As much as he needed a relief valve during those early years, a distraction from those beings was crucial. His teen years would soon arrive with all the formidable, heinous, decrepit creatures still inside, scaring his mind. As always, Greg intently listened inwardly of any sign of trouble from these unwelcome, scary guests. In the guise of seeming like other worldly beings to such a small child was indeed damaging. These detestable, demonic, dreadful creatures, Greg knew they had come from somewhere not of this earth. His parents said they came from the star studded Milky Way as they slipped through a crack during spring and summer storms every year. Lives lost centuries ago or hundreds of thousands of years ago came back, looking for a type of revenge. Ghoul and werewolf creatures looked for simple, easy targets to assist in total annihilation of this new place named Marcasite. Previous attacks by these atrocious, malicious, deadly beings haunted the First Nations People and probably the cave people who lived on these same lands.

Owing to the fact spring and summer sleep-outs relieved Greg from those scary dreams, they became an awesome retreat. The young ones were awake early, running around long before any parents came awake and aware. All of the aspiring future adult scientists, astronauts, or whoever awoke filled with tons of fresh energy. Summer sure brought out the best in everyone during those very warm dog days in July and August. Yet in another week, school would be out for two long hot months. Local swimming pools were very busy in the spring and all during the long hot summers. Some families went out to the local lakes to swim, fish, and camp on weekends to take in the hot sunshine. With lots of shade trees around to ensure no real sunburns could become serious for the kids. Kids were sunburnt from playing in the water with the sun reflecting back on them. At that time, they were all free to spend time as families wherever on weekends and on summer trips.

Greg remembers the trip with his parents when he was seven years of age. They headed to a park about three hours away from their home. Apparently, this was one of the places glaciers dropped huge deposits of sand. These sand deposits over time formed dunes from the strong prairie winds, whipping them throughout the years. In view of this, Greg never really saw or understood how this sand got here. Where did it come from? Any other area was covered with some trees and grasses. Not even in this desolate location did anything make sense to a young boy. Greg knew deep inside those eerie ghoul and werewolf creatures were more real as he sat in glacial sand deposits. Prior to walking and sitting in the sand deposits, Greg felt free of all those spirits or beings. Relief flooded his soul, heart, and mind finally becoming so relieved, very happy, and content. Yes, being here in this ancient site filled with historic artifacts made him smile. Finding petrified wood and bones from creatures older than anything he was aware of finally freed him of fear for now. Any release was welcome for Greg during that year of fear, dread, and scary beings attacking him at their will.

The three of them located a few small ponds of water in the sand hills as they strolled around. A little farther down the trail they found a lake for people to swim and cool off from the heat of the day. Tom Braden had stopped at the park gate and got a camping permit for a few days. Tom and Helen always loved camping and took Greg out often in the summers even when he was small. Greg was not aware of his parents doing this, as his thoughts were on other things. Maybe they found out about his thoughts and the images that haunted him? No way, because they were solidly trapped inside of him. Besides, this was a family vacation time for enjoying nature at its finest. Yeah, right, Greg figured what was, what will be, is going to be. Why worry about something he was not even able to do anything about? Yet Greg knew his young mind could be crushed under these creatures' constant torment. Fears caught up to Greg, making him lose his breath almost entirely that first day in the park. Greg was a very brave young kid, being only too scared to say a word to his parents about his ordeal.

These next few days seemed to pass quickly as the time came to leave the park behind in their adventures. Tom and Helen previously decided to head to another park about five hours further west on the highway right on the edge of the Rocky Mountains. Greg had wondered about the Rocky Mountains as he had seen some pictures on TV. They were like giant stone guardians standing watch over all the valleys underneath them, the trees, the vegetation, the animals of all sizes and species. All the many hours passed slowly as Tom and Helen took in the view along the road as they went. Greg fell fast asleep on the way to the park, curled up in the backseat with his head under a pillow. Tom and Helen let him snooze for the next few hours until they arrived in the outskirts of the park.

They woke up Greg; he was shocked by the sheer actual size of the mountains more than when he saw them on TV. Those rock-hard mountains resembled something chiseled from granite by ancient carvers. With snowcapped peaks and glaciers glinting in the clear, bright sunlight, Greg was amazed. How many centuries had these huge, dark, rock-strewn mountains been here without eroding away from the winds and rains?

Then out of nowhere, something dark shot across his mind. No, get away and leave me alone, he wanted to shout; however, he kept stoically still and quiet! Again he tried to shout, Get away from here and leave me alone. Not a word came out. Greg's mind did the talking for him as these shapes came at him over and over. Greg was scared and very nervous, as he did not want his parents to find out. He kept thinking they knew and took him on this trip to get him away from Marcasite for his own sake. For seven years old, he was smart enough to know and understand that he was being haunted. Ghoul and werewolf creatures found him again, which Greg was not able to figure out. Fear was turning his very tiny soul into a great pile of mush, scaring and searing him beyond belief. Greg did not want his parents to see him like this; maybe he could say it was car sickness? However, Greg felt the ice-cold feelings brought on by the ghoul and werewolf creatures being inside of him again. Just leave me alone and go back to where you came from right now, he really wanted to shout, except nothing came out of his mouth. How or why did they keep choosing him to come after anywhere or anytime? Was Greg marked from birth to be inhabited by ghastly, malicious, unholy intruders in his dreams? To Greg, it was feeling as if a beacon was inside his body to be honed in on by these disgusting, sick things.

It was just his mind waking up from a long, long snooze as those things attacked him. Greg knew deep down nothing good came about when these disgusting, unhallowed, gruesome creatures came circling around in his soul and mind. What's more, he felt stable, or was he feeling this due to being scared to death? Definitely being afraid and slowly processing the info may make sense. No one will ever know about his moments of being out there alone among the evil coming to this world. For being so very young, Greg Braden knew a lot about something trying to change him, for sure. Somehow, it never felt good knowing a part or one part of his future was going to haunt him. One may say Greg was a portal into the past or future, or just a vehicle for devilish, horrid, brutal creatures to enter into at will. At this stage, Greg was now seven years old and dealing with things no adult could or would comprehend and remain sane. Yet he hung onto reality with strength and courage beyond his youthfulness of his age group. Greg was concentrating on looking at the huge mountains to reduce the effect and strain of these ghoul and werewolf creatures on his entire mind and soul. Greg learned over the last year to build a strong willpower due to using it in many strange hauntings by monstrous, hideous, abhorrent creatures.

Maybe a spot in the Milky Way actually allowed these things to escape to attack the earth throughout time? Repulsive, fiendish, deadly beings were running amok in the very blackest, cloudiest nights of the stormiest seasons all over Marcasite. There were times when shadows could not be seen on the grass or the ground in front of people who were stupid enough to go out for a walk. The worst storms, according to the locals, opened the portals for ghoul and werewolf creatures to pass through from the Milky Way. Tornado-force winds tore the earth open to assist demons in order to help the foreign creatures to take people away. As the shrieks and howls grew in intensity, Greg crawled even deeper under his blankets during those storms. All youngsters and teens got scared and worried when the storms struck with such fierce intensity above them. As the loud, rolling thunder grew more ominous and the sheets of lightning flashed even faster, the rain poured down harder, and hailstones bounced off the house windows and the roofs overhead. Children were more apt to see the shapes of ghoul and werewolf creatures than older teens and adults on their windows. Tornado funnels twisted the darkness into a complete black blanket over the lands due to the force of the winds. Through the flashes of sheet lightning, people swore they saw frightful, macabre, harrowing creatures creeping about outside. The overactive imaginations grew as these storms tore at children, teens, and adults. How such terror and horror could exist in their world and inside their town scared everyone.

His first experience seeing one of the accursed, beastly, hellish creatures was in his closet during a storm. Scared would not be the right word for a six-year-old boy to behold such demon things. Hideous, barbaric, calamitous creatures were said to come out during the heaviest, wettest, darkest, fiercest storms every year from spring till fall. Greg became so scared he had hidden inside his closet only to find out it really was the worst place to be. Not at any time did he want anything eating him or crawling in beside him. All youngsters were really afraid of the infernal, unholy, petrifying creatures due to listening to stories late at night. Greg was worried they could take him away to some dark place and rip his body apart. A thought of never, ever seeing either of his parents again was a real fear inside him. Or they would never find him, as his parents said happened to many people before?

Greg knew all these stories had been passed down from the First Nations Tribes who told them to the first white settlers. His parents had told him many times of the history behind Marcasite and Gopher County. Greg kept recalling the stories, hoping the ghoul and werewolf creatures might understand how afraid he was and leave him alone. *Why are you picking on me?* Nothing allowed him to tell them in an audible way. Greg shook with fear inside, not wanting his parents to be aware of his suffering.

The family would spend another week trekking around the eastern side of these Rocky Mountains. Sharing the sights and sounds will be great memories for storytelling among his friends. They cooked the fish they caught, along with baked potatoes and vegetables over wood fires that made the food taste excellent. Pictures of everything they had seen and done took up all their rolls of film. Their holiday was wrapping up as they had to pack up the car with all their camping gear. About an hour later, the three adventurers left the park for home, heading east into the rising sun. As it rose higher, the sun shone hotter during the long drive home along the highway. A warm day was always welcome after a great holiday to keep the memories alive inside with no other thoughts interfering.

Greg prayed and hoped these ghoul and werewolf creatures were lost somewhere back there along the trails in the mountains. Their past identities were unknown, staying absent at all costs as Greg kept his mind closed. Shadow people were good at playing games at any time and place of their choosing. Greg felt the same way in regards to the fear within himself; it was personal and no one else's to play with. An ice-cold dread buried deep in his soul, so frozen not even a hot bath or shower could ease or erase these feelings. Any idea of covering up with extra blankets to try and relieve these symptoms was ridiculous. Ghoul and werewolf creatures were able to poke their heads inside the blankets baring their long, sharp, white incisor teeth in awful grins with slime dripping off, scaring Greg half to death.

Greg did manage to fall asleep on the way back home and slept like a log for a while at least. This was one time he seemed to escape the heinous, barbaric, calamitous aggressors within his soul and mind. Greg was yet to suffer from any sudden attack during their return trip, only feeling at complete inner peace, which was good after all the excitement from the first day of their trip when Greg awoke. Summer holidays were a time to feel good about as they went away in search of adventures, for trinkets, going fishing, camping, and all the good things. Yes, young kid wanted these days to arrive to get away from Marcasite and see other places. Coming home to swap good stories, experiences, and their fun-time summer exploits were going to be cardinal rules for Greg and his friends.

Suddenly, he felt a certain ice-cold dread filling his being from top to bottom. Greg lay there, not moving a muscle due to the fear of being woken with the ghoul and werewolf creatures crawling deep inside his small being again, not really wanting to alert his parents to his thoughts either. Scary images were appearing behind his eyelids yet he managed to squeeze them tightly closed. Why attack now, and how did they keep finding him? A far-off crack in the Milky Way or someplace really allowed them to find him at will. To all very young children, this was a very true and really scary reality. Greg was unable to even move one inch, pretending to sleep the rest of the way home. Someplace along the long highway going home, Greg fell asleep on the seat once again. This time, though, Greg had no more of those reoccurring nightmares the rest of the way home.

Time flew by as Tom Braden drove back home in one long, hot day in the sun to arrive in Marcasite. Tom, Helen, and Greg were all anxious to get home to get everything settled in fast. The evening was coming over the city as the barbeque was finally fired up for a meal of steaks, baked potatoes, and some veggies. Helen threw an apple pie together and put it in the oven really fast. Greg loved his mom's baking, as they all smiled from the hot, fresh smells and looked forward to all the great tastes of supper. Yes, barbeques took time to cook the coals to the right temperature while the apple pie cooked in the oven so everything could be done about the same time to eat dinner before too late. Tom, Helen, and Greg ate out on the picnic table in the backyard under another clear, starry sky. A hot, freshly baked apple pie was cooling while they ate, recalling a few events from the trip they had just been on.

Chapter Eight

The moon was full overhead, shining brightly amid the many stars and constellations above. Yes, a moon was good to watch as its different sections appeared throughout each month. The full moon was said to bring strange and odd activities to all parts of the world during that phase. As in past events of similar nature, the full moon got blamed for all the problems. Erupting volcanoes, storms on land and over water, tornados and hurricanes were some of the events blamed on the bright full-faced moon.

People looked back in old records about full moons that brought out the sordid, horrible, brutal alien intruders out of the dark. More trouble happened around the time of full moons than any other period of time annually according to most scientific report. The pull of the moons and the earth's gravity pulling against each heavenly body did damage to the Milky Way's lining in outer space. This actually caused various secret doors within the Milky Way to open releasing ghoul and werewolf creatures upon the earth. Storms that came along with the full moons were more violent, vicious, and deadly than others. Stories were told of diabolic, fiendish, beastly creatures being spawned from the Milky Way under the cover of the darkness of storm clouds. Could all this be true in accordance with the legends passed down from one generation after another?

All the storms came with such extreme fierce, gusting winds, walls of pouring rain, sheets of flashing lightning, rolling thunder, and huge hailstones. All this natural disorder could never explain the ominous attacks from depraved, harrowing, alarming creatures during the worst storms of the year from the spring till fall. Even as the full moon was being hidden behind those dark storms clouds, formidable, macabre, diabolic creatures attacked, taking whoever they wanted at will. Tearing, ripping, and gnawing on human beings and leaving bodies in open locations in the woods were their ritual habits. Stories from the Native Elders told of the repulsive, demonic, hideous monsters attacking their people, taking some away amid these bad storms. Native medicine men were the ones who drove these sick, horrible, twisted, vicious killers and kidnappers back to the other side. Their gods assisted in driving these vile forces back to the faraway, star studded Milky Way. Everyone was able to see the many stars in the Milky Way but not the hole for ghoul and werewolf creatures to escape from up there. Where was any opening that allowed these creatures to escape from way out there?

Could the opening be seen by the human eye, or was it hidden away from prying eyes?

As the legend says, every year, the ghoul and werewolf creatures returned to carry their rituals out again in the worst storms for six months. Marcasite was home for these ghoul and werewolf creatures to roam among the blackest, cloudiest stormy nights with sheets of extreme flashing lightning, loud, rolling thunder, pouring rains, hailstones thudding down from up above, tornado winds with huge funnel clouds twirling around faster and faster. Shadows of the morbid, accursed, marauding foreign beings were seen in the storms, searching for victims for a feast. Winds seemed to make the screams and howls become alive as if someone being torn and ripped apart. As the tornado winds churned faster, the ground was being opened up to help the depraved, pernicious, revolting creatures in locating hiding places for bodies. Imaginations grew more intense inside everyone's minds as the outside noises increased in fury. Fear gripped the souls of the residents of this town in each storm from springtime till fall. No one knew who would disappear next to be found torn, ripped apart, and gnawed upon in the woods along the highway to Goreville. There would be others who were taken away to be lost forever out there somewhere.

Greg wondered if the brutal, horrendous, grotesque creatures were part of this cracked door that opened right now as he looked upward. What if these dark souls became constant in his mind to drive him to an unstable life?

Greg just wondered aloud after his parents went inside. *Why me at such a young age?* Many years into the future, Greg would continue to see ghoul and werewolf creatures attacking him time and time again. Being shocked in this manner, his entire system might cause him to end up in the psych ward at the local hospital. Suddenly, he felt like being completely controlled by a foreign source from a realm far, far away. His screams were trapped deep inside once more with no release as these dark entities pulled at his sanity. These images were searing his spirit to the core for all time, each and every time. Tears came pouring down his cheeks as he sat immobilized with fear such as only he had experienced rolled over him again. Greg felt completely helpless as the creatures creased his soul once again that night. How could he keep the tough exterior alive while being afraid inside? His sanity was on the line right at this very moment as he laid outside looking up at the sky.

Greg's experiences of ghoul and werewolf creatures already slipping inside his soul over the last year hurt a lot. Tales from his grandparents and parents may have given his mind a scare. Or was it because his mom, Helen Braden, had a rough delivery when he was born? Greg never wanted or desired to find out why he became a portal for haunted spirits. Society's rules of disorders of the mind did not take into account the ancient tales of the known or of the unknown today. One day, research would indeed be required to establish these things as real or not real. Maybe reality was a state of mind based on an individual at a certain time or not? In time, Greg's answers would arrive from sources that haunted him already. Scientific ones were years away and might never be able to explain these ghoul and werewolf creatures! Greg was losing his mind slowly each time, and yet he hung onto reality at all costs. He had to, due to not wanting to lose his friends, which would make him an outcast. This fear alone kept him going forward more than anything else could.

Lots of school years ahead, fun, classes with friends, meeting many new classmates and teachers lay ahead for Greg Braden. These areas promised to build young Greg into a studious pupil, hopefully. Dreams of success filled every student in every class in every school in the city. The whole city was founded on dreams, faith, sweat, and belief in all possibilities. Yet at this period in time, life seemed like a dream to the young students of Greg's age in Marcasite. The students needed to adjust to sitting in their school desks, learning different subjects every day, to go from grade one to grade twelve, learning many subjects to turn them into well-rounded individuals. Creating smart, wise, ingenious adults who could contribute to society's overall greater good was what teachers did. Life seemed to stop a few of them from reaching the full limit of their achievement. Yet Greg had to actually concentrate hard to keep focused in classes. Fear and trepidations came over him at times during the days of instruction through each semester. Ghoul and werewolf creatures arrived with little or no warning to his soul and mind. Every day needed to be taken slowly and reservedly so for peace within himself. Not to alarm anyone or give things away, he would not be an outcast from his friends or classmates.

Making sure the right values were placed into the teaching plans was important. Teachers were left a lot of latitude when they drew up those lesson plans. Teachers went to school for four years to become able to provide the right stuff for young kids of all ages to learn. As being the ones responsible for the final marks the students achieved, they deserved the freedom. Plus, the recognition from their peers and supervisors gave added incentive to teaching staff and aides. Besides, learning how to cope with anxious or obnoxious students was a learned art. In that time of learning, no teacher ever learned to cope with what was coming to crash into Marcasite in the years ahead.

Greg and his friends were now finishing the fourth grade and were looking forward to relaxing for the whole entire summer. Kids and teens were looking forward to days of swimming, hanging out in the parks, playgrounds, and barbeques with parents and friends in their neighborhoods. Such activities never got old to the local young or to the parents as everyone enjoyed a good time. In fact, they had picked up on the need to please their parents this summer. In fact, most parents did remark they were proud of their children on how well behaved they had become. After all their kids provided help for planting flowers, mowing lawns, watering them constantly. The teens just shone with huge, broad smiles across their faces. Yes, everyone was just filled with pride and enjoyed the feeling of being happy with each person and every family.

Chapter Nine

Most residents had made plans to get out of the concrete and asphalt jungle for a while every summer. By now some families had cabins at the lakes nearby or set up tents there. Even the Bradens would eventually end up buying one of the last lake lots available. Not this summer, for some reason, Greg, Tom, and Helen enjoyed traveling the roads to see if the grass was really greener on the other side of the mountains. Greg had not got sweet on Janice Maribel yet. A very cute, blond-haired girl who lived down the block seemed to be very attracted to him. Greg never gave those thoughts any time in his mind yet, as he was still dealing with monsters. His thoughts were on the fear of being besieged by ghoul and werewolf creatures when being with his friends. Trying to hide this fear was not something to have as a skill, and he could only when he tried.

Any excuse to get away from his dark thoughts even at that age was a huge relief. As the family got further away this year, Greg actually relaxed a lot more. Greg felt the same as always toward the horrendous, foul-smelling, forceful assailants coming into his young mind. However, summer vacation got the fear withdrawn from him, which he needed. Maybe there could be hope from fear and trepidation as an adult? How this thought could make ghoul and werewolf creatures come alive indeed scared him to death. These ghoul and werewolf creatures were not supposed to come around until a dark storm struck the area. Most of the time, there was no storm when Greg was besieged by these horrifying, intimidating, raunchy killers. They enjoyed playing with his mind, soul, and heart for sure as it was like a game of tag for them. To Greg it was cruel, unusual, scary, and unnerving for any seven-year-old child to endure. However, he recalled very vividly one year ago when they attacked him in his closet during that severe storm. Greg was hiding in there instead of staying under the covers as he was told.

On top of this their vacation was in a huge, wide valley in southern part of the nearby neighboring province. Tom and Helen had said a huge lake was there amid the hills with lots of fruit orchards around it. Someone said a sea monster or a type of prehistoric amphibian monster lived in it. Stories meant for fun had the opposite effect on their son. Maybe the difficult birth was to blame for his activities from time to time? Greg knew all about monsters that hide in dark crevasses in every corner, especially inside of him. Having his parents tell him about a monster was nothing he expected, right out of left field, which was nerve-racking. How could a prehistoric sea monster still live in an ancient lake in these mountains? Was this so-called sea monster a relative of the ghoul and werewolf creatures? Greg knew the dark things brought him here for a reason to see this long-ago-lost creature. Why could he know all this at his age? He just tried to not scream out loud about it. Greg knew his parents had no idea of the unholy, hell hound, uncanny invaders that attacked him right then. He had to stay calm as could be without giving anything away to his parents.

Tom, Helen, and Greg had set up a campsite to stay in while they were at that huge, blue-green-looking lake. Tom and Greg set up the tent while Helen made supper for them. Helen made hamburgers, hamburger buns, with potato salad, ketchup, mustard, and with roast marshmallows for desert. After waiting for the coals to cool down enough, they cooked the huge white marshmallows. Greg was no different than other kids, as he loved marshmallows. They stuck to his fingers as he pulled them off the sticks used for cooking. Licking his fingers off of marshmallows tasted good, and his parents did not mind at all.

They always watched the night sky, looking for comets and meteors with bright red tails against the dark of space. The first of the night's beautiful falling stars, coming through the earth's atmosphere, burning up as they went along, was awesome. Tom Braden told Greg these objects had been flying through space for centuries until at last rushing through the atmosphere landing somewhere on the surface of the earth as meteorites. Greg wondered to himself if this was where all those ghoul and werewolf creatures caught their ride to here. After all, that would be a fast trip from the faraway Milky Way in his mind.

Greg's eyes widened with fear, experiencing something like being entered by foreign, evil things. These terrifying, appalling, beastly alien invaders had tracked him down once again in this faraway place. Indeed, these creatures were out, or it seemed they were out, after his sanity. After that, Greg went to hide in the tent, preventing any monster from attacking him or his soul. Tom and Helen asked him why he wanted to go sleep so early. Greg's mind was swirling with fear; he could not answer, and it would not slow down from this turmoil. Suddenly, Greg screamed at the top of his lungs as his parents rushed in to find him lying on the tent floor. Tears streaming down his young thin cheeks and fully realizing something was not right. Up till that point, Tom and Helen knew nothing of Greg's many inner fears and the trepidations he faced. Their son had held these fears along with the images of atrocious, loathsome, impious creatures inside for a few years already. Greg was still unable to tell his parents what was wrong or why he felt so scared to death. He knew the time had come to tell his parents about the inhuman, malicious, noxious creatures that attacked him in the closet last year.

The words of the doctor came back with a rush, hinting Greg may have problems because Helen had a difficult delivery. No one knew whether or not this or any other symptom may show up. It was not like he was dropped on his head. Something did happen that night when their son was born into this world. Difficult births happened from time to time, the doctor said. Nothing else could be said to the first time parents, as this was all new to the doctor. Tom and Helen seemed relieved but not sure about the future back then. All those years hiding the fears came full circle crowding back into their minds. Memories flashed like light bulbs in their minds, as the doctor told them in his words about Greg's hard birth. Helen Braden had a difficult labor that resulted in a breach delivery that could have an effect on their son as he got older. Tom and Helen kept having these words running through their minds all that evening and all night. Greg was normal since his birth—why all of a sudden these drastic change of events? One day Greg would find the courage to open up about the ghoul and werewolf creatures he saw and knew attacked him in his closet a year ago. Would his parents think he was crazy and have him admitted to the psych ward at the Prairie General Hospital in Marcasite?

After a restless night, the Bradens decided to stay for the mental safety of their son. The fresh air plus some activities definitely should alleviate some of the problems. Indeed, they really hoped for relief to come as soon as possible. Maybe after all, their vacations could something turn out for the best for Greg now. Tom and Helen still had no idea of Greg's experiences, let alone about any ghoul and werewolf creatures. One day maybe, Greg would open up about the fear, dread, and scares he had gone through, how these things entered into his soul, heart, and mind to torment him when they wanted to. Ever since that first night hiding in his own closet seeing those monstrous, gruesome, malicious creatures staring at him, licking their lips, the long, white, sharp incisor teeth, and those rolling eyes staring at him, Greg never forgot those evil, dreadful, smirking looks they gazed upon him that shook him so badly he wet his pajamas sitting in the closet hiding in that stormy night. Neither being able to move a muscle nor being able to get up to run away from them was still fresh in his memory.

Greg was good as new the next day running around just like a carefree kid. He did not show any sign or any form of trauma from the experience of yesterday. Tom wondered about this all that day as they toured the trails. Even after there being no sign of the lake monster, they had no clue what scared Greg so badly. Pushing the subject might force him to build a wall against reality. Over and above that, their son seemed very sane as obvious to both parents. Neither parent asked Greg about what happened the previous night in the tent. Greg was scared of some unseen thing, and they left well enough alone.

Later the family took in a tour of a wine factory and vineyard. Greg wanted to try out the fresh grapes on the vines. The adults got a free taste of the wines they produced, and the children were given a tour of the plants to taste the fresh grapes from the vines. Tom and Helen enjoyed those wines offered up today. At last, a freedom from worry came around, and the fun returned in the bright sunlight of the day. Everyone had real smiles in the crowd that afternoon as the sun shone overhead. A great day to be around others took the shroud of fear away from the Bradens, especially Greg. Tom and Helen's son smiled due to his parents being pleased to be outside in the daylight, tasting wine. A true feeling of peace existed in this mountainous location as the whole family smiled and enjoyed the fresh air.

Slowly, the afternoon was coming to an end, and the supper hour was nearing. In view of the time, they decided to go to a restaurant and eat. In fact, they were early enough to get a table right away before the big rush came. They got menus and took their time deciding what to order. Greg wanted a strawberry milkshake, his favorite shake as far back as he could remember. After the waitress took their order, they discussed their excursion of that very afternoon. Besides it wasn't every day they went on a tour of a vineyard and an entire winery. The great taste of the fresh grapes would be something Greg could savor for the rest of life. He enjoyed the juice as it ran down his chin at times he told his parents, which made all of them laugh out loud with Greg having the biggest laugh of all. He told his parents the juice shot out of his mouth when he chewed up his first grape. Yet he only had a couple of grape spots on his T-shirt from the experience. Then their dinner arrived, so they ate and kept talking. Everyone there felt eating the food under the evening sky outside on the deck was awesome. The restaurant deck actually did overlook the green, giant lake beyond that was surrounded by mountains on all sides. Yes, they found a very excellent place to eat that night. When their dessert arrived, the sun was just starting to touch the peaks of the mountains in the distance. There was a very gorgeous orange sunset to watch as they ate their dessert while talking a little bit. Tom, Helen, and Greg took in the awesome, bright, pink-colored evening sky for a while. Tom went ahead to pay the bill before leaving the restaurant with Helen and Greg.

It would be around nine o'clock when they returned to the campsite. Tom and Greg built a fire to cook marshmallows on later. Campfires felt good, which made nature seem much closer to them. After dark, the flames lit the area up and cast shadows on the tent and trees around them. Tom was telling Helen and Greg to look at the sky for shooting stars as they always came this time of year. Apparently, a meteor shower was going to take place that very night, the first one of about four evenings. Greg was the most excited of the entire family, except for the foreboding he sensed at times like this. Seeing shooting stars going over the top his head should keep his mind settled for the evening. Greg's mind just wanted to see the meteors streak across the lower horizon with their tails burning red behind them. As most young kids, he wondered what one would look like after it hit the earth, or what the ground would be like after one hit it. Do they create deep craters sending rocks and lots of debris flying around the area where they land?

The sky was black when the first meteor shot across the horizon lighting up the lower sky across the horizon. The red flame trailing behind seemed to create a huge explosion as it entered the atmosphere. Wow! Greg was not ready to move away from these sights now for nothing! When he was absorbed and got right into something, nothing took away his attention. These meteor showers never occurred back home in this fashion for a reason when this thought entered his mind.

All of a sudden, the macabre, horrendous, killing beasts pounced, entering his heart, soul, and thoughts. Greg kept still as a mouse as if a cat was looking, ready to jump on him. These beings crept further into his inner thoughts as the meteors came down. Once this show stopped, maybe the ghastly, frightful, intimidating creatures would disappear. Greg sure hoped so, as he was scared through once again, not wanting to withdraw into a shell, this being first night of the summer meteor showers, in the valley among the giant, granite-faced, solid western Rocky Mountains. With white, glacier peaks atop and down the slopes of every mountain in sight across the valley, the bright red meteor trails gleamed bright against the natural background of the mountain peaks. Meteor shadows flashed across the tops of white during the show occurring tonight. Ghoul and werewolf creatures came due to the crack allowed from these space rocks hurtling into the earth's atmosphere like that tonight.

What did those ghoul and werewolf creatures want with him? What actually transpired to bring them into him? Greg remembered the stories about creatures that supposedly came from the star studded Milky Way. Just then the revolting, grotesque, violent creatures started to spear his mind with such a force full of fear and deep trepidations he began to shake real hard. Just maybe his family had left a trail for these things to follow and catch up to them twice now? Greg was unable to get a grasp on this concept of being followed by unknown evil creatures from another place. They honed in on his being like a guided missile from afar into his life. How were the unspeakable, malevolent, demonic creatures able to find one young solitary boy wherever he went? Did they desire to kill him or just take him away?

At that time, his parents agreed their vacation had been a good one and would indeed have to end. The Bradens decided to take the long way home, hoping whatever attacked their son would be lost. Greg was their only child, and Helen was not able to have another child. After Greg fell asleep in the backseat, Tom and Helen starting talking over his situation. How to find out what transpired, and how to keep it quiet was going to require a minor miracle. Greg had to have hid this dark secret far inside his soul for it to occur so fast and abruptly. Tom and Helen could not fathom how Greg got through so much and had not said a word. Had they known could they have done anything to ward off the hideous, dreadful soul killing creatures? Greg was strong, brave and tougher than any other seven- or six-year-old they were aware of. Marcasite held some kind of a dark secret complete with the despicable, inhuman, harrowing alien beings. Their son, Greg, was one who had seen these creatures while hiding inside his closet during one severe summer storm. His parents were deeply concerned about the mental well-being of their son right now. As Tom and Helen mulled the situation over, Greg was sound asleep in the backseat not aware of the concern being expressed by his parents. Finally, they decided to leave things sit while they head back home along the highway to Marcasite.

Chapter Ten

Prairie General and their high quality staff of doctors needed to check him. Tom and Helen took him a couple of days after returning to Marcasite. The guise was Greg had picked up some type of flu on vacation. The psychiatric ward was just like new, with three shrinks on duty. The most highly regarded ones in their fields was the word. This surreal, unworldly challenge could probably push them beyond all their preconceived thoughts and ideas. Did educated people contain any sense of other worlds and beings that could exist therein? Time had come to find out in the Bradens' minds if so-called shrinks could help Greg or not. Tom and Helen knew that something was happening to Greg due to his lying in the tent after screaming out loud. Greg had not really fully explained why or who caused the attack that night. Would he be able to explain all what had taken place at the hands of the ghoul and werewolf creatures over the last year? His parents were unsure of how much Greg could handle before he broke down mentally.

The shrinks practiced and held discussions for moments just like this one. All their so-called combined education was astronomical and very much required right now. Textbooks and all research showed ghoul and werewolf creatures were taking over or trying to become the dominant force in Greg's mind. As a panel, the responsibility of predicting violence was of a great concern to them, which was, could these evil beings become at all violent toward anyone? Being informal and free thinkers, the case caused some problems right away. Would Greg hurt anyone at their urging, or were they just figments of a very young, overactive mind? A difficult birth by Helen may have been partially responsible for the present trauma in some manner. Greg knew none of these doctors could even fathom or understand sanely what he had experienced from these malicious, unholy, beastly creatures in his short life. Greg was seven years old and experienced more than these doctors would ever need to know. He was not going crazy, just simply attacked inside by those ghoul and werewolf creatures, the creatures that were unseen to all except the ones who had been taken away and killed or vanished into the blackness of the storms, Greg thought.

Greg was admitted into the Prairie General Hospital for observation in the psych ward. This was where Greg opened up about the things that were attacking him for the last two years now. At this time, Greg told them ghoul and werewolf creatures that had kept invading his soul, mind, and heart. All these evil beings were scaring him, filling him with intense fear and ice-cold dread since he was six years old. Still Greg did not feel good telling his story to anyone due to not knowing what may lay ahead for him. He knew he was not at all crazy, just plain scared to death of the ghoul and werewolf creatures. Greg explained the first time he saw them in his closet that night and the severe, summer storm that made him seek refuge inside his closet because of the noise from the lightning, the thunder, the rains, and the hailstones. Greg continued telling them he felt some kind of presence in the dark with him. Slowly, as he looked to his sides, he saw bright, white, sharp incisor teeth gleaming at him. Lips pursed in grins, drooling slop falling from their mouths. He was frozen to the floor and wet his pajamas in the closet out of intense fear. Greg was unable to explain how those things appeared in the darkness of his closet. How could he, as he was only six years old at the time? Now he was seven years old and still scared out of wits from the ghoul and werewolf creatures.

Dr. Ken Denton disagreed with the plan of attacking Greg with a magnetic charge of some kind. The patient was only seven years old. Plus, kids had overactive imaginations that provided the evidence found in textbooks. Dr. Denton felt his opinion was the correct one when it came to understanding Greg's problem. He felt

Greg just wanted more attention from his parents as the result of being an only child. Dr. Denton was wrong by a country mile, as the saying went. Dr. Denton could not accept the concept of ghoul and werewolf creatures being real. His mind had been mired in books for too many years to understand the reality of a seven-year-old boy.

Dr. Debbie Granton felt a more prudent way to proceed was to test the strength of the any unhallowed, repulsive, accursed creatures present. She was concerned due to the age of the patient. She believed Greg's story as being true, as she had done enough research into the tales of the ghoul and werewolf creatures in university. In scientific terms, there had to be a way to get these things to leave Greg alone. She wanted to really examine Greg more closely, maybe keep him for a few nights and days to monitor if these things came at him. While being held in their state-of-the-art facility in isolation, tests will be done in complete safety. She was interested in how they attacked Greg and what attracted them into him.

Dr. Wallace Drieger said more time was needed for research to find out more about these horrendous, terrifying, macabre creatures as being absolutely important. Basically, he agreed with Dr. Granton in her findings and determinations. Difficult situations called for other than the normal acceptable proceedings to achieve success. Holding Greg for observation and under constant watch just may provide some very important clues. Or maybe these things would not come around during his stay? This step was required and should be carried out with a lot of caution. Greg would be kept in an isolation room away from other patients for monitoring and his safety while he was here.

Next would come a meeting with the hospital board to get the needed authorization to carry out the tests on Greg Braden. Traditionally, most specialists like these can sit and come to some unanimous agreement. Additionally, at least two agreed with each other, and one had a different approach toward any or some type of preconceived medical condition the young patient may or may not have. The only hospital was Prairie General, which had only been opened for close to two full years. These psychiatrists had just come on board in the last six to eight months. Mind you, they learned at some of the largest, most prestigious universities across the whole entire country. Additionally, all were very eager to prove their educations were worth the time, effort to the hospital, the patients, and all the people of Marcasite and Gopher County. Their reputations were on the line right now with this first case in front of them.

Next morning, as the sun was coming up, all parties entered the hospital to get the final procedures underway. All the elevators ended up at the second floor to drop off all the board members, doctors, and secretaries all heading to the conference room today for a very important meeting. Administrators had set aside a full six hours in total to discuss the details in regards to Greg Braden. They had four big coffee urns and many items to eat brought up from the basement kitchen and instructions not to be disturbed until the six hours were up.

Meetings begin when someone says, so today was not at all any different. The chairman called the meeting to order and gave the order of speakers. Then the doctors would begin their long assessments of Greg Braden's condition.

Dr. Ken Denton would be the first speaker on the subject at hand. He made comments that Greg was characterized by a strange, cold, scary behavior and withdraws into a fantasy world. He could not say if Greg was mad or crazy. Otherwise, his mind was good, sane, and measured, within normal ranges on tests from last few days and nights. Dr. Denton had no explanation for the erratic horror Greg experienced that summer. At no other time had this occurred to his parents' knowledge according to any facts or based on any hospital record.

Dr. Debbie Granton needed to clarify that her co-worker needed to rethink his positions for a boy like Greg. Greg was a normal seven-year-old boy full of life with an overactive imagination. He loves the outdoors, the sleeping in tents, campfires, fishing, eating fresh cooked meals on an open wood fire. At that time of his attacks he was in dense wooded surroundings that were very unfamiliar to him. Ghoul and werewolf creatures could just have been shadows from the birds flying across the moon lite sky. Shadows always existed in the woods every night as far as she had found out. How could Greg's young mind explain these things at all or these very real, weird experiences so vividly? Dr. Granton believed Greg and felt he should be released to go home with his parents. There was nothing the hospital could do at this time for him, as he was not a threat to himself or anyone else. Still, she believed in the ghoul and werewolf creatures being real and not imaginary. It was possible Greg had been attacked by some of these creatures when he was six years old. Dr. Granton felt nothing would be gained by keeping Greg in the hospital any longer and he should be sent with his parents. Being at home with his friends would be good for him.

Dr. Wallace Drieger decided to take the same approach as Dr. Granton. He felt she knew her job and was more familiar with these effects on a seven-year-old boy. Children always had active imaginations from their early years even into adulthood. Greg should be given a chance to return home and live a normal life. Dr. Drieger also felt Greg posed no threat to himself or anyone else. Greg deserved to go home and lead a normal life with his family once again. Dr. Drieger had observed Greg in his room and saw nothing out of the actual ordinary occur. No attacks took place and hopefully the creatures that attacked Greg Braden would now leave him alone. He deserved to live a normal life outside with family and friends.

Greg got to go home that day, and he was happy he did not lose his mind. Doctors or no shrinks had any idea of the ghoul and werewolf creatures that inhabited his mind at times. He never felt completely controlled, yet one day those evil things just might take him right over the top! Dreams should not be real life occurrences by any means inside the minds of anyone. Greg needed to keep secrets from his parents, friends, and acquaintances for the rest of his life. No one would ever see him as a friend if the word got out among them. Imagining people pointing and whispering scared Greg just like the ghoul and werewolf creatures did.

Greg saw all his friends the next day and told them all about the trip with his parents. The things, places, and stuff they did seemed to fascinate all of them. Greg listened to all the stories his friends told about their adventures every summer. This time together every year filled them all with wonder from the tales that went around. Yes, excitement about whom had the best holiday story made them laugh and smile for hours. The afternoon soared by like a rocket going to the moon. All of them would regroup later on in the park down the street after supper. One of all their favorite places was this park due to the swings, sandboxes, and trees to climb at the park. They could lie around all day on the fresh-cut green grass and tell more stories from their vacations.

Yet no one had asked him about being in the hospital for the last few days after his return home. Greg felt relieved inside over that fact more than his friends or parents knew or felt. There was still a lot of summer time left to spend with his friends. Telling a real lie to his friends might not have been easy to do. Greg was going to do this, if need be, in order to safeguard his secret. Life was already tough on him without covering up this turmoil with a lie to his many friends.

Greg and Janice's friends included all of the following: Lenny Farfeld, Caden McDougall, John Wallis, Teagan Sannerman, Abbey Brown, Bailey Hutton, Barbara Williams, Valerie Stockton, Bambi Payton, and Adam Turco, just to mention a few. They all seemed to be very close with each other at any time of the day or night as they grew up in Marcasite. The bonds of friendship were formed at young ages as parents tried to pass this great knowledge onto their children. Besides, children were usually good at playing if watched and supervised.

Yes, the evening weather was nice, with the sun overhead sparkling like a diamond in the western sky. A clear blue cloudless sky could be seen across the faraway horizon. Still to come was an evening sky, filled with stars hidden away in the background of the Milky Way not yet showing through. After sunset, the stars would appear and majestically light up the darkness of the heavens with such awesome beauty. Every night they all tried to find all of the constellations up there in outer space. Activities like these filled Greg inside with an awe-inspiring wonder of what actually was out there amid the stars. God made all of everything in the heavens for people to marvel over for all eternity. Great summer evenings were the best to be outdoors for hours, especially on those cloudless evenings.

Clear skies showed the moon, the entire Milky Way, the constellations, all visible planets, comets, and meteorites.

Back then telescopes were small and built for people to sky watch in the summer or on winter evenings, and for bird watchers who really enjoyed catching a glimpse of their favorite wild bird perched upon a tree limb. Catching a view of a bird, sitting atop a feeder, eating seeds in the dead of a cold, white winter, made a great picture. Not all people owned telescopes to search the night skies. Anyone could see the expanse of the space with the naked eye, which was truly amazing. Asteroids, comets, and meteors were watched with the naked eyes. The constellations and stars too numerous to count shone in a cloudless night sky.

Greg's mind went into why these ghoul and werewolf creatures seemed intent to really disturb his world. No answers came for him then, as he was still filled with the awe and wonder over the dark night sky above. Shooting stars could be seen as they crossed the night just above the far western horizon. Other meteors could be seen streaking across upper areas of the faraway night sky. Yes, all of them enjoyed these sights, hoping that maybe one would land near them. Getting a piece of a meteor seemed an impossible dream to them because not one had landed here about ever. Dreaming about finding a piece of a meteor seemed to fascinate Greg and his friends through each subsequent meteor shower throughout the year. Greg felt otherwise due to his personal experiences with the unholy, harrowing, obnoxious creatures. Maybe they had hitched a ride on the back of one meteor cruising through the vacuum of space, which allowed them to attack him inside his soul, heart, and mind? He knew better as ghoul and werewolf creatures only came out during dark storms of the spring, summer, and fall. Yes, frightful, depraved, hellish creatures had unveiled themselves to him when he was six years old. Ever since, he was invaded by these beings from the Milky Way at their will and timing; he was always on guard. Greg had managed to keep all this hidden away inside himself, except for that one time. Now he needed to become a steel wall and let nothing slip out in front of anyone.

Later, after he was at home Greg felt those same eerie feelings coming on, the cold fear, ice-cold sweats just before the morbid, noxious, heinous creatures attacked him. Hiding in his room was an actual requirement to keep his parents from finding out again. Entering the psych ward seemed such a bad idea even for him ever again. After all the neighbors might find out, and then his friends might shun him forever. No, he needed to keep this inside like a solid cocoon wrapped up, protecting itself to become a butterfly.

Adapting to fear from the very unknown could not be easy for anyone, let alone Greg Braden. Sleep was at times a faraway fleeting, precious commodity when actual dreams scared him right to his bones. Any lifelike dream was completely and foolishly unheard of among his friends unless no one was going to tell of any such experience.

Greg would not allow anyone to get close enough to find out about these despicable, barbaric, fiendish creatures that haunted him at will. Not being able to explain it even to himself, how could he tell all his friends or his parents everything?

Those early times would be etched forever in his subconscious and conscious mind. At that time, Greg would lose memories of where his dreams took him. Nights were filled with lifelike dreams, feeling being far away from home with no reason for it. Ghoul and werewolf creatures caused some real despicable activities to actually occur from spring till late fall. Fear of the unknown in the night seared his brain, soul, and mind for life. Why him and not someone else in another place or time? He had more questions than answers crammed into his thoughts each and every day. Yet Greg knew these were only dreams and not reality at all. He always awoke in his own bed and not lost outside of town or any other place. Beginning to be sleep deprived began to cause him problems with his school activities and studies. There was no way Greg could open up about what he faced from these ghoul and werewolf creatures. His mind became to be haunted full time by visions of demonic, malevolent, grotesque beings. This was why they allowed him to live after the first visit at age six in his closet scaring him enough to pee his pajamas. Greg had to get through his current trouble and focus on his future in a good way.

A guidance counselor asked him what was going on at home. Greg said he was having trouble sleeping and said it was nothing. Preteens seemed to have those same problems from time to time. Greg was after all one of the top students in the school from an early age. All of his friends fell into the same range of marks and took part in most sports. The guidance counselor said okay, that nothing seemed out of the ordinary. The school never notified his parents about this particular meeting. Whatever the problem was it seemed to go away soon after this initial meeting. Greg needed to learn to conceal these problems better than he ever had so far. Building a shield against his fears at school in front of his teachers and fellow students was to become a top priority. Greg achieved this objective with hard work and determination every day at school and with his parents at home.

Greg had to learn to hide these feelings of fear and dread deep, deep inside him. Better coping skills helped him so nothing really affected his scholastic activities. Greg was just worn out from being scared to sleep due to the ghoul and werewolf creatures entering his body and mind. He also had become a very well-adjusted young teen after so many attacks from the ghoul and werewolf creatures. Greg needed to keep aware of his abilities to succeed at anything once he decided to. His very own natural-born inner inquisitiveness aided Greg in his studies and with his friends. All the abilities Greg had come from fighting a searing, spine-tingling fear unknown to anyone of his peers. Through all his experiences, he stayed strong, unflappable, and stayed cheerful as any young child should have been. He developed a hard inner core with a good, smiling outer side. He learnt how to hide his fears inside without showing any outwardly sign.

Next year they would all be advancing into Two Hills Junior High, entering the seventh grade. Everyone was excited taking the next step in their lifelong educational journey in life. First thing, being carefree when summer break was upon them was to be exactly what they needed. All schoolyards were still full of young teens playing all kinds of teen games. Boys were engaged in their baseball games, which was a springtime ritual each year, and girls enjoyed playing softball as much as boys enjoyed baseball. Any restlessness he may have harbored during winter disappeared at that time. Outdoor school activities stirred his soul allowing his mind to relax and taking in the smell of warm weather. Watching the trees budding around the schoolyard from the windows of his classrooms always grabbed his attention.

Chapter Eleven

Indeed, this was the first spring he started to take an interest in Janice Maribel from down the street. Janice was a very pretty, blond-haired girl who had been his friend for many years. Greg was never aware she had liked him for that many years previously. The pair would spend a fair bit of time together that summer as always just being close. Just being together sitting and talking in the sunshine in the local park. Two young lovers enjoyed going for walks and holding hands in the whole neighborhood, with broad smiles on their faces. Sometimes the pair stopped to join in a game of softball in the park. Young love was a great feeling that made Greg and Janice seem very happy. Greg and Janice had lots to share one day down the road.

Greg felt one time maybe those ghoul and werewolf creatures would attack his soul and spirit when Janice was there. Being unsure about how to handle any occurrences bothered Greg. So far nothing scary or unforeseen had happened; maybe being happy changed them or chased them away? Somehow Greg doubted his thoughts, as for sure as the sun shone every day. Janice kept him feeling very happy and contented through that first spring as a couple and being together. Janice seemed to have the very boy she dreamt about for years growing up. Greg was finally her boyfriend, and now everyone knew it. Yet everyone did know this was coming before Greg did. After all, the broad smiles on their faces ensured everyone the happiness was genuine and true. Even if they knew before he had become aware of her attraction to him that spring, it was no big deal.

Spring rolled into summer, and classes came to an end for the entire student body in Marcasite. Local swimming pools quickly filled up with teens and kids alike from morning to night. The smell of chlorine sometimes burnt their noses when they got caught up in a splash. The intense, insane laughter and shrills from everyone filled the air around the pool. All the splashes from the cool water got everyone out in the sun, fun-filled activities going on. Summer always brought out the best in people all over the place, whether in the city or in the country. No spring or summer storms had struck Marcasite since a while back. Evil was awaiting the time to attack once more and have their thrills with all the residents of Marcasite.

Greg knew this summer would be different than previous ones. Nothing had attacked him for a month or so now. His mind seemed centered on Janice and his friends as they played in the pool. He was hoping for the entire summer to be just like today. No more repugnant, hideous, monstrous creatures crashing through his soul and mind. Greg's sanity needed to be in check, especially in front of friends and classmates. Reality was in abundance right at that moment in Greg Braden's life. Janice especially did not need to see him at his worst as the ghoul and werewolf creature reached inside him and took over his soul, mind, and heart. Playing games with him since he was six years old and now he was thirteen years old. For seven years, Greg had managed to keep this dark secret from every one of his friends, his teachers, and even his parents for all those years, except the one intrusion that occurred on a summer trip with his parents when he was seven years old. That vacation ended with a trip to the local psych ward at the Prairie General Hospital.

Every summer his family took a vacation somewhere, and Greg always looked forward to it. However, Janice seemed sad over this happening, just as he did. Greg told her it was going to be for two weeks only and he would send her postcards. Janice perked up after hearing that being happy with Greg had been her dream for years. Young love was always fraught with sadness due to unexpected separations during the family summer-vacation times. Maturing and accepting disruptions were hard on teenagers due to hormonal genes changing. Greg would spend that last evening with Janice and his friends at Freedom Park down the street from their homes. Sitting in the park was a ritual every year after all the snow was gone and spring came into full bloom. All summer in the warm evening, their time was filled by playing on the swings, throwing baseballs, and sitting around talking on the grass. Just being there and hanging out seemed the greatest thrill of all through their young lives.

Two young lovers walked slowly along hand in hand to the park to join their friends that evening after supper. A lot of other parents saw them going along together, which brought many memories back to them all. Time really had not changed the appearance of young lovers being in love. Maybe their young children were growing up faster than they ever imagined was possible. For many parents, they had married their first loves of their lives back when they were young men and women, as Greg and Janice walking along with such innocence in their faces was overwhelming for most parents. Two teens who had known each other all their lives finally realizing they enjoyed being together. Greg now hoped this feeling of caring about Janice would rid him of those ghoul and werewolf creatures.

In that time as summer passed, the fall arrived, and school was back in. Greg and Janice were still together, which shocked and surprised some of their classmates. Jealousy came from some guys, as Janice was turning out to be a beautiful, well-filled-out, young female teenager. Girls were really jealous due to Greg being so handsome, and they wanted him. Greg and Janice laughed it all off, not taking the chatter seriously. Peer pressure was common with teens in schools anywhere in the world. Marcasite was no different in this respect, with the teens poking fun at each other. Joking around was okay, and nothing should be taken seriously in that way.

Little did they know their lives would take a severe twist soon. One dreary, dark, cloudy evening, a severe storm struck the entire area, with intense strong winds, the rain pouring down, hailstones pelting everything, sheet lightning flashing across the skies, rolling thunder roared overhead. Everything was swirling in huge circles as the tornado winds continued to grow and increase with speed, perfect timing with the cover for the ghoul and werewolf creatures to now attack at will. They were sneaking around, chasing through the winds looking for victims in town. Shadows seen among the flashes of sheet lightning as it opened up across the skies. Thunder rolled louder and more often filling the whole area like artillery guns going off. Rains pouring down and filling the gutters up as the hails stones bounced off everything outside. What caused these monstrous storms to suddenly appear over Marcasite? Were some type of fiendish, calamitous, hellish creatures skulking around out there in that dark, ominous storm?

Exactly two weeks after school started, it seemed as if Marcasite was lost to the elements from the dark side. Where had they been hidden for so long this summer since the last big storm hit in late spring? Except that storm never left anyone missing or dead, ripped and torn apart, and gnawed upon by incisor-sharp teeth from the ghoul and werewolf creatures. They had left everyone alone as the vicious, terrible storms wreaked havoc on the residents of Marcasite. Nerves were frayed by the next morning after the storm waned and left just as suddenly as it appeared. What damage had taken place overnight and who disappeared in the storm?

As always the unhallowed, beastly, petrifying creatures became hungry at the same times and swept through the town at will. All of the residents of Marcasite felt or knew inside that someone or more than one person was going to be lost that night. Fierce fall storms came in this same manner and ended with a death knell coming to call. Not what anyone needed or wanted to hear about after a storm like last night. Yet the time for death was never announced before hand by whoever caused it. People knew who caused the terrible, extreme, havoc, deaths and disappearances in Marcasite. Ghoul and werewolf creatures felt their time for a feast on human flesh had come. The noise covered up the attacks on any homes or the people inside them.

Teagan and Candy, the owners of the *Gazette*, would be out early to see the police about any strange happenings after this storm struck Marcasite. The *Gazette* had a responsibility to report on these terrible events and if any disappearances took place. Police Chief Harry Rook would as always be open to Teagan and Candy showing up to ask questions. The *Gazette* covered the deaths and disappearances with care about the families involved in them. People needed to be aware of what took place amid the storms that struck the town.

Early the next morning one of their classmates, Lenny Farfeld, was reported missing by his parents; he apparently just disappeared from his home—no sign of forced entry, no broken doors, no open or broken windows either. How could these abhorrent, monstrous, barbaric intruders enter through walls and take people away? Both of Lenny's parents were very shocked as their son had never screamed or shouted during his disappearance. Lenny was athletic and strong for his young age and should have caused some sort of noise. Lenny could have fought back, or was he just overpowered by the ghastly, atrocious, deadly invaders? Police had no clues as it was too early to have any facts, according to Police Chief Rook in this matter, even though police officials knew these creatures were responsible and unstoppable when they attacked.

A few days later, Lenny Farfeld's dead body was located outside of Marcasite in the woods off the highway north toward Goreville. One of the local farmers was out walking his dog when they came across the remains of a body among the dense underbrush. The entire area was all roped off so the local police and the coroner, Dr. Gabe Bridger, could carry out their duties without being disturbed. No more details were made available from the police, nor could Teagan and Candy get any more interviews. Many of the older police members saw this as another case of mutilation by the same type of ghoul and werewolf creatures. This new coroner was not around when the two young girls died years ago or when the deaths of two construction workers happened years after. Dr. Gabe Bridger had only just arrived in town a couple weeks ago and seemed to be getting his first lessons in the grisly deaths plaguing Marcasite. He would be plunging into a sickening mess of blood and bones spread across the open area in the woods. Locations like this were what the creatures left their ritual killings laying around in.

All the early residents had vivid memories of what happened in the past to Olivia and Hannah Samuels as well as the two construction workers. Marcasite stopped functioning after hearing of Lenny Farfeld's death and his body being found. A mourning period was implemented by Father Watson of the Catholic church. He was going to hold the evening prayers to be offered for Lenny and his family that evening. Father Watson expected the pews to be full for the prayer service later on that night. Death brought the community closer together, especially after a sudden, nasty, and unprovoked attack by some nefarious, deadly, atrocious creatures, as that was the only explanation anyone could fathom at that time. None of the previous terrible deaths were, nor could the disappearances of any others be, explained in rational terms.

These disgusting, despicable ghoul and werewolf creatures had come back for another feeding frenzy this fall. As always there were a few more deaths over the previous years before and since the construction worker's death, just not many in recent times, so this was a complete surprise coming once more upon Marcasite. Over the last ten years, the death toll stood at eight, not including the ones who were never found again. Were there any tourists who traveled through this area that may have disappeared and not been reported? Could these nefarious, obscene, accursed offenders attack people who were just passing by Marcasite? Was it possible for people to go missing with no trace and no one reported these occurrences to any police force?

How the ghoul and werewolf creatures managed to rip and tear bodies apart and gnaw on them to just scatter the bones around was a mystery. Remains were left right in the middle of the dense woods along the lone highway toward Goreville. Why only the highway to Goreville for a dumping ground for their various victims? Could they have used the town's location for previous centuries for scattering bones around? Was this their reason for them to keep returning and killing and taking others away? All the residents knew that some kind of forlorn, dark beacon was attracting the formidable, frightening, deadly raiders to this area.

Everything pointed back to those tales from the First Nations Peoples, who told them to the early settlers. Evil beings existed in this spot, doing terrible things to anyone who came around from spring till fall. For centuries these devilish, ghastly, revolting creatures made this area home to do degrading deeds to people. Storms brought deaths, disappearances, with people simply vanishing into the blackness of the stormy nights. No trace of some was ever found, and other bodies were torn, ripped apart, attributed to a wolf or a pack of coyotes. These tribes knew that no animal could ever be responsible for these horrible deaths. The First Nations knew ghoul and werewolf creatures caused the disgusting trouble as always.

The *Gazette* carried the story on the front page with all the information they had gotten from the police and the coroners offices. Teagan and Candy had been out to see the place where Lenny Farfeld's body was found. As reporters, they were allowed some access to the scene and were allowed to take pictures as well. However, they could not show the pictures of the remains of Lenny Farfeld in such a manner. The *Gazette* promised to keep on top of the story and let readers know about any findings in the next issue. All residents in Marcasite seemed shattered, shocked, and in disbelief over Lenny Farfeld being killed in a horrible way. The Marcasite police had no clues or leads in regards to what actually happened or how it took place. Any information would be released to the *Gazette* to be published as soon as it became available. Police Chief Harry Rook felt bad for Lenny's family, relatives, and friends who went to school with him.

The entire student body was shocked by this awful, terrible, dreadful, sudden turn of events, as a fellow student from their school was killed. Classes were suspended for the next couple of the days for everyone to talk and grieve over Lenny Farfeld. Vicious, obnoxious, abhorrent ghoul and werewolf creatures were out there amid Marcasite ripping, tearing, and chewing individuals to death. Such disgusting, horrible, grisly events occurred when severe storms hit from the springtime till late fall. Now with the devastating loss of yet another young teenager who happened in a huge storm that struck their community. The last time two young teens were taken were two sisters, Olivia and Hannah Samuels, from their home a number of years ago. The girls were stolen from their parents' home amid a very bad storm. Police knew something left long, deep gouges on their bones after gnawing on them.

The last recorded death occurred during the last period of a big expansion of Marcasite four years ago. A rugged, tough construction worker named Paul Jameson died during the last recorded major storm hit about a year ago. Before that a Ryan Renton, another construction worker, disappeared, and still his remains were never found. Marcasite carried a dark past along for almost every year or so, except now the killing and disappearances were happening more often over time. What made this occur now after a lull of activity in the last few months? Did a deep crack open in open space during this storm the other night to allow the ghoul and werewolf creatures time to feast on Lenny Farfeld?

Lenny's fellow students had plans to hold a memorial in the school auditorium for him. He was among one of the top role models and best athletes in the school, and he was very popular. Lenny was best friends with the following students: Greg Braden, Janice Maribel, Caden McDougall, John Wallis, Teagan Sannerman, Abbey Brown, Bailey Hutton, Barbara Williams, Valerie Stockton, Bambi Payton, and Adam Turo.

Being raised in the same neighborhood brought them to be close friends since they were kids. Hanging out in Freedom Park and playing together all the time made them a tight-knit group of good friends. Going to school from being in elementary school to junior high and now having Lenny struck down was awful. They needed to share the loss and mourning for their closest friend, Lenny Farfeld, in order to keep it together. Being at the school together with all the other students assisted the grieving process a lot. Lenny would have been there if it had happened to anyone else. That is why this event was so important to the whole student body.

Why would someone do this to such a great person as Lenny? There must be some crazy on loose in the city. Lots of new people had relocated to Marcasite over the last number of years. However, no one actually came to mind, and certainly no one from their school was capable of this despicable act of torture and degradation. The group made their way to Lenny's house to see his parents, which they needed to express regrets and sympathy for Lenny's loss to his parents. Lenny's extremely sad departure knit their bond closer as a group that fall. Best friends always stuck close together and grew together through thick and thin. None of them were aware of the worst times ahead for all of Marcasite in storms coming their way. As storms full of morbid, macabre, obnoxious creatures came, it was a complete surprise for anyone. The heavy carnage associated with them was such astonishing extremes for the residents as well. No one expected a young teen to be a victim of unworldly, ghastly, devious ghoul and werewolf creatures in this storm that night.

Greg Braden was fully aware of who and what caused these terrible, destructive deaths in Marcasite. He was the only one who had seen these dreadful, accursed, spine-chilling creatures in the dark of his closet. At least he was sure of that due to none of his friends ever saying or sharing any knowledge of seeing them. Greg still wanted to scream and run from those memories, yet he could not. He still knew he froze to the floor and wet his pajamas as he stared at the ghoul and werewolf creatures. Their huge, bright, white, sharp incisor teeth shone in the dark of the closet, showing slime dripping off their lips as they opened their mouths wide open. Greg was still scared these many years later and just hoped his friend Lenny died fast at their hands. Even if he wanted to, no one would believe him now after being in the hospital due to a wild imagination as a kid. Greg was still haunted by those abominable, despicable, calamitous alien beings ever since he was six years old. How many times they invaded his soul, mind, and body, Greg had lost count over the years.

Every student who knew Lenny attended the memorial for him at Two Hills Junior High School. Flowers and signs were put up by those students from his school, followed by a solemn ceremony with tributes given by his many friends and teachers. This was taking place the day before Lenny's funeral that seemed so surreal to them at such young ages. A very sad, touching moment for all of them as their friend was now gone along with his shattered dreams. Being lifelong friends, going to school together made this event even more poignant as that day went on. Tears flowed openly among all who attended that day for young souls were hurt, scared, and very fearful they could be next.

Everyone attended Lenny Farfeld's funeral service at the local Catholic church early the next afternoon. The service was a very solemn event as Father Zack Watson read from the Bible, and the choir sang a few hymns. Afterward, everyone followed the hearse to the local cemetery close to the edge of Marcasite. Students shared their grief openly as they passed solemnly by the open gravesite. All the citizens attending stopped to talk to Mr. and Mrs. Farfeld for a brief moment as they quietly went along. The church held a small gathering for the parents and teens after the service was over. It filled up due to many students and parents coming by for a couple of hours before slowly filing out. Lenny was going to be missed for a lot of years, especially by his family and relatives. His friends would talk about him and his many achievements for years to come as well.

Despicable, horrible, barbaric creatures took Greg's friend, Lenny, to get at him, to show what they were capable of doing to him. No details were being released yet about how Lenny Farfeld was killed and the possibility of whom. In the days to come, news would spread like a wildfire about how the ghoul and werewolf creatures, as told by the local native elders, had, in fact, come back. Marcasite was in for the shock of a lifetime; no one really ever understood how Lenny died, except the same way the construction workers died and the two young Samuels girls had. Original police reports stated it was known some kind of animal ripped Lenny Farfeld to death. Suddenly no one felt safe due to this stark, spooky announcement about an animal being to blame. There was no trace of any tracks or footprints belonging to any animal in the area or in the bush. Police could not announce to the general public about no animal tracks being found in those dense bushes where Lenny's body was found. Three other bodies were found, and one had completely disappeared from the face of the earth over the last five years. All of this was reported in the *Gazette* in every issue as the information became available.

Ghoul and werewolf creatures came from that crack in the star studded Milky Way as the First Nations elders had said. Greg was very sure about that in his mind and soul he saw them in his closet at six years of age. Establishing any real, secure thoughts of where these strange beings came from burned in his soul, especially since his best friend was dead and police just might think he was nuts if he told them anything. Greg knew being quiet had to be the only safe route right now, even though he felt he was to blame because those unholy, repulsive, foul smelling, long-toothed creatures had attacked him so many years ago. Greg Braden kept it all a secret inside for almost half of his life now. Just once, only when he was seven years old, the old fears, the searing torment, had become too much for him. After that vacation with his parents, Tom and Helen Braden had him checked at the Prairie General Hospital when they got home. Greg was actually pronounced sane a few days later to go home and have a normal life. Now after that incident, those people were indeed aware of Greg being invaded by ghoul and werewolf creatures. Who could actually think his experience might be important to the reality of what is happening lately? No one approached him or asked any questions that swept over him with a great wave of relief. Greg still knew who killed their best friend during the stormy night. He was just unable to say it out loud to the authorities yet!

Lenny's death was not due to beings of this earth. No wild animal had ripped and torn his friend to pieces in that manner—Greg knew this for sure. This had to be the result of those gruesome, harrowing, offensive foreign invaders that had the teeth to chew people. Greg was absolutely positive, as he shook with the ice-cold fear and trepidation for hours whenever he was by himself. Hellish, hideous, gruesome creatures had attacked him since he was six years old. Why they kept him alive, he could only try to understand; just having a play toy from time to time amused them. Greg kept remembering how they smacked their lips, with big ugly grins on their faces, rolling their eyes, showed him their bright white, incisor, sharp, teeth, while slime dropped off their mouths in his closet. This was something he would never forget for the rest of his life. Greg recalled being frozen to the closet floor and wetting his pajamas that night during the wicked storm. Creatures from another dimension returned to see Greg each time they came back to Marcasite to feast. In order to remind Greg there was no escape from the grasps of their reach.

School classes and life slowly returned to normal over the next couple of weeks. Lenny's death had yet to be solved, which still bothered all his friends and family. The city cops searched for clues for whoever or whatever did this sick, twisted damage to a young Lenny Farfeld. Greg was aware deep inside the police were completely clueless in the investigation of Lenny's murder. Greg knew the local First Nations had told white settlers these stories many years ago. Why were these tales and stories of evil ignored for all this time? Greg had his own stories of being internally attacked from the time he was six years of age. He still had never told anyone, not even Janice, about what he endured or what occurred during those bad times. Recalling how he saw those appalling, horrid, demonic creatures that first time in his closet as he hid during the raging storm. He was frozen stiff with fright, ice-cold fear ran through him, and he did wet himself sitting there, unable to move. No sounds came from his throat as much as he tried to scream, as if he was muzzled from doing so. Those memories still seemed so real and vivid to this day in his mind and soul. He could only imagine what Lenny must have endured at the moment he was taken away to be killed. Was he dead before being torn, ripped apart, and gnawed upon? Greg had many awful pictures going through his mind, which made him want to throw up.

Chapter Twelve

In the middle of October, another severe storm struck Marcasite yet again. Fierce winds came with torrential rains. Heavy hailstones, funnel clouds hammered the city. Lightning flashed, and thunder started to roll overhead. Just as before, the night was filled with dark shapes skulking about. The clouds formed shapes exploding into dark images on a blank white canvas. The sheets of lightning flashed; the thunder cracked louder than ever before in recent memory. The tornados tore as if ripping apart the countryside on their journey to hell. Severe storms of this magnitude always burned through everyone with the dreadful, malevolent, repugnant creatures skulking around. Thunder sounded similar to cannonballs being thrown down a bowling alley lane as the ten pins exploded as they were hit. Flashes of sheet lightning light the darkness only to leave and reappear right away again seconds later. Images could be seen in the bright light, or were the minds just overactive this dark, stormy night? No. Some type of abominable, grotesque, foreign creature was running amok out in the stormy darkness. They needed a victim or two to feast on this night to satisfy a real unending craving and hunger for warm human flesh. Ripping, tearing, and shredding the body and disposing of it in a certain location in the dense woods seemed to fit their ugly ritualistic behavior. Plus, others actually disappeared without a trace never to be found again.

People seemed to be missing as they had in previous times as told by local First Nations elders back in those stormy times of the distant past. Who was going to chase away these immortal, fiendish, unholy creatures back into the starry Milky Way now? Did strange, vile, scary ghoul and werewolf creatures actually exist in the real world of everyday life? Not one person seemed willing to accept the possibility of them being present right now.

Actually, repugnant, diabolical, vicious creatures were running amok on this very night. Yes, they always did on the bleakest, most-violent stormy evenings. Something gruesome was going to occur as the storms increased with power and the strength of demons whipping their chains around. Tornados kept roaring through Marcasite as if to pay back people for encroaching on private ancient burial grounds. Maybe the First Nation elders were right about the old stories handed down from their elder generations. In the southeast corner, this land was haunted by beings from the faraway, star studded Milk Way, who showed up only in the most unexpected ways and amid the greatest storms of the springs through the fall seasons?

Caden McDougall disappeared much the same way Lenny had gone into the darkness om the rainiest and the severest weather. Ghoul and werewolf creatures had snatched Caden right out from his house in the blackest moment of the storm last night. Mr. and Mrs. McDougall could not recall hearing anything from their son; he just was not there anymore. None of the family heard or saw anything out of the normal. No windows were open, no doors had been opened, and this shocked the McDougalls. With the extreme noise of the storm, those demonic, macabre assailants entered the McDougall residence, sweeping their son along with them into the violent night. The vile creatures did have centuries of experience of swooping down and taking people away into the worst of storms. Caden McDougall was just another victim for those disgusting beings from that other dimension.

Caden's body could not be found; it was if he just vanished into the dark corners of the netherworld. Police found a few faint blood spots in Freedom Park not far from the school about half way to his home. They never knew if that was his blood or not; they had no way of telling for sure. Rain had wiped out too much to know for sure what type of blood it was. Another teenager had gone, upsetting the town of Marcasite even more since Lenny Farfeld died. Now two teenagers were gone in the last two weeks amid terrible, noisy storms that swirled around

Marcasite. These storms created a complete chaos among an entire population of this prairie town. The jewel of their dreams was being shattered beyond recognition and repair in many minds.

Caden, like Lenny, was a very popular teen at Two Hills Junior High. He was well liked, fun to be around, a class clown who enjoyed making everyone laugh, good at most academics, sports, drama, and just about anything. His family took their loss very rough, as any parent would losing the second oldest of their children, a sure athlete for university sports as was his parents' desire for him. Now they had to lay him to rest in the cemetery beside his friend Lenny Farfeld. Yet his body had to be recovered before his parents would even think of holding a funeral for him.

Once again, Teagan and Candy got to work and looked into the disappearance of Caden McDougall. With no evidence of forced entry or any broken windows or bloody tracks, police were stumped once again. What transpired and who or what came and took Caden away last night? The *Gazette's* owners were just as stumped as the local police in this disgusting matter. Police were searching the same wooded area where other bodies were dumped before in the dark forest along the highway. No trace could be found close to where they had hoped to find any pieces of body parts. It would be many long days and many long nights before police would at least have one solid lead in any of these cases—not that any leads were going to disclose the nefarious, unspeakable, malevolent things that killed all those innocent people over the years, let alone Lenny or Caden who were the most recent victims of the hellish, dreadful, deadly storms this fall.

Greg and Janice were once again deeply saddened along with the rest of the student body. Why were the horrendous, demonic, barbaric creatures out to stalk and kill teens from their own school? Greg Braden would have traded places with his friends, except these evil things wanted to torture him, keeping him alive to drive him insane slowly without any hope he could save himself. Ghoul and werewolf creatures created havoc in the natural world order for their ritualistic feasts on human flesh. Greg knew this because of the fiendish, diabolical creatures tormenting him mentally without physical harm coming his way. Fear, tremors, and cold sweats came over him every time the spine-chilling, detestable, revolting creatures crept into his soul, mind, and body.

The ancient tales of hideous, detestable, heinous ghoul and werewolf creatures coming from nowhere had to be true as there was no other explanation. Late-fall stormy evenings were beginning to unravel the real world from the true seams of time. Monsters from the netherworld entered to carry out these extreme practices on the unsuspecting public on the earth. Ravaging on human flesh to satisfy a true, ritualistic craving for many centuries was too hard to understand by many. Yet, these abhorrent, immortal, loathsome creatures had, in fact, come back to have their ways with all people, just as they had done so for many centuries if anyone cared to take notice of their past behavior.

How many more storms would come to take Greg's and Janice's close friends or family members from them? Life was becoming unbearable for the young Greg Braden to accept over these two unexplained and unexpected deaths of his friends. Why had the abhorrent, loathsome, hellish alien beings not just taken him when they could have at age six? They did not have any right to take his friends away! Greg wished he could go back in time to the night in his closet and have these ghoul and werewolf creatures take his life. Maybe his friends may still be alive today instead of dying in this fashion. All of them had him cornered in that closet as he was frozen, with no voice and no movement, so why not take him? Greg Braden was going to suffer his entire life for that grisly, grotesque nerve-racking experience of being six years old, sitting among those repugnant, noxious, repulsive, and abhorrent creatures.

Once the skies cleared, surely sanity would return even if it existed in a fragile state for a long time to come. Marcasite seemed to be for unearthly beings to play with and toss residents around with excessive force during the stormy seasons. The serene quiet after helped everyone to relax to an uneasy, uncomfortable point. Losing two teens from the same junior high school following two gruesome fall storms left the whole entire community in complete shock and disbelief of what just took place. Small children were fearful to be left alone in their rooms at night even on the calmest of evenings. Sheer fright grew more embodied in the population as each night approached. How did anyone deal with such frightening stuff anyway? How did parents tell their children not to worry over creatures taking them away into the dark and killing them? Having their young children torn, ripped apart, and chewed up by ghoul and werewolf creatures was a nightmare for parents to deal with. Explaining some horrible things to young children was going to be extra tough. After Lenny Farfeld and Caden McDougall being murdered, parents felt the need to talk with their children of all ages. No matter how hard this would be to get across, the message had to be given out.

Ghoul and werewolf creatures created the chaos to hide behind the heavy cloak of clouds made entirely of black. Winds blew to hide the screams of the victims from all residents inside Marcasite in the southeast corner of Gopher County. Rains covered up marks of all trails if there was even any there to follow. Their town was becoming well known but for all the wrong reasons this fall. Death began to stalk Marcasite as the stories passed down from the local native elders were coming alive. This year the dreadful, demonic, atrocious creatures struck with more veracity, tenacity, and killing at will, scattering parts of some victims in the deep woods on the highway to Goreville. Other victims from past times were never found once they were taken away to a secret hiding place. This made the entire population believe in ghoul and werewolf creatures slipping through cracks within the star studded Milky Way.

A memorial took place for Caden in the gymnasium at Two Hills Junior High School arranged by the student body. Wreaths and flowers covered the west wall around his picture. All his best friends gave a short speech about him and their friendship. Tears may have run down every student's cheeks, but they all felt proud to know him. The school canceled all classes that were scheduled to resume in a couple of days to allow the recent shock to wear off a bit, especially with two students being killed in one-month period; nothing like this occurred in many years. Caden's funeral was postponed by his parents until his remains could be located.

Eventually, ten very long, tense days later, Caden's body was recovered outside of the town limits. Caden's body was found slightly further inside the woods where Lenny Farfeld's body was discovered. He was laid, exposed, open to the elements, with his bones scattered on the ground. Caden seemed to have been attacked by the same beings with long, sharp, incisor-like teeth that left, deep, gouging marks on his bones. A type of big creature with strong jaws had dragged these two this far out before attacking, ripping, tearing, and feasting on their flesh. Most residents felt acutely aware of the ghoul and werewolf creatures' abilities to do such horrible things to humans.

This very knowledge unsettled the bravest of the residents in town. None of the local police force members would admit to not having fear inside with what had occurred lately.

The reports of the local coroner, Dr. Bridger, would be available in a couple of days. Dr. Bridger needed to check all the marks on the remains that were recovered to ensure the same beings were responsible. Caden's completed pathology reports would be completed and examined along with Lenny Farfeld's for any clues. To Gabe Bridger with the highly trained eyes, the teeth marks and gouges in the bones were eerily similar. However, he knew no animals existed in this part of the world that could do this damage. Where did these things come from, was it like the stories told of beings from the star studded Milky Way? Dr. Bridger had two more deaths in two weeks and two teenagers with the same eerie signs of mutilation by those terrible ghoul and werewolf creatures. Bridger knew that no earthly animal was responsible for what happened to Lenny or Caden. Being a man of science and knowledge, he had to explain what he could and leave the rest up to the police.

The McDougalls wanted to bury their son soon; he needed to be laid to rest, after all. His family, his relatives, all of his friends, classmates, the entire student body, and the rest of the community needed closure from these brutal, terrible, troubled days. Once the coroner was finished, Caden's body would be released to the funeral home to prepare his remains for burial. This could take a couple of more days for Dr. Bridger to finish the entire course of his examination with a few extra tests to be done. Local police wanted to cover all the bases again like in Lenny Farfeld's death case. No one wanted to leave any stones left unturned in search of answers for these families during the recent spurt of degrading violence.

The Catholic church was packed with mourners who came to say good-bye to Caden McDougall. His family was at the front of the church, crying as the priest offered prayers for their son. A second young member of the same school was lost for no reason during a severe storm in the fall of that year. Father Zack Watson presided over the service as he had over Lenny's. Father Watson spoke of a smart, talented youth who was called home by God to watch over his family and friends. Even though everyone was hurting, they felt Caden was in a better place full of sunshine and peace. Everyone sang hymns and songs before the service came to an end. Father Watson offered prayers for the family, their relatives, friends, and the whole community during these wicked, trying times of late.

No nefarious stories were ever mentioned until the services and the interment came to an end. No one mentioned a word out of total respect for Caden's parents and siblings during this time of terrible loss for them. Everyone felt some long-forgotten, abominable, grotesque creatures had been awoken to be disturbed and released upon Marcasite. For some unknown reason, these malevolent, horrendous ghoul and werewolf creatures completely unleashed their fiendish fury upon all the residents of Marcasite.

What awaited all the residents of this nightmarish, dreadful, deadly place was hidden away from prying eyes. Marcasite had been haunted for centuries, with no end in sight, it seemed. None of the sudden deaths of late would ever be solved in this lifetime. No remains of the missing bodies were ever to be turned up in this wooded place along the highway to Goreville. Ghoul and werewolf creatures took real unspeakable fun and great pleasure in tormenting families by never revealing their secret hiding spots where other remains sat. From the faraway Milky Way, the sadistic, insidious, obnoxious alien beings just waited for the right moment to leap down causing turmoil and discourse in Marcasite.

After the service, a single long line of people filed out of the church to follow Caden's casket to the cemetery, another gravesite dug out of the cold ground for a young soul lost to something out there. A graveside service was held by Father Watson, laying him to rest in peace beside Lenny Farfeld. Everyone stood there, taking in the words being offered, not knowing if Caden was the last death they would face ahead. As everyone went by his casket, they placed flowers on top and offered personal prayers. It was a warm, beautiful, green, peaceful morning in Marcasite. Caden would have been proud to know he was getting one of the nicest, clearest mornings, just the way he loved it all for himself. He always loved the warm late-fall weather and the many different colors mixed with the array of associated fall flowers. Greg and Janice were among the last of his friends to leave the cemetery that day.

All of the residents went to the community center for snacks and a chance to chat with Caden's family and relatives. As sad as it was, people did manage to smile when talking and telling stories of him. His family and relatives felt good hearing about such exploits for such a young teen. He was looked up to among his peers, his teachers, and everyone was proud to have known him. His many friends came to talk with his parents and his relatives as they had met some of them over the years. Grieving was never easy for the families, and those close to the victims knew due to the manner of the deaths, time would be a close ally. Smiles crossed many faces as stories circulated about Caden and how good he was in and out of school.

Everyone stayed until the late afternoon hours that day, not wanting to leave and say good-bye. Caden's family still ran the local grocery store in town and would keep doing this. The McDougall family had stood tall and bore the loss of Caden well. Grieving was never easy, especially when a teenager lost his life so unexpectedly. With the support of the entire student body and the community, the family knew their son was loved by all.

Teagan and Candy were at a loss for information in these cases, except they knew what had done this did the same to other past victims. All deaths in Marcasite over the last number of decades were connected. Teeth marks were suspiciously of the same pattern, to their way of thinking. They were not doctors or coroners and with no type of information forthcoming for this part for their story. The *Gazette* was not giving up on any lead for a story, considering the untimely end of two young teens dying in the same weird, horrible, mysterious ways. Teagan and Candy knew from when Olivia and Hannah Samuels, Paul Jameson, Ryan Renton, Lenny Farfeld, and Caden McDougall these deaths were actually connected by a common thread. What was that odd connecting threads existing in their minds? Ghoul and werewolf creatures had to be the culprits in these disappearances and deaths in Marcasite. Russell Pagan wrote stories in regards to strange shadows of creatures coming out amid the terrible, wild storms from spring till fall. The Wellands believed Russell Pagan was actually onto something, writing stories in the *Gazette* about dark, unearthly beings, ending in the deaths and disappearances.

Repugnant, detestable, malevolent foreign creatures came and killed Caden the same way they got Lenny. Greg became aware of this deep inside his soul, just as he was when ghoul and werewolf creatures inhabited him over many years. Why had they taken his friends in this way? Greg was frustrated, scared, and had nowhere to turn for understanding or help. Telling his story was not the best idea, as he would be put away in the psych ward for sure.

Heinous, brutal, spine-chilling creations did, in fact, have the long, sharp, bright white teeth to rip and tear people apart. From the first time they showed their razor sharp incisors to him inside his closet, they made sure to open their mouths wide to show off their white, shiny, incisor teeth to a frightened child. Greg had recalled how these same ghoul and werewolf creatures kept smacking their thin lips, smiling evilly, scaring him completely, and jolting him back into reality. These exact, extreme, vivid memories haunted his soul and mind ever since. From six years of age, he hid those terrible thoughts inside his soul and heart from his friends and his parents. Being scared was nothing new for him any longer no matter the circumstances he faced.

Local police forces seemed stumped by the sudden deaths from the same neighborhood as Two Hills Junior High. Just in case the killer was a classmate of both teens, the cops talked to the student body as a whole. School officials and students knew no one at school was responsible for these deaths. The people of Marcasite were in their homes, trying to keep safe from the extreme rains, hailstones, sheets of flashing lightning, loud rolling thunder, and tornado-strength winds. Loud noises sounding like the earth was being ripped and torn wide open. City cops really needed to follow up on this to get into this investigation for these two deaths. The local authorities felt this was needed to make sure every student was aware of the real dangers. At least allowing the teens to voice their own concerns and to let them get some answers was the right approach in their mindset.

Students wanted to know why the cops thought one of them was the killer. This was a very ignorant, sad, sick excuse to treat all of them as subjects of the investigations into the deaths of their friends. None of them looked like the strange, shadowy, grisly ghoul and werewolf creatures, so why this exact line of questioning? Students felt the police were trying to place the blame on one of them that day. Teachers started to get offended with the way the talking was coming across to them. Police Chief Harry Rook soon stopped when he noticed teachers becoming increasingly upset. Chief Rook apologized for making it sound like accusations were being thrown around. He only wanted everyone's help in solving these deaths. Students felt insulted and betrayed by the cops in the deaths of their friends and fellow students today.

An entire city full of adults and kids of all ages were scared of being out after dark at any time. Local parks that were full of young kids were now empty as could be after supper, even in the early sunny hours of the evening. Parents kept their children and teenage kids inside long before the sun went down at night. Making sure all windows and both front and rear doors were securely locked so nothing could get in to take their kids away, even though parents were aware nothing seemed to stop ghoul and werewolf creatures from going through solid walls and taking whomever along with them, as if people became invisible with them to slip through the walls, doors, and windowpanes of the homes across the city. Any explanation was indeed plausible while investigating disappearances such as the ones that took place recently. The police and the coroner had no clues or any means to identify what really took place that night in the terrible, horrifying storm that shook Marcasite to its core once again. As in the past, no traces or trails of the barbaric, appalling, murderous attackers could be located anywhere. This town, indeed, was haunted by some type of demonic creatures from the Milky Way, according to the legends passed down.

Still a village grew into a town full of dreams of being a jewel on the prairies in the southeast corner of Gopher County. Stormy evenings filled with ice-cold fear as they waited for some type of monster to strike once again! Marcasite police started to feel the mounting pressure from all the community in these vile, despicable murders that remained unsolved. Citizens demanded to know what they were doing if anything. Town police responded, asking how could they arrest those things invisible to human eyes. No one saw any strangers skulking around in the bleakest, blackest storms, just shadows in between the sheets of flashing lightning. And residents were only hearing the shrieks, howls, and screams of the tornado-force winds ripping the earth wide open. The rolling thunder crashed high above, sounding like some type of giant bowling pins being smashed against a wall. Those noises covered up the cries of victims being hauled away by the twisted, devious, abhorrent ghoul and werewolf creatures deep out into the dense woods outside of town. The unlucky victims were to be torn, ripped open, and gnawed upon with the remains being scattered around in clearings. Then other people seemed to vanish into the pouring rain, hailstones, loud thunder, and sheets of lightning, never to be found again.

The police needed to get to the bottom of these strange, mysterious, insane sudden deaths. No police manual ever covered the unexplained beings from the faraway, starry Milky Way, let alone how to locate and capture these ghoul and werewolf creatures amid the storms. Fear had fully gripped each resident of Marcasite with such force no one was out alone anymore in public, not even on a nice, warm, calm evening with the sun still shining. No chances were taken for long periods of times till people felt the tension ease from the town. Such violence, mayhem, and murders took this small town by surprise every time, two teenagers now dead in the last two weeks with the local cops having no luck finding any lead, even though the effort was not wasted searching the area location in the woods where the remains had been located.

A variety of strange things may have come to roost here in this town of Marcasite, being built on so-called ancient ground. Greg Braden knew for sure these things came from a crack in the faraway galaxy. Janice still did not know about Greg's unexpected visitors from a heavy, severe storm when he was six years old. The faraway, bright starry Milky Way had been home to malicious, calamitous, blitzing creatures for centuries. Greg did understand from his experiences after being haunted inside for almost eight years. To say Greg was too scared to say a word due to being put in the nuthouse was not a desire he wanted or needed to share. Greg would keep his secret for the rest of his natural life out of fear of ghoul and werewolf creatures. He did not want to be torn and ripped apart and gnawed upon to have his bones scattered in the dense woods. Besides, he did not want to have Janice or any of his friends shun him because of his secret sightings of the monstrous, morbid foreign beasts.

Greg recalled his very first experience of seeing them while hiding in his closet during a severe summer storm. His parents told him to stay in bed under the covers in order to be safe. Greg became so scared he hid in the closet from the encroaching danger from the increasing storm. As Greg sat in there, some dark shapes started to appear as ghoul and werewolf creatures, surrounding him in there. Small children had the ability to see what grown-ups could not see. Greg was speechless, unable to scream or cry out with fear right then. He sat frozen to the floor of the closet for many hours before he was able to get up and return to his bed. This small frightened child of six years old wet his pj's while frozen inside his closet. Greg would not talk about or tell his parents until he was seven years of age. Why he had this experience would haunt him for the rest of his life. Greg's mind was cluttered with fear, trepidation, and no real understanding of why him at that time. Greg would continue to relive those traumatic events every time unexplained events occurred to those he cared about in his life or those times others were killed or disappeared due to the ghoul and werewolf creatures coming to inform him of their deadly deeds that just occurred. Frightening, appalling, revolting beings to others still crept into his world informing him as to their being present. Greg feared the ghoul and werewolf creatures more than ever now.

Furthermore, nothing was yet uncovered as to the cause in either Caden's or Lenny's death. Just some wild animal or something killed them, ripping and shredding their bodies into pieces. What caused these unworldly beings with razor-sharp teeth to run rampant during awful, darkened skies during the storms of spring and summer? The records showed that no earthly animal existed with these types of fangs that might cause such specific damage to a human being. Ghoul and werewolf creatures were only intent on eating flesh of human beings for some inhuman, twisted, ritualistic reason. With no real obvious clues as to where to find answers, police officials and the coroner were in the dark. With the evidence of past deaths that occurred during the storms over the years, nothing jumped out in leading any closer to solving these deaths and disappearances.

Chapter Thirteen

No explanation was given as to how they both ended up in the woods outside of the city limits. Just some kind of animal had come across their bodies and was obviously hungry and dragged the bodies into the woods. What guarantee could be given so no more teens would die in this horrible fashion? One police spokesperson was not able to confirm or deny if anything could be done. Public safety seemed to be lost on those sworn to serve and protect the residents of Marcasite. Teagan and Candy, the *Gazette* owners, did interview the police officials and came away with very little extra knowledge. As the information in their own files showed more understanding about what caused these deaths than police told them. When they pressed how someone took two teenage males from their homes no answer was given. How could anything dispose of their bodies in those dense woods with no trace for local cops to have no comment, which was becoming frustrating and unbelievable to all the citizens of Marcasite? This ice-cold fear, trepidations, and a deep-down feeling of being scared to death of the unknown grew more evident as the days passed into weeks.

City council was declared a group of dunderheads and idiots who were really incompetent in the eyes of the people. A civic election was coming soon with the mayor and his pitiful council surely to be on their way out. Marcasite needed people in office who cared, ones who were not scared to get things done. Most citizens knew deep inside no human was capable of providing protection against the ancient formidable, obnoxious, calamitous creatures from the faraway, star studded Milky Way. Yet the needed hope, guidance, and direction from elected officials were not forthcoming right now. The mayor and council of Marcasite should have provided a sense of being in control with the local police force.

The *Gazette* subscribers were used to reading about all these supposedly unexplained ancient graveyards underneath their city. Did any real, long-dead bones really exist or not? Did some things come from elsewhere in time and space among the stars and planets out there? Teagan and Candy truly believed ghoul and werewolf creatures came from the Milky Way where it was filled with stars and planets. They felt so strong in regards to their idea of the lurid, macabre, accursed creatures originating there that they ran editorials in the *Gazette*. Russell Pagan had written so many notes after talking to the early residents and the local native elders. According to the elders, their own medicine men sent these evil beings into a spirit world far beyond Mother Earth's boundaries. This was the way it was told to the first white settlers who had immigrated out here on the prairies. Teagan and Candy could find no trace of where the ghoul and werewolf creatures were allowed to cross back over at will. The First Nations Tribes said the ghastly, vicious, horrendous invaders broke through the barrier every year.

Teagan and Candy knew full well about the storms that blackened the cloudy skies above, the ferocious, noisy winds, the pouring rains, the flashes of sheet lightning, and the rolling, pealing thunder of those nights. The *Gazette* had old records from the early days of Marcasite, all filled with frightening, eerie storms with people disappearing only to be found ripped and torn apart days later or not at all in some cases. Stories were filled with the disgusting, despicable creatures running around among the darkest of the storms. Horrid, grotesque, demonic creatures showed only slight glimpses of themselves amid flashes of lightning, deep among the trees, along the streets and the parks all across the town of Marcasite.

They appeared in Gopher County at about the same time in shadows across the land on the horizon. Creatures from the Milky Way were hiding among the flashes of sheet lightning in those stormy nights. Rolling, crashing thunder aided them in keeping their footsteps from being heard amid the noisy, stormy nights. Some people attributed the loud noise to the stomping of the ghoul and werewolf creatures' feet on the very hardened ground. Tornados struck across Marcasite, seemingly tearing and ripping up the earth for burial plots of victims who would never be found again.

First Nations elders were correct with their legends of strange, ghastly, terrifying, vicious creatures preying on their peoples throughout time. Their own medicine men were said to have driven the evil spirits back to the other side where they belonged. Medicine men, as strong willed and powerful as they were, could not keep evil at bay for all time. Entities of morbid, heinous, banished creatures returned every year seeking vengeance for being sent away. As each occurrence came, the medicine men burnt herbs, danced, and chanted all day and night to get rid of evil beings. Sometimes, after many days the terrible, ungodly ghoul and werewolf creatures were driven back to the other side into the dark. Many of their people were lost and killed during all those storms in times gone by. Some medicine men told of some of the warriors having found bones with sharp, deep teeth marks on them. This was a very bad omen; the medicine men were the only ones who could drive the unholy spirits away.

The storms blew across the area for a few days and nights at different periods from spring till fall, just like a black force coming after human souls hiding among nature's mightiest fury. The innocent lives were swept away by unknown things during severe storms with great pouring rains, tornado-strength winds, pounding hail, flashing sheet lightning, rolling peals of thunder, and tall, dark funnel clouds, as if these beings actually caused the heightened fears to hide under a veil of darkness. Marcasite was being ripped apart with fierce, dark funnel clouds on their way down to the pit below. Shrieks and loud howls screamed aloud, sending out warnings to the population to stay indoors or risk their very lives disappearing amid the darkness. Even staying inside was not safe as people soon realized after Lenny Farfeld and Caden McDougall that both were killed by some unearthly creatures. How many more deaths will happen before a way was found to drive these ghoul and werewolf creatures back into the star studded Milky Way again.

Winter was coming with still no result to either of the latest deaths from any of the police work. Many people felt the First Nations elders and their stories were, in fact, accurate and should have been listened to. After all, the two teens disappeared during a raging late-fall storm. The *Gazette* owners kept finding old stories of people who were also snatched during past years in the dark of the storms from spring till fall. However, all according to past items, ghoul and werewolf creatures struck only in the first early days of spring to the late days of fall. There were no stories of any weird abductions or disappearance or deaths in any of the cold winter months. At least there were no recorded stories to be found anywhere among the newspapers office files. Maybe even before the first of the paper's issues were ever out in wide circulation, people may have gone away, never to return. Who really knew way back then with no newspaper to carry stories for people to read? Often people did travel alone or in pairs on horseback in those days. With no close place to call home, could many more of those weird, strange deaths have, in fact, occurred? There were no newspaper reporters either then to keep track of strange disappearances, which did not help solve any existing cases at hand. Only after Russell Pagan showed up to record history for posterity was a newspaper available. Russell did have a box camera that was heavy and hard to set up every time. He usually left the camera at the office unless he had a special place to visit on a given day.

The Marcasite police seemed stymied with their results or lack of any leads in either of the newest cases. No help was forthcoming from anyone because no one saw or heard anything on those fateful nights. Extensive searches came up empty-handed, even with the same areas being sifted through many times since. At this point, thoughts came to actually start to believe in the dark forces existing. Answers at times were found in the weirdest or strangest of places. Setting a trap for things from another dimension was not normal by any means, and how would it work? Still, some police members believed a real person was responsible for both of these deaths. Not everyone believed in the reality of ghoul and werewolf creatures coming around to visit the citizens of Marcasite. Many did believe the same evil beings were encroaching within the boundary of Gopher County to kill people. Conclusive findings were not among any reports the police had in their files from years ago or now. They needed to keep going and hope for a lucky break. These vile, wicked creatures had the history of attacking this area since time began if the police accepted it.

The *Gazette* publishers always poked around the police station for anything to provide their readers. After hearing about a harebrained idea for setting a trap, especially for some ghoul and werewolf creatures or other netherworld beings, they thought it was laughable at first. Other tales from the great grandparents who passed stories down were ignored but came back into their minds. Old police reports were incomplete, according to the police officer in the filing room, for one reason or another. No one was allowed access during this ongoing investigation even though Teagan and Candy wanted to assist. This was a public matter, as they had the right to know what the police were doing to solve these killings. Their pleading voices were left unheard, as it fell on the deaf ears of the cops, which surprised them both. A very arrogant attitude was not right at this point in time. The *Gazette* would carry this as an editorial in the next issue on Saturday for all to read. The residents needed to be aware the cops may be covering up the details of what occurred recently and in the past events. The *Gazette* got angry and carried a lot of clout with the people of the town.

The *Gazette* was published on Mondays, Wednesdays, Fridays, and a special edition every Saturday at noon. No matter what their schedule, the Wellands kept up their four times a week publishing duties for the general public. Sometimes there was not much rest at all for either of them since the last two teens died. Eating regular meals was another hardship even for the two of them during this cruel, hard period faced by all in Marcasite. On the evenings when they were getting the *Gazette* ready for publishing, they did feel happy, knowing all the people enjoyed the paper as much as they did. As usual after they finished they would have a hot cup of tea before retiring to bed for a well-deserved, good night's rest. Some nights, Teagan and Candy slept for five hours or less because of the demands placed on them, depending on whether strange events were unfolding due to any possible residents disappearing in those storms with wicked intentions.

Teagan and Candy always felt refreshed in the mornings, facing their beloved newspaper, just like two young lovers in the springtime in the warm sunshine of the days. Teagan and Candy Welland always woke up full of energy, wanting to get moving along with what the day offered good or bad. Love of running their newspaper kept them feeling alive, jubilant, and wanting more from each day.

Chapter Fourteen

The newspaper was ready to be put to bed for the issue the next day. Teagan and Candy printed enough for everyone in the city to have a copy. Ever since Lenny Farfeld and Caden McDougall were murdered, the circulation had skyrocketed. Getting these stories was getting to be harder with every issue, as not initially thought about was the time involved, with the trust and the rudeness of some residents. However, the reward was most people actually wanted to find out as much as possible in the *Gazette's* stories in every issue. Others actually wanted to assist in getting information out to the general public. Around the town of Marcasite, the *Gazette* was the only way to do this so slowly residents began to open up to the owners. Without the assistance of the residents, nothing new would ever turn up.

Every issue had a town-wide circulation that was reaching close to a thousand a week. In the rural areas, it was roughly two hundred every week. The *Gazette* was known as the only newspaper in circulation for the last one hundred years. The paper was founded when Marcasite was a dusty western village full of cowboys, bad guys, and sheriffs. Stories of cowhands following the herds to market for whatever they could get paid were commonplace. Long, dirty, dusty trails full of danger, especially when the lightning and thunderstorms cracked overhead, many a cowboy lost his life after being stomped on by tons of stampeding cows, steers, and bulls running wildly, trying to get away from the storms and whatever else was chasing them in the heavy pouring rains, huge hailstones, sheets of flashing lightning, and ear-pounding, rolling thunder. Shadows may have appeared in among the herds of stampeding cattle. Only those long-gone cowboys will ever be sure of what they saw out on the prairies then. Cattle spooked easy during any storm from spring till fall as the loud, rolling thunder would set them off, running amok. Tons of frenzied beef herds would stampede wildly across the fields and into the bushes. Some run into the hills along the edges of the ranches at the time in Gopher County.

The *Gazette* from the past was full of stories about cattle drives taking place on the open prairies in this area. Besides, people who owned the largest herds happened to own the largest of the ranches around the county. Gopher County extended some two hundred and fifty miles in all directions from the center. Marcasite was starting to be a small village on the edge of the prairies in the mid-eighteen hundreds. The *Gazette* carried editorials about the politicians misusing their influence to get what they wanted. The newspaper wrote stories of gunfighters hanging out on these ranches to push the small ranchers out of business. There were countless stories in the *Gazette* of those terrible episodes of the lack of law and order. The most corrupt of the politicians and the entire justice system was pushed along behind a wall of hired thugs. Real law and order would show up one day; until then, life went on for the residents of Marcasite and in Gopher County.

Another day, unnatural, disturbing, abhorrent creatures would unleash their own justice on some of those bad people. No records existed to show any untoward activity happening due to Russell Pagan and the *Gazette* not existing during those early times. Only those verbal stories that were handed down from one generation to the next truly existed. This depended on how much they had been twisted along the way. Not everyone kept the same story intact as they aged or the way it was told to them. People added or omitted parts of stories to protect others or themselves from harm. Such was life in those rough days, even before the ghoul and werewolf creatures were recorded killing and taking others away.

Teagan and Candy knew that other stories existed in the records packed away by Russell Pagan when he owned the *Gazette*. Tomorrow, with more time on their hands, the search would begin again into the depths of the crates and boxes. For tonight, sleep was required to refuel their bodies and minds to dive back deeper into history.

Teagan and Candy did believe in early to bed, early to rise, and had practiced this for many years already. No matter what transpired, a good night's sleep was required. Severe storms always kept them awake as they did for everyone all over Marcasite. Though Teagan and Candy were awake well past the midnight hour, a lot of times finalizing the newspaper for printing the following day, sleep was one thing they required if only for short periods of time in the darkness of the night.

The next morning, the sun was just over the horizon when Teagan awoke. His wife, Candy, was still sleeping beside him. Something seemed to have shaken him awake like a rag doll being played with and shaken by a child. Teagan looked around slowly as he did not want to miss anything if it was out of place in their room. Everything looked the same as the previous night; nothing was out of place. Was there something there or different, or is it just his mind playing tricks? By now he was sitting straight up under the covers. Waking Candy did not seem to be a good idea since he himself had no idea what to tell her or if he should. Teagan could never recall being woken in such a manner in his lifetime even as a kid. What just took place could have been the remnants of a dream he had it was surreal. Would the reprehensible, malevolent, dreadful monsters be playing with him for nosing around in their affairs? He was bewildered and decided not to wake his wife or alarm her in any way right then.

Teagan rose, got out of bed, and slowly, quietly got dressed for the day. He silently crept downstairs to rekindle the fire in the wood stove. Both he and Candy enjoyed a hot cup of coffee in the mornings, especially with a bottle of fresh cream they received from both George and Elma Franks yesterday. Teagan waited until the coffee was perking before going up to wake Candy. She might be very interested in his early morning visitor or the vivid dream Teagan experienced. Yes, she would indeed find it very interesting; it might even stimulate her mind this morning. She was looking forward to searching the boxes and crates for historical stories of the ghoul and werewolf creatures. Having fiendish, destructive, hideous creatures in their home may be disturbing if they had actually caused trouble this morning. Yet no other out of sort happenings showed up that morning or any other time inside their home.

Candy smelled the coffee perking as it wafted through their home. Teagan had also started making breakfast for the two of them. Both of them were handy in the kitchen just like in the newspaper office. He then helped Candy set the table for breakfast. They then had a cup of coffee before he finished cooking the eggs and bacon with biscuits. He then told Candy of the strange occurrence of an earlier moment that morning. Something had grabbed his foot and shook it like a young child shaking a rag doll, and he had never before felt things like this ever take place in his life. Teagan said maybe something was just saying to keep looking or searching for a clue. Candy figured

he was joking; however, she knew better when he looked
so serious. From the look in his eyes, she then knew it
unsettled his soul and shook him inside. Candy never did
ask why he refused to wake her up after this unsettling
event took place. Were these ghoul and werewolf creatures
warning them or trying to direct them in their search
for information? Could it have been the long-gone soul
of Russell Pagan trying to urge them onward in their
search for answers? Teagan and Candy felt some strange
happening had transpired that morning to wake him up.

Today was a research day for both of them at the office,
digging up more stories from the depths of the boxes and
crates called their filing system. Teagan and Candy felt one
day soon their need to buy a few filing cabinets would be
a good objective. After all, these wooden crates and boxes
were good ones with lots of wear and tear on them over the
long years of use. Many hundreds of stories existed inside
of each one, hidden, stored carefully, and snugly put away,
only waiting to be pulled out into the bright light of the
day to be read one word after the other ensuring the reader
never lost interest in the item. Stories were meant to be
attention gripping, eye grabbing, and needed the readers
glued to the pages, as they were deadly and weird in so
many ways. Storms filled with black nimbus and cumulus
clouds, tornado funnel clouds, pouring rains, huge
hailstones, bright flashes of sheet lightning, peals of rolling
thunder providing cover for the ghoul and werewolf
creatures. Everyone enjoyed a great item about what

transpired during those storms along with what happened to whom.

Russell Pagan indeed did a fantastic job of reporting every happening in Marcasite back then. Teagan and Candy enjoyed reading his old items from the eighteen hundreds, tales with how people just vanished into the depth of the blackness of the storms from spring till late the fall, bodies swept up to a secret location to be torn open, ripped apart, and gnawed on with the remains being left lying in the woods to be found. Others would never be found again in this earthly plane. These grainy boxes and graying crates of varying sizes held the entire history of the village of Marcasite and most of Gopher County through the great eyes of Russell Pagan. Teagan and Candy had their own unique manner of putting reports in order since taking over the newspaper. The *Gazette* owners bought a few metal filing cabinets with drawers to hold all the newest documented stories in place. Looking through Russell Pagan's system made them realize their items also should be stored in the new metal cabinets. Teagan and Candy never seemed to have much extra time for binding Russell Pagan's stuff. Reading through the meticulous, well written accounts of the times intrigued the pair, which consumed a lot of time during the days spent researching for hidden clues from the past.

Since the two local teens, Lenny Farfeld and Caden McDougall, were killed by things said to resemble shadows of ghoul and werewolf creatures, the discussion turned to storms that ravaged Marcasite and Gopher County in those spring, summer, and fall months of long ago. Strong winds drove towering funnel clouds, torrents of rains, huge hailstones, sheets of flashing lightning, and the rumbling peals of thunder.

Yes, they did believe in strange beings like these demonic, unholy, petrifying ghoul and werewolf creatures during those stormy nights, screeching, screaming, howling winds as the tornados tore through the entire county on their way to hell, the rains pouring down, the hailstones hitting so hard on their roof it was really deafening at times. You could only see through the rain for more than a few inches at best. Hailstones sounded like a baseball team pounding balls against a wall for batting practice. The thunder came out with a loud explosion like a cannon going off. Lightning seared their souls as it allowed shapes to run rampant in the flashes in the storms of the night. One giant organized campaign of hurt was unfurled upon Marcasite each and every time a storm struck. This caused these disgusting creatures to feast on human flesh, tearing it from bones and gnawing on the bones leaving deep gouges in them.

Yet no one said a word due to a strange agreement that keeping quiet was the best option in these situations. Would anyone look at one another like we had a mental disability if we all suddenly shouted about seeing ghoul and werewolf creatures showing up amid the worst storms? Any harm brought upon them would be self-inflicted, and that was no good. Besides, life was awesome, except from the restraints of being attacked in Marcasite, all the fresh air and with the freedom to go where you wanted to at any time. Who could ask for more than that, except for the freedom of fear from some devilish, unhallowed, horrid creatures? Shadowy, vile creatures that attacked during those fierce storms from spring till late fall inside Marcasite, ghoul and werewolf creatures attacked without any restraint. Life changed each year as these unearthly, revolting, detestable creatures came again to perform their ritual feasts on the residents.

They recalled certain storms when the devilish, barbaric things sprung to life among the huge hailstones, the tornado funnel clouds, the pouring rains, the flashes of sheet lightning, and the loud peals of rolling thunder. As being young teenagers themselves way back then, fear gripped at their innocent souls, almost as if the very fabric of the world would rip apart amid this freakish summer storm to unleash the evil images upon them. Fear pulled at them as if the same thing was happening again right now. Reliving moments from their younger past bothered them for an unknown reason as ice-cold shivers ran down their backs, just maybe the thoughts flooding back from being teens seared them more than either of them realized till today.

All four of them, Frank and Myrtle Thomas and Teagan and Candy chatted about life back when they were young and how hard it was. Their talk turned toward the topic of horrendous storms and the damages caused in terms of property and to the human costs involved during and after they struck. No one had a good explanation as to why this area was hit every year for six months. The two couples became so engrossed in the topic, time swept by very fast. For dessert, they had apple pie with fresh whipped cream, which kept the voices going on. Lots of stories were told by their friends that they were never aware of before today.

They were informed of dark, ominous cloud formations starting to appear as if the devil's brigades approached them. Swirling dust storms arose from tornado-strength winds blowing across the land, rain pounding down so fast and with such fury no one could see through it. Hail soon followed with stones the size of baseballs wiping out entire crops, and it did smash a lot of windows. Ghoul and werewolf creatures had arrived from another place, skulking around among the storm. People actually disappeared out in the village of Marcasite even back then. Most of These individuals that were taken showed up deep in wooded areas torn, ripped open, and chewed upon. Skeletal bones were left often scattered around on the ground as a warning to whoever found them. Other people who disappeared were never found again anywhere in this world. No trace or trails would be found as if they just vanished into thin air. Devilish, infernal, deathless raiders took their prizes and disappeared with them back into another realm.

Teagan and Candy became fascinated with the tales as they ate. Could they have forgotten about these regaled stories from the days of their youths? How was it now they recalled listening to their grandparents tell such episodes, holding them spellbound all afternoon at times? Now bringing these stories up with Frank and Myrtle eased them back into another time. Everyone at the table felt the uneasiness from those days during those raging infernos of the stormy season. Where had this tornado with winds that sounded like screeches of demons tearing the earth to shreds on their way down to the pit below come from? No one would ever know where the destructive, wild, appalling high winds came from.

They decided to spend a few more hours with the Thomases before heading back home. Both of their minds and souls seemed ready to burst from the fear of being caught in the village late at night. Neither one wanted to be out there should one of those freakish storms came down from the sky above this evening. After all, they had a forty-five-minute drive back home to safety of their house. Writing and filing any stories was going to have to wait for the morning to arrive. Once again, sleep would not come easy due to the unsettling fears that had come alive inside each of them. A very pleasant visit ended with such an eerie dread, making them sick with shock of the unknown. What really hid out there amid the storms causing the many deaths and disappearances and tragedy to many families? At some point during the night, Teagan and Candy eventually fell asleep, snuggled close together for safety.

Chapter Fifteen

After breakfast the next morning, they still recalled being stuck inside during such a freakish storm. The extremely intense, strong winds with torrential rains and hailstones crashing down on everything caused lots of property damage. Loud, howling, screeching noises seemed as if something was trying to gain entry as the tornado funnel clouds were gaining speed so fast and ominously. Their vivid memories recalled those flashes of sheet lighting, the crashing thunder overhead occurring as they wandered backward through time. The sounds from the thunder reminded them of the cannons at the circus as they were shot off. Marcasite seemed to be marked for a type of destruction from some of the diabolic, spine-chilling, frightening creatures. A strange, powerful dark force came and attacked them more so than in any previous year. Teagan and Candy felt the worst was yet to come for the residents of Marcasite.

Once the pair arrived at the *Gazette's* office, both immediately began spending the next several hours typing out the many segments of documented segments to fit together in the paper. Teagan and Candy had searched the records to find the main source of items from the long-ago past. Yes, every issue needed to be laid out for their readers to become absorbed in them. Somewhere a true gem did exist to scare and hopefully get someone to talk out about things that were held inside—two teens had been ripped apart by ghoul and werewolf creatures from another world in this seam of time. Did our star studded galaxy exist for things to sneak through and attack our planet? Russell Pagan just might have hidden such material away in his crates and boxes of old copies and notes. The *Gazette's* owners felt one or more residents may hold a key to opening this mystery up.

Greg Braden was the one person who knew the answers to these sick, horrible, despicable crimes. Two of his best friends were killed by something from the deep cracks of the star studded Milky Way. Ghoul and werewolf creatures with sharp incisor teeth capable of ripping and tearing people apart and gnawing on the bodies they attacked during those fierce storms. No trace was ever located as they never stepped on the ground in any of the locations. The weight of their victims seemed nothing to such beings who floated in and around in the tornado winds, with the torrential rains and hailstones. The loud rolling claps of thunder with the extreme screaming from the howling winds echoing off the outer parts of the homes scared everyone. The town was completely covered in black, becoming full of light for only a few seconds as the flashes of lightning flew across the clouds like a box of sparklers going off in sequence in all directions. The noises in this storm sounded close to a cacophony of different types of instruments blaring at once.

Yet Greg Braden knew because he had been invaded by these sinister, fiendish, odious creatures since his childhood. After all, he had seen the shrinks at the hospital and kept a secret all these years. Greg felt the fear grip at him over the years as those things entered his body and soul. Why he was spared never made sense throughout all this time. Greg was a lot stronger than he felt, as his spirit never gave out during these attacks. Often his thought took him back to that first attack in his room. Panic, fear, ice-cold sweats ran right down his backbone and through his young body as he reminisced, scared to death of something he could not see or identify for the first few minutes until some shapes became clear and he saw ghoul and werewolf creatures with sharp, incisor like teeth, grinning, sneering and scaring him. Slimy goop, dripped down from their gaping, wide-open mouths, spilling all over their chins just to instill fear in a six-year-old child. Greg could not move or scream, he knew from that time, knowing he wet his pajamas while frozen to the floor in his closet. Those fears and doubts about his sanity and not wanting to admit he saw the barbaric, foul smelling, fiendish creatures then or now worried him.

Neither Janice nor anyone of his friends knew anything of the visitations placed upon him. Greg was aware of being shunned by them should any knowledge of his adventure ever come out. In addition, possibly being accused of being party to the deaths of Lenny and Caden was way too much for him to fathom, guilt that was unduly his alone as no others who may also know had yet ever spoke up. Elders who lived through such atrocities in those past years told their younger generations of all this. Somehow it all seemed to fall upon the deaf ears of each generation and more so as time progressed. Now these legends passed down crept suddenly back into the forefront of everyone's thoughts. Greg knew more about ghoul and werewolf creatures than anyone in recent memory. Why he did was driving him to extreme thoughts as he got older. Greg knew keeping his sanity was urgent for his future life. He also knew keeping everything a secret from anyone in his life was vitally important. Greg would never allow himself to go back into the local psych ward at Prairie General. One visit in a lifetime was enough. Greg understood this now, looking back, being wiser.

All police forces were stymied, stumped, and bewildered as they had no leads or ideas or what direction to go in. Complete with feelings of being lost in the woods, alone with something evil shredding young teens apart was no good. Why had this happened and what managed the creatures to disappear into thin air? Both Lenny's and Caden's families needed answers; none were available as yet. The Farfelds and the McDougalls were very angry over all that was not taking place. Police Chief Harry Rook knew his force really was doing everything it could in these matters. None of these atrocious murders caused and carried out by these unholy, pernicious, outrageous blitzers would ever be solved. Police officers did their due diligence in each investigation to the best of their abilities. Residents were still not at all happy with the results turning up no leads, even if they felt the brutal, barbaric, hellish beings could not be stopped.

No one knew what the ghoul and werewolf creatures looked like who were responsible except for Greg Braden, himself a true victim. The only difference is Greg was allowed to stay alive to be haunted every time a death and disappearance happened in a storm. A lifetime of this would take its toll on a young six-year-old that now was in his teens. Greg had grown used to shielding the facts hidden inside his own soul from all his friends, especially Janice Maribel, his girlfriend. His parents only knew of one incident when he was seven years old during a camping trip. He never planned on opening up to anyone about the experiences with the detestable, brutal, horrid creatures. There were a few moments when Greg wanted to tell someone except he was unable. He felt tortured by these creatures working on his mind, soul, and heart. He had already lost his two closest friends to the ghastly, deadly marauding raiding crew this fall. Yet fear prevented him from coming forward to tell what he knew.

Local police seemed to be hamstrung with doubts of everything and nothing at the same time. Searches had been carried out systemically with no results. Both storms washed away any and all traces of evidence of the crimes. Somehow there had to be a trail or a sure sign of something taking place; however, there was no sign at all, except these cases scared everyone into submission due to the abhorrent, grotesque history behind them. No one could say that a trace of the hideous, reprehensible, demonic raiders did exist. Greg Braden had seen them, and he was the only one still able to see them out of all the residents in town. He was just too embarrassed to come forward to describe these repugnant, obnoxious, grisly creatures to the police.

Police were beginning to believe the elders should have been listened to. Elders knew the history of the entire area from the time of the glaciers through each successive epoch until today. Every generation received tales handed down about the past to keep them for all future generations to come. Along the way, people lost some respect for their elders and the legends that were sacred among them. The Marcasite police knew they were lost in the search for the killers of these residents. Over the years before the death of both Samuels girls until today, no one had been identified as the killers. Long before the first recorded senseless, mutilating deaths took place, the ghoul and werewolf creatures were blamed in accordance with the lore that stood for centuries among the local tribes on the prairies. Storms caused cracks to open in the star studded Milky Way, allowing ghoul and werewolf creatures to stalk the lands for human flesh to feast upon. The first white settlers were informed of the tales as passed down from the First Nations Tribes. These horrid, detestable, vicious alien, killing creatures came back time and again to carry out their deadly, ritualistic, feasting raids upon the residents living in Marcasite.

Tom and Helen Braden were among thousands of residents completely unaware of all the old stories of the area. Had anyone said something, then someone could have talked to the local elders. Curiosity was needed to find out, but even the cops kept quiet about all this. Well, because fear of the people stampeding in and out of Marcasite was not needed during this investigation. Peace and tranquility was required in order to resolve these two vicious, unprovoked, ugly, nasty murders and keep everyone safe from further harm and happy in Marcasite. In other words, the cops wanted to keep a tight lid on things.

Tom and Helen felt Greg's condition when he was younger had nothing to do with any of this. Whatever attacked Greg never came back, as far as they were aware of. Greg had not told his parents about those freakish dark things coming back or how often they had. The eerie feelings of fear, the ice-cold shivers, seared him to the inner being in his young soul. He felt that despite anything he said, nothing would have prevented the deaths of Lenny or Caden. Although Greg was deeply saddened by the loss of his friends, there was nothing he could have done to prevent it. This young teenager shook with fear and cold, knowing he should have died when he was six years old. Yet the creatures enjoyed playing with him like a toy, which made him want to tell someone; however, being shunned and locked away stopped him each time.

Greg had, over the last few months, spent time reading about the history of Marcasite, looking for an explanation as to what was occurring. Somewhere in these books existed signs pointing to strange happenings during this eerie, scary, dreadful spring and summer storms coming to do harm. Did these beings enter from a crack in the Milky Way to come skulking around? Bringing along with themselves tornado winds, torrential rains, huge hailstones hitting the earth and sheets of flashing lightning crossing the skies throughout the nights. Thunder roared like huge bass drums being shot with cannonballs. Pitch blackness enveloped those nights, frightening everyone as the storm continued unabated. Shadows were seen skulking around amid the storms, screeching and howling with the winds, growing in strength. Gray images were seen amid the flashing sheets of lightning across the sky, scaring every resident foolish enough to look outside their windows. There were numerous references in books about ghoul and werewolf creatures existing that caused gruesome deaths among the people. Deaths and disappearances happened within extreme storms from the spring till fall every year.

Greg realized this is what occurred on those two separate evenings when Lenny and Caden were taken. Old legends from the elders of the area should have been listened to instead of being ignored. Why would top officials refuse to listen to information about ghoul and werewolf creatures from the Milky Way? Greg's own experiences made him aware of the dangers ahead if he kept searching. He had to look further into these facts before anyone would hear from some hysterical student sixteen years of age for now.

Telling Janice or anyone else at this moment was not good he figured. One of them just might think he was just plain out of his mind. Greg knew he was onto something at that moment. He began to wonder how many other books existed on these topics and thinking about doing research at the local library after school might be a good thing. However, Janice might want to know why he was going there alone. He just might have to tell her about his own stories after all. The two of them enjoyed solving mysteries while doing school projects in the study halls together. Janice and Greg had done lots of research in the past few years in many subject areas. In and out of school searching their souls, thoughts of how they felt being together. Still, Greg was scared to tell Janice in regards to his haunting experiences by ghoul and werewolf creatures. Janice might actually think he was being silly or going crazy. He could not take that sort of step at this time for the same sane reason inside of him.

Winter crept up on the city much earlier this year as the snow slowly came along with the cold weather. Still, Lenny and Caden's murders went unsolved as time was going by. Evil creatures according to local lore never appeared in the winter months. Maybe the police would solve the latest two outstanding cases. However, no one believed they would or could. No suspects had been found or indicated, according to official responses to the *Gazette*. Teagan and Candy followed this case and all other stories they found in the old records. Plus, all the local residents had their share of old legends passed down from their elders.

Chapter Sixteen

Everyone became interested in the many winter activities to take their minds off the harsh current problems. Each winter there was hockey, skating, broomball, curling, sledding, and tobogganing events. The city had built indoor rinks and arenas at the right time, because they were always busy. All of the citizens felt good when they were having family fun and carrying on like kids. With the two local hills by the schools, skiing and stuff was always going on for kids and adults alike.

In mid-November, a huge winter storm struck unexpectedly with winds and huge snowdrifts plied up all over. The snow falls continued for days closing in on four days of long-ago, strange winter activity. It wasn't until the streets were cleared a couple of days later that someone noticed that an empty vehicle sat on the side of the street. No one was thought to be inside of it, and no trace of any identification was located in the vehicle. The street clearing crews called the local police to come out for it. All this sick, horrendous, twisted damage had to be done by those unseen ghoul and werewolf creatures. The car was full of snow due to the doors being open, which seemed strange to the police officers.

It would be another two days before police found out the white, two-doored, empty vehicle belonged to a couple from Marcasite. Alex and Abigail Walton had just moved in to a home in Marcasite about a month before. Two more deaths; were they connected to the earlier deaths in the past? It would take police another half day to find a body buried inside the Waltons' own vehicle, just on the street along Crown Park as the city crews cleared the sidewalks for the pedestrians to walk through. It was downtown, and everyone enjoyed the stroll through it on warm days all year long. Now an ice-cold fear took over as the citizens gazed at the park differently, no longer a place of warmth and greenness, just a place of death and wanton destruction.

Alex Walton died in the same manner as all the previous victims had—being, ripped, torn, and gnawed to death by some evil beings with sharp teeth like those ghastly, destructible, heinous foreign creatures. The only exception was his remains were left in his vehicle in town instead of along the highway to Goreville. Was this a new terrifying way to let the residents of Marcasite know winter could now be dangerous for them? No more freedom from the snow and cold of winter from the ghoul and werewolf creatures inside Marcasite.

An autopsy would be done at the Prairie General Hospital for a cause of death. What did remain of Alex Walton's body would need to time to unthaw first, which was going to take a couple of days. At least some of the body seemed to be there inside the clothing attached to the frozen seats. Alex Walton would be the first recorded death in any winter month from these ghoul and werewolf creatures. Marcasite seemed to be doomed year round now from unseen evil beings from the faraway Milky Way. Dr. Gabe Bridger indeed had his work cut out for him. Once, he removed the remains from the heavily frozen car, once it thawed out, work would begin. Then Alex Walton's vehicle could be turned over to the police. This was the third death and autopsy for Dr. Bridger since arriving in town in the fall. He wondered aloud in the autopsy room what was actually taking place and why had he come here?

Those same days, the car was towed to the police station to be searched for any and all evidence. Maybe something may show up to make this case easier to solve unlike the other cases that remained open. What were they facing and why this year suddenly cropping up with such violence? How many elders had said things would happen if the legends were not paid attention to? Police officials had forgotten about what their historical records may provide. There were a number of unexplained deaths dating back to the mid-eighteen hundreds for sure. A number went unsolved due to lack of staff during that late period of time. Others went unsolved due to the violent events surrounding those cases even back then. Storms of severe, sudden force and intensity came out of nowhere, and people died. Bodies were torn, ripped apart, and gnawed upon by some unknown creature not from an earthly source. This was contained in the police files at headquarters going back almost a century. Police officers scoured through long-ago reports of strange death and disappearances caused by some ungodly, grotesque ghoul and werewolf creatures. They only showed shadows of themselves amid the worst storms of the spring till fall. Now the first recorded winter death and disappearance had just occurred in town.

Marcasite was a town in turmoil already, and now it just became more inflamed. People were on edge more than ever due to another unexplained death and disappearance. Two new recent residents of their city for one month, and now both were gone due to some unexplained, untimely circumstance. Weary minds began to wonder with the winds and blinding snow that may have just has caused another sick, sad situation. What came during this windy snowstorm to harm the people of this death-sickened town? Never had any single attack been recorded during the winter months in Marcasite leading up to this month. Winter snow clouds kept the huge star studded Milky Way and the ghoul and werewolf creatures hidden inside. Horrible creatures were dumping violence along with lots of snow upon the tired helpless residents of Marcasite.

Those unexplained strange, ravaging, summer storms creating havoc and deaths were one thing to deal with. Winter storms with sudden deaths associated with them became a new breed of fear for residents to behold. The *Gazette* started running stories from their old historical records in the fact no deaths happened in the winters. The editorials bashed the police and the local mayor, as everyone felt they were not forthcoming in the truth behind what was going on. The Wellands felt strongly in editorials in their own paper and boldly spoke out loudly, being good newspaper people. Teagan and Candy were rational thinkers and believed the public at large deserved better knowledge. The public required a strong advocate to raise concerns on their behalf in the *Gazette*. Why was the information more guarded in this case by the authorities than in other ones in the past? People should be told about the results of any findings for their safety.

They would go after the real story with full vigor and strength of their newspaper behind them. This year was going to an extreme harsh one to live through for the population of the Marcasite. In the last four months, two teens and two adults were killed in a basically good community built for families. Tales from the local elders and their ancient legends crept into everyone's minds. Teagan and Candy printed information in every issue as they found it about how the town had been attacked in the past. These twisted, sick, disturbing activities, the haunting disappearances, and the deaths of people across Marcasite were wrong. Cold-weather deaths and disappearances were just not found in any records from the files of Russell Pagan. Marcasite became a scarier, frightening, and deadlier place that very winter. No one would feel safe this winter after the last attack by the repulsive, obnoxious, ghastly ghoul and werewolf creatures under the cover of white flakes and winds.

Winter had just started, and two lives were taken from them, and the fear deepened. A full ice-cold dread sliced the citizenship deep to the bone. No one went out unless with the company of others for safety's sakes. At one time, no one cared or worried about all the nonsense of unseen beings. No one ever went missing in the winter months before. Now the strange evil had inhabited their town in the deep, cold, snowy winter months. What was taking place to this jewel that was their home? Residents wanted to feel complete safety for their children and themselves. November proved being clear of the dreaded, frightful, calamitous creatures would not be. Now many wondered what lay ahead in the months through the rest of the winter. This town was built to become a jewel on the prairie; instead it was a wasteland of death and disappearances. It was too overwhelming for some families to handle anymore. Police figured some people were ready to move out of the city due to the deaths. That really was the case, as a few families did leave town because of the deaths and disappearances. The general thinking was everyone wanted to see this horrible business go away.

Police held facts back in their records that similar deaths occurred in preceding years. No leads for suspects were ever traced or found in any of the locations in the deep-wooded areas on the highway to Goreville. What had caused these deaths never left any trace in the dirt or snow. How would the police locate the monsters responsible for the many unexplained deaths and disappearances in Marcasite?

Vicious winter snowstorms and high winds had never been known or confirmed to cause such deaths. Police were stumped with no ideas on how to proceed in these two sudden winter deaths. Did Mother Nature indeed actually play a huge hand in these terrifying deaths? Something very foul caused climatic conditions with one person being torn open, ripped apart, and chewed to pieces. Where did such creatures exist in the unknown world of the cracks in time? Did an ancient ruling beast exist who brought all of this down on today's population, some type of retribution for building a town on an ancient grave site left by murderous, demonic, barbaric creatures? Old tales told of ghoul and werewolf creatures striking in the summer were common, not in the winter months. No stories had been passed down from one generation to another about strange deaths in the cold of winter. Now the worst fears were coming alive for the residents of Marcasite, as their world was tossed upside down in the dead of the cold and snow.

Many unanswered questions existed with no plausible excuses to reply to. Some type of reasoning needed to come back before everyone went crazy. A very uneasy fear of the unknown increased as the days passed slowly by that November. People did wonder when and who was going to be next for being led to their deaths this winter. Hiding inside their nice, warm homes was not safe even in summer months, as vicious, beastly, lurid creatures could invade the indoors. Winter came with absolutely no place to feel safe from the disgusting, twisted ghoul and werewolf creatures. Going to work and sending their children of all ages to school stressed out the parents across town. Life needed to go ahead with the same sort of happiness regardless of the circumstances. Fear should not hold anyone from going forward in showing their family's true bravery. Winter or summer, they all faced the same unforgiving, diabolical, atrocious creatures in storms together.

Marcasite seemed to be the greatest place to live not many years before. After the town came about, some dark, evil beings crept around among the residents, which began to definitely scare them, picking and killing citizens off at will during some of the worst storms in recorded history. Sinister feelings came mostly during severe, rainy thunderstorms when shivers run up and down their spines. At times an ice-cold dread often filled them up. Now the same ice-cold shocks came as winter was taking people away to be ripped apart, torn open, and gnawed upon.

One body was left behind in a car, and one was yet to be discovered as the result of the latest incident.

Abigail Walton would be found in the snow on the edge of the dense woods along the highway to Goreville. The same place the other victims were located in that area of the woods along the highway. Abigail's bones were strewn around the red-splattered area of snow like discarded leftovers on the side of the road. Her bones showed deep, long, wide gouges just like all the previous victims displayed. Local police knew they were dealing with the same killers as before over the years. Fresh snow splattered with red blotches of blood and not one footprint of any kind, how did these creatures get around without leaving any clues for them to follow? A deep sense of frustration and despair set in not just on the residents but on the police as well. How do you defend against something you do not see or hear? The victims were possibly the only ones with the ability to see the ghoul and werewolf creatures before being killed.

They still did not know Greg Braden could see these dreadful, demonic, hideous ghoul and werewolf creatures. Greg was haunted more as time passed over his predicament of being able to see what others could not. Those huge, long, incisors-like teeth scared him to death, the grins, the rolling of their eyes, and the drooling goop falling off their mouths. Greg felt he could be next in line to be a victim. Greg knew those creepy, evil, nasty beings kept him alive for a purpose that he was blind too. Still, being scared if anyone accidentally found out about the secret he held inside most of his life. No matter what, Greg kept it locked away and would pay dearly over the years. Life created this problem, and his soul kept trying to fight back to survive the damage intact.

Recent memories of their families happily frolicking in their yards and the local parks still existed. Yes, Marcasite was a paradise on the edge of nowhere, just not the one they all wanted it to be. Sudden, strange happenings invaded their gem of an oasis, changing it forever, right before their eyes. A certain charm that had existed to bring these people to the jewel called Marcasite, seemed to be gone. Maybe one day everyone would calm down enough to resume a happy contented lifestyle in Marcasite. If this wanton death and destruction would just vanish back into the star studded Milky Way where it came from, all the residents could relax and have normal everyday lives with family and friends. The *Gazette* continued writing stories about past times filled with terrible storms wreaking havoc from bygone eras.

Teagan and Candy still went to interview the local elders where and when they could. They were going to see Kelly and Dawn Brown from Marcasite. Both of their families resided here since the village was established. If anyone knew about the lore and history of this place, the Browns did. The two newspaper owners always phoned ahead to say they were stopping by for a visit. Kelly and Dawn seemed very happy to tell stories concerning the legends surrounding the town. Great unheard tales told by good storytellers were always welcome for the owners of the *Gazette*. Sipping hot tea and eating fresh biscuits on a cold winter afternoon was a welcome respite for both Teagan and Candy—no better substitute from the office cluttered with files than going visiting in town in the winter.

In fact, the tea was ready when the Wellands arrived, complete with hot biscuits fresh from the oven. Yes, it was going to be an interesting afternoon, sitting in one of the oldest homes in the town, an original solid-brick home built before the turn of the century in 1890. The brick work was excellent, and all the chinks were well filled, with no leaks appearing to show up. Kelly and Dawn lived in their three-bedroom house with a kitchen, dining room, sitting room, and very comfortable front porch. Indeed, every place was better when they had front porches back in the day. Most homes in Marcasite did have those front porches attached to the houses.

Teagan and Candy waited for the Browns to have a seat before sitting down and serving the tea and biscuits. Manners seemed always to be best success in pursuing topics of any kind. Stories they were after could only be had by a caring approach. Fear existed for almost eight months this year, to be exact. Kelly and Dawn knew about the stories from their parents and grandparents. Neither of them seemed to be bothered by the unknown evil in Marcasite. Kelly and Dawn had some strange experiences to share when periods of awful deaths occurred. Even back then no one had the answers the elders said—evil could never be seen only felt. Others said that during those vile, fierce storms with tornado winds, pouring rains, lightning, and thunder, shadow creatures skulked all about. Through broken seams in time or cracks in the star studded Milky Way, ghoul and werewolf creatures crossed over in stormy times. Kelly and Dawn Brown were shocked and completely surprised, hearing this story of two local residents being killed in early November. Neither could recall hearing such horrible, disgusting, murderous actions of the fiendish, destructive, diabolical creatures in a winter season. This was the first time in November that the winter did not provide a safe haven from bad things due to the cold and snowy weather.

When Kelly and Dawn were just young, impressionable kids, storms came and went. Some were really terrible, scary ones that left a scar inside their memories and on their souls. The Browns were recalling those vicious, extreme winds howling, shrieking like creepy, deadly banshees yanking the earth to pieces, such torrential rains falling so hard it was impossible to see outside. Flashes of sheet lightning flying across the cloudiest skies, interrupted by rolls of the loudest thunder ever heard in the history of the village. Teagan and Candy sat spellbound as they kept listening to these stories from long ago. Their parents and grandparents never told of any winter storms creating this type of havoc or deaths. Kelly and Dan simply said the news seemed to put them on edge due to hoping for a peaceful winter. The couple wanted a winter free of deaths, disappearances, and pain for the residents of town.

The *Gazette* never mentioned such events even in any old records dug up so far, which meant Russell Pagan was not able to cover everything. Candy took notes, as Kelly and Dawn retold these storms as if they were actually happening as they spoke. The fear and adrenalin rushed straight through each of them as the minutes passed. Their eyes exposed their souls filled with the trepidation from those black, noisy, cloudy evenings filled with complete and utter terror. Their childhood fears buried deep inside came pouring out in this cold afternoon into Teagan and Candy's ears. The Browns were blurting the words as fast, as they could not get them out of their mouths fast enough. Dawn was having the most trouble saying anything in a coherent fashion. Kelly was watching his wife very closely, with all the affection of being by her side for forty years now. The conversation tailed off, as a short break really was necessary especially for Kelly and Dawn. A rest and a drink of tea with a shot of brandy seemed to be a magic cure. Everyone smiled as the hot tea and brandy went down. Yes, Marcasite's old family traditions came in handy in certain moments during any time day or night.

A half hour later, the Browns continued with the tales from their parents and grandparents stockpile. According to their family history, these storms happened every year.

Kelly had mentioned these storms happened to bring more of the terrible, horrendous, vicious creatures upon Marcasite than elsewhere. However, the storms took life after life in one storm after another. The storms usually lasted from spring to the fall. There seemed to be anywhere from one to maybe around three deaths due in one six-month period. Now this was something the Wellands were aware of as owners of the *Gazette*. The amount of deaths really did vary each year due to the strength of the storms. Not every storm caused deaths and disappearances to occur inside the limits of Marcasite. For an unknown reason, the burden was lifted at times, allowing life to keep going forward unbroken. Kelly and Dawn knew more history than Teagan and Candy were aware of about how these ghastly, morbid, brutal creatures caused damages and death.

Teagan and Candy would need to research their archives to see how many deaths were reported in any year. Why had any unexplained deaths not been reported or recorded in the *Gazette* or in the police records? Now armed with some new information they could approach it from a new direction entirely. Where these records existed of other people actually disappearing from Marcasite and Gopher County was a real mystery. After all, humans never just left without any trace, or could they? Both of them wrote and jotted down various notes in regards to the many mysterious happenings. Research required an awful lot of reading, thinking about, filling out the ideas, and seeing the fine details from witnesses stand points. Teagan and Candy talked over every issue as they went through them, acting as sounding boards for the *Gazette*. The Wellands felt it was important to do the best work possible for their readers in each story that was published.

Later, once the interview was finished with Kelly and Dawn Brown, Teagan and Candy headed back to the papers office. The next issue had to be put together and readied for printing, another late evening for the *Gazette* before it would be put to bed, as the phrase went. Every story was meticulously laid out according to the way it would stand out. Making sure nothing was ever misquoted or attributed to the wrong source, professionalism was their one reason for the huge success of the *Gazette*. No one appreciated bad reporting or lack of quality less than the Wellands themselves. Being the sole newspaper, being correct in the reporting process, had to be paramount. Both of the Wellands took this business very seriously and knew everyone relied on the newspaper for the best coverage possible. As the *Gazette* owners, the two pored over pages and pages of notes to make sense of stories that needed to be told. Teagan and Candy knew people from all over were really very perplexed with these deaths. Wanting to help quail the nervous reactions was first and foremost to them. Newspapers had a duty to assist the public in the understanding of all things in their area. Reporting and covering these horrible deaths in town limits had a bad chilling effect on everyone. Marcasite was the main source for the unseen ghoul and werewolf creatures striking in force constantly from spring till fall. This was actually occurring more often than ever before in their records or Russell Pagan's records at the *Gazette*. Teagan and Candy were thinking of this while preparing the next issue of the *Gazette* to be printed and distributed for the residents.

In addition, finding out about all the strange deaths going back a hundred years or so got to them, interviewing those who were told about the fierce storms, rushing winds, hailstones the size of small rocks, with pouring, blinding rains, rolling peals of thunder, sheets of flashing lightning, black clouds filling the skies, and figures skulking, appearing as if out of nowhere. Strange, eerie apparitions who looked were the spine-chilling, harrowing, petrifying creatures gave them bad feelings of trepidation. Was all that just shadows playing on the minds of the residents out there? What hid among the sheets of flashing lightning during storms scared everyone. Deaths and disappearances took place shaking the whole community to the core. Yet they only took place from spring till late fall, never in the cold winter months till now. What changed this year to allow the deaths and disappearances to continue into November? A phenomenon occurred, and no one noticed it in the sky above the town. Something did take place that was indeed no good at all for the people.

Being out in the country in late evenings was refreshing, with the breezes and all the real, wonderful smells. However, there was a fear of the unknown appearing on the back roads on the way home into Marcasite. Teagan and Candy Welland knew enough of all the local history to be aware of the dark, even being adults. Storms got brought up swiftly, fiercely out of nowhere with tornado winds, torrential rains, huge hailstones, sheets of flashing lightning, lots of loud, rolling thunder. Neither one wanted to be the next ones to disappear in the dark, eerie storms now that this was mid-November and the last snowstorm lasted four days, leaving behind one dead body buried deep in the snow bank hidden inside a vehicle. The other body turned up torn open, ripped apart, and gnawed upon in the woods along the highway to Goreville days later. Inside the dense woods was a blood trail that police followed to find Abigail Walton's remains.

Alex and Abigail Walton were recent residents of Marcasite and did not deserve to die in this fashion either. Why those two, in the first winter storm deaths recorded in Marcasite, was to say shocking and surprising to all. No one would forget this year's early November's first strange occurrence as the winter went on. Would any more people disappear or to be put to death by some disgusting, horrendous, long-toothed creatures? Why only people from Marcasite for those beings from the star studded Milky Way? Maybe some type of unknown animal still existed from prehistoric times, coming around to pounce at will? If it was, there was never any trail or prints left behind, which soon ruled out any animal from an earthly plane being responsible.

Alex and Abigail Walton brought the death toll to four since the beginning of the fall, and that was two months ago. Lenny Farfeld and Caden McDougall had both died in similar manners, having been ripped apart, torn open, and gnawed upon by something very nasty. Their bones or parts of them were strewn around in the woods among the dense woods along the highway to Goreville. All of the dead body parts were located in this same area of the woods on this lonely stretch of highway. A long-ago group of beings enjoyed their feasting of human flesh here in the wooded area, just like this was a ritual for them that lasted a long time here in Marcasite. No one understood why such disgusting, murderous events needed to occur here. Marcasite was built to be a gem in the southeast corner of Gopher County. Along the way, a sudden change in the air happened, and people began to disappear from their homes in town. Bodies were found torn open, ripped apart, gnawed upon, and left tossed around in the woods outside of town. Everyone really required fast answers to the sick, twisted events of late. Police officials had to provide an explanation, which was their responsibility, and the time had come.

Chapter Seventeen

December started the way mid-November took off, with a huge snowstorm blowing in from the southwest. Winds swept the snow around to the point no one was allowed to drive on the streets. People were advised to stay inside at home or at work until the snowstorm blew away completely. Schools were closed early that morning, as no one wanted students stuck in the huge buildings with little or no food or water. Snowfalls of eight inches or more were being forecasted for the town of Marcasite that day. This all turned into more than a two feet over the next four days and drifts of four feet in places. Winds kept blowing for days, up to seventy miles an hour for the next few days, similar to the past summer winds. No one was able to recall such snowfalls or the winds blowing with such force occurring in Marcasite. The place was under siege from a twisted, strange phenomenon indeed this entire year.

The temperature dropped to minus forty with the wind chills and kept dropping as the winds gained more of their strength overnight. Four days after, the winds and the snow stopped like a timer shutting both of them off. Street crews were sent out to clear paths for people to drive their vehicles around. It would be at least a couple of days before the streets were cleared; that would allow drivers out. All residents were asked to please shovel the snow off sidewalks and sand them to be safe from slips and falls. Some houses were snowed up to the front doors and needed some additional help from the town to get out. The town sent out extra snow crews to help out those who needed it. Most crews were busy all day long, going from one door to the next across the town, knocking on each door to ensure all residents and their families were safe and sound, clearing snow away where they were required to do so along sidewalks and steps to reach the front doors.

One such crew could not get an answer at one door, so the town tried to get the people on the phone. No one was answering the phone there, and the caller figured that people were stuck at work still. The call was sent to a crew close to that office site to see if the people were, in fact, okay since both of the couple worked at the same building downtown in Marcasite. Dean and Madison Taylor owned a small insurance company out of a nice location in the heart of town. No one who was stuck in the building for the last four days remembered seeing either of them. All the staff from other offices figured they went home early when the snow began to fall, just before those winds really gusted, picking up severe strength later that afternoon, and they hoped not to get stuck outside.

Police were sent to the Taylors' residence to see if they get in to find out anything in their strange disappearance. This was starting to look like all the other nasty, strange events with people being taking away. Police went to their home and knocked on both of the front and back doors. Crews had cleared the snow from the walkway around to the rear door while they waited for the cops to arrive.

Of course, there was no answer, which was not unexpected for police did not figure they would be home safe and sound. Dean and Madison Taylor were gone into the dead of a winter snowstorm. They forced their way into the garage at the Taylors' home to find their vehicle parked inside. Next, the doors needed to be opened to have the home searched for any signs of them. Dean and Madison were not inside their well-kept, neat bungalow. No mess or broken items anywhere, it was just like they left it earlier to go to work, no dirty dishes or any food out on the countertops, which was weird and strange. Why was their car parked in the garage beside the house? The couple seemed to vanish eerily similar to every other past case. Not being at work was one thing, and going away with no trace was another matter entirely. None of the past disappearances made any sense, and this one did not either.

Police would indeed have another case of a disappearance on their hands that would not be solved.

Many times, crimes would take months or years to find clues in order to resolve them. These bodies, especially when dealing with ghoul and werewolf creatures, just showed up torn open, ripped apart, and gnawed upon when the creatures wanted to leave them. Winter could provide good cover for hiding from the dark things of the night, considering these unholy, accursed, macabre beings could hide in any type of weather now. Summer storms only showed shadows in the flashes of sheet lightning. How could anyone see a shadow against a backdrop of white canvas? No trails or footsteps, no blood from within the Taylors' home or from them, were ever found. The wind had whipped the snow into a real frenzy for twenty-four hours straight during those nights and days. Piles of snow were close to four feet high or more in some spots and two feet high in a few others across Marcasite.

Teagan and Candy Welland, as owners of the *Gazette*, picked up on these latest victims or apparent victims of some disappearance. Everything pointed to the same things being responsible for taking the Taylors away as all the others. Neither had any proof from the police or from any source, just so much seemed to be similar in every way, except this time bodies appeared to be gone. Teagan and Candy knew in past cases bodies were gone, taken and never found again. Could this be one of those cases where Dean and Madison Taylor may be gone forever? At least they did not leave any kids behind to be devastated by their sudden and unexpected loss. The Taylors had been insurance agents in Marcasite for close to five years now. Now it looked like their business was gone away, along with them, for no reason. Ghoul and werewolf creatures really were getting to all residents of town at any given time this year. Four deaths in three weeks of this winter, and the fear was just beginning. Six deaths since the fall now and not one clue had so far been located, except the same deep, long gouges on the bones of the victims.

No one knew what would happen from one day to the next, scaring them and making them concerned for their safety. Cold weather and heavy snow was one thing to accept; now they had to worry about the scary, diabolical, obnoxious creatures attacking Marcasite. What was going on with their dream of living in a safe, clean, friendly place that was the gem of their eyes? Most people felt the weird, dreadful creatures would stop their murderous rampage soon enough. None of this extreme, murderous tirade made sense to the community, not even the police. How do people guard against these untimely attacks by these repulsive, grotesque, deadly foreign beings? This would never be easy now or at any time. Creatures from the faraway Milky Way were hidden by the dark in the storms from spring till fall. Those same disgusting, abominable, brutal creatures were being hidden behind the heavy, deep, windswept, white blankets of snowfall. All this fear was being driven by the deaths piling up this year compared to other years in Marcasite.

Greg Braden was one of hundreds of students who had to stay at home due to the heavy snowstorms. He really enjoyed sledding and skating in the winter times. As all his friends did. When he found out about the Taylors' disappearance, he knew automatically the same creatures who attacked him did this. Greg shook with fear, knowing they should be gone in the winter months. He became scared, fearing they would come for him this time and take his body away as well. Greg still had not figured out why he was allowed to live while others died or disappeared forever. With the deaths and disappearances taking place this winter, he was concerned about his family's safety; he knew they all could be next.

Six deaths since September and it was only early December. Marcasite was indeed being stalked with deaths and disappearances, taking a huge toll. An oasis was not supposed to turn out this way at all, especially with the planning, sculpting, and building that had taken place over many years. No satisfactory explanation ever came out as to why people died or just vanished into thin air. A star studded Milky Way held the key to the mystery that engulfed their paradise in this southeast corner of Gopher County. Local native elders had passed this knowledge onto the first white settlers who come out west. In turn, this was passed down to every generation in the newcomers to the plains. This winter was the first to have deaths and disappearances attributed to the ghoul and werewolf creatures.

Greg Braden was the only person with an actual sighting of the ghoul and werewolf creatures, at least in his mind and his eyes. Frightening, horrid, macabre foreign beasts had found him when he was six years old hiding in his closet from a wicked storm. They exposed their grotesque, disgusting, foul smelling, brutal intruding bodies to infuse fear upon Greg. However, they enjoyed their experience so much, they kept returning to amuse themselves, scaring him over and over again. Wherever Greg went, they found him to sear his young soul as far as they could. Now especially, since fall of this year, he felt as if he was going to lose his mind. All these deaths for no reason in his teenage mind, and why had they not just taken him? Greg seemed lost in thought during those winter storms with the havoc being wreaked on Marcasite. He felt to blame for what happened to all these people, because he could still see the ghoul and werewolf creatures, only he knew fear kept him from saying a word to anyone. The fright of being blamed for the deaths, disappearances, and shunned by his friends made Greg keep things hidden deep inside his soul.

The snowfall from that storm would be cleared from all the streets within the week after it came down. Schools, businesses, and all activities returned to normal once everyone was able to get around once again. A shroud hung on the residents of town as the cold and the darkness of winter came on them early every afternoon. Not that everyone disliked winter or all of what it offered in the way of family activities. Regular, fluffy snowfalls were common and enjoyable as residents young and old were outside.

Lately, most people stayed inside unless they had to go somewhere important. Every resident knew no safeguard existed against being taken away by those despicable, horrid, daunting foreign attackers. Severe storms from spring till fall had proven this true time and time again through the years. Lives were shattered this winter due to the happenings that they never expected in the coldest months of the year, a first time for everything and no one was prepared for what had taken place and what could lie ahead.

A funeral for Dean and Madison Taylor would be up to the family if they wanted to hold one at all. As their bodies were not yet found in this fresh covering of awful, deep snow in this last blizzard. No one knew where to look for the bodies of Dean and Madison Taylor to begin with. The woods held too much snow to send search teams out there as maybe the search would take place in the spring. Their home and car already showed no remains existed there. Police were stumped for clues and had to do something in regards to this latest pair of disappearances in order to calm the general public, except the residents knew the deaths were caused by some beings from the faraway Milky Way. A crack allowed these ghoul and werewolf creatures to get out and reach earth. Police officials were tight-lipped about this all the time for fear of looking like fools. For now, they just hoped what was causing all these deaths would just stop and go away.

The Christmas season was fast approaching, and everyone wanted some peacefulness to come to Marcasite again. None of the older residents had gone through periods of this dark, inhuman killing that plagued the town right now. Town officials had put up Xmas decorations in hopes of lifting up the spirits of the residents. Store window were lit up with all kinds of displays this year. Everything possible was being done to help people adjust from the gloomiest year ever. All children needed to know Santa Claus was coming as always. Schools were going to put on Christmas pageants for the students and all their parents. This seemed to bring a sense of calm to those in Marcasite and eased the tension all around.

Christmas pageants went off without a hitch, as everyone had a great time attending them in every school in Marcasite. Teachers heaped the praise upon the students instead of taking it for themselves. Students smiled as audiences clapped and clapped some more for their shows this year in each school. Every student felt a huge degree of self-pride from all the elementary to senior high students. They realized their performance was the best they ever held for a Christmas pageant. For some of the students, this one would be their last one as the next spring would be graduation time for them. For now, they felt only pride in doing this as good as they could. Schools were going to be closed as of tomorrow for the two-week holiday break.

Spending time away with family and friends was looked forward to every year. Classes would resume again in the first week of January all across the town.

Christmas was a great celebration for everyone in and around Marcasite, as many visitors came to town, all for one awesome Christmas carnival held over the holiday season to brighten the spirits of the residents and visitors alike, complete with ice sculptures, sleigh rides pulled by horses, snowman making contests for kids, ice fishing, downhill skiing, tobogganing, hockey tournaments and more for all ages. This was the first of many future Christmas carnivals to be planned for Marcasite, in relief from the cold and to have fun in the snow. If this first one went off really well, with everyone involved having fun, the next year was going to be a better one. Hopefully, the visitors would love all the activities, and the residents could have a great time outdoors. Children of all ages were going to be red, rosy-cheeked, and warm inside, smiling, laughing and cheerful, just the way everyone wanted success to look like after the year they experienced.

Christmas morning, better and brighter as everyone opened the many gifts from under their Christmas trees, being at home feeling so jubilant with the families around with a great day ahead seemed surreal. The smell of roasting turkey invaded every room in all homes close to the kitchens. A typical Christmas feast with all families was mashed potatoes, green peas, carrots, turnips, stuffing, and gravy. There was a lot to be thankful for as they sat down at the tables that evening. Many stories of past Christmases went around as was the tradition in most homes. A lively conversation at times made them smile and laugh out loud while they ate their meals. Desserts would consist of lemon meringue pies and mincemeat pies along with fresh whipped cream.

All around, no one left the table without a full stomach at suppertime on that special day. Children, teens, and adults were content after a great Christmas Day spent together, just a relaxing family evening to look forward to sitting around watching some TV or listening to Yule time songs on the radio. Sucking and eating some Christmas candy at the same time on that evening, being spoiled with candy on Christmas night was special and made everyone feel good.

Marcasite's mayor, Harold Holden, was going to open all the festivities for Boxing Day morning on Main Street downtown in front of a huge crowd as they had hoped and planned for this day long ago. Time had come to show the best of their Christmas carnival to all who came out. Boxing Day was going to be a fun-filled day of activities across town as the festival got going once again. The weather was warm; the sun was shining brightly above Marcasite and all the people down below. Sleigh rides were full all day long as some grandparents took their grandchildren with them, as other people climbed aboard. Sleigh rides took about half an hour to go around the downtown area of Marcasite. The stores were all adorned with Christmas displays in the windows for all to see. Christmas decorations hung from streetlight poles along the streets to make it look entirely like a winter wonderland. Children and teens slid down the local hills on toboggans; adults and others skated on the local outdoor ice surfaces made for the carnival while other people skied down some hills and still others did cross-country skiing in the parks in town. Hockey games were held in the indoor ice arenas all across town.

A refreshment stand was set up to keep everyone of all ages warm and happy, from hot chocolate to hot toddies for the older people. Boxing Day was the best of the carnival so far as the activities were excellent on a warm, sunny day. Not one person, young or old, was actually disappointed at all; in fact, they had trouble concealing the happiness. Being there was an awesome experience from the start of the day. Boxing Day evening, the town planned to hold a giant bonfire in Freedom Park to commemorate the first Christmas carnival in Marcasite. This was going to be the best of highlights in the day's long list of activities for young and old. Everyone could come to roast wieners and marshmallows that night along with drinking hot chocolate for the youngest and hot toddies for the older ones. The forecast called for a cloudless night with cool temperatures just around minus five. Plus, sleigh rides would be available for a couple hours before it all got underway that evening.

Thousands of residents and visitors turned out to take in the huge event in Freedom Park that night. Adults, teens, and children were raucous, happy, and glad, and had no problem at all showing all these feelings. Later, before the festivities were to end that night, a fireworks display was going to take place, with thousands of flashes as the rockets shot off, followed by lots of different bright colors spreading, across the sky. Some seemed to drip slightly, slowly, downward to the ground. Others kept shooting smaller rockets exploding in a fast sequence of colors high up in the sky. Overall, the night's light show was something no one would forget, at least they felt this way. It was all over for Boxing Day just after midnight and time for bed for all those who stayed out. Tomorrow would be another day of celebrations for the people who attended the first day's events. The Christmas carnival still had a few days to go before it would be all over for this year.

A pancake, waffle, and egg breakfast was planned to be held on Main Street this morning as cooks were up and out attending to the duties. Volunteers were setting up a number of the heavy cook stoves, getting the pancakes and waffle stuff made, and the eggs needed to be fried as well. Bacon was also available, courtesy of local food stores that supplied most of the goods for that breakfast. No one would be turned away or sent away hungry during these morning cookouts. Their morning was sunny, chilly, yet hospitable by most prairie standards in the winter months. There must have been close to two thousand people who came to eat breakfast this morning. People from a few close by villages arrived to take in the first breakfast of pancakes, waffles, bacon, coffee, talk, friendship, and closeness built up over the years. Neighbors and friends came together in a spirit of harmony, enjoyment, and fun during the Christmas season.

The day was filled with a few of the same activities as the first few days of the Christmas carnival, except that some schoolkids were putting on Christmas skits for everyone. The local town hall had the largest capacity, so they held them there. Shows told the story of the birth of Jesus Christ, where he was born, and that he was the son of God. He was born in a manger in Bethlehem in Israel a long time ago. And how a real, bright star showed the three wise men to where he was in the manger. The audience loved the entertainment so much they provided a standing ovation for their efforts. More than a dozen shows would take place during the carnival, and many more spontaneous standing ovations were heard.

The first Christmas carnival ended, and the entire town of Marcasite gave thanks to those who came out for their efforts. Mayor Harold Holden was very proud for those who gathered to see the shows by the students. The mayor gave huge thanks to the organizers, suppliers, stage workers, and many others who assisted in the carnival. Yes, big smiles and hearts full of happiness was reward enough from all the guests who were here. Town officials told everyone sitting that morning that next year's

Christmas carnival was going to be just as good or even better. The town could hopefully carry out these plans in advance for next year's Christmas carnival. All of council were full of anticipation and excitement for the following year's Christmas carnival.

New Year's came and went in Marcasite without any tragic, strange deaths or incidents thus far. No one was on pins and needles waiting, as the happy feelings gathered during the first Christmas carnival still kept them warm inside. No fears were shaken up or stirred up in any form in town so far. Maybe, these astounding, repulsive, diabolic alien intruders had taken a sabbatical for the rest of winter. Hopes were very high, and people did not want the worry going into a New Year. The last year was so gruesome, awful, and deadly with no relief from the despicable, brutal, calamitous ghoul and werewolf creatures in those severe storms. Along came the incredible windy, cold, snowy winter carrying with it the same unseen evil. Why did these cruel, monstrous, inhuman creatures love wreaking havoc on their gem of an oasis? Could this be the last time anything happened in anyone's memories or in police records or in records of the *Gazette* in the winter?

Chapter Eighteen

January was cold, snowy, and with strong, gusty winds so far to begin with. This month may have a real good surprise in store for all the residents of Marcasite. Schools were set to reopen in a few days, and the children, teens, and teachers were looking forward to going back to their classes. Once everyone was back into a routine and comfortable, time would pass easy enough right into spring. Surprises happened, because that was what they were, and one was coming soon.

A snowstorm that was far worse than the one before Christmas hit a week later with severe force. Winds, snowfalls, and drifts of snow a few feet deep piled up again across town. Schools were closed before students left their homes, and most if not all businesses shut down. The fear slowly sunk in, thinking someone or some people would be lost, once again crept into the hearts of everyone. In all storms, it felt like a trigger was yanked, thus creating a loss no one ever got over due to these devilish, atrocious, hideous alien creatures attacking their jewel of a town. Why did they need to keep approaching and chasing all the residents of Marcasite?

It seemed to be a long time as the days passed before the storm blew itself through the town of Marcasite. Clearing the streets was Mayor Holden's first priority and making sure people were safe. How could anyone disappear in a whiteout like this? Maybe all the residents with their own children were, in fact, safe and sound in their homes. Town officials would know in a few days how long it could take to clear all the snow from all the streets and have it all hauled away to the dump place to wait for the spring sun to melt it all away or the heavy rainstorms to help.

Two days later, one person was located in a car, torn wide open, ripped apart and gnawed down to the bone by the same horrendous, monstrous, abominable foreign beasts. His name was Hank Farley; he had lived with his wife, Heather, and their two sons, John and Howard. Why only him and no one else was taken to their deaths? His family would be badly shaken by his awful, dreadful death during the first snowstorm of the New Year. How was anyone going to tell his family Hank suffered the same death as many others? Police needed to the notification of the death to his wife and family. Hank's remains were taken to Dr. Gabe Bridger's office for examination. Dr. Bridger seemed to be sickened more each time he saw such tragic deaths.

Hank Farley was a partner in one of the local grocery stores for the last five years. He worked there for close to four years before buying in as a partner. He believed in the need for good produce, good food, and good dry goods for everyone. They operated Cherry Creek Grocery with the greatest customer service outside of the big cities like Goreville. Bill Hood needed to be told of his partner's sudden death in the snowstorm two nights earlier. Police Chief Harry Rook decided to inform Bill Hood about the demise of Hank. The two had a great business sense and a common touch with all their customers and suppliers alike. Harry Rook had known both men for many years already, and he felt an obligation as friend to talk to Bill. He knew that this was not going to be an easy task to carry out today.

Teagan and Candy received the terrible news from the police in Hank's death. The *Gazette* was ready to print up an issue tomorrow, and all the details of Hank Farley's death would be and needed to be included. All residents had to be informed that their mutual problem makers were back once again. Nothing seemed to keep them away from town; no storm was bad enough to stop death in its tracks, no cold frigid enough to freeze them out, not enough snow to bury them deep within the drifts or winds capable enough to twirl the creatures back into the skies above. Ghoul and werewolf creatures knew they had been invincible against anyone in Marcasite since time began. No one or nothing ever stood in their way and never would. As always, their natural feeding ground was here for them, and time always proved this true. Why, was the question on everybody's minds. Over and over, this was mulled through the spirits and souls of all in Marcasite as the death toll climbed over the last four months.

Mrs. Heather Farley, their two sons, John and Howard, and the family on both sides decided to hold the funeral service next week after all details could be worked out. A gravesite needed to be cleared and dug in the local cemetery at the Catholic church. Father Watson was called upon to conduct the service by the family of Hank Farley. He had a week to gather the family history from what he knew of them. They had all been regular weekly attendees over the last nine years at the Catholic church. Father Watson was becoming over whelmed by the sudden number of deaths and disappearances over the last number of months. He had done a number of services since the first one last fall.

Greg Braden was still the only person in Marcasite with the pertinent information about these demonic, dreadful, hideous monstrous creatures, because he had seen them and continued to see them every time someone was killed or taken away. They haunted him at will, taunting him to go crazy or to laugh at his inability to do anything. Ghoul and werewolf creatures knew no one was going to believe a teenager with crazy ideas. Greg had been to the new Prairie General Hospital and put in the psych ward once at a younger age. Those horrible, vivid, fearful memories of hiding in his closet during that one very fierce storm had stayed with him. Greg kept recalling seeing those bright, sharp incisor teeth, the slime dropping from their lips, the grins spread across the faces of the evil-looking ghoul and the werewolf creatures with him. Greg wet his pajamas in the closet that night, as he could not move; he was frozen to the floor. As soon as he did move, he jumped up, ran out of the closet, climbed into bed, and stayed awake the rest of the night. He promised himself to never leave his bed during a storm ever again. Greg shook with fear all night long, as any six-year-old would do.

Finally, the day for Hank Farley's funeral arrived as everyone from town and Gopher County packed the church. Father Watson led the people in prayer for Hank before his wife, Heather, gave his eulogy. Heather was a very strong person who now had to look after their two sons, John and Howard. Tears streamed down her cheeks, but she never faltered in her eulogy. The church choir sang a few songs and hymns before the casket carrying Hank Farley was carried out of the church. It was then the huge overflowing congregation started to file out. The graveside service was simple and brief, as the family asked for it to be this way. A reception was going to take place in the community center to accommodate all the people who came out to say good-bye to Hank Farley. A sad, yet warm feeling filled everyone as they expressed caring, loving words in being the only to accept Hank's death. Being strong in front of his widow and children was important to all those there.

Greg was the same age as Hank's son, John, and had some classes together at school. The two of them were more or less acquaintances in school and out of school. Greg was into sports, and John was not. Howard Farley was on the school swim team and was a strong swimmer. That was all Greg knew about the two Farley brothers, from school and from town. All of them lived a few blocks apart and seldom had contact, not like Greg's other friends who lived close by. He could not explain why this happened, not being familiar with John and Howard Farley.

Another week passed slowly, as the edge of fear seemed to exist openly among everyone in and around their town. Death from the unknown never got used to being accepted ever in this age or before in any time. Marcasite was built to be an oasis on the open prairies for people looking for a great place to call home. Instead, they found a place filled with hideous, malicious, unholy creatures. Death and destruction came out of storms from early spring till late fall. Now the trail started to come in the winter months as well now. Yes, the tales passed down from a century ago were becoming true all over again. Why, was the most common question. Thorough complacency overtook the residents of Marcasite during that time period. However, their dreams were not fading now as something the First Nations elders spoke of did attack this area. The stories mentioned ghoul and werewolf creatures sneaking through cracks in the star studded Milky Way, amid the storms of the early spring till late fall. Not one mentioned deaths and destruction amid the winter time before, only that these experiences lasted from the springtime to the fall. All residents were hoping this year could bring the much-needed relief from worry that came with the storms.

Teagan and Candy Welland were still looking for information surrounding the disgusting, fiendish, calamitous killers. Even as they kept pressure on the local police forces, nothing was forthcoming. Neither of these veteran newspaper reporters could explain how there was no clues left behind. The only marks were gouges on the bones of the victims that were recovered. Other victims still had never been recovered after they had disappeared. Vanishing into the netherworld of the star studded Milky Way in outer space surrounding the planet. Or possibly being buried deep beneath the earth's surface as the tornado-force winds struck in storms from early spring till late fall. As the sounds from the howling, screaming winds as the funnel clouds ripped the earth open to bury victims. Now this winter activity raised more questions than answers as to what happened to the people who disappeared. Where did they end up in the ice-cold weather and deep snow? The *Gazette* was still printing stories of what happened from the past and present. Just a simple and definite lack of information in regards to any deaths in the depth the winter months. Russell Pagan, as good as he was, did not have any recorded deaths from the beginning of November till the end of March.

The *Gazette* was still being published four times a week and sold out as always, and people read every issue. The coffee shops were full of residents talking about the different stories inside the paper. Any weather or good weather reports were welcome news for everyone in town and in Gopher County. Nice weather made people feel better and often took away their worries and concerns. Teagan and Candy received their reports from the national weather service by wire. The *Gazette* believed in this method, as it was cost effective for their thriving newspaper businesses. Keeping costs down meant not having to raise prices for their customers.

School had resumed, and life was back to normal these last two weeks for the students and parents. Winter weather stayed calm, with no storms or snowfalls, which made life bearable as well. Kids of all ages could play outside in the fresh air at school, and after school, there were lots of activities for them. Marcasite almost seemed to be that jewel of an oasis in the winter and summer of their parents' dreams. Could this period of awful death and destruction have run its course? Time was the only answer for anyone who thought about what may happen next.

Chapter Nineteen

Suddenly, the last week of January, another severe snowstorm hit Marcasite with even more force. The storm knocked out power and heat to most of Marcasite that day and into the next couple of days. Many of those affected were being housed in the community center as the power and heat were running on generators. Getting people there continued to remain a huge problem for rescue workers as they fanned out in those hardest hit areas. Children, teens, and parents were stuck in cold houses hopefully with warm blankets and clothes until rescuers got to them. The community center had beds for five hundred people each on the main and basement floors and food for all of them. Father Watson kept the residents hopes upbeat with many prayers and stories of goodwill.

Police and firemen went door to door through each neighborhood, taking people to the community center. Early the next morning, most people had been accounted for in the badly affected blocks hit by the storm. The last few homes were being checked, and in the last one a rescuer made a grisly discovery as two bodies were found, torn, ripped, gnawed, and strewn around the house. The bodies were what remained of Dan Walker and Karen Walker, and their daughter Heidi Walker seemed to be missing. At least, it appeared neither one suffered before dying at the hands of the diabolic, treacherous, barbaric creatures. All the usual clues of teeth marks left on the bones of each victim gave up the real evidence needed. Bodies torn open and ripped apart were the other clues always present in these cases. Police officers and the local coroner, Dr. Gabe Bridger, were there all that day. The remains were taken to the morgue to be examined by Dr. Bridger. These fierce storms were bringing more death and destruction into Marcasite for some unknown reason. All top town officials were stumped by what was taking place this last year especially.

Since fall, the death toll stood at two; now it was nine, one disappearance and still counting as time went on. There had been four deaths years earlier in Marcasite. Two construction workers and two young teen sisters had lost their lives. In total eleven deaths and now two disappearances had occurred in the last number of years, which was so sad indeed to have to accept. No one knew of any defense against these abhorrent, dangerous ghoul and werewolf creatures that attacked at will. How could they slip through cracks in the star studded Milky Way to kill people? According to local legends, this had occurred many times over the past centuries. Now all they needed was hope that the end was near for the feeding frenzy and the taking away of people. What may lie ahead was just as scary to the people to think of or believe could occur. All residents of Marcasite were scared witless enough for their family's safety. A dream of the jewel on the prairies was being stripped away from them all. Their great grandparents had settled here as they had been deeded the lands before leaving their homelands. As parents they had a dream of coming to a new land and raising families on the prairies of the west. Now it seemed so muddy, scary, even filled with fright, as death, disappearances, and destruction could occur at any time.

Greg Braden's family had not been part of the original migration westward in those old times. His parents, Tom and Helen Braden, moved to Marcasite after it was being built so his dad could work. Greg still could not figure out why these horrible, detestable, murderous creations allowed him to see them. Why did they not kill him or take him away instead of torturing him all the time? He knew they visited him every time when death and destruction struck Marcasite. He saw them, their bright, shiny, incisor sharp teeth, and the drool dropping from their mouths as they showed that disgusting grin. All this did was scaring him, searing him through every time they appeared to him. He should have stayed in bed that night when he was six years old. Now being fourteen years old, Greg was even more afraid of those things that haunted him and

Marcasite. One day he just might lose his mind over these terrible, haunting deaths, disappearances, and destruction taking place. He could not tell anyone for fear of going into the psych ward for a long time. And he also felt the shame of believing he could see what others were not able to see. Greg shook all over from the fright that thought brought upon him. Was he to blame for every all the nefarious, revolting, abominable death and destruction that was taking place in Marcasite?

Meanwhile, the local police still had no leads or clues as to why these things came here to cause the problems they did. Most other cases were solvable; these ones were not going to be solved. All they could do was wait and do their job, clean up the scenes, and make life better for those affected if possible. Reports were filed away as nothing more could be done. Victims who were found were buried and the two others were still listed as missing.

Teagan and Candy Welland kept up their vigilance in search of clues in their files that Russell Pagan left behind. Most of the papers had been gone through and stored away in metal cabinets. Others were still in wooden crates and boxes, as their time was being spent on other areas of research. Plus, keeping up printing four issues very week did not leave much time for anything else. Both of them were getting worn out from all those terrible deaths, destruction, and the disappearance of the young Heidi Walker. Never had they felt as utterly depressed as now over any event in their lives. Being able to cope with trouble and able to report it was always their dream in life. Now the strain seemed to be getting to them right now. Everyone in town and around Gopher County was feeling the same way, they knew that much. How could they not be? People had their own unique way of handling death, destruction, disappearances, and life. Still, these latest events were the hardest to face with the ghoul and werewolf creatures attacking in the wintertime now.

Funerals for Dan and Karen Walker were held in the days following the initial police and coroner's investigations. The bones of the bodies were released and readied for burial to be put in caskets at the funeral home. The service was going to be held at the community center to hold the expected crowd of people attending. Heidi Walker still had not been found, which upset all the residents in and around Marcasite. Father Watson, the Catholic priest, was officiating for their funeral service. As Father Watson offered prayers, even he was struck with a knot in his throat over such senseless acts of depravity—two parents both killed viciously and their daughter disappears into the depth of the snowstorm. The community center was full of people, most with tears in their eyes. Others lost inside their souls with thoughts of dread and fear for what had happened. A choir sang hymns, with most of the others singing along with them. After the service, the two caskets were rolled out into the waiting hearses. People followed in their vehicles to the cemetery for the graveside service for Dan and

Karen Walker. Everyone went back to the community
center for a gathering to remember the latest victims
and their daughter. Marcasite was indeed full of caring,
loving people, even if they were scared witless right at the
moment.

Out of respect for the family, all schools and businesses
shut down for the day so everyone could attend the
service. Not everyone was going to fit into the community
center at one time. Some people stayed home until they
knew the graveside service was going to take place. Then
everyone gathered around the graveside in the cemetery
for the final services by Father Watson. This last service
was the most solemn of all in recent memory for all those
who were there. After, everyone went their separate ways
to find some type or kind of solace somewhere. Most
families went home to be together and talk about what had
happened once again. Maybe this could help them all get
some relief from the fear they all were feeling right now.

Tom, Helen, and Greg Braden went home like most
everyone else had after the graveside service. Greg
knew more than anyone else, yet he could not open up
about all that he was aware of. That inborn fear of being
scorned by Janice, his girlfriend, and all his friends was
too much for him. His parents would indeed put him in
the local psych ward at Prairie General Hospital again.
He had sworn never to go back there, no matter what the
consequences were going to be. These ghoul and werewolf
creatures unveiled themselves to him in his closet at age

six. Greg's parents were very quiet as they all sat looking and watching some black-and-white TV show. He did feel relieved they never asked any more questions about his long-ago experience with the ghastly, nefarious, horrendous foreign monsters. He just might be too scared to answer them. Greg somehow felt responsible for what took place, and in other ways, it was not his fault, he figured. Still, he could never shake the fact the terrible, hellish, reprehensible creatures haunted him, each time they struck during a storm ever since he was six years old. Why only do this and not take him away or kill him?

The whole town of Marcasite were feeling trapped inside a world of fear, trepidation with unknown dangers attacking when they desired. No one had yet to figure out a viable reason their homes being such a desirable place to provide the needed food for the demonic, odious, hellish creatures to feast on. No one ever would find the explanation behind all the death and destruction hitting their small jewel of a town. After all, people came back after the last long drought to have homes, to have work, and to have families, not this wanton death and destruction that was striking all of them more often in such a short span of time. Police officials were stumped, confused, and very bewildered by all that happened. What could they do if the beings could not be seen or heard? Not one clue ever turned up to lead the police toward any killers, where they came from, and how to catch them. Nothing changed so far; something had to!

Greg Braden remained the only one in town with the intimate knowledge of these ghastly, heinous, brutal creatures in how they looked. He had seen them too many times over the years as they increasingly got to his mind and soul. Who else knew of these of these evil beings, other than himself? All Greg was aware of, every one of his friends were petrified when someone died in such an awful, terrible, disgusting manner. As they could be the next victim for these heinous, horrific, malicious creatures being torn open, ripped apart, and gnawed upon. Then having their body parts thrown around. Young kids and teens alike were the group most frightened by this type of activities occurring in town. Their friends and family had died or disappeared in such a short period of time over the last four months. He felt the same fears, the ice-cold dread going through him, and the fact he saw them while no others did!

Teagan and Candy had recently located a few old stories from the records at the *Gazette*. Stories somehow remained hidden until one day they searched in a real creative manner going through each one slowly and deliberately. Among the old crated stuff, the two of them came across were some old, odd, brown-colored newsprint. What amazed both of them was not the color of the paper but the stories on it. The date was from the late eighteen hundreds in regards to one family being attacked and a couple of members disappearing. Severe summer storms actually existed even then, and now they had some more actual proof. Proof now existed of those repulsive, grotesque ghoul and werewolf creatures taking people away into the dark of the worst storm on record of that time. Russell Pagan covered stories of storms happening, people being killed, and the ones taken away somewhere. The point was they had never found one like it at all earlier in this time period after spending hours digging through these records.

The date was June 14, 1884, in the village of Marcasite in late afternoon; the skies were clouded over. Then tornado-force winds, torrential rains, sheets of lightning, and rolling thunder struck overhead. Never had such a storm hit the area till that day, according to the story in the *Gazette* of the day. In the morning, once the storm was over, someone noticed their neighbors were not around. Both parents, all four children, were gone as if they had been swallowed up in the storm. A search was started for the family in hopes of finding them wandering in the streets or hiding in the livery stable or another building. No one was able to say why they left the safety of their home. Russell carried this item on the top of the page that very day. He felt it was important to let the citizens know of what took place the night before in their village.

According to the stories the name of the family was Mr. Louis Hamilton, Mrs. Freda Hamilton and their children, Doug, Allan, Brenda, and Betty. They found all but the bodies of Brenda and Allan Hamilton outside of Marcasite along the road to Goreville. All bodies showed signs of being torn open, ripped apart, gnawed upon, and strewn around in a small clearing. A story such as this was the earliest one they had come across to back up the death and evil destruction taking place from spring till late fall. Also, the story explained the legends passed down from the native peoples were true, as Russell Pagan now had the proof.

Now Teagan and Candy finally had the long-lost proof with the old, brown-colored paper from June 14, 1884. The police might be interested in seeing this clipping, so they headed over to the police station. The *Gazette* owners were right, as the police chief was actually very interested in this old story. Anything to help explain all of the unexplained deaths and destruction in Marcasite was welcome. Now the newspaper owners felt the police should share any information with them. Working together could lead to a way of aiding in warning residents of attacks from the hideous, detestable, murderous foreign killing creatures. No one was jumping to such foolish explanations at this exact point in time. First of all, who knew for sure where these beings came from? Did they actually sneak through cracks in the star studded galaxy above? Nothing seemed to prevent the diabolical, vicious, odious intruders from gaining entry into homes attacking residents and taking people away into the deep woods.

Teagan and Candy returned to their office to make this old, brown-paper story come alive as the first page of tomorrow's *Gazette*. Everyone was going to be very shocked and surprised, even scared, by the finding of that story from June 14, 1884, in the *Gazette* by Russell Pagan. At least, past history was coming true all over again that proved beyond any doubt of ghoul and werewolf creatures existing at that time. Inside this edition were more stories of recent deaths and one disappearance. Police still had no leads in those cases except to say that now they believed in stories handed down from the past.

Winter weather was going to continue for a few more months before spring would arrive for Marcasite. Residents remained just as aware of their surroundings at all times, day or night. Family safety became the most important issue for those who had them; for others their safety drove fear deeper inside. Too many deaths and too much destruction had so far occurred in Marcasite. For a town that was built as an oasis on the rolling hills of the southeast corner of Gopher County, life turned bad. Instead of total, joyful happiness and contentment, they faced fear, death, disappearances, and severe storms all year around now. No one knew what to expect anymore as time slowly crawled along in the cold depths of winter.

January came to an end without any further incidents of storms or ghoul and werewolf attacks. Most citizens felt the calm before the storm was always out there, waiting for complacency to set in again. Awful, cold winter winds blew right through everyone, no matter how warm they dressed. How they hoped for warm weather to arrive without thinking that could mean severe snowstorms. Marcasite had been buried under enough snow already this winter. Too much fear built up with the deaths and disappearances taking place over the last four months since October began.

Chapter Twenty

February came in calm, warmer, and no snow, as everyone breathed a sigh of relief, which was wrong. None of the residents could fathom what was coming along at them in a certain manner. February thirteenth, the night before Valentine's Day and one of the worst, most severe snowstorms of the winter slammed into Marcasite, dumping even more snow and blowing winds of over seventy miles an hour outside. Valentine's Day was going to be a sad one indeed for all in Marcasite. Everyone hunkered down inside their own residences to wait out this current snowstorm. Of course, most thoughts were more centered on who would be gone or dead. Maybe this time no harm was going to befall their gem of a town. Morning or days later, news would spread around in this for sure as always it did. Residents needed to learn to never let their guard down when a storm hit the area. How could such evil attack Marcasite in this horrible, terrible, horrendous way?

A few days later when life returned to normal, the street cleanup began from one side of town to the next. Sidewalks and steps were shoveled by the owners of the homes, all due to being good people, getting exercise to wear off some of the fears harbored deep inside of each of them. No bad news had been delivered by the *Gazette* today, so that was good to know. The next issue was due out the day after, and until then, everyone breathed easier. Just maybe, Marcasite was through with all the deaths, disappearances, and the destruction by those indestructible ghoul and werewolf creatures.

Early the next morning, the Wellands' phone rang, waking them up from a peaceful slumber, almost startling them. The police chief was on the line saying he needed to talk with them as soon as they could get there. It was bad news once again, which was better delivered in person. He wanted it in that way in those days for the *Gazette* to handle the release to the public. Teagan and Candy Welland rushed down to the station house as fast as they could after grabbing a quick coffee. They could not function without caffeine in any circumstances, especially bad-news days.

Harry Rook, the police chief, was waiting in his office for them with a few senior officers of his staff. Harry told them that Hal and Hilary Laxton had seemed to be gone from their home this morning. They had no children and no relatives close by to Marcasite, and the search was already underway for them. Hal and Hilary Laxton were two local teachers from Robert Brown Senior High. They taught history, physics, and science for the last eight years there. Hilary taught drama classes, and Hal was a basketball coach, and the students were going to be shocked. Every parent with teenagers there was not going to like the news either. Harry Rook figured if Teagan and Candy could get the news out in today's *Gazette*, it would make life easier. All they could do was try to maybe run an insert for the issue as it was running already. Both the Wellands headed to their office to get busy.

The *Gazette* was late getting out to the public after the insert was printed and placed inside. The coffee shops seemed busier than usual that afternoon as Teagan and Candy made their rounds. Everyone was anxious to read all about the news from the storm over the last two days.

Life was becoming too predictable over the last five months, and that began to cause too much hurt to people of all ages. A buzz circulated around every coffee shop and home once the news sunk in about Hal and Hilary Laxton being gone. Were all these deaths, disappearances, and destruction going to take place for many more months? No one knew that answer. Nerves were frayed almost to the breaking point, especially now.

Residents wanted answers from their police chief and his officers. Things were out of control, with no assistance from their police or town officials. Frustration, fear, and outright being scared brought most people out the next council meeting. Mayor Harry Holden was on the hot seat as the community leader. He was to ensure the police did the right things in the deaths, disappearances that happened in Marcasite were taken care of. The entire members of the town council took the flack as well as Mayor Holden—all were equal in blame. People paid taxes, which counted for police protection from harm of any kind. No clear-cut answers were arrived at in the meeting that evening in the town offices in any matters brought forward. Nothing could be done; however, the mayor would not admit this to the public. Because to create chaos and turmoil was unneeded at this time due to the deaths and disappearances that took place over the last number of years. The last five months have been the worst in the town's history, and no answer to end it would ever be found.

Greg Braden, after reading about the teachers from Robert Brown Senior High, knew he should go say something to his parents. However, he did not have the stomach to face them or undergo any tests as to his mental stability, as he alone knew what those repulsive, morbid, accursed alien creatures looked like with those long, bright, white incisor teeth, the drool dripping from their mouths, and the evil grin spread across those disgusting faces. Everyone knew what they were capable of, as they showed that over and over—tearing, then ripping, gnawing, and throwing body parts around in the woods along the highway to Goreville. In other cases, people just disappeared, never to be located again. For some unknown reason, the ghoul and werewolf creatures had secret hiding places for certain victims to do whatever they wanted to. This explained why no trace was found of a number of bodies after the attacks took place. Out among the star studded galaxies lay a secret liar filled with human trophies on display for ghoul and werewolf creatures to salivate over.

Greg Braden did not know where any secret hiding places existed, only that he truly was haunted every time the ghoul and werewolf creatures came to Marcasite. He still had not told Janice Maribel, his girlfriend or any of his friends. His school marks and extramural activities were not affected over the many years due to being stressed out. In the beginning, he suffered from some shock, dismay, and fear, as his marks dropped for a while. Once he got his bearings and took control of his soul, mind, and spirit, he came into himself. No one could see he'd gone through this horrible trauma in his life since age six and beyond. However, he felt full of guilt as the death and disappearances continued to grow around him. He knew deep inside there was nothing he could do to stop the ghoul and werewolf creatures from coming around. Fear had him by the throat that very day as he read about the Laxtons. *Why,* was all he could muster from within his thoughts. Many people died and others disappeared and Greg could not assist in easing the trouble. His sanity meant more to him for some reason than any who would believe him. How could he admit to the residents, his friends, and classmates he was able to see the ghoul and werewolf creatures that have been killing and taking other people away? He was not able to due to being shunned and maybe locked up in the psych ward again.

After a few days, the search for the Laxtons was called off due to lack evidence of their bodies being out in the woods. Police Chief Harry Rook called the *Gazette* to let them know the search was called off. It was the same as in all past cases; no trace was found of their bodies in their home or cars. Two more bodies were added to the growing tally of those who have disappeared in those calamitous, vicious, abhorrent storms. Whether they were dead or not, no one held that answer, as much as the pain created by the loss grew and burnt into the very hearts and souls of the residents of Marcasite. The heinous, obnoxious, lurid foreign invaders had to have a grisly hiding place for those who disappeared. Unknown types of horror, torture, pain, and hurt could be inflicted on all of them in that location. People, young and old, hoped for the bodies to be found out there one day. No one deserved to be taken and never returned to their families.

The *Gazette* was going to run the full story in the next day's issue. Hal and Hilary Laxton were good teachers and cared about their students, which they had found out. After the eight years teaching, most students knew them by sight in the hallways. All of their fellow staff seemed much shaken by such terrible news in regards the two being whisked away. Yet not one of them had any explanation as to why this was happening to their oasis in town. Everyone recalled the stories of the ghoul and werewolf creatures being handed down from one generation to the next. Now the teachers at Robert Brown Senior High did finally accept the tales as true facts as the happenings were taking place today. Over the last five months, all the strange deaths and disappearances finally sunk in for them. Why had they not accepted the truth a long time ago? Probably due to being educated not to accept the unknown things in life without first questioning and then finding solutions to them.

Teagan and Candy had all the information to run the presses for the entire issue of the *Gazette* coming out tomorrow. Time to put the paper to bed had come around and to get some food in their stomachs along with some tea, especially after a long, tiring day of interviews and taking in sad news from people in the community and at the school, including students. Being good newspaper people was their lifeblood and enjoyment as well. They had to admit all the deaths and disappearances in the last number of months were just overpowering them. The Wellands were never the type to give up in the face of any adversity, especially now when people counted on them more than ever. Stories were what readers required, no matter how bad the news was or could become. Anything to do with the destructive, barbaric, malicious alien raiders may scare residents, but they needed to hear it anyways. Nothing bad was ever going to be left out of their paper.

The next morning, the *Gazette* needed to be packed up to get ready to be taken to the coffee shops and stores around Marcasite. Residents were always waiting for the paper when it came out in the mornings. Coffee and reading seemed to go hand in hand as the morning talk increased. Amazement and frustration filled the air wherever the paper was read; residents were just plain fed up. Yet somewhere they believed their gem of a town could survive through the current events. After all, they all settled here just like most of their grandparents and others had done. Marcasite became a shining beacon of beauty from the rolling hills of southeast corner of Gopher County, rising from the dusty ground of the prairie allowing all things to sprout and finally mature, just like a dream planted so many decades ago forged by workers who helped Marcasite into the light of the sky.

Sitting or standing in shops and stores chatting about the worst times in memory seemed to help them alleviate the pressure. Relaxing was important as anyone would agree with if the deaths, disappearances and destruction ended for good. Being around friends and acquaintances always helped ease the pressure from their souls. As everyone knew each other in a small town, Marcasite residents were no different, especially with all that had taken place over the last five months or more now. Sticking together and not leaving their dream homes was the only way to survive the current troubles. Most were here when the town was still clean, before the ghoul and werewolf creatures started to come alive to take over their oasis. Unknown and unseen fears became very unsettling among the population of adults, children and teenagers. These two latest deaths were just due to being here and not being willing to leave.

Ghastly, hideous, brutal creatures had a terrible, horrifying way of staying for five long months each year. That time was very close to ending in some people's hopes and wishes in their minds. Other people felt very different due to the extent of all the deaths, destruction, and disappearances since last fall. During the construction of Marcasite, a couple of deaths had happened and even more since then. Some other residents thought all that took place was just payback for trespassing on ancient ground. The *Gazette* had carried stories from when the latest string of deaths and disappearances began to happen. The only ones who knew how long the destruction, deaths, and disappearances would last were the barbaric, atrocious, horrendous long-toothed creatures. An unnatural desire to feast on human flesh while taking other ones to a faraway location to torture and devour on their schedule. This seared the residents to the inner depths of their souls more than anyone could admit out loud.

Yet there was more belief in ghoul and werewolf creatures coming from the faraway, star studded Milky Way. A crack existed allowing these beings to attack at will with intense killing sprees and taking other people away for some unknown reason. All this was in line with the tales passed down from the native elders to the first white settlers about strange deaths caused by ghoul and werewolf creatures, beings that came during the worst storms of the year from spring till late fall. The medicine men drove them away to a faraway place they believed was the Milky Way. Medicine men were the most powerful in their tribe, as it fell on them to ward off evil, undesirable beings. They danced, calling on their spirits of the gods to assist them in giving them much needed power for hours and hours. Even after many people were torn open, ripped apart, and gnawed upon with their remains scattered around inside the dense woods, other people disappeared and were never seen again among their people ever again. Periods of death, destruction, and disappearances only lasted from spring till fall every year. According to the elders and the medicine men of the local native tribes, they had lost hundreds of people through the centuries.

No one knew how the ghastly, fiendish, obscene, murderous attackers escaped to come back to kill, haunt, and attack their town at will. Did a crack actually exist in the Milky Way for them to come back in the worst storms of the year? Now in the dead of this winter, they were out doing their demonic, repulsive desires to people. Marcasite residents were now always on edge as no one knew or wanted to know when a storm could strike. Worry, fear, strife, and utter concern for what lay ahead shook them all. How could one guard against an enemy like those nefarious, odious, detestable ghoul and werewolf creatures? As they could enter through any wall, any door, and any window without leaving any marks, traces, or trails. Marcasite seemed to be on their radar screens for many sick and twisted unknown reasons. A town built smack dab in the middle of a hunting ground for despicable, terrible, outlandish foreign creatures. Described due to the long, deep, teeth gouges on what bones were recovered from the remains of the many victims. Guesses were all the coroners and police had at best, with a scarcity of clues left behind. Still more victims were out there somewhere, never to be recovered or found again. Over the centuries, how many people had, in fact, gone missing in these incredible, deadly, reprehensible storms of such intense ferocity? Hundreds or thousands, who actually knew the true number accept those brutal, devilish, diabolic slaughtering alien beings?

Greg Braden was still not saying a word as he was scared for himself and his family. What could he do to help? Not one of his friends seemed to know anything about them. Greg could not ruin his family's life over seeing beings no one else ever saw. Sixteen years old now, and for ten years those grotesque, repugnant, hideous ghoul and werewolf creatures had shown themselves to him. Right from the first time. He always had an explicit memory of being in his closet, frozen to the floor and wetting his pajamas that night. How he wished he had taken his mom's advice and stayed in his bed. Instead, he became overcome with fear and decided to go into some place dark. This was a huge mistake for any six-year-old child to make. Especially during such a fierce, lurid, hellish, stormy night. Greg knew those beings were going to haunt him. Trying to drive intense fears deep within his soul. He felt at ease with the one person who kept him going forward who was Janice Maribel, his girlfriend, without whom he may have ended back up in the local psych ward again.

One day he would have to face his distracters, in some way, to help stop the deadliest torment coming at Marcasite. A heinous, unspeakable, horrid crush had hit Marcasite over the last five months with nothing to stop it from continuing. Till that day came to open up, all Greg could do was be quiet. Fright outweighed all other options for in his fear-driven thought patterns. A deep, cold, fiendish feeling he held inside since he was six years old seemed to be overcoming any willpower he possessed. Plus, ever since his two best friends, Lenny Farfeld and Caden McDougall were murdered Greg carried that with him at all times without showing any outward signs. Inside, he was ready to fall apart, yet Janice could not be aware of his knowledge of what caused the deaths, the destruction, and all the disappearances over the years. Greg knew he would lose her and all his friends by opening his mouth now. He chose to keep silent until a time came to be brave enough, strong enough, and ready enough to say something.

All of his friends were just as scared, just as frightened, like never before in their young, short lives. School was the only idea they dreamed of, to seek out peace and quiet with no more harm coming toward them or their families. Winter was one season that usually held lots of fun and excitement for all. Now just a cloud of dread, fear, cold, spine-tingling chills all day and night held them. What happened to the wonderful, beautiful, loving town they remembered from their younger days? As those memories were still alive inside their souls, they should grab hold of those to keep them close. Being younger than their parents should provide them with more of a comfort zone, which was nonexistent now.

Two very slow weeks passed without any incidences of snowstorms or extremely strong winds blowing through Marcasite. Life was relaxed once more, almost to the point everyone who desired it could feel the peacefulness of the moment. Good weather was holding up the spirits of everyone across the whole town. February could swing great, warm winds in called Chinooks, which came from the west. Snow melted and it felt like spring maybe coming next month; at least it did feel this way, kids returned to playing outdoors, skiing, tobogganing, skating indoors and on the outdoor rinks. Laughter from the kids and teens filled the parents with hope that had been missing for just about five months now. The days had more sunshine as each one passed, and they warmed the hearts of residents as spring should now be only six weeks away. Sunshine was starting to feel great after the dark times of the winter months had almost buried the residents in total despair.

Chapter Twenty-One

March was a month that came in like a lion, or it would go out like a lamb, or vice versa to most residents. As everyone waited for the snow to melt and the sun to help make all things green and regenerate all life. A time when the air smelled fresh, with the warm breezes sweeping across the prairies leading the way to Marcasite, drying the ground off and taking away the snow and ice from the area. Dreams like this were weeks and weeks away, yet dreams were very important after almost six months of trouble, all those bad deaths and disappearances that struck Marcasite since October of last fall into this New Year. All people needed and wanted was a normal life with their families for fun and real enjoyment. Time was going to tell them on its own terms, sort of due according to the timetable the ghoul and werewolf creatures set. No schedule was put out for residents to look at from the disgusting, unseen, creepy creatures. They came whenever they wanted and needed to inflict pain and suffering on Marcasite. Their feeding frenzies caused severe turmoil when they showed up in town these past six months.

March crept into being with thick, white clouds over top Marcasite on the first of the month. Snow came down slowly as the morning sun looked to be a shadow from the other side, a day filled with promise so far as no winds or any calls for snowstorms to strike. Snow would fall peacefully all day long, accumulating in piles of close to a foot deep by late afternoon. The white clouds never seemed to look any different as daylight was almost half over for the day. Schools closed early to allow the students and staff to go home due to the heavy accumulation of snow. No one had felt anything to fear, no doubts of being safe, and thoughts were good. Everyone then knew for sure March would go out like a lamb, as the saying went. Kids of all ages played in the snow as they made their way home along the streets in Marcasite. All the pent-up pain, fear, hurt, and the loss seemed to slip away that early afternoon. Teens and children just enjoying being outside as if nothing bad had befallen Marcasite. Times such as this were few and far between for everyone since last October.

March first's snowfall continued to slowly come down into the evening hours, long after the sun went down. Light, huge, fluffy flakes built up on streets, sidewalks, and steps all over the town of Marcasite once again. Nothing seemed out of the ordinary, except the air was a little warmer than it should have been. Early spring snows brought a rise in temperatures and more dampness to the air. Snows in March were typical, with strong wind gusts drifting and piling snow up all over town. Streetlights seemed to be half hidden by a blanket of white as the evening crept along into the overnight period.

As everyone awoke the following morning after the snow had stopped coming down earlier during the night, piles of snow were built up along the streets, sidewalks, and on the house steps. People could be seen outside shoveling to clear their walkways, steps, and driveways. The temperature was colder due to a strong wind still blowing, so everyone was dressed up very warm to guard against freezing their skin. Inside the homes in Marcasite, moms were getting their children dressed for school that morning. Parents also made a hot breakfast for their families to enjoy the start of their day. Mornings spent around the table seemed to be keeping the spirits up in cold, snowy weather.

Schools opened a little late because the streets were not cleared that early, and many of the students missed school that morning. During the winter months, small class sizes due to the storms were a normal occurrence in Marcasite. Those who missed a few classes at times usually got the needed class information from friends or other students. Teachers provided all the classes of students with extra time for assignments to be handed in due to storms taking away from classes. Marcasite had the best schools and teachers, which made them very proud of the students who achieved good marks all through the years. During the real bad times when ghoul and werewolf creatures struck students did well, the students had to concentrate on something other than all the deaths and disappearances coming to Marcasite over the last six months. Teachers found ways to keep their students focused on learning in the classes they taught. Having fun and not being too strict during those critical times seemed to help ease the attitudes.

Marcasite had been safe from any harm for a number of weeks now, and maybe this was going to continue. Spring had not yet arrived and the snow could be hiding other victims deep under it. Adults went about doing what they usually did to keep their families happy and contented, trying not to worry over what was out of their control at times like this, although the dreadful feeling was always present due to what had gone on since last fall in town. Those awful hideous deaths, the incredible destruction, and the horrible fact disappearances happened to spook them more than anyone could have imagined took a huge toll. Marcasite was supposed to be a gem of place to raise a family in complete serenity, happiness, and peace. Some revolting, diabolical, fiendish ghoul and werewolf creatures found them trespassing on their personal feeding grounds. Now the worst of things was being carried out on them for no real reason they understood or knew of. Most residents remembered when peace had been here before the last depression struck across the country. Still, the older residents had memories of unspeakable deaths and disappearances taking place back then in those days. Minds tended to not always recall the same terrible events and who could blame them?

Older residents thought of the times when those who left returned to Marcasite for a better world to live in. People slowly came back home for work, to raise a family, and others came back from a world war overseas. Even those people felt a type of dreadful, horrid, offensive beings watching them return one by one. A lot of people recalled thinking dark forces followed them back along the roads and railroad tracks to Marcasite. A dusty, small populated village on the edge of nowhere was looking a little worse for wear and tear than when they had left it long ago. Residents either knew or slowly began to hear about all the weird happenings while they were gone for the last decade. Anyone who had not stayed definitely was soon aware of the bootleggers setting up stills out in the countryside in Gopher County.

There was that ever-present feeling of being watched ever since as a bad, evil presence had kept watch on the town. Over the years, deaths, destruction, and disappearances came to life just like tales passed down from the native elders. During the depression, nothing strange ever took place in Marcasite that was in any way connected to the recent events. Teagan and Candy Welland, who ran the *Gazette*, could not recall any stories related to such evil, terrible trouble in that time period. As empty as Marcasite seemed to be with a war, a depression, and lots of dust storms taking place, the *Gazette* published no less than once a week. Teagan and Candy figured nothing had happened during the depression as the weather was so hot, dry, and dusty, and nothing grew, except dust devils, big, brown tumbleweeds, and thistles that were everywhere in those days. Tumbleweeds blew through the streets, across roads and fields. A feeling of being seen by unknown or unseen forces was always present for some reason. This eerie, awkward sense of something keeping watch unnerved the residents ever more internally.

When cleaning up after the latest snowstorm, the remains of a single body was found in a back alley on the edge of town, frozen to death. The corpse was thought to have been under the snow for some time and needed to be thawed off at the coroner's office. Parts of the body were gone, and other parts were stripped of all the meat, muscles, and tendons. Deep gouges were shown on other bones of the body, which was the same as all other deaths. Police and the coroner had no idea of who this person was, as no ID was found on the body. Whoever it was had no criminal record and was not in the system for any reason. March became a complete disaster for police and the coroner's office. Lots of old unsolved cases had piled up, and more came in every month now. The police could not admit they were beyond their scope with all the investigations yet to be carried out. However, they had to keep going forward with the belief these killings would stop very soon. No one could ever accept this after the last number of months now being the worst in recent memory.

Unjust deaths occurred too often over the last number of years in Marcasite, and why, no one could explain. What had the residents done to have all this unfolded upon them in this cruel incredible manner? All they had wanted was a gem of a place to live and raise a nice family on the prairie. Among the slightly rolling, green-covered hills of southeast Gopher County on the vast open land. Now their dreams were being shattered, and no end seemed in sight from the attacks by ghoul and werewolf creatures. Still the residents galvanized their spirits to put up a wall to keep the evil at bay, as if that would stop these vile unseen beings from coming to do what they desired when they wanted to. A feeding ground for beastly, horrible, gruesome creatures existed where Marcasite stood, this was a real huge, privately owned feasting lounge for these extreme, disgusting, terrible, horrible beings. People would agree to stand together and do what it took to stop the attacks. Just what this would take was something else that was out of their hands and thoughts.

Another week crept past as the police tried to find out the identification of their victim and where he had come from. Finally, they got their break; a man matching his description was just reported missing from Goreville a while ago. His name was Hugo Perez; his family said he went to work and just never came home that day.

How he came to end up in Marcasite seemed to be the mystery around all of this. Police never located any vehicle belonging to his company in the limits of Marcasite. How did he come to end up here then? Had he been scooped up by these ungodly, odious, demonic creatures and brought here? Hugo, it turned out, was a regular delivery driver for a transport company from Goreville. He drove a load of parts down for a local car dealership before he went missing. Police finally found the truck in the industrial park, half buried under a huge pile of snow. He was just at the wrong place at the right time for the detestable, fiendish ghoul and werewolf creatures to come feed once more. Another victim belonging to those demonic, diabolical, horrid creatures from the star studded Milky Way.

Hugo Perez's remains were sent back to Goreville to his family for burial the next day once the last bit of paper work was done. Police officials still seemed very tight-lipped over all the deaths in the last year. People wanted protection from these insidious, barbaric, macabre monstrous creatures. After all, they paid taxes for protection, did they not? Even the mayor's office was taking tons of heat from the residents. Frustration was mounting as the death toll continued to climb from one year to the next. All they wanted was their dream of a jewel to come true once and for all. Sadly, the nefarious, abhorrent, dreadful killers knew better than to let anything happen to their desires for feeding in their private lounge called the town of Marcasite. Hugo Perez was just another victim chalked up to the twisted, barbaric, brutal ghoul and werewolf creatures killings.

Chapter Twenty-Two

Winter was hanging around as March was only half over for them, and spring was a way off. Snowstorms were predicted to hit Marcasite in the next few days, so all residents got ready. More death and disappearances were going to happen, as they always did. Dread, fear, and just downright terrified feelings filled everyone in these last days of March as this newest storm struck. Winds blowing fiercely and snow falls so deep blowing through Marcasite like never before. The worst storm in decades finally smacked into them head on and continued for two days till the winds died, the snow stopped, and the temperature dipped to minus thirty. Drifts piled up over three feet high across town, so everyone was having trouble getting outside of their homes. Who was going to clean up the great drifts of snow if all of them were stuck moving around? However, some street workers were able to get some snowplows on the streets within a couple of hours. It would take about three days before all of the residents were able to go about their daily routines. Most schools and businesses were shut down through this entire time period. The worst snowstorm in many years hit them full force, head on, and people survived it to see life continue.

Everyone felt someone was dead or gone away or more than one after being stuck for the last two days of this storm. Now they had to get their sidewalks cleared to the doorways to get out. Their only activity was going out to clear the walkways and driveways around their homes. Still, that nagging pull of the subconscious mind drifting toward what may have occurred during the time while the snowstorm was howling down on them. The residents of Marcasite would indeed find out in due time of the latest misfortune to strike. Ghoul and werewolf creatures never lost an opportunity to feed whenever they could, especially under the cover of snow or rainstorms. Why should the people be scared over this latest storm? No one enjoyed having friends, relatives or neighbors killed by vicious, atrocious, abominable beings from the faraway Milky Way. One thing they all were aware of, such beings did not come from earth, and they were sure glad they were not the unfortunate ones. Who could tear open, rip apart, and gnaw on human beings in this fashion? Not anything from this planet is all the residents had agreed on this thought many years ago.

Once all schools and businesses reopened, a head count was done to make sure all were present that day. Of course, some people were missing, which was the entire

Hill family; not one of them had shown up, no kids, no parents at work, so they called the police to let them know who was missing. Marcasite police went to their home to find it empty and no sign of struggle having taken place. Where did they go and what took them? Police brass knew the answers for their questions. The ghoul and werewolf creatures struck again under the heavy blanket of snow with the fierce winds behind it.

The highways were still very treacherous; however, a search of the usual area needed to be carried out. The sooner they did, the faster answers would be forthcoming, and evidence could be gleaned from the site. Search teams spread out along the area to slowly go over the snow path for blood drops or bone fragments, bones, and clothing. Hours stretched out so slow that day in the cold woods when one team found the remains of all four victims. They were found scattered across the empty space amid the woods about a quarter mile inside that snow-covered trees. All the searchers were overcome with grief as they looked at the slaughter of innocent lives, children taken before they even had a chance at life and parents gone before they experienced all they could have had. Some searchers would need to talk with grief counselors who were coming to be normal occurrence. Anyone who was on search teams always found his or her own way to deal with things, while others needed some form of help. When these latest deaths took place, it was real hard to accept the gem of a town was so disgustingly evil and vilely decrepit.

Teagan and Candy Welland found out shortly after the remains of the Hill family were found—Mark Hill, his wife Carla, and their two children, daughter Jasmine and son Albert. This was an actual first for these ghoul and werewolf creatures, attacking, tearing, ripping, and truly mutilating everyone in this family. Deep incisor teeth marks were left behind on the bones scattered around deep inside the bushes along the highway to Goreville again. Teagan and Candy felt this area must have meant something for these ghoul and werewolf creatures. The victims were found in the same geographic locations along the lonesome highway to Goreville, just not in the same spot all the time, which was significant in one way, they had thought. As usual there were never any footprints other than the blood drops, small bone fragments, a few complete bones, and some clothing scattered around. Everything seemed to be routine in this crime scene; nothing varied from past sites.

The *Gazette* needed to run a new edition tomorrow, so this would be the lead story on the front page. As much as they dreaded to tell the residents all the gory details, they had no choice, as the Hill family had lived in Marcasite forever in their minds and anyone who knew them. A family bio was very important to tell all their readers who knew them or not all about their family. Mark Hill was a carpenter and had worked on many buildings in Marcasite over the years. Carla Hill was a librarian at the Marcasite Central Library right downtown. Jasmine Hill wanted to be a figure skater when she grew up and had been doing it for the last seven years. Albert Hill was a good student who wanted to become an engineer after high school. Now the entire family had been wiped out by the ghoul and werewolf creatures that plagued the town for many decades.

Now they all would be laid to rest in the next few days in a local cemetery. As they were all Methodist, they would be buried in the main city cemetery, which was a beautiful green-grass-covered location in the summers. Now it was completely topped with huge mounds of fresh white snow. In a few days, the snow would be scraped away from the ground to make way for four gravesites. A green rug lay down to cover the dirt and the snow around the sites for the peace and comfort of the relatives and the mourners.

As the funeral service started, the residents had already filled the Methodist church to capacity. Every pew was taken and more people stood at the back and sides to take in the service. Never had so many come to pay respects for one family before due to all four members losing their lives. Reverend Ken Faulkner officiated over the mass and the graveside service that day. Everything was very solemn throughout in every detail from start to finish. The day was cold, and those who came to Cemetery shook with cold shivers; however, they never left till the entire graveside service was over for the Hill family. Still at that point to truly believe a family of four were killed by these nasty, despicable, heinous ghoul and werewolf creatures was really terrifying and truly unbelievable.

The church held a gathering in the community center for all who wanted to come mingle afterward. Everyone who attended the services came out to talk and try and cheer up the entire community. After all, life was going to go on for the rest of them at least that was possible at that time. Conversation was light-hearted and warm, but it hurt to be there for that one reason. No one mentioned the ghoul and werewolf creatures during that gathering that day. Thoughts were on the ones who were gone and the effect they had on the residents of Marcasite, how they had brightened up their time together watching the town grow and how their children grew so fast, which was good therapy for the entire population to expand upon after such great sadness. Grief could take away happiness for way too long, but Marcasite had been through so much in the last year especially. Talking with people they may not have seen in some time kept some pain away. Laughter slowly crept into the community center that afternoon as people started to smile openly. Everyone stayed late into the afternoon as they enjoyed the company of friends, acquaintances, and neighbors.

Now they realized why they loved living in their jewel of a town—because of the closeness and kindness they found. Bonds were formed as the village grew into a small town a long time ago, how families started up, how kids played together, went to school and played together. Yes, they had lots to be thankful for, except the bad moments that lately came too often. No one really understood why they were being attacked by the morbid, depraved, noxious creations. What had they disturbed or created to allow this dreadful death and disappearances to happen? Did the Milky Way actually split open a crack and allow these beings to come down and hit Marcasite at will? Feelings of deep anger, frustration, disgust, and hurt were with them always this past year. What could they do to get rid of these curses that befall them? Maybe one day an answer could be found to assist in helping their beleaguered town. Otherwise, their lives were going to be very much full of these kinds of trepidations, fears, and deaths that no one needed. Life was supposed to be happy, pleasant, and pleasing here in their oasis on the prairie. However, all they found was a giant hole filled by the horrid, repugnant, murderous alien beings who loved to feast on human flesh at will, which was wrong to them.

Their world returned close to normal later that week after the funerals for the Hill family were held. Life had to get back into a routine to save their sanity. Schools filled up with students and staff as they all felt relieved for now. Businesses had full staff levels once again, as they knew what had happened allowing people time off. Marcasite was a very caring place to live with the kind thoughts handed out under very trying circumstances. A breather was, in fact, required for the whole town to relax from what life did. Days later, the smiles, grins, and good-natured fun returned to the people one more time, a typical, classic syndrome as each recovery followed one calamity after the other. Strong-willed, caring, ever hopeful people dreamed of being safe, happy, and contented in Marcasite. Their gem of a town was built for them to raise their families to be away from harm.

March was into its third week as a spring thaw with a warm breeze hit the area. Snow was melting as the nice warm sun shone all over. Spring was finally here, and winter was finally coming to an end for Marcasite, maybe a spring snowstorm left to come sometime in the next week or so. Everyone was happy with the nice weather right now as the snow was softening up under the early sunny heat. Puddles were slowly forming in the ruts in the streets from the vehicles driving back and forth. Not enough water that made people gets splashed by vehicles going by. Water was a hazard every year as it ran off from the melting snowpack along the streets. Sunshine was lasting longer as each day passed now, and all residents could smell the fresh air blowing in from the west. Cheer was replacing gloom among the people as well. Spirits started to be uplifted as the days got longer as March drew to a close.

The sky was clear and blue over Marcasite in the southeast corner of Gopher County as the week went along. Warm weather seemed to stay in place instead of the deep cold and snow in the recent past. No one was complaining about wearing fewer clothes these days in town as the temperature increased slowly. After the winter cold and snow, it was a relief to be hot enough to wear spring clothes. Complacency could be good or bad at any time in those weary days between spring and winter. Winter may return one more time with a severe blast of cold and deep snow. Every year it seemed old man winter was cruel, mean, and nasty enough. Maybe this year was going to be different, as spring would clear away the mess of snow and turn things green. Hopes never faded after long hard winters, except this past one was the worst ever. Prairie people were a hardy bunch, surviving droughts, famines, and ice-cold winters in the past decades. The bright life burned inside each one of them, which they got from their parents and grandparents.

Winter was forecasted to blow back in overnight with a lot of snow, maybe a foot or so if the weatherman was correct. Winds could be blowing close to thirty-five miles an hour or more overnight. Around eight o'clock that evening, the snow started to fall slowly at first as the breeze was just beginning to pick up. In the morning, the snowfall was still coming down, and the news said the schools would be closed for the day. Business owners were not going to open and have employees drive in such terrible winter road conditions. How could anyone drive with snow blowing about like it did in a storm? Except most residents knew deep down death at the hands of ghoul and werewolf creatures was out there. Too many times over the past months, people were killed and disappeared during snowstorms. For the first time ever, winter was when dreadful, malevolent, destructive foreign raiders struck according to all records. This winter the deaths left residents with no peace of mind to live among all other humankind out there. Why was their world upset and blindsided by demonic, appalling, petrifying creatures? The two graveyards in Marcasite seemed to have fresh places for coffins to lie in.

Chapter Twenty-Three

Today the town was buried under eighteen inches of snow and drifts of up to two feet in some areas of Marcasite. A typical springtime phenomenon occurred in the southeast corner of Gopher County where their town was. Strong winds did the most damage, covering streets and sidewalks under deep banks of soft white snow. Once the storm subsided the plows would come out to clear all the roadways. Sanders were going to be out after all streets were done one by one to keep drivers safe. Schools would reopen when it was the right time for students who walked or were driven to attend classes. Every precaution was taken due to the eerie, scary, death knell that took Marcasite by surprise all winter long. Families needed to do fun activities while they waited for the storm to end. Another day off was always welcome in the colder months, staying indoors where it was warm and dry.

The spring storm ended later in the afternoon in time for the last rays of the sun to come out. Evening was a little cloudy yet, and the breeze was still brisk across the whole of Marcasite. Somehow, was there an eerie calm waiting for the discovery of a dead body or more? Was someone missing from their home, taken away by the dreaded ghoul and werewolf creatures once again? Fear was the biggest weapon these beings had on the people of Marcasite, going back many centuries before any town was built on that exact location. Any questions in regards to anyone being killed or missing would, in fact, be answered very soon.

The day after the streets were cleared, the police received a call about no one being seen at a certain address. The owners had not cleared their sidewalks or the driveway at their home. Two constables were dispatched to see if anyone was at home. Once they arrived, they got through the snowdrift on the sidewalk and went up to the front door. As they knocked and waited for the owners to open the door, they felt a chill go up and down their spines, just another sure sign something was amiss inside the residence of Rick and Mary Raffert. A locksmith needed to be called to pick the lock for them to get inside for a look around. The curtains were completely closed in the house from their vantage point at the moment. No lights were on, as it was still dark enough to use them at this time of year in Marcasite.

It would take some time for the locksmith to show up due to the bad driving conditions today. They both went back to their cruiser and waited in the warmth and then called in all the information they had so far. Once inside the home, more would, in fact, be known about whether anyone was in or not and what could have happened to them or if they left some time before the neighbors noticed. How could they get around when most streets were blocked? A snow plow had come and cleared the street leading up to the Rafferts' home for the officers. The two cops talked over what they knew in regards to the Rafferts and the belief they could be somewhere else. Due to the other outstanding cases of deaths and disappearances, they could not rule out ghoul and werewolf creatures being responsible.

About forty minutes later, the locksmith arrived and let the officers inside the residence to search for the occupants. Both constables took their search one room at a time throughout the complete residence. Of course, no one was home, and there was no sign of any struggle having taken place. They called in and asked for the crime scene team to check everything out, as too many cases had occurred this winter already. A number of other police officers showed up to help check the property and garage where the vehicle could still be inside it. Yes, their car was still there, and no one was inside it. Another eerie case seemed to be handed to the police with no evidence or foot- or fingerprints. There was no sign of their bodies on the property either in the front or backyards. All the snow was shoveled off the yard to be sure nobody was underneath. What happened baffled the officers on the scene as always. How were they going to stop this, let alone catch some things that do not leave clues behind? These gruesome, ghastly, harrowing deadly beings that came from another dimension through a crack in the Milky Way, could it be impossible? Rick and Mary Raffert were nowhere to be seen on their property inside the house or outside under the snow. A thorough search was carried out digging in the snowdrifts to ensure no one was buried underneath on their property.

Once the news broke and the residents became aware of another couple of deaths taking place, fear was going to run rampant again. Ice-cold shivers crawled through their souls as the knowledge that it could have been one of them. A relief was apparent even though these despicable, nefarious ghoul and werewolf creatures struck some other household. This seemed wrong and foreign due to feeling extremely sad over the loss of two of their neighbors. What was going on in their town, and why were so many horrid deaths and disappearances taking place? After the last five months of the toll increasing, more anger, frustration, pain, and fear was being expressed to the mayor, the council, and police officials.

The *Gazette* covered all these depressing, horrifying details in every issue for people to read. That seemed the only way to cover the sordid events that were taking place across Marcasite since early October of last year. Times like these always hit Teagan and Candy Welland hard, as they felt the same level of anxiety, same level of fear, same level of insane doubts of this going on and no faith in the destruction ever coming to an end in their days. Their private opinion was never expressed to anyone outside their home and office. Private thoughts and discussions between the two of them were just that. Being husband and wife for many years and newspaper people, they had many talks over stuff, including the strange happenings, deaths, disappearances, and many other stories that circulated in their paper. Teagan and Candy may have talked with friends at certain times in regards to the deaths and disappearances. The pair never sounded scared while being in public, which was a skill learned over time to help. Reporting on the deaths and disappearances were taking a toll on the Wellands this winter. Never before had things occurred in the usual still of the ice-cold winter months.

Teagan and Candy went to talk with Police Chief Harry Rook later that afternoon in regards to the latest event. Chief Rook had called them as he usually did in these deaths and disappearances. He wanted to know if the story could be held until the next issue came out, which would be Saturday afternoon's special issue, and they said okay, if that was necessary. Harry Rook wanted time to have his officers do a grid search and look for any details to help in the intense investigation. The *Gazette*, being the only newspaper, would receive exclusive rights to the details for the story. They felt as if saying no would just hamper the relationship they had with the police chief for a story, something that was close to any newspaper's heart, and that bond could not be broken. Time was on their side, and the two of them went back to their office to get some stories ready for Saturday's special issue. The following morning, there was still no news from Police Chief Harry Rook. This, under the circumstances, was not strange, as there were times when bodies never turned up during the initial search and were found many days later.

Search teams fanned out along the highway to Goreville, as it was the dumping ground for dead bodies. Snow was deep in spots as expected after a big storm in the woods, which acted as a net to catch it. All the search teams knew the usual spots to look at just in case the routine was the same. They looked for the tell-tale red blood spots on the fresh, white snow crust against the brown of the trees, a painstaking process for the searchers whom worked in hard places as the sun glared off the snow right back at them. By the end of the first day, no sign was found of any bodily remains in the exact locations. Just maybe these two people were taken to another place and would never be seen again. The next day, all the search teams would be out at daybreak to begin looking once again until there was no reason for hope of finding any trace of bodies or bones or any clothing or blood inside the wooded areas.

Life carried on as the residents dug themselves out from under the huge snowdrifts around their properties. The kids and teens played outside in their yards, never venturing far from their homes. Fear had taken hold of the community once more, even though the sun beamed high overhead. The winds were very strong, cold, and unforgiving even in the springtime on the prairies, a bite so hard, deep, and it hurt if one was not dressed warm enough. Could this be those ghoul and werewolf creatures having another laugh at the expense of the people of Marcasite? Thoughts may run wild with the winds at any time of the year. Right now all anyone wanted was the snow to be cleared away from sidewalks, steps, and driveways. Streets were slowly being cleared up as the day went on after the Rafferts disappeared from their home. Everyone wondered what happened to them as they tried to keep busy for the time being. All these unexpected deaths and disappearances since last October till March were too much on the whole town. No one was able to stop the terrible, extreme hurt, tremendous pain, and excruciating grief that struck Marcasite since then. People wished and prayed they could stop the death toll from climbing any higher than it was. The police were not able to fend off the heinous, horrendous, brutal slaughter by these creatures that were their responsibility.

Search teams were gathered at the police station first thing the next morning in order to get their search grids. Certain areas were more important to look at than others due to the certainty something was going to come up. The weather should be warming up today, and the sun would be shining brightly overhead. Sunglasses were going to come in handy in those conditions out in the woods. Once all the teams were set, they headed out the doors to get into their vehicles. Heavy gear was a necessity in those dense woods and deeply snow-packed areas they were going into today. They all knew it was going to be slow going through the day, as all searches were in this place. Maybe this time no one was going to end up being torn open, ripped apart, and gnawed upon. It could be a simple case of individuals disappearing into that faraway place the demonic, dreadful, fiendish ghoul and werewolf creatures took certain victims. A special place used to stash people for ritualistic feasts to be held at a later date. Where the brethren would be comfortable, far away from prying eyes of any humans who could interfere with what would be done.

The sunlight was starting to fade as the search teams made their way back to the central meeting location. All their vehicles were parked in the same pull out on the highway to Goreville. Again, no team had any results from another exhausting, empty, day-long search tramping through woods and knee-deep snow. They would go back to the station and compare notes for a while before leaving to go home for the night. Everyone had to come back again the next morning and lay out another search grid. Volunteers and the police officials knew the searches need to be carried out with extreme caution and care. If the missing people were members of their own families, they would expect nothing less be carried out. Nothing less

than a full, exhaustive search of the entire grid area would
be acceptable for the right reasons, no matter how long
it took to find or not find Mr. and Mrs. Raffert or their
remains. They could be buried under the snow that came
down and had been blown around covering the openings
in the woods.

Chapter Twenty-Four

Greg Braden was still in Two Hills Junior High and doing really well in all the classes he took that year. Even with the deaths of two of his best friends last October, he had kept himself together. Greg was still the only one who had seen these gruesome, ungodly, abominable ghoul and werewolf creatures to his knowledge. Those ugly, scary villains with the long, sharp incisor teeth still haunted him to no end. He swore that every time someone died or disappeared they paid him a visit just to let him know they had not forgotten him. Greg was very much aware he could never say anything to his parents or anyone else about still seeing those creatures. He was never going back to a psych ward ever again in his life. Flashes of being in his closet at six years of age when he first saw them—why had he not listened to his mom and stayed in bed that night? Now as a teenager he knew for some reason it was all supposed to turn out this way. However, this just made him more frightened of what his future held. These destructive, diabolical, repulsive ghoul and werewolf creatures were going to keep feasting on the population for many more centuries to come. He knew they would return to see him time and again over his lifetime; every time they came for a feast he would see them next to him in the dark of the storms. And now he saw them this entire winter beside him in the dark of night with the snow coming down outside, letting him know they allowed him to live to torment at their calling and in their own despicable, unspeakable manner.

Greg's only way to survive was to throw himself into school studies. Plus, Janice Maribel was still his high school sweetheart, which he enjoyed very much. She had a good effect on him once he realized she liked him. All his friends seemed to know before he did, he recalled many times. Young love crept up on some, and he was one of those teens. Whatever it took to shake those memories and visits by more of the devilish, malevolent, malicious foreign beings Greg would do. Going crazy seemed a real scary, mind-blowing situation to face. Yet these things wanted him for some unknown reason and kept him alive when they haunted the town. He was fortunate school got canceled today, as he seemed unsure if he could face anyone after the latest news. He always seemed to feel responsible for the deaths and disappearances of people. How could those obnoxious, appalling, lurid creatures do this to him, wreck his life and destroy his future if he allowed them to get to him in any manner? Yet Greg felt it was helpless to fight something as evil, dreadful, and scary as those creatures from the faraway Milky Way. Why did they not just leave him and Marcasite alone? He then remembered to phone Janice as he had promised her he would. Bringing up enough courage to the level that allowed him to hide his fears deep down inside, he dialed her number. Janice and Greg talked for almost two hours that afternoon, which was good for them. Relief flooded Greg inside as Janice made him feel like he was important in her own way. Greg always felt good when he talked with Janice since they got together.

After he got off the phone with Janice, Greg had a shower to warm up some more, as he felt a cold chill coming over him, not the same cold chills when the ghoul and werewolf creatures came to call on him. This spring weather felt uncomfortable to him and probably everyone else in town. Lots of other residents, young and old, had been outside in the day's snow and cold, just not going anyplace, just staying in their yards for the time being until more was known about what happened the night before. Marcasite had already lost its shine as a jewel and an oasis on the prairie landscape long ago. Now the full impact of what a teen Greg's age knew and saw hit him before he took his shower. He knew he should say something to the police, but he was scared of being put in the psych ward and shunned by his friends for life. The hot water felt good, but the chill remained burnt deep inside his soul when he felt this way. Greg stayed in the shower for a long time, thinking about how stupid he was to feel scared of opening up about what he knew. That was the end of his thoughts, as he needed to stop thinking such things before he lost his mind.

School and work resumed again a couple days after the last snowfall and disappearances of the Rafferts. No trace had yet been located of them, and police were still following up on all possible leads. None of the Rafferts' relatives had heard from them in the last few days either. This seemed to worry the police chief and his staff at police headquarters downtown. Search teams were still scouring the woods along the highway to Goreville for any remains. None had been located as the search grid had been expanded a number of times. They were down to their last set of coordinates in their search area, and hopes were fading fast, as time was running out. If nothing could be found, then it was a case of being taken to that place where ghoul and werewolf creatures hid them, trophies stashed away for some type of gruesome, painful ripping apart, tearing open, and gnawing at their pleasure. Such thoughts left all those involved with a terrible, utter feeling of real hate, complete disgust, and helplessness. There were still a few hours of daylight left to keep looking for today in the woods. A couple of more days and the whole area will have been searched in its entirety, and that was a lot of places.

When the search was called off for the day, the teams again returned to the Marcasite police headquarters downtown. Everyone reviewed what they saw as clues in this situation, which were zero—no footprints, no snapped branches, just fresh snow and deep in places. As it was possible the remains were, in fact, buried under the fresh snow cover out in the densely wooded areas, they might have to wait for the snow cover to melt off if nothing came up in the next couple of days. Still, hope had not faded as the evening settled in and everyone went home. The search team members went home with some enthusiasm down inside left for the following day.

That evening, all residents prayed for a happy ending to the matter of finding the missing couple. As much as all the deaths since last October bothered each and every one of them, no one was going to move away. Hope gave encouragement to people in even the most difficult of times. Besides, they had all heard the stories passed down by one generation to the next. None of those tales scared them; after all they had experienced, fright was not the word. Being next or having one of their family die or be taken was more to the point of life. Something had occupied this place long before human beings took up residence on the prairies. Taking up residence in this area came with being of strong and willing type of character. This was being tested beyond belief by these terrifying ghoul and werewolf creatures. According to all local tales handed down from the first generation to come out here, the First Nations people told of frightening, murderous, beastly beings from the faraway Milky Way, attacking them from spring till fall. Their medicine men danced all night long during the storms when they struck. They were able to send the ghoul and werewolf creatures back to that faraway place at the Milky Way. They could not keep them at bay for any length of time, even though they hoped to. Many people retold these tales among their families when troubled times came around. Anything to aid in helping relieve the fear of the unknown in the dark was welcome, and as parents, they had no choice.

The next morning came, and everyone awoke with a good feeling about it as their families got ready to face it. Children of all ages got dressed, ate breakfast, and dressed for the cold weather for the walk to their schools. All students had to catch up for the days missed, just like the teachers needed to play the same game. Not one student seemed to be scared or worried in any fashion. In fact, they enjoyed being there at all times, and learning fascinated them. Nothing seemed to slow down this encouraging trend by the students in every class in all the schools in town. Teachers felt it allowed them an escape from the grim reality of the times they faced. Ghoul and werewolf creatures were never mentioned in classes anywhere in town.

The search teams returned to their grim task in the densely wooded area outside of town along the highway to Goreville. Hopes were very high as the day was warmer and the sun seemed to beam more brightly overhead. Just the signs they all needed to fulfill their need for a successful finish. Finding the remains or bodies of the

Rafferts somewhere today because it felt good. Just luck might be on their side this day as they crawled through the thick over grown bushes. They happened to come to a wide opening that was not on any map, and sure enough, some body parts were spotted. Blood spots were spread all over, some bone fragments, other bones, and some body parts with clothing attached were found. There seemed to be two bodies, but then everything needed to be bagged and taken back to the coroner's office at the morgue. The recovery effort took almost three hours of work by all members of the team. Once all the bagging and tagging was done, the evidence was taken back to the vehicles for transport back to Marcasite. These horrible, noxious, hideous ghoul and werewolf creatures were hiding their victims deeper inside the woods each time. They had centuries of practice, according to local legends, and now there was no one who doubted this procedure.

Once getting back to the rallying point, the search teams put all the bags into their vehicles and headed to the coroner's office at the morgue. The coroner would be busy most of the night to come, as there were lots of parts to identify. Everyone involved hoped this was the remains of the Rafferts. No one wanted to have another death to explain and another search to carry out. Police Chief Harry Rook then called Teagan and Candy Welland to tell them the news about the possibility of finding two bodies. More would be known tomorrow after the coroner was finished his agonizing work. The *Gazette* had already published the

Saturday edition, and the next one was Monday. The news was going to be late, so probably Wednesday's issue could carry the story. That was the best anyone was going to hope for as a positive identification on both bodies, which may take time.

Teagan and Candy needed to soak in the bad news that both the Rafferts were indeed killed. This should have been known by now after all the evil things that had happened in Marcasite since last October. Something made these creatures blood thirsty and very hungry for human flesh. Neither of them knew or had any clues of what had set these ghoul and werewolf creatures off in this latest rampage. Being intelligent human beings with lots of experience with weird events, deaths, disappearances, and destruction, all this confused them. Teagan and Candy had to find an answer for this dilemma before any more people lost their lives. Maybe another trip out to visit the local First Nations People and talk it over with them again was required. Someone must have the ability to get rid of these demons for good; at least they hoped so. Once again in the morning, they would make a fast trip out to visit the First Nations' chief and his medicine men if they were able to, as the Monday issue of the *Gazette* needed to be run and sold. Maybe Tuesday morning was going to be the time to go. They had their hands full for almost six months now as the deaths climbed and the disappearances piled up in Marcasite.

Every month something did happen to unsettle the entire population of the town, as deaths occurred more than any disappearances. Though some were never found, their loss was felt very deeply. Coffins were buried with very little bones or no body at all in them due to families needing closure. Local police were doing what they could to keep people safe from natural harm. These ghoul and werewolf creatures were so unstoppable. Evil creatures feasted and hid bodies like playing a game of hide and seek, except it was real. Beings from the star studded Milky Way broke free from a crack in some dimension to attack the earth at will. Deadly storms from early spring until late fall brought the ghoul and werewolf creatures down upon the residents of Marcasite. They were hiding under the cover of the darkness, amid the flashes of lightning, showing only shadows. Were they real or just imagined in the minds of everyone who witnessed the extreme of it all? The tornado-force winds sounded like the earth being torn open to help hide victims or release more demons to help. Roaring, rolling thunder sounded similar to thousands of feet stomping the ground to dust. Pouring rain assisted to hide the unhallowed, frightening, diabolical creatures amid the cloudy night storms. Winter was the time to relax and enjoy nature at its finest.

This winter was the most disturbing ever against the residents as the revolting, fiendish, calamitous intruders never let up. According to local legend, no strange, eerie creatures struck in the cold, snowy winter months. Why suddenly did they pick this winter and why the increase in the number of occurrences? Many people were torn open, ripped apart, and gnawed upon by the beastly, unhallowed, morbid aggressors with long, sharp incisor teeth. As always the tell-tale signs of deep, long gouges were apparent on the recovered bones from the sites in the woods. That highway to Goreville held some significance to these evil beings, some type of ritualistic dumping grounds for who knew how many centuries already. How come the heavy snow and extreme cold enticed something so bad to kill and take away other human beings? Spring right through to the fall was the normal period of activity for these extremely despicable, grotesque, diabolical ghoul and werewolf creatures. Now the entire year became one extreme time of fear and dread, as there was no escape or hiding from them.

March ended and April was upon Marcasite, bringing warm weather and light rains. Winds assisted to slowly melt the street ice and the snow on the ground. The air smelled so good for the first time in many months. Warm winds from the southwest were always welcome in the early spring as everyone shed a few heavy jackets. Kids were outside, more just to run around in the sunshine, playing silly games. Parents were less tense in letting their kids outside even in after school. Younger children were watched by their mothers or babysitters during the days. Evenings were still spent doing family activities until the ground dried up more. Once the parks were dry and opened again, then children of all ages would be seen swinging, sliding down slides, playing in sandboxes, and just having fun.

However, every parent knew snowstorms or sudden thunderstorms may strike at any moment. A blue sky was nothing to worry about on such a beautiful, warm evening in April on the prairies. Any signs of dark or heavy white clouds might spell trouble on the horizon, which no one was looking forward to the level of deaths and disappearances they caused to the community. For now, all they could do was take in the fresh air and relax with their families. Marcasite was going to be their oasis in which to raise their families in peace, quiet, and serenity. Now those things had them on edge all the time for almost half a year. Trying to take time outs to enjoy the parks was hard however for their kids they would. Kids and teens seemed to bounce back from hardship more than adults for some reason. This could be due to parents retaining the grief and pain longer when people died at the hands of the ghastly, heinous, brutal foreign assailants.

Greg Braden was one teen carrying around the scars from the hideous, loathsome, unholy alien creatures inside his soul. He had been seeing these demon things since he was six years old. On a night when a severe summer storm struck, he hid in his closet only to be visited by them. Figuring he was alone, some things showed themselves to him in the dark inside the closet. Ghoul and werewolf creatures with bright, white, long incisor teeth showing grins with gooey stuff dripping from their mouths sat beside him. He was unable to move, being frozen to the floor and scared as could be. Greg wet his pajamas that evening before they left him alone, and for a while he could not move. As soon was able, he ran like any real scared kid and jumped into his bed, hiding under the blankets for the entire night. The memory of that night was going to stick with Greg for his entire life. The raging, reprehensible, barbaric invaders seemed to come back after him, no matter where he was. If he was on summer vacation with his parents, they followed to scare him. Instilling fear at all times seemed more like a game for those ghastly, terrible, demonic creatures. Greg would only be checked out once at Prairie General Hospital's psych ward. After, he swore no one would ever find out about those faraway visitors attacking him. His friends meant too much to him, and especially Janice, his girlfriend, could not know either.

Greg lost two very close friends to those ghoul and werewolf creatures last October, and he felt responsible. Having knowledge that no one else had seared him, keeping him on edge even though eventually managing it. Still, one day Greg might have to step forward to tell what he knew. Could he face being committed to the psych ward for a long period of time if he did? Just wondering made him doubt his own sanity, because no one will believe such a story from a teenager. Greg had no answer how to stop those creatures or send them back to wherever they had come from. Maybe keeping his information to himself for the time being was the best answer. Plus, he would be at home with his family, friends, and Janice Maribel, his girlfriend. Exactly where Greg wanted to be right now was very safe, comfortable, really content, and extremely happy. School was a lot of fun, intriguing, and he was a top student in all of the classes he enrolled in.

Marcasite police still had no answers as to what, who, and if they could do anything to stop the incredible deaths and disappearances. With no evidence other than the long incisor teeth marks on the recovered bones, they were at an impasse, and the residents were fed up, scared, and feared for the safety of their town. Never had such events been so recorded in history as these were. Local legends had attacks going back as long as the First Nations Tribes lived out here, tales passed down from one generation to the next and to the first white settlers who came out west. Police Chief Harry Rook knew the legends were true, just as every resident knew. However, he was unable to bring himself to admit publicly due to being stubborn. As police chief, he could not face some things he was not able to fight or arrest. Privately, he was confused and mystified by the sudden increase in ghoul and werewolf creatures attacking Marcasite this past six months. Harry Rook wished that such beings had stayed in that faraway place instead of doing harm to people. At the same time, he felt there was an answer out there somewhere.

April was very quiet for the first week before the rains came to wash away the snow and slush from the town.

Memories of many past springs were welcome when they all planted new flowers and trees, and gardens increased to make them feel awesome once again. Just this one would be a safe one with no ghoul and werewolf creatures coming down to attack them. Everyone wanted to have fun with no more worries, just that enough was enough right now. Thoughts of green lawns, fresh blooms from the flowers, trees coming into bud and fresh smells in the air brightened up the entire attitude around town. Renewal was always looked forward to in April and May as the greens, many varied colors, and the fruit trees bloomed. Marcasite was a very beautiful sight in the springtime, as people drove or walked through the neighborhoods to view the sights. People no longer felt shackled by the cold, snowy conditions of winter. Being free to go where and when they wanted was a much needed therapy that spring brought out for sure.

Light rains fell off and on for the next couple of weeks continuing to wash away the grubby look of winter. The deep-down dirt needed to be recovered with a new cover of a fresh, cleaner-looking world. Rain water was heated up and soaked back into the heavens to fall again and again. In between, the sun was shining brightly overhead to heat everything and everyone up, which is what was needed after such a cold, snowy winter as people looked forward to a hot summer. It was not long before the world starting looking like a whole new place for all to live. Marcasite seemed to be returning to its very early beginning when residents first came to town. Just maybe this spring life was going to be back on track for these people in Marcasite.

Chapter Twenty-Five

As April neared the middle of itself, a severe storm was forecasted to hit Marcasite in the evening that day. Sure enough, people figured the worst as these storms caused the most damage, deaths and disappearances. Marcasite seemed to be besieged by these vicious, detestable, fiendish ghoul and werewolf creatures amid these storms that struck at that time as well. People were on edge, and they were ready to face the onslaught of what nature had in store. However, this one storm came with such force it caught everyone off guard. Rain pounded down so very hard, large hailstones dropped sounding similar to a bass drum, lightning flashed faster, rolling thunder echoed constantly, and the tornado winds were harsher than ever. Figures seemed to creep through the ever-quick lightning flashes, searching for a feast among the residents of Marcasite. This storm would last for another twelve hours before it was all over.

In the morning, the air smelled so fresh after the long rainstorm, and things were damaged in some places. Hailstones broke a few windows here and there in a few houses and a number of businesses downtown. The hail hit the hardest in the downtown central core for some strange reason. Streets were a little flooded in those same places, as the system had trouble keeping up with the downpour. Otherwise people seemed to accept some things in their lives. Later that day, someone reported his neighbor was not seen since they'd had coffee the previous evening.

Police were sent to check the situation out at the address of Harold Banks. As it turned out, he was single. Harold was an assistant manager at the Marcasite Bank branch downtown. He was seeing a teller from the bank by the name of Trudy Wheeler. Trudy had her own place in town, and they saw each other away from work. Trudy and Harold had been in this arrangement for close to a year now. She was lucky to be home the night Harold went missing, as the police informed her about Harold the next day. Trudy took the news hard as expected by the officers who informed her that morning. She needed time off work to get over the sudden loss of her boyfriend, and the bank gave her time, which meant no one else would be gone or dead somewhere.

This was going to make the investigation a lot easier for them now. However, his body was not in his premises as the police had hoped for. A cold fear gripped all those at the house as the body may turn up in the woods along the highway to Goreville. This was the usual result after searches were conducted in the area of the residences. Search teams would be set up to comb the wooded grids as always. Many bodies were found spread out in open places within the dense wooded areas inside the brush. This still seemed to be a weird type of ritualistic dumping grounds for the ghoul and werewolf creatures. Police Chief Harry Rook often thought of how many deaths actually occurred over the centuries at their hands. Harry Rook would be shocked if he actually knew how many died.

Search teams may have to be very careful, as the snow was still deep and now very soft on top. All the rain that fell had done its work to help aid in hiding Harold Banks's body in the snow-covered landscape. They struggled through knee-deep snow all afternoon with no success or trace of anything. The search was called off due to the evening setting in, which was disheartening for all of them. Tomorrow would be an early start and hopefully a better result in the end.

The members of the search team met back in the morning at police headquarters to plot their grid searches. Each team was designated a certain grid to cover in one area before calling for any new grid coordinates to cover. Each team then headed out to the highway to Goreville for the day ahead. Each leader was in charge of eight members on the search teams. They all carried a radio to let every team know if anything was found or recovered and where. Two teams were dropped off at on the starting of the grid while the other two were sent to the top end of the grid. Both teams worked toward each other all day out in the dense woods along the highway to Goreville.

Searches started as soon as they arrived at their destinations on the highway. The long walks ahead were not looked forward to, except the weather was going to be warm. At least maybe a good sign of finding some remains today was all that mattered. Somewhere deep inside those dense trees was Harold Banks or his remains. Each step was uneasy, as they kept sinking into the soft snow cover. No one wanted to have a sharp wooden branch go through into his or her footwear. They placed one foot in front of the other, looking from side to side to see something out of the ordinary. Searchers looked for signs of blood spots or clothing or bone fragments or some bones or human body parts intact. The sun was high overhead in the early afternoon, starting to reflect off the snow, causing trouble seeing clearly. Sunglasses were being pulled out to be worn in the sunlight. The dark-tinted glasses would make it a bit harder to see blood droplets or blood trails in the snow in darker areas. Plus, they needed to take it a little slower, as the snow was getting softer under their feet.

One hour after another, they passed through the search grids played out that morning back in town. How much longer before they would come across a blood trail or any signs of Harold Banks? Searchers knew their work was difficult enough, trying to bring closure for families. They were responsible for finding and locating a person or body or remains of people, which they were real good, having done this so many times already when anyone went missing from Marcasite. Having never found anyone alive was hard to take every time when the searches ended. These ghoul and werewolf creatures seemed to have no cares or concerns when it involved death or disappearances. Neither left any trace of any prints or other evidence behind, other than long incisor teeth marks on the victim's bones.

Another fruitless effort went away with no results locating Harold Banks remains or body parts. Tomorrow, once again, would be an early start with new search grid coordinates to be laid out. A certain pattern seemed to repeat as to where remains may or may not be found in those woods. Ghoul and werewolf creatures actually enjoyed leaving what little remained of people in different locations to throw them off the track. They admitted that after many centuries of practice, the evil beings were good at that. Still, what needed to be done was the harshest yet. To locate any remains in dense, forested places was tough enough in dry conditions, let alone in deep, soft snow. Snowshoes of varying types were used to keep from sinking into the deep snow now.

Early the following morning, the teams met at the police headquarters to get everything set up for the day's search grids. This was day three into a missing-person situation, and all those in the room knew no one survived these things. Of course, this point was stressed, because there was a first time for everything in their world. The mood was a very positive one as they set out in teams heading to their new coordinates along the highway.

Upon arriving, they got suited up and made sure all gear was being carried along with them. Radios were ensured to be on the same channel for contacting each other in case anything turned up, as all understood today could be the day to finish off the futile and daily searches for Harold Banks. He needed to be found and buried somewhere if his family came forward to claim his body. Still, no one other than his neighbors knew him or talked to him, other than his coworkers at the bank and his girlfriend, and they were willing to claim his body for burial. Harold did not live close to most of his coworkers at the Marcasite Bank. In fact, he and Trudy lived almost halfway across town from each other. Maybe they enjoyed the distance for some privacy between themselves, away from prying eyes of other staff members. It seemed to work for the two of them until that night the last storm hit.

Every search team entered the dense woods and the deep snow once again with renewed vigor this morning. As always, they fanned out about three feet apart across a straight line, or straight as possible through the woods. They tried not to stumble along as they sunk into the softer snow and the mess of small twigs below the surface. Eyes scanning the areas from side to side slowly foot by foot was the best way. Somewhere out there in front of them was the body or partial remains of one Harold Banks. As those ghoul and werewolf creatures may have torn open, ripped apart and gnawed on him here. Or they could have taken him away to their secret hiding place from where no one ever returned from. No one ever understood why only a few people got taken to that place or why. Searchers had these and many other thoughts going through their minds at times like today. Of course, the main reason was the locating the remains of Harold Banks. Nothing else really mattered except keeping focused and on target in their search efforts.

A few hours later, all teams stopped for a short coffee break and to give them some rest in the warm weather. Time just to enjoy the fresh, warm air and get reinvigorated deep within the woods surrounding the teams. All of them knew in a few hours the body or remains of Harold Banks needed to be located today, as the search grids were narrowing down to the last few they had left. An all-out, extreme effort needed to be carried out today for Harold Banks and the sake of everyone involved. Residents of Marcasite were getting concerned he would never be found at all. Team leaders called for all members to resume the search once more that day in the warming temperatures.

Right at that time, the people fanned out in a straight line across the whole area to be combed through. Daylight would last for another four hours or less from that time, so it was going to be a long afternoon. Shadows came and went in the woods, which were a usual manner with the sunshine high overhead. Eyes darted back and forth, looking for any sign of blood, bones, or bone fragments or body parts with clothing attached. Anything to indicate what could have been or not have been what happened to Harold Banks was of importance. One hour passed with nothing appearing to any searchers along the grid lay out. Three more hours or less to go in the woods and all wanted to end this futile effort for finding Harold Banks. No one was giving up as they pushed further inside the dense bush and snow along the highway to Goreville.

Back in Marcasite, life was going on as normal as could be for all residents. Businesses and schools were open, and that was good for all concerned. People were beginning to learn to accept such deaths and disappearances caused by those events. Mayor Harold Holden believed this was a testament due to the strength and will of residents in town. Marcasite was built for families and businesses. Trying times brought them closer together, and this event was no different. Smiles may have become more forced; however, everyone gave a great effort to be neighborly. Schools were full of cheery kids and teens across the town as they carried on. Children of all ages were the future lifeblood of Marcasite, and nothing really bothered them, not since the deaths that hit two local schools anyways in the last six months. Two students and two teachers all fell victims to the vile ghoul and werewolf creatures in the depth of severe storms that struck Marcasite. Still, everyone bounced back from the pain and grief as always and this

time once more. Their world was still going around in
the warm sunshine and the bright moonlight. Now the
death toll stood at seventeen since last October. Mayor
Holden had a serious problem that faced his town right
now in the last six months. How could such deaths and
disappearances keep reoccurring in Marcasite?

Sunshine was brightly gleaming through the windows
in homes, schools, and businesses all over town. Spring
seemed to be approaching fast and the feeling within
everyone almost glowed outward. The air became so fresh
with the dampness of the melting snow of the passing days.
Another few weeks before spring would be in full swing
across the entire southeast corner of Gopher County, of
which Marcasite was the largest town for people to exist in.
Snuggled among the rolling hills of the prairies of the area
made it unique and special place. That is why everyone
in the past said it was an oasis and a jewel of a place to
live and raise a family. A real gem was created for just
being contented and happy forever and ever on the land.
Marcasite did not lack for want or need, as everything was
there for all of them.

Some dreadful, hideous, atrocious ghoul and werewolf
creatures existed before anyone lived in this area. Even
to this day they came under the cover of darkness amid
storms of such force to kill and take away people. All
according to traditional tales passed down from the local
First Nations Tribes to the first white settlers who came out
west. Every year, these tales said terrible things occurred

during the storms from spring till late fall. And the tales proved to be accurate, except never had any deaths or disappearances occurred in the cold winter months. What changed a creepy, evil desire for these ghoul and werewolf creatures to come feasting in the coldest times of the year? Where did these bad, horrible things come from in the first place? Did the star studded Milky Way provide a slight crack that allowed them to slip into their dimension? Over the centuries no answer was ever found that made sense to anyone in that regard.

The search teams were still going through their grids, with another couple of hours of light left before returning to town. Most of the area had been gone over already with no results showing up. No one was giving up as hopes were still high among them as their leaders pumped up the energy level at all costs. Today is the best day for finding Harold Banks or what remained of him. Another hour passed ever so slowly before one team found one awful, grisly sight ahead of them. They called in their team leader who notified the top officials who came over. At least they believed the remains could be of human origin and most likely Harold Banks.

Now the task of picking up and bagging the pieces for evidence became of real, absolute importance to the teams in the field. Nothing was to be excluded from being grabbed and put in the evidence bags. For some searchers, the scene was too much to take in. And they asked to be relieved from it. Which for a couple that day, the requests was granted due to the extreme violent manner of death shown once more. After everyone was finished the remains were taken to the vehicles responsible for transporting them to the coroner's office in Marcasite.

Marcasite's coroner's office knew its responsibilities in this and other matters, having gone through so many. Dead bodies or parts of them were becoming second nature over the last half a year. Never had Dr. Bridger saw this much destruction to human beings in his life before moving to this town. Had he known, maybe Marcasite would have another hardy coroner in his place. As always he braced for the worst in all cases when people were taken away from their homes or disappeared. Now that human body parts were located and being brought to his office, he got ready for them. This was another very twisted, sick example of someone being torn open, ripped apart, and gnawed on again.

Examinations of the remains were going to take place the next morning at the morgue in town. The coroner was told that Teagan and Candy Welland from the *Gazette* were coming down for the results tomorrow afternoon. Police officials were going to attend as well the following day. Information was required to add to their files in order to solve or look for means to end this string of deaths and disappearances. Such destruction of many human lives and the loss of others was becoming overwhelming for the cops and all the residents. The single biggest strain was placed on the coroner's office to come up with what caused the deaths in these cases. The rest remained up to the police force to find the culprits behind them.

The newspaper owners knew full well about how hard such death and disappearances caused destruction to their community. As owners of the only local newspaper covering such sordid details every time was not easy for them. The two of them felt a real strong responsibility to the public at large to reveal all that was good for them. In some cases, they were not to expose certain details by police order due to the terrible condition of the remains of some bodies. Any disappearances were reported in every issue of the *Gazette* during the week when they happened. Teagan and Candy would go the local morgue the next afternoon to hear what the coroner had to say that they could print. Seeing bodies torn open, ripped apart, and gnawed on was nothing new anymore for them.

One o'clock the following afternoon, everyone who needed to be present in the morgue assembled. All the remains were laid out on a green cloth covered by a white sheet, and once the white one was removed, a hush fell came over the room. This death looked all others, the same extreme violence, the same tearing, the same ripping of body parts, and the same long incisor teeth marks on the bones. A morgue was cold to begin with, except today they felt more cold than normal. Harold Banks could have experienced more pain than any of the others for some reason. The coroner seemed to believe the muscles and tendons were pulled apart more slowly on him. His bones showed even more intense grinding due to suffering at the hands of the ghoul and werewolf creatures, as if Harold needed to be taught a lesson that was unknown to anyone present. Cause of his death was no different otherwise in any regards.

Both of them had another very sad story to explain in the next issue of the *Gazette*. Tonight was going to be a rough one for Teagan and Candy as they prepared the story about Harold Banks. Trudy Wheeler had been informed of her boyfriend's death by Chief Harry Rook after his remains were located. Both knew their responsibility was not going to be an easy one on the feelings of those affected by his loss. Certain details could not be told to keep people from getting even more scared by his passing. Nothing about his suffering more than anyone else was to come out in any story. Neither Teagan nor Candy wanted to lose the respect built up with the police and the coroner's offices in town. All they wanted was an end to such twisted deaths that plagued their hometown for way too long now.

Almost one year of extreme, solid violence had passed at the hands of those ghoul and werewolf creatures and why? Marcasite was a feeding ground for a devilish, horrendous, calamitous presence in many centuries past that continued to the present day period for what sick, twisted reason was unbelievable for many. Teagan and Candy carried all the deaths in the *Gazette* since they owned it. They had read Russell Pagan's stories he carried when he owned the local paper and they were all sickening to them. Now there was another item to fill the front page in tomorrow's edition for the readers to take in again!

The *Gazette* was finished late that evening as Teagan and Candy went home to get some supper made. Then follow it with a hot cup of tea, some talking and a good night's sleep. Getting up early to pick up the paper to go sell the issue at the stores and in the coffee shops was routine. As always, they enjoyed going around visiting different locations, talking to the owners, friends and customers in town. All the local stores held copies for the customers from Gopher County who wanted one. These owners knew from their experience that expanding the customer base paid off and besides they grew up with most of the people in town and the southeast corner of Gopher County that they covered the news for. One of the better parts of their trips was warm weather, sunny skies, which did bring some smiles to people.

After the paper was finished selling out, they returned to their normal business activities of finding more information about the unexplained deaths and disappearances. Dropping by the local police headquarters seeking information about Harold Banks awful death felt hard on them. Still, Teagan and Candy had that responsibility to the overall general public, no matter how tough it became. Chief Harry Rook talked with them for quite a while in his office in the late afternoon that day. He was able to locate a relative who had agreed to come collect his remains for burial. Harold Banks was from a small place in a smaller county about five hundred miles away to the east. The relative did not want to talk with the press about what happened. Teagan and Candy agreed to the wish of the relative to leave things be in that regard. Otherwise, there was no lead, which was always the case in all the strange, horrible deaths in Marcasite.

Life was going to be rough for Trudy Wheeler after losing Harold Banks and all her coworkers finding out. No one said a word to hurt her or bruise Harold's reputation as assistant manager at the bank. Both were hardworking employees doing their jobs that they were hired for. Harold would indeed be missed by all of them at the bank. Trudy had to just relax and take one day at a time to grieve. In fact, she put in for a leave of absence for a week, which was granted.

The Marcasite Bank was short two employees for now until a new assistant manager could be hired. Trudy would return in a week, and others were willing to take her shifts at work. A recruitment program was put in place to find the next assistant manager for the bank. Who knew how long that was going to take? Besides, the bank could function without one in place for the time being. Business was brisk, even through this period of time when Harold died. Residents needed to carry on with their normal, everyday life as well as the bank did.

Spring was coming, and the snow started to melt, causing puddles to fill the streets and yards across the town. Everyone seemed to be more upbeat as the days got warmer and the snow retreated. It would not be long before life was renewed, all things would turn green, plants and fruit trees would bloom and other trees would bud. An awesome time of year for all residents of Marcasite as hope returned again. This always reminded them of their jewel of an oasis on the prairies that they dreamed of. Fresh air blew into town to aid the snow in melting away. Soon life was going to be fine, without any more pain or grief, is what they wanted.

Springtime brought rainstorms and turned the snow into dark brown messes along the streets and homes. Yet the rains were needed to end the snow covering the ground across the whole town. Everyone also felt deaths may come back under the cover of the black cumulus and nimbus clouds in the skies. The ghoul and werewolf creatures hid under the pouring rains, the flashes of sheet lightning, and the rolling thunder overhead with the huge hailstones pounding the roofs of the houses. Shadows would appear in the darkness outside to scare anyone who dared to look. Nobody, of course, admitted to doing something so foolish. People knew hellish, diabolical, odious assailants swooped around in the winds, amid the flashing lightning, and the peals of thunder to grab somebody to feast on. Maybe more than one person would get taken away in those storms in the springs.

Over the last five months, the residents had their fill of unexpected, terrible, horrible deaths caused by those unseen fiendish, demonic, alien beings from the Milky Way, a faraway, star studded galaxy that allowed those things through a crack to attack Marcasite. This was all according to local lore passed down from the First Nations to the early white settlers who ventured out west. Great grandparents handed the stories to their next generation, who did the same thing. Not one generation missed hearing about the evil, scary, dreadful ghoul and werewolf creatures. Everyone needed to be aware of what existed out in the storms when they struck Marcasite. No one was safe from their haunting, hunting feasts as they slipped through walls, windows, and doors without a trace. People vanished into thin air, never to be seen again, while others were less fortunate. Those were found torn open, ripped apart, and gnawed upon with long incisor sharp teeth. No wonder the level of anxiety increased as the storms approached, especially over the last twelve months. Local legends failed to have any deaths and disappearances included during the cold, snowy, winter months of all the many centuries before. For some reason these insidious, dreadful, murderous foreign beings seemed to be allowed through a crack in the faraway Milky Way this winter. Storms from spring till fall were violent with extreme heavy rains, huge hail, sheets of flashing lightning, and roaring peals of thunder. Only the death toll and the missing tally increased more this past seven months than any other period of recorded history.

Bright, warm sunshine increased every day in the month of April, which made residents very happy. An end to winter cold and snowstorms with hope looking at them in the face felt so good. Most residents were ready to have their gem of a town resurrected from the ashes of death, disappearances, and destruction it caused. An ugly cover of that dirty, brown snow covered most of the ground still. Strong west winds and light drizzle was coming soon to aid in wiping it away. Springtime smelled awesome as the breezes blew softly across the town from west to east. Snow banks slowly melted more every day in the warmth of the sun arching higher in the sky. Puddles were running into rivulets of small rivers along the curbs of the streets. Vehicles splashed water up when they passed through them without warning the people who often got soaked. Some people became upset, while others laughed over it. A renewal time for everything and everyone as was the custom since the beginning of life after the last great ice age. Smiles were good for the souls of all the residents in town these days.

Chapter Twenty-Six

Temperatures continued to climb, as April was about to come to an end in another few days. A storm warning came out in the late afternoon with rain and heavy wind warnings with it, just like any spring storm. Most residents hoped for nothing bad to befall their jewel of oasis of Marcasite during the night. It was around five o'clock when the storm hit full force into them. Severe, heavy rains coming out of black cumulus and nimbus clouds, the extreme strong winds, flashing sheets of lightning across the skies, followed by loud, rolling thunder overhead. Maybe the obscene, morbid, accursed creatures would not come haunting and hunting for their feast tonight? However, this being the first real storm of spring, they were going to arrive when the time was right. According to the schedule they maintained throughout time, sadistic, savage ghoul and werewolf creatures from another dimension broke into this one for feeding on human flesh. Gnawing down to the bones leaving long gouges to mark the fact it was them. A true tell-tale fact left in all cases of sudden deaths during any storms, that was, if any bones or body parts were dropped off in the woods along the highway to Goreville.

As in most past stormy nights, someone was gone from their home in Marcasite without a clue left behind. Another teenager disappeared during the night, leaving behind both her distraught parents and one brother. Jane Goodworth was only fourteen years of age, with no history of running away, a good child, a great student, with many friends in school. Her fellow students at Knob Hill Junior High School in Marcasite were going to be very shocked. Her dad, Bill Goodworth, was a lawyer with his own law practice in a four-floor office building downtown. His wife, Elaine, worked as a fashion designer in a top clothing store down the street from him. Her brother, Paul, was sixteen years of age and attended Winters Senior High. The family was really shaken up, scared, and frightened about where she had gone. Not one of them heard any noise, no disturbance, or anything that aroused any suspicions. All the noise came from the terrible storm going on outside, which may have covered up other noises.

Police Chief Harry Rook dropped over to talk with the family as soon as he got the call about their daughter disappearing. Nothing could persuade him otherwise as to the cause of the situation his department faced again. Chief Rook needed to reassure the parents everything possible was going to be done to find Jane. No guarantees were spoken of finding Jane alive; however, everyone knew she maybe dead already. Harry said his department was actively organizing searches to spread across town to look for her. He got a list of friends who may have known where she had gone. That information mostly was to keep the parents upbeat due to the large number of deaths over the last seven months. Fear was already in the family's eyes, and no more bad thoughts were required at this point. Marcasite's police chief said his duty required him to go back to headquarters to oversee the teams and aid in setting up the search grids. Bill Goodworth thanked him for coming by to talk to them; plus, they wanted him to find her, no matter what the final outcome.

Chief Rook knew full well that Mr. Goodworth might have felt the ghoul and werewolf creatures stole their daughter, Jane, amid the extreme, noisy storm in the evening and night previous. Harry returned to his office and talked with the search teams to get them out looking right away. Since the location of other finds occurred along the highway to Goreville then that was a good place to begin. Gear was loaded into the transport vehicles and the teams climbed into other vehicles to leave town. Everyone was on their way within three quarters of an hour.

Upon arriving, they disembarked from the vehicles and unloaded the equipment to carry it on their bodies. Every person had handheld radios to communicate with one another as they entered the dense wooded places ahead. The sun was hidden behind clouds today, which made it harder to see clearly in some spots. Flashlights could be used to provide the extra lighting needed. The snow was really soft, so the progress was slow and steady all morning. After three hours of no results, a break was called to have a drink of coffee, tea, or water with some dry food. Anyone involved in these searches required a high energy level at all times. A half-hour rest period, then once more they set out in their grid pattern spread across the heavily treed areas.

Everyone's eyes looked from right to left, keeping their heads down for clues on the snow, on a tree twig and the bushes. Another hour passed as the sun started to slowly come out high overhead on the searchers, allowing natural light to filter through the dense leafless trees to the snow bound ground below. Just before three o'clock, one person found what seemed to be some blood spots ahead on a trail. That search team closed ranks to find the next spot when a clearing about six feet around was spotted. Some small bones, fragments of others, and bloody parts inside part of clothing were found. Search teams need not look any further for Jane Goodworth, as they located her remains that first day out looking for her; it seemed so cruel, cold, and sick for a young teenager. All the search teams went through this period every time they went out after a disappearance following a storm. Except the death rate kept increasing along with the toll of those disappearing from Marcasite.

Word of the location of Jane Goodworth's remains was passed along to the Police Chief Harry Rook. Now Harry Rook had to get together with her family and tell them the sad news of Jane's death. Also, he needed to inform them the ghoul and werewolf creatures took her away from them. No one needed to be told of the damage inflicted on a lost loved one at their hands. Too many deaths manifested with undesirable and great horrible damage occurred in this area for centuries. This teenager was now the third to be killed in the last seven months. *Twenty-three people either dead or missing now in the last number of years*, he thought. Each time he became required to call upon a family with bad news the more he dreaded having to do so.

Chief Rook drove over to the Goodworths home to inform them Jane's remains were found this afternoon. Now they would be able to plan a funeral for her to lay her to rest in the cemetery of their choice. He just told Bill it looked similar to the previous deaths that had occurred. Elaine and Bill were very thankful their daughter was found this fast and early today. Her brother, Paul, never talked; he just sat there with an unbelievable stare on his face. He carried an almost blank look of denial of his sister being dead, let alone by the horrible, accursed, macabre intruders' hands. Harry Rook never overstayed his welcome in those trying times for families.

Bill and Elaine would be busy for the next few days, making arrangements for burial and then contacting family members outside of Marcasite. Many tears would be shed in the hours ahead by phone. Neighbors stopped by to offer condolences and help in anything they would need. Father Zach Watson from the Catholic church was called to drop over to talk by the family. The Goodworths were Catholics and attended church regularly every Sunday. Both parents and their son needed some guidance with the damage done to them by those hideous, murderous, despicable ghoul and werewolf creatures. How could Jane be killed by the horrible, brutal, malevolent forces in a spring storm? Too much hurt had just overpowered the household once they knew Jane was, in fact, dead. Such unimaginable destruction happened to others, not within their family, was what they thought. This pain of loss caused the three of them to think insane thoughts about what caused her death.

Three days later, on Thursday morning, a funeral was held at the local Catholic church for Jane Goodworth. Again every pew was taken with residents of Marcasite standing where they could fit. Father Watson presided over the service with opening prayers for Jane and her journey to heaven. Jane was looking down on her family, hoping they know God calls each one of us home when it is our time. Her dad gave her eulogy on her short life on earth, providing her accomplishments, dreams, and hopes in life. Jane wanted to go to heaven if and when she passed away. All her classmates and friends were present in the church as her dad spoke about her. Tears ran freely due to the pain felt by all of them at never seeing her again. Jane Goodworth had a full life ahead of her yet; she was taken way too soon for a reason no one could understand.

Once the church service ended, the coffin carrying Jane's remains was pushed down the aisle toward the doors. A hearse was waiting to take Jane to her final resting place at the Catholic cemetery. Father Zach Watson carried out the graveside service before all those present placed red roses on Jane's coffin as they left. Bill and Elaine asked everyone to come by their home for coffee, tea, and food after.

The Goodworth's house brimmed full of people for the rest of Thursday as everyone came. Talk seemed light and cheerful to assist the family in a terrible loss of their youngest and only daughter. Life actually brought communities closer together in these times of trouble. Friendships grew tighter, and neighbors were closer throughout the town of Marcasite each time. People slowly stopped coming over around four in the afternoon on Thursday. Bill, Elaine, and Paul were tired, even though they had family members from out of town visiting. Those left seemed to be a little happier, knowing many other people cared enough to show up after the services ended.

The Goodworths had family stay for a couple of days after the funeral for Jane. At that point, everyone needed to get back to work and their own lives. Spirits were high even then as good-byes were said to one another. Letters and phone calls would have to be good enough till all had a chance to visit again under more favorable circumstances in the future. Great times brought out the best in the Goodworths, even if this time was a deal of sadness and pain for all of them.

Spring carried on into May as most residents replaced old plants with new types of flowering species. Fruit trees had come to blossom throughout the town just as other types of trees budded into leaves. Green grass was perking up as the sunshine became warmer every day that month. People felt more alive in the heat of the days and warm evenings as the days went by. No one had any thoughts of storms or ghoul and werewolf creatures coming to knock at Marcasite's inner doorways. Laughter filled the homes, streets, stores, schoolyards, and local parks in those hot springtime days and evenings. Skies had been clear and blue for about two weeks with no end in sight, according to weather reports. Residents were busy doing work in their yards, getting things in order for the summer ahead. Grass needed to be cut weekly, and plants required watering constantly in the early morning hours. Watering grass and plants early avoided them being burnt in the hot afternoon sunshine.

Once summer break arrived for their children, their lives would be more hectic. Trips to their cabin at the local lakes on weekends kept parents hopping all the time. Long summer road trips were always welcome, with most kids wanting to enjoy seeing different parts of the country. Kids loved the scenery of the rolling hills to the majestic western mountains when they could. Eastern trips showed the flatter plains giving away to hillier country in the next place.

One thing these trips avoided was the severe summer storms that struck out of nowhere on Marcasite thus meaning none of those who went out of town could be killed by ghost and werewolf creatures. Coming back to find friends dead at the hands of those deadly, grotesque creatures often shattered any peaceful and contented feelings from going away. No one had control of whether or not who was next to be killed or taken away. Still that eerie feeling came if had they stayed one of they may have perished. Yet most families remained unaffected by the ghoul and werewolf creatures striking out against their town. Being spared from death or a disappearance did not mean that no one was free of the effects from them. Pain was the same from loss of friends to loss of family members in town.

May was followed by June with the warmest weather since last summer rolled right across Gopher County. The swimming pools were filled to capacity, which made children, teens, and parents extremely happy. Evenings spent at a pool as the sunshine continued to pour down on them all seemed beyond reality. Screams of joy and fun filled the air around every swimming pool. Nonetheless, someone would get sunburn in the heat of the days and evenings of early June. Still, everyone remained unconcerned about such matters, as cool fun was the only thing on their minds. This made sense considering the extremely high temperatures so early in the summer this year. No one complained about this; in fact, more were feeling great to be out in the sunshine, as the winter dropped a lot of snow and cold temperatures on Marcasite. Most residents wanted all the hot weather that was offered to the residents. June could be real strange month, weather-wise, due to lots of unexpected rainy days helping to make things grow.

In the middle of the month, a welcome cooldown swung over the town as clouds covered the sky. Later in the afternoon, blackness appeared in the clouds overhead of Marcasite. An unexpected storm was brewing with possible heavy rains, huge hailstones, sheets of flashing lightning, loud, rolling peals of thunder, and strong, wild winds along with it. This just occurred as everyone got ready for the evening just in case. A weatherman told of a system hitting not far from Marcasite, and it was going to strike the town within a couple of hours from now. Residents were told high winds were a huge part of the expected storm, and they should seek shelter someplace safe. Everyone knew this was going to be impossible due to expecting the ghoul and werewolf creatures to attack. The worst of storms brought them along to take people away. This had occurred in these types of severe weather systems in the summers and in the past winter months. Residents prepared for the worst that evening once again inside their homes across town.

Sure enough, roughly two hours later, the storm slammed into their town with greater ferocity than any other system had ever delivered. Rain drops poured down, huge hailstones hit so loud the roof seemed to be crashing in, sheets of flashing lightning swung across the skies, and peals of roaring, rolling thunder crashed overhead louder than a cannon. Residents kept their heads low, trying not to move believing the nefarious, inhuman, unholy beasts were creeping around. As this was the worst ever storm to strike Marcasite, people knew those disgusting, unseen beings must be hungry. Someone, or more than one, in fact, would be gone, having disappeared before the storm ended. Several hours later, the storm subsided, and everyone tried to relax. Yet not on person dared yet to look outside through a window in case a ghastly, brutal, abhorrent ghoul or werewolf creature stood there in the quiet, waiting for one last victim before leaving Marcasite alone till next time. It would be many hours later before anyone opened his or her curtains to see if the sky was clear or not. After the sun had risen, people started to look to make sure their families were all safe and sound due to the severity of last night's storm. Everyone hoped that no one ended up gone from the safety of their homes. Wishes of hope and goodwill were sent through prayers to all residents of the town.

Chapter Twenty-Seven

Police received a call from a home where a husband was missing; his wife said he went to check their house. He did this during the early hours in the morning, and then she fell asleep, having been awake for the entire night. Police officers went to the home to look around to see if any trace could be found of the husband. The police officers were aware nothing would show up as a sign of trouble. Too many scenes like this one had been examined with no results coming forward. Fred Perry was gone without a trace into the darkness of the early morning hours. Mabel Perry, his wife, was distraught when she found out for sure Fred had disappeared. He was not the type to just walk out of their home during a storm. Mabel and Fred had been married for many years, and he would have never left her this way. The police officers understood and believed her story of what transpired that morning.

Teagan and Candy Welland received a phone call from Police Chief Harry Rook about another person being gone. He asked them to come down to his office for an exclusive report for being the only newspaper in Marcasite. Harry Rook informed them a Fred Perry disappeared from his residence some time earlier that morning, saying his wife fell asleep because she was tired from being awake the whole night. Apparently the storm began to wane early, so he went to check to make sure everything was all right in their house. When she woke up, he was gone and not one idea of what happened.

All three of them knew the impious, feral, unholy creatures were extremely quiet carrying out their searches for human flesh. Monsters were hiding among the chaotic noise of the storms, under the sheets of flashing lightning and loud peals of thunder. The pouring rains and hailstones bouncing off roofs caused even more noises to cover up the attacks. Ghastly, monstrous, malicious foreign beings were sneaky, crafty, mean creatures, to say the least. In fact, the creatures were just incredibly nasty, vicious, and monstrously vile toward the victims they managed to steal away. The gruesome, heinous, hellish creatures tore open and ripped apart and gnawed upon people, feasting on human flesh at will. Then they would scatter the leftovers in open areas deep inside the dense trees along the highway to Goreville.

Police Chief Rook wanted them to run a story in tomorrow's issue about what happened to Fred Perry.

He insisted they talk to his wife for more background
information and have a look around if she let the two
of them. For some reason, he was worried about Mabel
Perry, as he wanted her safe, they felt. If swinging by her
place could ease his anxiety, then of course they would
do it, as Teagan and Candy told Harry that was their first
place to go after leaving his office. He seemed relieved they
were going to take him at his word and check up on her.
Their families had been friends for some twenty years,
he told the Wellands before ending the conversation due
to work concerns. They both made to thank him for the
information and help he provided to them for the story he
wants to see run the next issue of the *Gazette*. Anything to
keep the good partnership with the police chief growing
was all right with the two of them. The reporters left Harry
Rook's office and walked out to their car to head to Mabel
Perry's home.

Teagan and Candy drove over to talk with Mabel Perry
about Fred's odd disappearance to help ease her sadness.
Both had seen too much up close and personal in the areas
of ghoul and werewolf creatures killing and taking others
away. Now to do something to assist a fellow citizen of
town felt right. Mabel and Fred Perry lived on the west
side of town in a one-level bungalow, a nice-looking white
house with green, manicured lawns, good-looking flowers,
with fruit trees spread across both yards, front and back.
The exterior of the home was modest but very inviting and
comfortable to both Teagan and Candy Welland.

Once they arrived, something made them feel uneasy, maybe because someone was no longer here. Being aware of disappearances that usually turned out to be actual cases of bodily dismemberment bothered them still. Mabel must be a very strong person, they thought, as they approached her door to knock on it. After knocking, Mabel opened the door for them, and they told her who they were. Mabel said she knew that they owned the local *Gazette* newspaper. Teagan and Candy smiled, being surprised by her knowledge without ever having met before in person. Mabel asked them in to have a talk with her today about her husband vanishing, fully knowing why both of them had showed up at her door today.

Mabel ushered Teagan and Candy into the front room to sit down in comfortable chairs that were there. Fred and Mabel enjoyed having some soft furniture to relax inside their house after a busy day. She was going to make coffee for all three of them to keep herself occupied, they imagined. Just a light conversation carried on until their coffee was served by Mabel.

The very first question Mabel asked had to do with those ghoul and werewolf creatures that were supposedly attacking Marcasite. She wanted to know if they really existed out there and actually could kill and take humans away? Teagan answered by informing her all the information and past medical results indicated this, in fact, was true. Whatever caused the damage did not come from earth. No one had any idea of where other bodies were taken that disappeared into thin air. The *Gazette* would report any information and details as always in these situations. Mabel seemed puzzled with her husband's sudden vanishing from the home they shared for twenty-five years, as if he ran away into the tempest of the worst storm ever to strike Marcasite. Teagan and Candy Welland knew the pain and bewilderment she was experiencing right now. After so many deaths and the disappearances the two of them covered, the same pale, white, fear on people's faces did look the same.

Mabel said she and Fred thought they heard a noise in the house like someone sneaking around. Fred went to investigate. Mabel was tired, and as she laid there trying to hear, her eyes slowly closed on her. Being awake with others in town due to this extremely noisy storm most of the night, sleep was needed. Mabel did not mean to fall asleep; when she woke up, she called for Fred. She never heard Fred answer her call for him. Now fear gripped her, yet she needed to go look for her husband. Mabel told them she searched every room, and Fred could not be found anywhere. Mabel said she became hysterical without any sign of him inside their place. Why did he leave to go search the house that night and end up going outside maybe? Mabel said she called the police right away to report Fred missing. Nothing else she could have done, Candy told Mabel to ease her guilt. Teagan and Candy talked with Mabel for a couple hours before heading back to their office. They told Mabel to call if she needed to talk to someone at any time day or night.

Since there seemed to be no damage to anything, no forced entry, no broken windows, etc., Fred and Mabel's vehicle was in the garage. In similar cases of sudden disappearances, police were stumped with no evidence at the scene. The extremely ungodly, demonic ghoul and werewolf creatures were not leaving any trace of themselves at all. Police officials called the search of the Perrys property off for now. No use upsetting Mabel Perry any further today, instead it was time to begin other work.

Teams were sent out to look around back alleys, parks, and other places within Marcasite that might hide a body. Maybe this occurrence would turn out for the better, was all Police Chief Harry Rook hoped for. Hours went by as his officers searched every nook and cranny in town for any signs for Fred Perry. Around four o'clock, the heavy search was abandoned due to no leads turning up—no blood evidence, no strange foot prints, no weird finger prints, nothing at all anywhere. Once more, deep anger and frustration hit home, because everyone would soon know the truth again. Ghoul and werewolf creatures struck during the worst storm to ever hit. Taking away Fred Perry from his home amid the calamity. One more victim attributed to the brutal, dreadful, calamitous creatures that attacked during the latest storm.

Mayor Harold Holden and Police Chief Harry Rook needed to send a message out to the citizens of Marcasite and one that would ease the deep-seated fears built up over the last nine months. Since the total number of deaths and disappearances grew as time passed, they needed action that only the two of them had the power to enforce. A draft of the script was drawn up and given to them to proofread. The next evening the mayor and police chief would talk to the people of Marcasite in a public gathering in Freedom Park at six o'clock in the evening. Hopefully, the sun could shine overhead and make the event seem better than just sad and surreal. Still a meaningful message of hope, tranquility and the dreams of returning the jewel of Marcasite back to life. Both men were skilled public speakers, as their duties required it. Mayor Holden was the more factual consummate speaker with more years of experience than Police Chief Rook. Between the pair, the crowd was going to be pleased by both men taking a leading role in recent occurrences, not as if anyone really had stepped away from it during the previous nine months of turmoil. This was the worst stretch of deaths and disappearances to strike Marcasite in recorded history.

Both leaders spoke at length about the future and what it held for everyone young and old alike. Whatever tragic circumstances held them, both reassured residents it would soon go away. Marcasite was a place built full of hope, dreams, and the promise of pleasure to raise families on the prairie landscape of the southeast corner of Gopher County. The town was amid the low, rolling hills in that area where winds blew across from west to east, all from spring till late falls. The town grew from the dust of the prairie landscape back in the mid-eighteen hundreds into what they now saw. Marcasite was a magnificent place full of life, a great beautiful oasis just for the residents to enjoy and grow into a better, happier place in the future. Each day always promised a better future for the people who made this town home from the very start.

Mayor Holden talked about the great and wonderful things everyone accomplished so far in town. A great future lay ahead, and nothing would stop that dream from happening or taking place, now or ever. Plans were being made to increase the number of businesses and manufacturing jobs for graduating students to come out of local high schools. Businesses were offering full time work positions giving young people the opportunity to raise families and stay around Marcasite instead of moving away. People had many choices of what to do with their lives in town if this was what they wanted. Young men and women could go to college and come back for a bright future to raise a family, buy a house, and grow old at home. Taxes were low, prices were low, and everyone was happy when family came first in these days. Mayor Holden explained he was extremely proud to have been here all of his life. His family, like most others, had planted roots here almost a hundred years ago.

Police Chief Harry Rook outlined the opportunity his department offered to young men and women in police work—learning to track unknown things, chasing crooks, conducting long searches, and regular police work. He had the mayor's backing to build a highly efficient police force, required to accomplish the goals of keeping this town crime free and people safe from harm. Chief Harry Rook knew this was a great opportunity to gather new personnel for his force to combat these gruesome, degrading, murderous ghoul and werewolf creatures; just a thought that he never uttered out loud to anyone in case he sounded strange. Chief Rook spoke for close to half an hour about everything in his speech word for word. He received a loud round of applause for which he felt good over.

Mayor Holden gave the last few words and thanked all the residents for turning out for the talk in Freedom Park. This park is a magnificent green space in the heart of Marcasite, yet close to some neighborhoods. Mayor Holden gave thanks for the wonderful blue sky under which the town had gathered. As he finished up, he also received a loud round of applause for coming out. These residents felt better, even if no real hope was in sight to end whatever was out there. Ghoul and werewolf creatures probably would keep coming regardless of any assurances from the mayor and the police.

Chief of Police Harry Rook knew a full-blown search needed to begin the next morning, so the call went out for volunteers. A couple hundred turned out first thing the following morning. For the most part, everyone had experience from previous searches, and those who had none were filled in. Novice search team members were set up with those who knew the ropes in the woods. Equipment was handed out and explained how to use it, especially radios. They required searchers to be on one channel with each other at all times in the dense woods. There were enough new members for teams to cover more ground by going in two directions. Two teams started on the edge of Marcasite while the other two teams went out five miles further out to work back to the other one. Once search teams had their leaders in place, everyone got into vehicles to head out to the same highway to Goreville.

A nondescript piece of highway, for some sick, twisted reason, had become the real, official dumping grounds for body parts scattered inside the dense woods. Ghoul and werewolf creatures were ritualistic, repugnant, malicious, beastly beings from the faraway, star studded Milky Way galaxy. No area was exempt from being searched as open spots were not always indicated on previous maps. New clearings or openings seemed to pop out at them every time they entered the woods to look for someone. To the dreadful ghoul and werewolf creatures, this became big games of hide and seeks. They hid bodies, and the searchers would need to find the parts of what was left over from their feast. Locating the place where the bones and the fragments of bones and body parts and clothing could be was never easy. The volunteers just walked through their grids each and every day. Nothing more could be done by them at this point.

People stretched out three feet apart between each other on both sides of the highway to make sure the ground was covered thoroughly. Eyes needed to be pointed toward the ground, glancing from left to right. Search teams were placing one foot in front of the other in this dense bush, so the going was tough. The day's heat again would be hard on everyone, even with every searcher carrying water bottles to keep hydrated. With the deep cover of trees, it was still very hot and dry in the woods. These people placed one foot in front of the other every few seconds, scanning the ground around them, looking for any sign or indication of blood spots or any trails of any sort. Clothing could be caught by a tree limb as a body was being carried and left hanging on the limb. Nothing would be overlooked or passed by without being positive; that is why the teams had radios with them.

Two hours seemed to pass like ten hours inside the dense underbrush of the wooded areas along the highway. Searchers had to be careful not to trip, break an ankle or a leg during those times out there. Today was slow going, as the foliage could hide blood spots or the splatter of blood very well. In the snow, it was easier to see red spots with no cover from the treetops. Summer never allowed the exact qualities as winter during searches for any people who disappeared from their homes during extreme storms. Being able to keep concentrating all their effort on the task could be overwhelming at times. An hour later, the head search team leader called for a half-hour break from all activities. At this point, rest was needed to regain some strength from the walking that morning. New search members' nerves were a little on edge, not sure about what the focus was anymore, except Fred Perry had a wife mourning for him and who wanted to lay him to rest if possible.

Once the rest period ended, everyone got started to head out again from where they were deep inside the woods. They already covered close to a mile, with still more distance to go. Being reinvigorated, the mind and eyes worked fine as everyone got going through the same routine. Eyes darted from left to right as they placed one foot in front of the other across the forest floor. Slowly as possible, they went forward, making sure not to overlook any sign or indication of blood, clothing, or bones. The search was getting close to end for the first day with no results, which was typical in some cases. In other cases, no remains were ever found anywhere, just like certain bodies just up and disappeared into thin air during those horrible, extreme storms of summer and this past winter in Marcasite. About half an hour later, both teams met up and the search was halted for the day. Searchers returned to town and gathered at the police headquarters. After that, everyone went home to their families for the night. Just maybe a good night's sleep after the sickening events over the last two nights and today would relieve the stress.

The next morning, search team members rose as the sun came up to get an early start on the day's effort.

Another grid was laid out for each team to cover, which had to be just as carefully done as the previous one yesterday. Everyone knew the importance of finding the remains today due to the possibility Fred Perry may never be found. Each day's search became that much more important. Mabel Perry was all alone without Fred, her husband, by her side. If she could bury his remains, at least she would have some comfort from this terrible ordeal. Searchers retrieved their equipment and climbed into vehicles to head out to the sites to search this morning and all day long.

Another five miles from where the second team started to work back to the first team was the point to begin. The first two teams were dropped off, and the second two teams were taken up to their positions on the highway. Each one trudged into the woods and again stretched out three feet from each other over the forest floor. The morning was cooler than yesterday; however, the breeze may change or stop at any time during the day. The order to start walking and looking came over the radios. Each person took one step at a time, with their eyes glancing from left to right and looking downward to the ground. Everyone was in a light mood, wanting to find any remains so the search would not end in futility again as yesterdays had done.

Minute after minute slowly crept past, and the trees were just as thick with every step taken. Somewhere a hidden open spot might appear with the remains of Fred

Perry scattered covering the ground amid it. As gross as the thought was, many of these searchers had seen the remains of too many residents out here. An hour passed without any indication of anything so far. The teams kept the slow pace going for another hour; still nothing came up. Everyone wanted to go for another hour before taking a break for lunch. At that point, no one had come across any signs of blood, blood trails, bones, bone fragments, and clothing filled with human flesh. A lunch break was called for the members of all the search teams out in the dense woods.

Searchers lay back, resting; some closed their eyes, and others drank water as if they had none left inside their bodies. Hot weather could be hard on people when you are slowly walking and looking for things in the woods. Breaks were very healthy and allowed the mind to focus again. The eyes needed to be closed for a few minutes to get rid of the cobwebs of the ground coverings they looked at almost constantly. Having some food after a long morning was, in fact, an order to survive in the afternoon's warmth ahead of them. Other people talked about their families, hobbies, anything to break the monotony of the search. New and old members of the teams had different ways to relax during their breaks. Once more the call came to start the afternoon search came over the radio, which felt good as everyone felt rested up. Search teams gathered up their equipment and headed to the line to start out again. No one was going to walk to fast in order to find any sign of Fred Perry's remains in the afternoon hours. The sun was high, and the temperature was climbing with all the humidity in the woods from the heavy rains. Besides taking each step slow was the only method to locate the signs they were looking for out here.

Teams spread out across the forest three feet apart again before moving ahead with the search. Mentally everyone really hoped to find Fred Perry's remains and end the search today. They knew it was important but kept any negative thoughts inside their minds and souls. Searchers always tried to remain focused on what was directly in front of them and not too far ahead. Having skills to find the smallest blood spot, blood trail or even a piece of clothing was important in helping to locate body parts and the clear area where remains actually sat inside the woods. Every step was carefully taken to ensure that nothing was overlooked or missed. No voices came over the radio, which meant no one so far had found anything. An hour passed and still no call on the radio, and the searchers needed some relief soon. At any moment, someone may call on the radio to let them know what was left of Fred Perry had been found. Till then, all the teams kept going one step at a time through the thick woods. No one lost their focus on the task at hand, though the quiet wore on them at these times. Being specialists at conducting searches after having done many over the years, these individuals had homes, families, and normal responsibilities back in Marcasite.

Another hour went by before a short break was called over the radio in order to give people some much-needed rest. Top search leaders felt the same level of frustration as those out in the woods. Nobody deserved to be torn open, ripped apart, mutilated, and gnawed upon by those ghoul and werewolf creatures from another dimension. Why had they chosen Marcasite and its residents had been a question without an answer. Nor did anyone need to be hidden in some desolate spot in the dense woods along this highway to Goreville. Others should have been left here instead of being taken away to some location unknown to anyone. Most of all, team members wanted the deaths, the disappearances, and the destruction of families to end. These thoughts went through the heads of the searchers while they conducted their activities each time. Their work was never easy to carry out, no matter the circumstances behind the search.

From the top search leaders down, they knew keeping everyone motivated and focused was very important this afternoon and that was the reason for the breaks being taken at those intervals. To keep everyone in good spirits and wanting them to remain looking through thick bush and dense trees for remains and anything else to end this search was justified. Fred Perry's body needed to be found today just because it was better to find it soon, rather than realizing he could have vanished into the darkness of the storm.

Twenty minutes later, the call came to regroup and spread out to start again for the final push of the day. Everyone was ready for the last assault through the rough brush and trees, looking for signs. They all wanted to find Fred Perry's remains to take him back to his wife, Mabel. Then the search teams could go home to rest with their families, or they would be back early in the morning to search again. No one wanted to go home emptyhanded again today. Fred Perry was their responsibility to find, and they were dedicated to that cause. Nothing ever allowed the searchers to give up, except when the exercise was proven futile.

The search teams set out once more across the forest with a goal in mind to find any remains of Fred Perry. He deserved better than to lay in the dense woods far from his home in Marcasite. Searches kept that vigil looking down from left to right as they went along. Radios were on the same channel, waiting to hear a voice calling saying yes they found him. An hour passed, and people felt tense now as time was going against them today or maybe not. Step after step needed to be taken until something showed up or the radio call came in. Searchers were very careful now, as daylight was going to be precious in these dense woods. Trees would reflect the amount of sunshine from coming down into the area they were looking into. Everyone still had about forty-five minutes until they met up with the other search team coming toward them. Once they arrived, a much saddened walk would occur all the way back to the vehicles waiting to take them back to town.

Just before the time was up, the radio call came in that one of the teams on the other side of the road located his remains. Their search had come to a sad ending that day deep in the woods off the highway to Goreville. Maybe there was significance to bodies being dropped off along this highway. Still, Fred Perry had been found, and his wife would have closure now. Mabel would be able to bury her husband with the dignity he deserved after their long and happy marriage. For now, his remains were being picked up and bagged for the coroner, Dr. Gabe Bridger, to examine. Protocol was something that needed to be followed in all deaths, no matter what. These types of killings bore the identical methods of severe cruelty, demonic sickness, and sadistic means. In each death, the bodies were torn open, ripped apart, mutilated, and gnawed upon then left hidden in spots only ghoul and werewolf creatures knew the reason for.

The *Gazette* had come out the day before with news of Fred Perry's disappearance from his home during the last storm. Nobody really needed to know this was worst storm ever to blow into Marcasite in recorded history. Widespread damage from heavy winds, hailstones, and a number of flooded basements in lower areas of town. Residents faced a real daunting task in recovering from the overall effects of the storm. Still, another person gone with no trace intruded on the minds of residents. Marcasite became a very dreadful location to raise a family, to live, and to work. Yet no one wanted to leave the dreams held so closely inside each of them behind. Fear seemed too much, although hope of surviving kept them going through every day.

Now Fred Perry's remains had been located, and another terrible, sickening, horrible death had been solved. Ghoul and werewolf creatures swooped in during the worst storms at will to create chaos, death, and disrupt life. A normal existence faded slowly as time passed, especially over the previous nine months. Nerves had been shredded with the precision of a surgeon as the deaths piled up along with the disappearances. This carnage needed to end before the town became a plain blight to the future of it. How could local police combat things they could not see? These unearthly beings that attacked under the cover of the most severe summer and winter storms causing havoc among residents of Marcasite. Who had the ability to enter homes with no signs and taking victims with the same unseen signs, making anyone invisible going through walls and windows along with them?

The *Gazette's* next issue carried the full story of Fred Perry's body being found in the woods along the highway to Goreville, except the details of him being torn, ripped apart and gnawed upon being left out. Respect for his widow, Mabel, was heeded along with all of the families who lost members in previous attacks. Nothing would be gained now by revealing what everyone knew already due to the publicity of what the conditions of such remains were being found in. Repeating every detail made Teagan and Candy sick even after having covered so many stories that were connected in this demeaning, disturbing manner. Being good reporters with the respect of the residents helped the pair through it all. People needed to read about what happened to come to grips with the reality of it. The *Gazette* was still the single media outlet in Marcasite for everyone. The *Gazette* carried comprehensive stories in their issues, covering everything possible. Nothing was left out unless the public good could be put at risk by revealing certain details. Plus, no families needed to know what happened to their loved ones at the hands of the ghoul and werewolf creatures.

Fred Perry's funeral was well attended by most of Marcasite, as everyone there could relate to the loss incurred. Mabel Perry walked with her head held high to show the strong will carried inside her soul. Those in attendance were struck by her composure at Fred's funeral. They imagined the horrendous torture she suffered waiting for this day to slowly come around. Everyone hoped by being here for her that would ease those difficult times ahead. Father Zack Watson did the funeral service for Fred Perry inside as the sun shone outside the church. Once the church service ended, the people followed the coffin out to the hearse to be taken to the Catholic cemetery. Everyone followed the hearse in their cars as it slowly drove along the streets. The graveside service was carried out once the residents arrived. When Father Watson was done, then people filed out past the coffin containing the remains of Fred Perry. Mabel stood there watching as people placed single white roses on her husband's coffin. A gathering was going to be held after at the church in the basement for those who wanted to come.

The legends passed down from local native tribes were ignored by most people. Now the entire population knew the stories were indeed accurate and factually true. There could be no other plausible explanation for all these deaths to occur in these manners? Throughout the history of Marcasite evil existed causing death, disappearances, and destruction in the lives of local First Nations Tribes. Those deadly, formidable, macabre intruders kept raiding after Marcasite came to be a village with immigrants from other places. Legends were passed down to these new people about ghoul and werewolf creatures from the faraway Milky Way galaxy attacking everyone. Nothing could stop the macabre, unholy, inhuman hell hounds, and the residents knew hope was their answer. One day maybe these creatures would go away back to where they came from for good, an empty wish, but how could they expect those dreadful beings to leave them in peace? The residents felt a real spiritual need to find an answer and real quick.

Chapter Twenty-Eight

People from Marcasite had always been very tough through the lean times of the many droughts, wars, and almost becoming a ghost town. Tumbleweeds and brown thistle used to blow around their streets. Marcasite had become a good-sized town, which everyone had dreamed of for many decades. Just the deaths and disappearances seemed so out of character for their gem of a town. Pressing forward into the future undeterred had to be the only answer for them all, as past generations took this approach and stuck it out to start a village on the edge of nowhere. Despite the appearances of horrible, lurid, disgusting ghoul and werewolf creatures seemed to be here now a way to often causing deaths, disappearances, and destruction to families. Residents would regain their resolve to stay and keep their families in Marcasite, having seen the dreams of an oasis built in the low rolling hills here in the southeast corner of Gopher County.

The bright yellow sun seemed to rise every morning from the far eastern horizon over Marcasite. A bright blue sky above was a backdrop with wisps of white clouds here and there across the canvas. Trees were covered with full green leaves; lawns were deep with lush grass. Yards showed an extraordinary array of flowers of all types and many colors to brighten up the look. Spring and early summer turned the town into a beautiful garden of paint strokes across Marcasite. People of all ages were out enjoying the warm evenings after work and kids as well after school was out for the day. Those dark times seemed to fade from memory during the good weeks, especially in warm, sunny weather. Attention was on having fun in the outdoors, playing, and barbequing and family activities. School would soon be out for the summer again, and for two months the kids and teens would have free rein.

The *Gazette* owners, Teagan and Candy Welland, followed up on each and every death, disappearance, and the destruction it caused to the town. Their paper was scooped up when every issue came out. They had to hire teens to sell the *Gazette* thus allowing them to free up some time for researching, putting stories together, and printing the paper. Teagan and Candy did go out to coffee shops to sell at times to visit with residents and get feedback. Good newspaper reporters never stopped carrying our appointed duties to the general public at large. They had to interview the police chief, his officers, and the mayor and the council to find information for stories to carry. Public announcements were always what they offered in each issue and pictures of different gardens from across Marcasite were very common all summer long. Teagan and Candy filled other spots with past local history stories that seemed to be a favorite with the residents. People chatted about things from the *Gazette* throughout the days and evenings.

June was an awesome month for everyone in Marcasite with great weather and school slowly winding down for the year. Most students had exams of one level or another to look forward to in the next two weeks. Every year would finish this way until their own educational journey ended for each one. Studying usually happened during school hours or in the evenings at home under parents' supervision—no fun until all work was done and the kids and teens knew this. Each day was like crawling through hot sand on their bellies when they wanted to be out in the fresh air. Students wanted to be playing baseball or some other game in all the local schoolyards across town. Yet receiving passing marks or good marks was worth the thinking power and studying time required.

The final exam was finished, and now the only thing left was to come back to get their report cards in two days' time. All students were free to do what they wanted, and with the hot weather, everyone went to one of the local pools to cool off. Summer was going to be a wet, fun-filled everyday thing along with vacations to places far away from Marcasite. These activities made the kids and teens appreciate the summer breaks more every year as they grew up. One day, after high school graduation, they would all be adults and maybe go to university or college in another place. This year another group was going to leave high school, headed to work in town, university or college somewhere. Good times and bad times, still everyone seemed proud of being where they were right now. Marcasite would always be their home no matter where they ended up living in the future.

Two days had passed fast, and now the time to go back and receive their report cards came. Classrooms were filled up that morning, and then the teachers called each student by name to come up and get his or her report cards. Once that was done, school was dismissed until September, and that was it for the year. Students emptied lockers, filling up backpacks with stuff, and headed home in groups, talking, laughing, and planning activities as usual. A warm, sunny day to end the school term on this year was welcome news. This day was looked forward to ever since spring rolled around this year. Now they were graduating and going into another grade in the fall, which was two months away.

After going home to drop off what they had to, all of them grabbed swimming clothes, big towels, and whatever else, heading to a pool. Greg and his friends always went to the pool in Freedom Park, which was the closet one from their neighborhood. It was only a few blocks from it anyway and the largest in town. Long, hot days playing in the water and drying off in the heat of the sun was a lot of fun. Getting suntans or sunburns never really did matter to them during summer breaks or in the early spring heat of May or early June due to living on the wide, open prairies. All kids and teens enjoyed being outdoors in the summer sun, never worrying about getting burnt up by the bright, hot sun.

Not one person felt like recalling the horrible year of deaths, disappearances, and the destruction caused to Marcasite by these deadly, marauding ghastly intruders who came when they felt their burning need for human flesh overcome them. Their mayhem seemed to fill them with some kind power over ordinary people. The damage done was by tearing open, ripping apart, and gnawing upon the body parts; it really was gross, to say the least. Huge gouge marks found on bones indicated long, sharp, incisor teeth biting the meat, muscle, and tendons off. Invisible killers lurked in the dark of storms for nine months, including being under the cover of snow this past winter. Ghoul and werewolf creatures floated through the air due to no footprints ever being located in any place. Those things disappeared into thin air along with the many victims they took. Adults probably thought about all this more than any young person did. Greg Braden was the one young person who seemed to be able to survive the extreme fear of seeing those horrid, gruesome, noxious, intruding beings. Life did go on and would have to for all concerned to be normal. One day again, life would trip the release pedal for fiendish, macabre, unhallowed creatures to come haunt Marcasite again.

Summer weather was amazing right through into July of this year in Marcasite. The fresh breezes were light just enough to keep the midday heat a bit cooler for everyone out in the areas. Pools stayed full all day and evening as young and old played in the water to stay refreshed. Other families had taken off on annual vacations to distant locations in other parts of the country. Those still here took full advantage of what Marcasite offered for activities in the hottest months of the year. Parks were full as many families took in a full advantage of outdoor cooking areas for supper. Kids played games and ran around in the grass, chasing one another. Teens would sit in certain places away from their families for more privacy. Girlfriends and boyfriends held hands as they sat or took slow walks while waiting for their suppers with their families.

Chapter Twenty-Nine

Greg's family was soon leaving on their annual trip to some place never before visited, which became the custom over the years. Tom and Helen Braden felt by doing this they shook whatever followed Greg when he was young. As Greg had never mentioned those beings again and never screamed out loud again after going to sleep, it had worked. There had been many summer trips taken over the years since that moment occurred. Their son was a normal teenager, good grades, loved sports, and had many friends and his girlfriend, Janice Maribel, who his parents liked very much. Janice and Greg were fine with being apart during the summer break due to going away with their families. They had the entire year to spend time with their friends and to be alone together when possible.

The Braden family was going up into the northern areas to do some camping where it was really hilly, full of trees, bears, and many other wild animals. The family was really actually looking forward to going out to the boonies. Greg enjoyed the outdoors, the fresh air, and the cool morning breezes in the hills. Tom Braden needed to take time to enjoy this break with his wife and son because he always worried about the ghoul and werewolf creatures attacking his family. Now the woods, fresh air, and the chance to do some good fishing with his son seemed to be the medicine he required. Their trip passed very fast, and they once gain returned to Marcasite with lots of memories and renewed health. The Bradens got home in the late afternoon that day after an early start to a long drive from the last stop the night before. Everything was unpacked from their vehicle and taken into the house. Then it was put away before doing anything else before supper. Talking while doing this allowed them to retell stories of the trip, which made all of them laugh out loud. Family activities were not only fun but should be important as well. Tom, Helen, and Greg always believed this brought them so close together as a family.

Greg called Janice while his mom made supper to let her know he was home from their trip. He told her a few stories about the fishing he and his dad had done and how big the fish actually were. They agreed to talk in person after supper in the park with the rest of their friends. Greg had a huge smile on his face when he went into the kitchen, and his mom knew why without asking. She wanted to know how Janice was doing and if her family took a trip yet this summer. Greg told her they had not gone yet, would not until the start of August. Helen said he would get by just like always, as it seemed neither family went away at the same time, not that she could ever recall besides supper needed to be finished on time if Greg wanted to go out soon.

Greg decided to do some reading to pass the time before supper, and he knew he would have to help his mom set the table. Greg did not mind as it would allow him not to do dishes so he could go out sooner with his friends. Everyone sat down to supper and talked some more about their trip. The weather was still very warm outside in the early evening hours for today in Marcasite. No breeze was coming through the open windows in their house either. Summertime came with no breezes at all some days; people called them the dog days of summer. Greg could never understand this saying, as dogs did not like hot days. His parents just laughed at him for not getting the fact it was just a joke, sort of, about the weather. The Bradens continued with their supper, talking, laughing, and enjoying the time together as always. Once they had supper, Greg gave his mom a hand clearing the table before asking if he could go out. Of course, he got the reply he wanted, so off he went to visit with his friends.

Summer evenings in Marcasite passed slowly as the sun took long arcs across the sky above. As at most times not a breeze came from any direction in the hottest times of the year, not that anyone was going to complain as they could go to a swimming pool for a dunk in cool water.

Most families took advantage of the opportunities to enjoy the warm nights and swim in cool water. Marcasite did feel like the oasis on the prairie during those times of the summer, a gem of a town that was made to be enjoyed by all the families, and they did when they could. Bright sunlight glittered on the surface of the pools across town as kids and parents splashed in the water. Some people caused huge waves and loud splashes as they jumped off the diving boards. Shouts of glee, happiness, and joy echoed all over each swimming area in town.

Other residents went to one of the local parks to spend time with family and friends in hot weather. Lying down on the cool, green, grass under the cover of the tree tops was a great, relaxing way out of the direct rays of the sun above. There seemed to be a lot of teens out in the parks, playing games, or sitting around in groups talking. Everyone had activities to keep them busy during those good, sun-filled evenings in the summertime. Marcasite came to life in the golden sunshine of the spring and summer months. Their jewel was reborn this year, especially after the sorrow-filled nine months that just passed. All those bad events were far from the minds of everyone, for now at least. Many parents talked about moving into newer homes, planting grass, flowers, and gardens in their yards. Now their children were either in their teens or growing up fast. Most children were going to the elementary schools and all the way into high schools across the whole town.

Summer seemed to be the best in part of living in
Marcasite to everyone who lived there. An oasis of green,
low, rolling hills showed off the flowery town like a painter
doing a complete canvas to hang in a gallery. Yet some evil
beings came around to ruin life for the residents and their
families. Just as they hoped for serenity and peace for the
summer, a storm would strike to collapse those dreams.
Still, a very ideal scene of people from all age groups
having fun in the sun existed in the third week of July.
No one really gave storms a thought until a cloud or two
showed up in the sky; even if that gave relief from the hot
rays of the sun pouring down on them. No storm had been
here since the middle of June when Fred Perry died at the
merciless hands of the morbid, accursed, depraved ghoul
and werewolf creatures. Right now everyone enjoyed the
awesomeness of summer in the sunshine and the outdoors.

Teagan and Candy were busy putting together
issues full of stories for the residents to read, with many
unexplained reasons as to why and how the ghoul and
werewolf creatures got around through walls, windows,
and doors. Maybe a door was left unlocked or a window
was not closed all the way? Walls never showed any
damage of things going through them. Everyone knew
the unholy, malicious, beastly foreign beings only showed
up under the cover of the dark skies of the storms. Now
this past winter they hid under the white blanket of snow
as it came down. Being dark shadows to the human eyes,
they roamed, taking people to kill and hiding others

somewhere out there in the netherworld. Filling in details from these deaths and disappearances kept them both very busy all the time. The *Gazette* still needed to be printed for sale four time a week, and they had a very fast-paced work week still, though both remained enthusiastic about being the best reporters. The local paper owned up to its reputation to their faithful readers in Marcasite and those who came in from Gopher County to purchase each issue. Russell Pagan was probably looking down from heaven with great satisfaction of how Teagan and Candy still carried on with his traditional publishing ideas. People wanted to read about everyday happenings and the unexplained activities that haunted their town.

Families were still going on planned vacations this month to enjoy the great outdoors of their country or maybe down into the neighboring country to the south if they wanted to every year. Janice Maribel and her family were heading down south for the first time this year, which was interesting for them. She and Greg Braden would be apart for two weeks again, for a total of four weeks of not seeing each other. Life just was that way due to time allowed away from work for their parents. This would mean Janice was going to be able to tell Greg and all their friends of the adventures of that vacation upon her return home to Marcasite. Telling stories from summer trips was a ritual as they grew up together as a way of being older and wiser teens of the world.

These teens had been good friends for many years: Janice Maribel, Greg Braden, John Wallis, Teagan Sannerman, Abbey Brown, Bailey Hutton, Barbara Williams, Ken Williams, Valerie Stockton, Bambi Payton, Adam Turo, Bill Wade, Pierre Gratton, Tad Breland, Greg Lewis, and Isaac Stedman. These stories that were shared kept them going for months after their annual vacations, not that anyone tried to outdo the others, just telling honest tales. These friends still talked about Teagan Farfeld and Caden McDougall, who passed away last fall. They all missed their best friends very much since last fall's terrible storms tore them away.

Chapter Thirty

August was already upon Marcasite as the hot weather hung around, which everyone enjoyed very much. What a summer it was so far—no storms or any rains falling down from the skies above. Clear blue skies everyday kept the entire population happy as they all continued to play in the pools and parks in town. This was one of the best summers to come to Marcasite in many years. Barbeques were usually cooking at least two meals a day for most families this year. Open pit fires in the parks, with grills on top, allowed the families to cook their hot dogs, hamburgers, or steaks, and even baked potatoes, which were all very tasty. Some families cooked marshmallows for dessert on the same fires. They needed to put the fires out after using the fire pits. Every park had a source of water to drink and to use for putting out hot fires. Fun times created good memories to be retold over a lifetime with family and friends.

Sometime overnight, some extremely dark cumulus and nimbus clouds moved in overhead, lightning flashed, thunder rolled, rain poured down, and hailstones fell hard against everything. People woke with a scare, knowing full well the ghoul and werewolf creatures were being recalled to haunt the town again. Summer had passed so far with no storms; now all of a sudden a dreadful, noisy storm struck. The residents knew the shadows were going to be seen among the flashes of lightning outside in the pouring rain and hailstones. Who would be gone this time after the storm left its mark? Deadly, diabolical, vicious creatures loved the dark, wet weather to feast on human flesh.

Ghoul and werewolf creatures struck when their need was at its greatest until the hunger produced an attack and ended when it was satisfied. These same fearless beings snuck out of the Milky Way Galaxy, using the diversion of a severe storm hitting Marcasite with full force. No forewarning was given to the residents about the imminent, heavy, crushing blow coming along. Hideous, grotesque, brutal creatures crept in the storm creating panic and total distress among the whole population. Murky-like shadows appeared amid the flashes of lightning in the dark. People swore it was those atrocious, malevolent, barbaric creatures out there being seen. Otherwise, no one actually saw a thing according to any resident of the town. No trace was found and no footprints located in any location due to the heavy rains and the hailstones wiping them out. This made total sense to the local police officials who had no other explanations for what transpired each time.

Again, a storm hammered Marcasite for many hours overnight and into the early hours of the morning. Lightning flashed continuously, peals of thunder roared overhead, rain kept pouring down, and the hailstones slammed into things, and the damage was done. Each storm seemed to be a taunting from the revolting, hideous, monstrous assailants showing who was in complete control. Not one individual person would dispute this fact, especially after so many deaths and disappearances taking place. One and all knew a sick feeding frenzy resulted in somebody or more than one person being gone. Once the storm lifted and the sun rose up above the horizon to give light to the people, then the fear could subside. Only at that time could all the towns' residents be sure their families were safe from harm. Hope existed for all their neighbors to be safe and sound as well after this storm.

Rain still fell long after the sun came up that morning, which dampened the mood for the people throughout Marcasite. They knew out there someone was gone from his or her home or maybe more than just one again. At some point, everyone would read it when the next newspaper came out. Marcasite lacked a local radio and TV station, which meant relying on the *Gazette* for news. No one minded, because the *Gazette* came out four times a week, enough to satisfy the hunger for news and other important matters for residents to read up on. The rumor mill actually ran faster than Teagan and Candy could publish the *Gazette's* next issue. It did not take long ever to find out in small communities for some reason, even though the police usually found out first. Maybe the sight of police cruisers in front of residences gave the news away. The *Gazette* publishers were always filled in once the police knew the facts behind what took place.

Police Chief Harry Rook got the call after getting into his office that morning about another strange disappearance. Zach and Fanny Neil were unable to find their son, Ron, in the house this morning. His parents told police Ron was home that night as he came home on time every night. No noise was heard of anyone walking around or coming or going from the house all night. Then again the thunder probably covered up a lot of noises overnight in the storm. Ghoul and werewolf creatures apparently took only one young soul from his home. Zach and Fanny Neil told police that Ron never had gone outside during the night previously to their knowledge. He was a good teenager with a great outlook and attitude about life. Ron had many friends in the community and at school who he was around most of the time, except when he was home. His parents were asked to call to see if his friends had heard from him this morning. Police were going to go ask some of his closest friends about where he may have gone. Hopefully, he did not end up in the hands of the accursed, harrowing, obnoxious invaders during the incredible storm last night.

Police Chief Harry Rook called Teagan and Candy Welland to let them be aware of what may have happened again overnight. Neither of them seemed to be shocked by the news due to all the strange deaths over the last year alone. The *Gazette's* next issue was due out tomorrow; they informed Harry Rook and the story was going to run as the headline on page one. This became the spot for all the sudden disappearances and confirmed deaths of people at the hands of the ghoul and werewolf creatures. Teagan and Candy hated running stories regarding teenagers who just left their homes without a trace of evidence. Nothing was worse in their minds to any family than seeing this story being told on the front page of the *Gazette*. Both of them had a duty to report all disappearances and strange deaths in the newspaper. The newspaper never released the way the bodies were torn open, ripped apart, mutilated beyond belief, and gnawed upon.

The police combed through a list of all Ron's friends and could not find any sign of him out there. They all said he went home last night, and no one had seen him since. There was no problem as far as they knew of. Ron was a great friend and classmate to all of them not one of them thought otherwise. Police searched inside town limits for him, and nothing showed up. They knew a search of the wooded areas outside of Marcasite along the lone highway to Goreville was required again. Except if the body was just taken away, no trace would ever be found due to past outcomes. Ghoul and werewolf creatures had a habit from time to time of just removing someone from existence to their hiding place for a private feast. Keeping those remains for whatever reason not one able-minded person could accept or understand. Police Chief Harry Rook asked for volunteers to come the next morning to the headquarters to make up teams to go out looking for Ron Neil. His officers called all past team members, asking them to come and maybe recruit a few more to bring along with them.

First thing when the morning police shift started, search teams were set up, each with a leader in charge. Police had made sure vehicles were on standby to take everyone out to the search areas for the day. Everyone had water, food, a radio, and a map to keep in their grid patterns in the dense woods. They also had on ponchos, for the trees would be very wet from the heavy rain left over from the storm. All of them would also be stretched out three feet apart in those woods along the highway. Most people who had participated in past searches were acutely aware of the danger of overlooking things out here. Blood trails could be washed away or covered up by leaves or other under growth, especially following a heavy rain. Going slow was the most important step in trying to find evidence of any thing pointing to where Ron ended up. Ghoul and werewolf creatures never left one footprint or any forensic traces during their murderous rampages or despicable kidnappings in the past. Their victims never seemed to leave any easy trail for the search teams to follow along. Time and perseverance were the only methods in finding any remains, if at all possible.

That first day went by slowly, and the men were getting tired of slogging through wet trees, even though the hope was very strong. Once the day was half over without any sign of any remains, some new members were feeling the pressure of getting closure for the boy's parents if possible. Others who had more experience just told them to never worry, as time was the key if those ghoul and werewolf creatures left the remains out here to be found. Some past searches went on for many days before any conclusion came along not always with good news for the families. An end could be found; only effort and time need tell the outcome for the victims involved.

A lunch break was called at that hour to rest the teams up for the afternoon walk through the dense woods. Spirits were fine among everyone searching that first morning, with the energy level superb, according to the leaders of the individual teams. Search grids were checked on the maps to ensure every inch was covered, which needed to be done earlier in the morning. As the afternoons grids were tougher grounds to cover, with thicker, denser trees and shrubs to pull apart to look into for any signs of human remains, blood trails, and pieces of clothing. These areas had been combed over many times in the past months and over many years due to these ghoul and werewolf creatures. Search leaders knew that keeping up momentum and spirits pumped was the absolute importance out in the wet, green canopy of trees.

After a forty-minute rest teams stretched out and stepped ahead once more with their eyes going from left to right, never knowing yet always hoping to find some sign of remains as soon as possible. Raindrops fell on them from high above as they made their way in those heavy, thick trees. Pushing aside the thick brush to see inside in order to step through it, ever searching for blood trails and clothing, in the back of their minds, they feared a silent attack from an invisible enemy from another dimension amid searching for torn, ripped body parts and other remains. As no attacks had taken place during any searches, however, there was first time for every event to happen. A damp, chilly afternoon made all team members needing a hot coffee break to warm up a bit. Once the coffee arrived everyone helped themselves to steaming cups along with sugar and cream if they wanted. Their midafternoon stop would last for twenty minutes, just enough time to warm the insides with hot coffee. The sun still had not come out so far that day; maybe another rainstorm might be nearing its way along. Under the canopy of thick, green foliage, it was hard to see the sky today up above. The left over rainwater still covered their ponchos, and the cold would soon set in again.

Again the teams set out to watch the forest floor, never losing hope of finding any remains to put an end to the search early. Rain and cold weather would take its toll in a few days if nothing turned up. The storm last night probably washed away any signs due to light rain still falling into the late hours of the afternoon. Sunlight could poke through the cover of the green leaves of the trees here and there at times. So far today, not one ray of sunshine appeared anywhere, just cold, drops of rain dripping on the men looking for Ron Neil's remains. As the hours wore on, the men were wet, tired, and starting to slow down the pace as they crept on to reaching their goal. When the men kept moving forward without interruption, things would be all right by the end of the shift that day. Each pair of eyes was focused on the ground and slightly ahead with each step. Hour after hour, they inched their way straight through the dense forest and brush in front of themselves.

That day seemed to be close to being over when a radio crackled from a team working back toward the others. Ron Neil's remains may have been located about half a mile from the first teams. A relief followed by a surge of sadness gripped the search teams knowing the Neils would never watch their son mature. At least their son could be buried with dignity and the relief of being found. Not one person walked away without some pain over this senseless death. Ghoul and werewolf creatures caused untold grief and pain to satisfy a twisted, perverted sense of killing that no one understood. Twenty-five deaths were attributed to those dreadful, brutal, murderous alien creatures that most people were aware of in Marcasite over the years. The *Gazette* had reported on all these untimely deaths that struck during severe storms from the spring till fall. As well, this past winter being the first one when abhorrent, hellish, calamitous aggressors attacked murdering some and carrying others away to a secret fortress in the Milky Way.

Ron Neil's remains would need to be bagged up and carried out to the coroner's wagon to be taken back to his offices. As usual, there was not much left of the young boy's body in the woods, just signs of it being torn, ripped, and shredded apart as they feasted on him out in the forest. Long, deep gouges could be seen on what bones were left whole or those left in parts from long incisor teeth digging into them. Bits of clothing were found attached to some pieces of the body parts, which was hard to take for people doing this work. Individuals needed a strong stomach while picking up body remnants after ghoul and werewolf creatures got through with them. Work of this nature would take hours in order to ensure nothing was overlooked or left behind. The Neils should have every piece of what was left of their son to bury. Plus, the coroner needed to do his examination to figure out if the cause of death was the same as in all past deaths. From just a simple once-over of the remains, it was obvious to even the untrained eyes that those unholy, dreaded, barbaric alien murderers did it. Dr. Gabe Bridger had seen his share of mutilation since he came to this town to be the coroner.

Police Chief Harry Rook received the call about the location of what remained of Ron Neil late that afternoon.

He was not really shocked due to so many unexpected deaths and disappearances in Marcasite over the years. Harry Rook felt very sad for his parents losing their only child to some horrible creatures from another dimension. Harry took a couple of his top officers with him to tell Zach and Fanny about finding their son. He still had some trouble carrying out the part of notifying parents and family members after the remains were located. In some instances, no bodies were ever recovered due to these ghoul and werewolf creatures taking them away to a secret hiding spot. The drive over to the Neils' residence only took about ten minutes at that time of day in Marcasite.

Harry and his top two officers accompanied him to the door of the house when Harry knocked on it. Zach Neil opened the door, and he immediately knew the reason for him coming over. He asked them all to come in and sit in the front room while he got his wife, Fanny. When they entered the room, both burst into tears because they knew their son was dead. Harry Rook still had to inform them their son did die from being killed by the same creatures who haunted Marcasite for many centuries already. Harry did not go into detail, except saying the coroner would release his remains when his examination was complete in a couple of days. In the meantime, they could make funeral arrangements and notify family to attend as well. Anything the family needed or wanted, Harry Rook would assist them in any way possible. Zach and Fanny thanked all three for coming over to let them know and how glad they felt his remains were found so quickly. Zach and Fanny wanted let all the people involved know they appreciated the time and effort from them. Harry and his men would tell the search teams they were glad they found their son's remains that first day. Harry Rook and his two men left the Neils' home and headed back to their police headquarters downtown. Their duties were over for now; the only things left were going through the search team's notes for future related activities out in the dense woods.

The search team leaders were busy putting together the notes of the grid search done by their men out in the dense woods and brush. None of them seemed relieved to any extent, only glad it was over this quickly. These strong men knew that in many other searches, days could pass before any remains were ever found. For some strange reason, no attacks occurred during the search activities out in the forest, probably due to the ghoul and werewolf creatures wanting them to locate what was left of different bodies. Remains were never put in the same locations, as they changed it up every time. Like a game of hide and go seek for those involved in the searches. Why these locations along this lonesome part of road toward Goreville for a dumping grounds? Too many questions kept rolling through their minds, and no answers came up for them or the police. The heinous, atrocious, unhallowed attackers created fears that became deep set within the minds and souls of the residents. The searchers had to deal with the outcomes of the ones who were taken away by these demented, vicious, disgusting creatures. Being out in the dense woods looking for and finding what remained of the bodies left behind; all the details were included in the reports put together by the team leaders each time, and no one left anything out when they did these papers up, regardless of the desire to not upset those above who read the paper reports later on with the full details.

Zach and Fanny Neil were Methodists and were going to have Reverend Ken Faulkner officiate for their son's service. The Methodist church held just as many parishioners as the Catholic church down the street. The date for the funeral had yet to be finalized as the remains of their son had not been released by the coroner. Dr. Gabe Bridger needed to spend another day going over his body parts before releasing them. The local funeral home would be notified to come when he was finished. The Neils thanked him for taking his time and understood the reasons for it. They both read most of the reports in the *Gazette* about the other bodies that were taken. The *Gazette* had an agreement with Police Chief Harry Rook to never divulge the complete details of what the remains looked like when they were recovered. The residents only knew the sanitized versions of the bodies being found.

Marcasite was shaken up once again as the terrible news spread across the town after the *Gazette* had published a story in regards to Ron Neil's disappearance. This coincided with his remains being located in the woods the same day. No one expected that anyone could ever survive from being kidnapped by those grotesque, despicable, odious ghoul and werewolf creatures. Once everyone, young and old, would soon find out that Ron Neil had died, that was going to be hard to swallow, another person ended up gone with no end in sight to these unexplained, sudden and horrible disappearances ending in death. Marcasite, in the thoughts of many, was not the gem of a town they dreamed of when it was being built. Marcasite should have been the jewel on the prairies their parents had planned on; instead, it became feeding grounds for hideous, ghastly, killing creatures. Local legends had been passed down from one generation to the next about severe storms striking while filled with devilish, detestable, horrendous ghoul and werewolf creatures. Nothing seemed to have changed over the centuries here in the southeast corner of Gopher County, except for the town of Marcasite had rose from the dust-filled and desolate prairie lands into a wondrous, beautifully colored place.

Teagan and Candy were informed by Police Chief Harry Rook about the body parts of Ron Neil being found. He told them his parents were already notified and the town now needed to know. No details of his remains were to be released in any future articles in the paper in any issue at the Neils' request. Both Teagan and Candy agreed to keep concerns secret from the public for the family's desires. Funeral arrangements were pending till the coroner was finished his investigation. This could take another day before the body parts would be released to the local funeral home. The rest of the details were going to be sent out by Zach and Fanny Neil once they were finalized.

This gave the *Gazette* owners an extra day to have their next issue ready for publishing and hopefully complete with details of the funeral arrangements. If not, then a special flier could be needed to inform the residents of the details for the service and burial. Teagan and Candy waited patiently for the Neils' call for information about Ron's funeral. Both had learned early on not to be pushy in delicate situations with families regarding deaths or disappearances of loved ones. In other cases, none of the family was around to tell them or the police a single word because they were never found. Bodies just vanished into thin air, taken away to a faraway secret location out among the star studded Milky Way for a private festive ritual with the brethren.

Chapter Thirty-One

The *Gazette* carried stories from the early days when Russell Pagan began reporting on people disappearing during those awful, deadly, severe storms that began occurring from spring right through to the fall. Russell Pagan knew all about the local legends passed down from the First Nations Tribes when the white man came here. They told of how some type of horrendous, abhorrent being from the faraway Milky Way, slipping through a crack and taking their people away. Russell became one of thousands who believed in the legends behind these stories over time.

Not one person had actually seen these atrocious, barbaric, horrid foreign creatures, except maybe in amid the flashes of lightning streaking across the skies above. With the rolling thunder crashing overhead, people knew something was stomping around, looking for a feast of human flesh. As the hailstones pounded, sounding like hundreds of feet stomping on their roofs above, unending rain poured down to soak the ground in low areas, causing slight flooding even then. People found out after the very first such storm someone or more than one disappeared from their homes. Yet they remained refusing to leave this area of Gopher County, determined to build a community for future generations to be proud of and continue to grow it.

Teagan and Candy were proud of continuing the reputation Russell Pagan started so many decades ago in the past. Marcasite residents enjoyed the newspaper and all the great stories it ran four times a week. Good or bad, the coffee shops and restaurants were full of chatter about the strange happenings in Marcasite. Homes and offices became a way of keeping people aware of the events taking place as well. No one seemed to miss out on buying any issue of the *Gazette* when it came out, as everyone knew who had died or went missing, while others were related in some cases. The *Gazette* constantly sold out every issue four times a week as it was published and delivered.

The next issue of the newspaper would inform the residents of the funeral for young Ron Neil. Zach and Fanny Neil needed to finalize the last details for his burial with the funeral home and the Reverend Ken Faulkner at the Methodist church. Teagan and Candy agreed to hold the presses till their call came, no matter how late that evening.

Any funeral was always well attended by most residents due to having experienced the terrible feelings of loss, because the town had grown really close over the years. Way too many times the funerals were for young teenagers who died at the daunting, hellish, brutal beasts' hands. Any of those who were killed was bad enough for the residents to handle, except the younger ones upset everyone. They lost a chance at a full life and the happiness it provided. Ron Neil was another one who would never have the experience at the full opportunities life offered.

Teagan and Candy were still in their office at the *Gazette* at close to ten o'clock that evening when Zach Neil phoned. Teagan took down the details by hand as he received them. Then he doubled checked to ensure he got all the details of it right before hanging up to proceed to get the paper ready. Teagan and Candy set the letters for the presses and ran them through to print out the stories and one sad obituary about Ron Neil. Their son's funeral was going to be held the day after at the Methodist church at ten o'clock in the morning. Everyone was welcome to attend the funeral along with family members.

With the interment of the casket containing Ron Neil's remains taking place in the local Marcasite cemetery just a few blocks from the edge of town. The Catholic church had a cemetery just a couple blocks down from the church itself. Both churches were located about four blocks from the west side of town. The day following tomorrow, another huge crowd would fill the Methodist church to say good-bye to another youth taken before his time.

The *Gazette* came out the following morning, even though Teagan and Candy Welland were up most of the night, preparing the *Gazette*. Distributing the newspaper woke them up as the fresh air livened up their spirits, even though their eyelids felt they were being weighed down with sandbags and the tired lines of missed sleep showed. As the day went along, the couple brightened up until the last copy was sold. Once that had happened, they went home to get some rest before having to get up again. Teagan and Candy were fully intending to go to the funeral the next morning to support the Neils. A lot of the local residents would come out to support Zach and Fanny Neil and their relatives at Ron's funeral. Everyone usually turned out to be there for every family affected by the deaths over the years in town.

Tragic news always spread fast as the residents found out exactly who died, as it was often unknown until the paper came out. Maybe a few close friends or neighbors were aware of who. Still they had kept the information private, which was the need of families in that moment of knowing a loved one was gone from their home with no trace. A sickening feeling came across knowing those ghoul and werewolf creatures had crept in under the cover of a storm, striking so swiftly and without any noise. Who really knew with the tornado winds blowing, the roaring thunder overhead, the pouring rains, and huge hailstones coming down? Silent, deadly, virtually invisible killers entered amid the outer turmoil; no one could have prevented any tragedy from occurring. These had to be indeed the most disgusting details of what and how the ghastly, nefarious, hideous beings operated from spring till late fall every year. Except, this past winter they hid under a blanket of soft, white snowflakes amid the extreme blizzard conditions to take people from their houses.

The morning for young Ron Neil's funeral came, with the sun shining with a lot of warmth and a gorgeous, clear, blue sky above. Everyone arrived at the Methodist church a little early to fill every pew inside with standing room only at the back. A very quiet, somber mood penetrated the people as they sat waiting for the casket to come in. The funeral home arrived, and everyone stood as Reverend Ken Faulkner lead the casket into the church. Once his parents and relatives were seated, then the service would start for their son, Ron.

Reverend Faulkner gave a blessing for Ron Neil's soul in his journey to heaven to be with God and Jesus. The choir sang some hymns, and the congregation followed the words along with them. Zach Neil gave the eulogy for his son, which made everyone smile and sad at the same time. His young son should have been allowed time to grow up and enjoy life, which did not happen. However, Zach told those who came out that Ron would want them to be happy and look after their families. Zach broke down at that point and stopped and returned to his seat. The loss was too great for him, Fanny, and his relatives to go on any longer. Reverend Faulkner knew it was time to say one last prayer for Ron before going to the cemetery. The casket was slowly wheeled out of the Methodist church into the bright sunlight.

After the hearse was loaded with the casket, it started a long, slow procession across the four blocks to the cemetery. Reverend Ken Faulkner provided the solemn graveside service before everyone strolled by the Ron Neil's casket to say a final good-bye, even if they did not really know him. All those present had felt a connection due to either having lost some one or knowing someone who died under the identical circumstances. Afterward, a gathering was being held in the local community center for those who wanted to drop over. In fact, everyone did show up to lend support to Zach and Fanny Neil and the family relatives who came to Marcasite to attend the funeral.

People in Marcasite were very good-hearted people who felt the hurt each time someone was taken away by those ghoul and werewolf creatures. No one knew or understood the reasons why their town was haunted by such vile, dreadful beings. They really needed to reaffirm Marcasite was built to be a gem on the prairies to raise a family, creating complete happiness for all. Past generations planned the town as an oasis in the small hills in the southeast corner of Gopher County. What actually became of this dream seemed to be too crazy to accept any longer. Yet no one suggested leaving Marcasite behind due to the thought of knowing other people would just move in. Leaving others at the hands of those ghoul and werewolf creatures sounded cowardly in reality. In time, an answer just may be found on how to rid themselves of all those evil beings once and for all. How this could come about seemed overpowering, which drove their spirits even more toward this goal.

August was usually one of the best summer months of the year, except it was prone to severe storms. Already one young person died after being taken by those ghoul and werewolf creatures during one storm. After that particular storm struck, the weather had stayed very hot, sunny with little wind or not even any breezes blowing. This was very typical dry conditions for the month of August in Marcasite. Their town was located down in the southeast corner of Gopher County. Could it be that such conditions aided in the horrid, atrocious, abominable raiders' vast knowledge of the next time to strike upon Marcasite? Did they have the ability to sneak around searching for a way to attack as the entire local weather turned bad? Local legend told of these despicable, ungodly creatures coming in through some cracks in the star studded Milky Way during severe storms. Having a perch high above the earthly plane definitely would provide an excellent vantage point to look down from. Marcasite must have been a sight they honed in on since time immortal.

Chapter Thirty-Two

Teagan and Candy Welland were busy working on the next day's issue of the *Gazette* for readers to enjoy. Their offices were hot from the presses working full speed to get it printed on time. The machine had been improved on to put the pages together instead of doing this by hand. This just increased the heat inside the building during the heat of the summer months. Their love of being newspaper reporters always drove them to being the greatest they could be. There were getting to be many more stories and advertising in their newspaper over the years as well. The readers never complained about the quality of the great stories inside or the ads in the paper itself. Teagan and Candy were very proud of the venture that originally was started by Russell Pagan. He was a real-life hero to the two of them, as he brought to life the actions of others through words in the paper. His old box camera snapped pictures he displayed among the many copies of old papers he stored in the office files.

They were carrying on with his tradition, his pride, and his determination he showed during his time as publisher and owner.

The following morning, Teagan and Candy rose early for breakfast before going to gather every printed issue of the *Gazette*, bundling them up, for delivery, then heading out all around town to coffee shops, restaurants and offices. People, as usual, were waiting for them with huge smiles and their hands out with money for a copy of the newspaper. This was a very enjoyable time for the Wellands four times a week in the community, seeing all the smiles and warm greetings waiting for them.

After the paper sold out, Teagan and Candy decided to go out for supper that evening to celebrate just as they used to when they first became owners of the *Gazette*. Both needed a break from the routine of cooking at home, and going out gave them a certain feeling of belonging more than anything else. Seeing friends and some of their good customers from Marcasite who operated the restaurants made these outings worthwhile for this couple. Being kind and friendly was never a bad idea, because both Teagan and Candy had lived in town for many decades now. They knew everyone who lived in town due to all residents buying copies of their paper. Some of the newer residents were unknown to them as in one or two previous deaths. Marcasite was still expanding as more people moved in for work and to raise families.

The evening was warm; a slight breeze blew across from west to east in town. High above, the only things visible were some light clouds scattered against the blue sky. Swimming pools were filled with kids, teens, and parents in those hot spells in the summer. Local parks always filled up around suppertimes, as families desiring to cook out over open fires. Most families probably had barbeques at home; just being in under the cover of the trees gave some relief from the heat. Any break that shaded areas provided was always welcome, especially during extended heat streaks like the one that gripped the area for over ten days now. Most people really wanted rain to come cool off everything before it dried out completely. Fear was apparent, as most were aware the worst storms followed these periods of hot weather, bringing ghoul and werewolf creatures down upon them all across Marcasite with no warning except the storm effects themselves.

Sometime during the night, great cumulus and nimbus clouds rolled in, full of rain, hailstones, lightning, and thunder. The first strike of lightning made the dark of the night come back to life. A loud roar of thunder cracked, waking up the whole town from a deep slumber, letting them know a storm had arrived. Rain poured straight down before the tornado winds picked up, driving it against the windowpanes of the homes. Huge hailstones hit the roofs, sounding like bass drums being struck with fury. Flashes of sheet lightning kept coming and going, as the thunder roared ever more loudly from high above.

If anyone looked outside, they might have seen shadows of ghoul and werewolf creatures running around in that weather. Feasting time was once again in front of them, and fear definitely grew as the noises increased outside. How could any human being try to tell one noise from another inside or outside during this storm? The residents with children may have checked to make sure they were all right in their rooms. Others with no children just hugged each other, hoping the daunting, accursed, unholy creatures would skip by their houses in that scary, stormy night. No one would get any warnings if the ghoul and werewolf creatures decided to visit with them. This was never part of the deal with evil, dreadful beings from the Milky Way ever!

The storm continued for many hours, and as a result, no one really got any more sleep than they had previously. All that ruckus and noise kept going on ever since the first flash of lightning and the loud crack of thunder that followed. These storms seemed to hit the town of Marcasite regularly far back into history. Everyone was scared out of their wits the longer the storm went on into the morning hours. The sun should have been out, yet it was hidden behind black storm clouds still. Rain still fell with no let up, sheet lightning flashed, thunder still rolled overhead, tornado-strength winds continued, and the huge hailstones were pounding everything on the ground. Surely, all those ghoul and werewolf creatures had already taken someone or were still putting their feasting order together out there.

Whatever the reason, people became so afraid of the great blackness from the storm clouds above. Soon, maybe the storm would let up and go away from Marcasite and leave them alone once more.

All residents felt the same way regarding the outcome of this overnight storm hitting them so hard. Late August's heatwave brought terrible weather along with it as suspected by most everyone, except no one thought an extended summer storm was on the agenda at all. Still, someone or more than one person could be gone already or being taken away right know. No one knew why the storm continued for so long into the morning, with no end in sight. The roads could not be used because the rain and hailstones were blinding, just looking out through windows of the houses. They just stayed indoors waiting out the storm, hoping not to be part of the customary ritualistic menu for the dastardly, grotesque, impious invaders that morning.

A couple of hours later, the weather seemed to ease up a bit, as one of the worst of the summer storm passed by Marcasite. Clearly, this would not be a good day for this town again after last night's severe storm. This storm was not expected when the residents went to sleep that night due to the sky being clear. Stars could be seen high above, shining ever so brightly in the dark of space as a backdrop. Everyone just wanted another peaceful evening in Marcasite, which seemed normal during the recent heat wave in August. What they received was the opposite of their dreams during that night. Now all anyone could do was wait to hear who had been taken away amid this storm. Fear had become only too common during these horrible, deadly storms in Marcasite over the years after the ghoul and werewolf creatures made people aware they existed inside the dark of the stormy nights. No one felt safe due to these noxious, unnerving, grisly blitzing creatures going through walls, windows, and doors. How could the residents come to grips with such despicable terrors, never knowing when or if their families or even they may disappear into the scary, eerie, flashes of sheet lightning, roaring thunder, pouring rain, and pounding hailstones? People could be taken away to be torn open, ripped apart, and gnawed upon in the dense woods along the highway to Goreville. Maybe they would just vanish into thin air along with the many hideous, revolting, horrible ghoul and werewolf creatures from the faraway Milky Way.

Hours later, somewhere in Marcasite, a friend, neighbor, or coworker might become aware of a person not being around. After that, the police would know about this tragic event from the terrible storm the night before. Police Chief Harry Rook would inform the mayor before calling the Wellands on the phone. A certain protocol had been set up from the first time such deadly occurrences hit Marcasite. This dated all the way back to when Russell Pagan owned the *Gazette* in the village. Turmoil was not easy to accept as it happened and to whom it took away.

No one was immune to the dreadful effects caused by those horrid, hellish, fiendish creatures. The only way to cause awareness was to have it published for the residents to read. The *Gazette* provided the only tool available for the mayor and the police chief to convey the required information around Marcasite.

Teagan and Candy Welland woke up at the same time as everyone else did when the storm slammed into town. Thunder roared, shaking the houses on their foundations, trying to climb right inside beside whoever lived in each one. Flashes of sheet lightning shot across the sky, with more thunders crashing overhead continuously. Raindrops of the large size came down upon the rooftops, and huge hailstones hit like a hammer hitting an anvil outside. Tornado-force winds tossed everything around amid the storm that night, causing havoc beyond reason. Fear penetrated through the souls of every living human being and all animals big or small. The Wellands felt the knowing of the foreign, marauding, unhallowed creatures being present for their time of feasting in the dark stormy night. They knew a phone call would come that day sometime, as it usually did. If another deadly unexplained disappearance took place, it was their responsibility to report the situation through the *Gazette*.

Today was the day to prepare tomorrow's issue or publication and under these awful, bad trying circumstances may take some extra time. Nothing had to be rushed following those creepy, eerie, frightening nights shaking the population to its core. Teagan and Candy just had to wait for the phone to ring and alert the pair of what took place overnight in town—who disappeared or how many had gone away in silence inside the thundering noise of the storm. For now, the Wellands could only get other stories ready to put in their next issue of the paper. The day crept by as noon came to Marcasite and still no phone call. This should have felt good; instead, it hurt, waiting and knowing that fear would come to life.

Around two in the afternoon, the phone rang at the office of the *Gazette,* and Teagan and Candy found out the horrible news. Chief Rook needed them at his office to find out the rest of the information as it came in. Teagan and Candy headed to police headquarters right away; being punctual was important in these occurrences. Who had disappeared was shrouded in mystery due to Harry Rook not telling them. The seasoned pair of reporters would soon find out exactly who had gone into the dark of the storm. Even after covering so many terrible events of this nature, nothing ever prepared them for the findings. This afternoon was going to be one of the toughest outcomes to face for everyone involved.

A family of four had disappeared from their house sometime during the severe, sudden storm of the night before, Dylan Huston, age thirty-four, Greta Huston, age thirty-three, and their children, Aden Huston, age thirteen, and Kloe Huston, age eight. No evidence of forced entry, not any opened windows or no rain under any windows, all doors were closed, with no dirty shoeprints and no damage of any sort showing. Inside the house, nothing seemed to be disturbed, which became evident as the police walked through it. Room by room, the search yielded no clues at all as to what took place. The only thought was the detestable, grotesque, demonic ghoul and werewolf creatures indeed struck once more under the cover of the storm, the four members of the Hustons gone into the darkness of the severe weather last night.

Teagan and Candy actually were shocked about the whole family of four disappearing into the black stormy night, even though they both were awake all night with the rest of the residents of Marcasite due to loud, roaring thunder, the flashes of lightning across the sky, rain pouring down and huge hailstones hitting like never before. Just knowing that four individuals were gone came as a complete surprise to both. Getting as many facts down in writing was important as the story needed to be factual. No matter how sad and gruesome the disappearances could be, people had to be told. The *Gazette* held a great responsibility in getting the news out to all of Marcasite. Once Teagan and Candy gathered all the best information they could, it was time to go back to their office. The pair of journalists then thanked Police Chief Harry Rook and his men for talking to them and hoped to hear if more information came in. This was going to happen, they were assured by the police chief.

Teagan and Candy quickly set the printing press for running all the stories. The latest breaking news story would run on the top of page one, because people needed to be told. The Hustons were friends and neighbors of many other residents in town. Both of their son and daughter had attended Rabbit Hill Elementary in Marcasite the previous year. Aden was getting ready to turn fourteen in a few weeks. He was looking forward to going to Two Hills Junior High School this fall. Kloe was eight years old and still going to Rabbit Hill Elementary School. Their family's dreadful end would be out in the *Gazette* the next day, except no clue as to where they went appeared in the story. The Wellands could not say why; neither could the police offer any opinion in that area of the investigation. The presses ran for most of the evening to ensure the next newspaper would be out in time for morning. Teagan and Candy were able to go home to have supper and relax for a few hours before returning to check the stack of papers out.

Meanwhile, the police were trying to figure out what happened with the Huston family and where they could be. As the evening wore on, most of the police officers felt they had been down this road before in other disappearances in Marcasite. Police Chief Harry Rook called the coroner, Dr. Gabe Bridger, to see if he would take a look around their house that night. Dr. Bridger said he could do that for him and agreed to meet him there in half an hour. The two agreed to meet then at the Hustons' house to look for stuff that others may have overlooked.

Doctor Bridger had proven abilities in forensics going over fragments of bones, bones themselves, and pieces of bodies left inside clothing. He identified the same deep gouges in samples of bones turned up from all the other searches. Being a coroner was supposed to be a routine type of work, except here in Marcasite it was not. Nothing in his training made him ready to face the types of mutilation and destruction people went through before they died. Ghoul and werewolf creatures really were savage killers from another dimension, as no other explanation existed. Dr. Bridger had done over twenty-some autopsies on remains of bodies since he came to town a number of years ago. Those deaths struck him very hard, especially any involving children and teens. Any ordinary autopsies were just easier to handle in his opinion due to his work ethic, understanding, and responsibility.

Doctor Bridger met with Police Chief Harry Rook and a few of his men at the Hustons' residence. Nothing had been removed or changed since the first officers arrived on the location earlier that afternoon. Chief Rook allowed Doctor Bridger to walk around the entire house for himself giving him free rein. With his trained set of eyes, he might be able to come across a clue to get things moving. If not, then a search of the usual spots inside town needed to be done very soon after. For now, this house was the main crime scene until the end of any search for remains turned up something.

Gabe Bridger took time going over each room, as he was asked to be thorough during this walk about. Initial searches gave him a breath of fresh air in dealing with the results of missing people and, in certain cases, entire families. Nothing held him back in dealing with clues to assist in ending things whether in a positive or negative way. To him, results were what mattered in clearing all cases. An hour and a half later, Doctor Bridger had not even found one single clue as to what took place or where the Hustons went to. Police Chief Rook admitted it was a long shot and thanked Dr. Bridger for his help.

Police officers fanned out across the whole town, looking for certain clues to get this search over quickly, except everyone felt deep inside those ghoul and werewolf creatures struck amid the eerie, noisy, freaky storm last night. After such a prolonged hot spell, something bad was due to enter from any storm surge hitting Marcasite. Another strange deadly disappearance took place with four members of the same family going into the stormy night. Police officers carried the knowledge of the missing with them during every search from beginning to end. No matter what the outcome, all these deaths caused by those ghoul and werewolf creatures could not be prevented. No one had really seen those beings other than as shadows in the flashes of sheet lightning in the crazy, wild storms.

Every cop believed in evil beings that existed in their town since the legends were passed down from one generation to the next. Too many times missing people turned up torn open, ripped apart, and gnawed upon. Other times, missing people never showed up ever again due to just vanishing along with the ghoul and werewolf creatures. Storm surges came to allow the hunters from the Milky Way time to fulfill their needs for a type of carnivore feasts and future private ritual meals. The local cops carried out the initial searches in town due to the immediate need to end it right away.

Later, just before dark, the search was called off to allow every cop to go home and rest up for tomorrow, as search teams might have to be assembled once more to go into the deep dense trees along the highway to Goreville. This area had been the dumping grounds for those depraved, appalling, morbid aggressors for centuries long before any highway existed. The forest was known for being home to creatures feasting on human flesh and leaving small fragments of bones, whole bones, and pieces of bodies in blood-soaked clothing. These were only the ones who came back to their families in parts to be buried. Some people never returned after being taken away amid the horrible, terrible, life-altering storms that struck Marcasite.

Police Chief Harry Rook needed to decide before morning what time to call for volunteers to create four search teams. Four teams covered more ground than two ever did in one single day. One entire family was out somewhere, lying in a spot where these ghoul and werewolf creatures knew about. Harry Rook never had trouble gathering people to go on search missions. Marcasite seemed full of very caring, responsible, community-minded residents willing to help those in terrible times. He knew the number of searchers would be futile in locating the Huston family alive. Past experiences showed how the disgusting, horrid, dreadful ghoul and werewolf creatures either only left parts of bodies behind or no trace of individuals were ever found. Harry had very little sleep, tossing and turning most of the night, fighting with demons from another dimension, knowing full well his decision and timing would be seen by the whole town.

Shortly before dawn, he decided to let his wife sleep and go make some coffee to think a bit more. Caffeine woke him up due to his mind being tired this morning from a pitiful fight against invisible enemies. Harry never won any of those battles during his sleep or when he was awake. How would today be any different in finding four bodies or remains of them? One thing was for sure: he needed to go to his office early to get his top officers together to call for volunteers. Setting them into teams was the senior officers' job, so they were able to cover as much ground quickly and efficiently in the dense wooded area along the highway. Harry decided to make breakfast before going down to the local police headquarters. Time seemed to slip by as he cooked and ate his food before putting on his uniform and leaving his home. Harry would arrive at his office by six o'clock that first morning after the family disappeared.

Harry and his senior officers met in the main boardroom and drew up plans of who to call first till the last name received their request. Also, search grids were planned once phone details were set up with other police officers. Most everyone knew where the search should start along the highway to Goreville. No one really understood why this stretch of road had been the drawing spot for ghoul and werewolf creatures. Ancient tales told how the evil beings came through a crack in the Milky Way. Now the day arrived once more to look for remains of their deadly attacks in the dense, green, wooded places. Tall shrubs, moss, and grass covered the forest floor this made it very slow going. Harry and his top team ensured every nook and cranny of the forested areas would be covered until results were at least left without questions. All of those present also knew some people would never be found alive again, no matter how long the search went on or how many acres of the woods were searched thoroughly every day. Outcomes had to be either all bad or just unknown in some cases families needed to accept this. Harry Rook along with his men started gathering their team members that morning in order to be out just after lunch.

Everyone gathered at one o'clock that afternoon in front of police headquarters to be set up into teams and to get their search-grid maps to cover. Trucks were ready to take them all out to the starting point on the outskirts of town. Here at this place, two teams needed to be dropped off. The other two teams went up another mile up the highway to work back to the first team. One team covered each side of the highway in order to cover as much ground as possible every day. Each team had a leader assigned who coordinated all the search team activities to get maximum results without anyone getting lost. He kept in radio contact every fifteen minutes with his team members. Team leaders called the coffee breaks, lunch breaks, and quitting times once Harry Rook and his top men informed them. When the radios, work gloves, water canteens, and other equipment had been handed out and stored away, the teams could begin.

The afternoon sun shone brightly even in the dense canopy of the treetops among the trees. Team members stretched out three feet apart in the green forest with lots of thick underbrush to walk on. The afternoon sun shone through in some places in the green canopy of the trees above them. Temperatures inside this dense forest were cool, which enabled less water to be drunk up. People walked as their heads were focused downward, with eyes going from left to right. Slowly, teams managed to step ahead looking for any clues on the forest floor, a tree limb, or a shrub branch. No one was in any hurry to get ahead of the game, because they could relate to the fact people disappeared and died, to be found by residents like them who joined search teams with no questions asked when the call came. Right now, everyone needed to remain focused on trying to find clues to end the search today. Daily goals had been a fact in every search that had taken place for missing people from Marcasite.

After about an hour and a half later, a coffee break was called so teams could sit and relax. Their efforts had been good, even though nothing was found yet in the woods this afternoon. Resting for twenty minutes might liven up the spirits more than Harry knew or hoped for. Team members talked in low voices, if they talked at all, maybe just taking in the peaceful quiet of this place, listening to birds chirping among the treetops from their nests, probably having older chicks with them. Once the break was over, it came over the radios for everyone to get ready. Teams seemed to be full of energy and rejuvenated as the search got underway. Their search grid had been half covered in an hour and a half today. Now they had to keep going with the same level of effort walking, looking, and ensuring that nothing was out of place.

Four teams in total walking through the dense woods along the highway to Goreville one more time. How many deaths need occur before those deadly, gruesome, murderous creatures decided to leave Marcasite forever? Close to thirty people had now disappeared due to the ghoul and werewolf creatures attacking their town during some of the worst storms ever. That number was only from the time the young Samuels girls disappeared following a severe summer night storm. Forty-eight team members were out searching for a family of two adults and two young children. Unthinkable tragic events brought these brave men out into the thick trees to hopefully find remains of the Hustons. Thoughts rolled through each member heads about finding the family before another day would be called for. No one wanted to actually face the reality of finding the Hustons torn open, ripped apart, and gnawed bodies lying in the woods. Possibly seeing some bloody body parts inside loose clothing, lying scattered on the ground, made them sick and scared at the same time.

Minutes seemed to pass ever so slowly out in this dense forest of trees searching for the bodies or remains of the Hustons. The summer heat was beginning to get through the canopy of treetops. Sweat began to come over the team members, the more energy it took to keep going forward, looking down, eyes glancing from left to right. Daylight in August will last for another few hours, even though the search would end long before then. The teams needed time to get back to the highway from the trees, shrubs, and where they were. Another ten minutes before the search could be stopped for the rest of the day and people were looking forward to it. These volunteers were worn out, sweaty, and very hot after walking through that mess all afternoon. Finally, Chief Rook called out to stop the search and asked everyone to return to the highway right away. The trucks would be waiting for them to bring them back to Marcasite. He told everyone they did a great job, and he was proud of the effort put in. Harry hoped that everyone would come out tomorrow to assist in the search for the Hustons.

After the volunteers arrived back in town, they took their equipment off and stored it for use tomorrow. Canteens were to be taken home, cleaned, and filled with cold water for tomorrow morning. Team members went home, showered, put on clean clothes, and really looking to relaxing with their families that evening. Supper was a good time to talk, laugh, and appreciate being alive with each other, though no one asked about whether or not the Hustons had been found. Some things were not to be discussed with family especially at mealtimes.

Chapter Thirty-Three

Hopefully, that night would be quiet, and the town could sleep and rest up for another beautiful day tomorrow. August nights usually had slight breezes in them to cool off the air from the heat of the days. Marcasite was not bothered by strange activities for that night as the residents slept. A lot of men had pushed their way through the dense forest searching for the Hustons. Now they were asleep with their families, which is all anyone desired for now. This was a peaceful night for the residents of Marcasite among the low-rising hills of Gopher County. The town was a beautiful gem to live in when life felt good and was, in fact, good. Their gem of a town existed in a sparkling light with the moon shining down upon them.

That night passed along without any sudden awakenings as the sun rose, and within an hour, alarm clocks started to ring across town. Search team members needed to have breakfast and report for duty again. Every one of them made sure they had grabbed the canteens of cold water to bring with them. Each one headed to police headquarters for receiving the search grids for the day. Once the details had been covered, each of the teams headed to their trucks to be taken out along the highway to Goreville. A fast start to the day was necessary to get as much ground covered as possible. It took about fifteen minutes to have the first two teams arrive at their locations to begin, and another ten minutes to drop the second teams off. Today was going to be just as hot as yesterday in the forest, which meant taking things slow. Concentrating on each detail of the areas around them and in front of their eyes, they kept going forward, moving one step at a time, keeping focused on trees, shrubs, and the ground cover for anything amiss. No strange sight would be overlooked due to a possible clue being present. Hour after hour, it crept by with no results so far from any team on the radios. A call for a break came out from Chief Rook, because he knew they required it. Having been involved in many such searches, Harry did seem to be aware of the needs of those who volunteered. He looked after the men very well in fact, which is how he became police chief in town.

After a twenty-minute stop, these teams began the slow walk through the dense trees, thick shrubs, and heavy ground cover. All searchers wanted to find a clue or sight the remains of the missing family. That is why they volunteered to be out here and wanted to just provide peace to their town and the relatives of the Hustons. Being focused and going along at a steady pace aided in finding a blood trail on a leaf, or bit of clothing snagged on a tree limb, or a pointy shrub at least. A forest could hide things for centuries before allowing it to be found by anyone. Search team members knew how valuable locating clues were in locating the remains of missing residents. They also knew that, at times, people were just vanished along with the ghoul and werewolf creatures into the star studded Milky Way.

The morning hours came to an end with no sign or clue of the Hustons anywhere in the woods. Lunch hour was something these volunteers sure needed to refresh their batteries and to think about good things. Just being able to kick back and stop worrying about all those things they have no control over. Their families were alive and well; unlike every family directly affected by death from within a severe summer storm. With this awful past winter being the first recorded deaths of people killed by those ghoul and werewolf creatures. How could they harm innocent people, especially young children? Most of the volunteers were trying to keep occupied with good thoughts, however, it was hard with no results in finding any remains so far, even though the search was only a total of eight hours old. It was a must to be successful to locate all four members of the Huston family. Others looked over the search grid, mapping where they went through this morning, to double check no area was not covered.

Team leaders mingled around with each other till just before lunch hour was over for the day. They all returned to their individual teams to talk with everyone, ensuring spirits were high, knowing the afternoon would be long, sweaty, and tough going inside the trees, thorny shrubs, and ground cover. Team leaders made sure the volunteers had full canteens before starting out again shortly. Plus, all teams received new search grid maps for the afternoon's walkthrough. These searchers had been through this many times, except the new members who joined for the first time. The seasoned veterans took them under their wings to help them along. It was never easy to get used to walking in the dense wooded areas along the highway to Goreville.

Fifteen minutes later, all teams were called to be ready to move out once more into the dense trees, shrubs, and the leafy, twiggy ground cover. Not one of these volunteers had a look of defeat on their faces. An hour break allowed them get the feeling about searching and finding any remains of the four family members of the Hustons back. Search teams spread out in their formations to enter the woods. This would be repeated for many days before the remains of at least two of the Hustons were found in a small clearing. There could be remains of all four scattered around the ground inside that spot.

Team members were pulled back as Dr. Gabe Bridger and police officers picked up and bagged the body parts left on the forest floor. Even Dr. Bridger was not able to say with any certainty there were four bodies lying here. At least he might be able to after taking them back to his office and examining the bodily remains. Dr. Bridger wanted to be right, as always, before saying yes or no in this case. The last seven days were frustrating for all the volunteers and police officers. Dr. Bridger required that all bodily remains be picked up, no matter how small they may be. This could take a few hours as he and the many police officers checked through the trees, thorny shrubs, and the ground cover as this became the most important part of any findings—the recovery of all the remains.

Around four in the afternoon that day, all remains had been picked up and bagged for the coroner to check out, after which they were transported back to the office in town for examination at Dr. Bridger's office. He could not be sure exactly how long it would take to figure that he had bones from the Hustons, or how many of the Hustons were present in his cold morgue. Dry, Gabe Bridger worked late into the evening before leaving for the night and going home. As he drove along the streets, he thought of how many times he examined remains from the victims of the ghoul and werewolf creatures. There was always the sure tell marks of deep gouges in the bones and signs of tearing and ripping on other body parts left behind. Parts of people were left inside clothing at the scenes, just to make searchers sick to their stomachs. The stench itself after seven days, or any amount of time, was unreal and overbearing for anyone. Being a doctor and a coroner, he accepted the stench as part of his work in the morgue. Cutting open bodies was part of his work and he liked to find the cause of death in normal cases. Ghoul and werewolf creatures simply caused death by just tearing open, ripping, pulling bodies apart, and gnawing on them. Dr. Bridger felt a pang of fear due to living alone for most of his life. He drove slowly along till he reached his house and parked his car in the driveway.

Dr. Bridger checked his mail before entering his home that night and, as usual, he did not get any exciting letters. His mind seemed to be on the Hustons and all the others in Marcasite who were taken by those ghoul and werewolf creatures. He was remembering why the town was built, from stories he heard after moving here—everyone wanted a gem of a place to raise a family and have a good place work. Marcasite was supposed to be the gem on the prairie landscape—instead, it turned out to be haunted by those harrowing, brutal, morbid creatures. As the legends told, they came from a crack in the star studded Milky Way during fierce storms from spring till late fall every year. That was, until this winter, as they struck under the white cover of snowstorms.

Gabe Bridger made himself a light supper, followed by a hot cup of tea, still thinking of such terrible deaths befalling the good people of Marcasite. He always woke up early in the morning no matter how late he fell asleep. When those severe storms struck he was wide awake like everyone else in town. His last thoughts were of if he was the next victim for the ghoul and werewolf creatures. It was almost eleven o'clock that evening before he was able to fall asleep.

The town came alive the following morning, just after the bright, warm sun rose over the eastern horizon. Today would be another hot day in the last eight since the last tragic summer storm struck. The *Gazette* would be out in a few hours, full of the information in regards to the Hustons being found. At least the search teams hoped this was the case for all four members of the family. No one survived after being taken away by the ghoul and werewolf creatures during any storm. Most were found, others were never located in the dense woods along the highway to Goreville. Coffee shops in town would soon begin to fill up with customers waiting for the *Gazette* to be delivered. Residents enjoyed reading the many different stories, even the bad news of late. Teagan and Candy Welland were on time every day. In the morning, when the paper came out across town, the stores had their copies delivered when they opened the doors for business. The McDougalls' store had been good at selling copies of the *Gazette* for many years to customers who dropped by from out of town. A couple of small stores that opened up also sold issues of the *Gazette* for Teagan and Candy. Every store like these helped everyone to keep up with latest news available.

Dr. Gabe Bridger was awake and arrived at his office before seven o'clock today in order to get his work started. He knew figuring out what belonged with other parts to try and identify who they had found was going to be tough going, even after doing so many of the same autopsies on other bodies after they were torn open, ripped apart, and gnawed upon. Usually he worked on two bodies, now he needed to work on four, if, in fact, they were here in the morgue with him. Dr. Bridger knew this was going to take a lot of time to assemble these pieces into any type of skeletons. Plus, Police Chief Harry Rook would phone him to get an update if he had one to offer. Teagan and Candy Welland from the *Gazette* needed to be informed about any update when it was available. This could be put into an issue for distribution to the residents of Marcasite and those who lived close by out in Gopher County.

Dr. Bridger was aware a lot of the residents knew the Hustons and wanted to know if all four were found yesterday in those woods. Bridger also wanted to know who was here with him in the morgue. Right now, all he had was bags of remains, which was not unusual in these deaths attributed to those ghoul and werewolf creatures over the years. Yet, he seemed unsure about who lay on his cold morgue tables this morning. He set about trying by opening the first bag and setting the contents out, one piece at a time. Dr. Gabe Bridger had to check the size of each remnant of bone with another, as to the length and diameter. He needed to follow this procedure for every bag of remains that was in the cold freezers reserved for dead bodies in the morgue. His cold freezer drawers were filled with bags of remains found in the woods the day before.

His task seemed insurmountable when he started this morning, however, work had to be done and he was the only coroner in Marcasite. Just maybe, the entire Huston family was in his morgue keeping him company today.

Police Chief Harry Rook phoned Dr. Bridger just before noon to inquire about his initial progress in this case. Dr. Bridger told him that he could not draw any conclusions as to if all the family had been found. In a day or two, he might have more of an idea of who was, or who was not, found yesterday. Dr. Bridger told Chief Rook if he found out before then he would definitely phone him. Dr. Gabe Bridger asked Harry Rook if he could release his finding to Teagan and Candy Welland. Chief Rook told him he would take care of the release in regards to information for the public's consumption. This ended the very short conversation between the two gentlemen for the day.

Anyone who had read the *Gazette* found out that it was possible that bodies found out in the woods might be the Hustons. Nothing concrete was offered in the story, just hope that the search was, in fact, over. Dr. Gabe Bridger was conducting the autopsy to ensure the entire family was located in that small clearing. People talked over the story that day at work, trying to find comfort in the knowledge the Hustons were all found. No would ever refuse to volunteer to go search again if called on. Civic pride and the responsibility of doing the right thing always gave them a push forward, because they knew people would volunteer if anything befell them or their families. Marcasite's residents had always been there for each other with an endless caring attitude. The sick, sad news always struck the residents very hard each time an incident occurred.

Dr. Bridger carried on his excruciating work all day long into the early evening hours the first day. He often got carried away with what he was doing. He lost track of time in the morgue. Still, he did not know how many of the Hustons he had visiting with him on the tables. So far he knew at least two bodies from the bags of remains he had gone through, even if it was parts of two of them. Dr. Bridger decided to call it over for the day and go home for some much needed rest.

He knew he was hungry and would drop by a restaurant, eat supper, then go home and sleep for the night, because he felt mentally worn out today. Tomorrow would bring new challenges to his approach in putting the skeletons together for the Huston family. This weighed heavily on his mind at the moment, due to this being the worst case of death and mutilation he had faced to date. Gabe needed to be ready to answer Chief Rook's questions as well. Teagan and Candy Welland would also need an update, if possible.

Gabe Bridger cleaned up and stored the skeletal remains of the bodies he had in two drawers in the coolers. He cleaned himself up and changed his clothes to get ready to go have supper. A treat was always a welcome respite from the routine of everyday life of being a single coroner. However, he was unable to take his mind away from the task he faced at the morgue. How many of the four family members actually were there in the bags still to go through? Gabe knew he had parts of at least two adults of the family laid out in the drawers so far, but did he have the children as well, inside the bags in the coolers, yet to be uncovered? Dr. Bridger fell asleep still lost in thought over his dilemma at work.

Morning came soon for most people around town in late August, as work still needed to be done every day. Kids and teens were still out of school and could sleep their life away for now. Businesses needed to open on time and have employees show up to run the places. It was another beautiful, sunny morning with a clear, blue sky this morning, which would make the residents happy. The pools would be doing a brisk business, as kids and teens would swarm them once again. Summers were great whenever the weather was awesome in the southeast corner of Gopher County. Times like these reflected Marcasite as the true gem on the prairie landscape. This was the dream for the founders of the small village nearly one hundred years ago. Today, the place had turned into a good-sized town with lots of residents, schools, businesses, and everything they needed.

Gabe Bridger awoke at six o'clock in the morning as always, which was a long habit in his life. He arrived at his office by quarter to seven this morning to get an early start on his recreations in the morgue. Gabe would spend today fitting together the skeletal remains into the best forms possible. Dr. Bridger wanted so much to have all four members of the Huston family laying in the cold drawers inside the morgue. Time was the only way to answer this burning question inside his soul. He did not like putting the damage from the ghoul and werewolf creatures into skeletal forms. Bridger knew some parts of the bodies would never be in the bags of remains. They were devoured whole by the beasts from the faraway Milky Way during their feasts on human flesh. Gabe knew he could only do what was possible, and that was going to be good enough. He got into doing his morning's work right away without wasting any more time thinking about such things.

Dr. Bridger pulled out the drawers where the two adults were laying since yesterday and checked the bones and bone fragments for anything he may have missed. In his mind, he just wanted to be sure that the remains were two adults instead of two young children. He took a few minutes to carry this procedure out before going any further. Then, he got out another bag of remains from a cold storage drawer to go through. He carefully placed it on the third table in the well-lit room. Dr. Bridger carefully opened it up, not wanting to drop any stuff out on the floor.

Once he got going on this bag, he realized that some more of the first two bodies were inside this bag of remains. Again, he had some painstaking work ahead of him, piecing the bones into place. Cleaning the bones and bone fragments off was slow to say the least, but today he felt good doing it. The fleshy remains he placed in other containers for the local funeral home to deal with later. By noon, he knew that Dylan and Greta Huston were indeed among the dead in his room in the basement of the hospital. He also was sure at least the other two members of the family were among the parts in other bags of remains. He just needed more time to go through the other bags of remains left inside the drawers in his cold storage. Maybe by the end of the day he could announce to the police chief and the mayor that the Hustons had been found. This would not take place until he was completely sure that all the remains came from the entire family. This could take another couple of days before the skeletal parts were laid out, identifying four bodies.

Dr. Bridger received a phone call around one o'clock in the afternoon from Police Chief Harry Rook, inquiring about his findings so far. Gabe told him no firm details could be released until further examinations were carried out. The two talked for a few minutes before Chief Rook hung up to allow Dr. Bridger to return to work.

Dr. Bridger kept his slow pace all afternoon, carefully picking his way through each bag of bodily remains. One small piece and one more clue each time as he searched, cleaning the bones and bone fragments off. Bone fragments he cleaned by putting them on screen-like instruments to allow the water to run over them without taking anything else along. Then, he set them out on clean, white cloths to dry while he went back to cleaning the next batch of remains. Hour after hour, until a bag was finished, before he got into placing the parts into a skeletal form. He enjoyed this part of his work, because he was helping out the family, friends, and neighbors of the Hustons. Besides, his work was never boring living in Marcasite—it was just sickening with all the deaths and disappearances.

Teagan and Candy Welland awaited a call in regards to the results from Dr. Bridger, when Harry Rook would call them. For now, they were preparing the next day's issue of the *Gazette* as was their customary work. They had lots of stories in this issue, from remains being found in the dense woods along the highway to Goreville, to other local news —like the fact school would reopen in another week from now. Would this school year be any different than last fall? The Wellands packed as much into each issue, with a lot of punch and snap inside the stories.

The fact that no news came in about the Hustons was no real surprise for the two veteran news correspondents. The next time the *Gazette* came out, there would be time to get the article inside the paper on page one. The residents would want to know, to set the town at ease in their disappearance. Were the entire family dead, or did others just vanish into the depth of the storm? Many more questions were unasked, but answers became the most important thing right now. Teagan and Candy kept focused on preparing the current issue for printing later tonight. Once it was set, then they would run the presses and go home for supper. After supper they would return to the office to check on the process and ensure no snags occurred while they stepped away. A few hours later, everything was done and the printing presses started up to run once again.

Chapter Thirty-Four

Greg Braden was in his room at home, waiting for his mom to call him to help set the table for supper today. He had been out with his friends, and Janice was with him as well. The two young lovers were inseparable nowadays, which seemed to suit both of them. No one minded seeing the pair walking around holding hands or kissing in public anymore. *It was just normal,* he thought as he lay on his bed. The day had been full of cool activities at the local pool in Freedom Park. No one complained about the hot weather; as the water kept them feeling great in the afternoon. Late August temperatures were made for good times for all ages in Marcasite—not a cloud in the clear, blue sky above the entire town.

Greg's mom called him just a few minutes later to come and help her arrange the table for their evening meal. His father would be home from work soon, and the family enjoyed eating the meal together every night. They ate breakfast whenever possible, depending on if Tom Braden had to leave for work earlier than normal. Just then, Greg's dad walked into the house, and he said hello to everyone. He said he could smell supper through the big, open kitchen windows from outside. Helen served the food, and even Greg loved the odors of the food fresh from the oven and the fried steaks. A great meal with fun conversations began as they sat down to eat. In about half an hour, the food was gone, and they all felt full due to Helen being a wonderful cook.

Greg sat and talked with his parents for a few minutes before starting to clear the table with his mother, which did not take very long to clear and put away the other stuff into the fridge. Then Greg went to lie down to allow his stomach to settle a bit because he felt stuffed. He asked his mom and dad to make sure he was up in an hour to go meet Janice and his friends down in Freedom Park. They told him they would ensure he was out the door by then, and the three of them laughed.

Greg lay down and just thought about the Hustons who were taken away and hopefully all had been found. He still felt he was the only person in Marcasite with the knowledge of what these ghoul and werewolf creatures actually looked like. He had never shared this knowledge with his friends due to the fear of being shunned, pointed at, and talked about behind his back. Fear and panic had played a huge part in the beginning when he first saw them in his closet that dark, stormy night. He was still haunted as the ghoul and werewolf creatures came by as they attacked the town during each severe storm. Greg managed to survive these deeply aggravating, tense moments when the ghastly creatures looked him up in his room. He never did figure out why Marcasite was being besieged by the ghastly creatures during the many severe storms. Thinking allowed Greg time to come to grips with the predicament he faced in life. What could be done to make sure they stopped? Greg was not sure about a cure being available. He would have to step out of his cocoon one day should one become possible in the future.

Time seemed to pass fast when his dad yelled for him to get up to go be with his friends down at Freedom Park. Greg was grateful for the sudden break back to reality from his train of thoughts. He rushed out of the house after saying good-bye to his mom and dad on his way.

Dr. Gabe Bridger knew he had the four members of the Huston family in the morgue by his side today. He felt shattered inside, knowing such terrible, disgusting pain was inflicted on these loving people. Gabe knew his work was far from over in this case due to having a few bags of remains to go through yet, just to be sure that all the skeletal forms could be put together for each family member. He was not going to finish the work today, as he had worked enough late hours. Now it was time to go home, get some food, and then sleep the night away. Tomorrow was going to be another hectic time ahead for him to finish the skeletal forms off.

Marcasite was a quiet town tonight as kids and teens played outside until the time came to go home for their bedtimes. The swimming pools and parks were full of people as always on the hot August evenings. A warm breeze blew across the town, helping to dry off those who were at the local pools. The parks allowed Greg, Janice, and their friends space to play games in the evening air. The clear blue sky was what anyone could ask for in the late summer months. Once the sun was going down, everyone headed home to be safe from the ghoul and werewolf creatures should a sudden storm arrive.

Teagan and Candy were getting the printed copies of the *Gazette* ready for delivery in the morning, bundling them up in packs for the stores, the delivery teenagers, and themselves to take around Marcasite. Everyone was waiting for answers in regards to the Hustons being found in the deep woods out along the highway. Was the entire family located that late afternoon two days ago? Who would have just disappeared into the dark, stormy night to never be found again? The *Gazette* had the latest news for the readers who got this issue. People need to be informed of the newest developments in the case, and the *Gazette* never let them down. Teagan and Candy had these many questions and thoughts going through their minds as they wrapped the bundles together this evening. Once this business was done for the night the Wellands' would go home to have some tea. After that, the couple would retire to bed for the night's sleep.

Every resident in town was fast asleep for that entire night of late August, which was good in those bad times. Yes, the whole town would not be awoken from their slumber until the alarm clocks rang in the morning. A hush fell over Marcasite as the slight breeze was the only noise heard. No birds or owls were heard overnight either, which was different due to being in a place where such noises were heard. The southeast corner of Gopher County had no secrets from the night any more. All had been shown over the years in each severe storm, which created terrible events. Tonight was very quiet and solemn in Marcasite as everyone would sleep peacefully.

The sun rose as the alarm clocks started to ring, waking people up in every house across town. It was time to get up and get ready for another day's work in every business in town. The *Gazette* was coming out this morning and people were curious as to what the headlines said. Residents rushed to get to the coffee shops and the stores, or waited for the delivery boys to get their copy of the paper. The news could not be gotten fast enough on the days when the *Gazette* came out since the Hustons had been taken away from their house during the last storm. Speculation ran wild following these disappearances taking place over the years in town. The *Gazette* started arriving on door steps, in coffee shops, and on the store steps early that morning in town. Teagan and Candy knew people were aware of the Hustons possibly being found in the woods a couple of days ago, now they would know for sure. Gossip ran rampant with news whether it was true or not in these cases, when the ghoul and werewolf creatures swarmed the town during the stormy evenings and nights.

Dr. Gabe Bridger woke up feeling refreshed after getting a solid seven hours sleep last night. He needed a hot shower to wake up and get ready to go to work again today on finishing his autopsy on the Huston family's remains. He would have to talk with the mayor and the police chief today some time. Once the final details were taken care of so he could positively identify all four members of the family he would make the needed call. He had lots of work left before he would release the family to the local funeral home for burial. He had breakfast after showering and getting dressed in a business suit for work this morning. Gabe then drove to the hospital to begin his search for more bones and bone fragments in the last bags of remains that were brought into his office a few days before this.

He entered the hospital through the main doors. As always, before he got too far the police chief stopped him in the lobby to chat with him. They continued to his office where the talk carried on for a short period of time. Dr. Bridger could not yet say he had all four members of this family in his morgue. He hoped to say for sure by late this afternoon if he had the time to get his work done with. Harry Rook just wanted to ensure that the four members of the Huston family were, in fact, found. He did not want to have any more upset citizens on his hands. Bridger informed him again that once he knew for sure he would call right away with the findings. The two men parted company ten minutes later, both headed to their respective work places.

Dr. Bridger went into the morgue and put on his white uniform to start preparing the last few bags of remains. He knew today had to be the final one in this horrendous case of mutilation. Gabe then uncovered the two partial skeletons he had pieced together, along with the skeletal remains of two others. He thought that was the probable scenario right now as he looked at them. Next, once he could pull his eyes from the forms in front of him, was to open the remaining bags. A huge start first thing in the morning was not so unusual in this place anymore.

Gabe placed one bag on a clean table covered with new, fresh, white sheets to begin the painstaking work of cleaning bones and bone fragments to place in some sort of order. He did have two other tables ready for skeletal forms, just in case. Nothing was real easy, checking through the pile of mess from the bag dumped upon the one table. After doing so many autopsies on partial body remains, he was somewhat an expert now. This was nothing to be proud of—having the largest death toll in the county. This time he thought more about his reasons for wanting to finish today than any trivial matters.

Just before lunch, he knew that all four bodies of the Hustons were, in fact, lying beside him in the morgue. Shivers ran down his pine at this realization right at that moment, about how cruel life was. The ghoul and werewolf creatures cut down one entire family of four with no doubt about it. Dr. Bridger knew he had to call the police chief right away to inform him of his findings as the result of the autopsies. The bones were all ripped off, torn apart from the bodies, and gnawed upon by long incisor teeth. Deep grooves existed on every bone and bone fragment he had examined this morning. He had only one lone bag of remains to look through still, yet he had conclusive evidence the entire Huston family were all indeed present and accounted for. This stuff was sick in its own right, but being the first one who was aware of the results made him ill. Being the coroner in Marcasite was the reason he took the job years ago, before he became knowledgeable of these types of deaths.

Gabe Bridger would wrap up his autopsies on the remains the next morning, once he had all the parts he was going to have for four bodies. This was not very many to say the least, due to the ghoul and werewolf creatures chewing most of the bodies up. Now Dr. Bridger was able to let the police chief and the mayor know for sure that his work was indeed done. And the Huston family's remains would be released to the local funeral home for the next of kin to have them buried. He actually was looking forward to making the calls today. Finally, he had something to feel good about after so many dark, edgy days suffered by the residents of Marcasite. Dr. Bridger made the calls to release the burden from his own shoulders as well.

Passing the news to the mayor and the police chief felt better than any therapy could possibly do. Both men were pleased by the results from his autopsies on the bags of human remains found in the woods that day. Harold Holden, the mayor, and Harry Rook, the police chief, both praised Dr. Bridger on his excellent work ethic and the awesome final results. Harry said he would pass the news on to Teagan and Candy Welland at the *Gazette* as soon as the conversation stopped. The town would be happy to hear the news in regards to the entire Huston family being found in the woods along the highway to Goreville.

Harry Rook made the call to the *Gazette* owners to inform them of the latest update to run in the next issue. Both of them were relieved to get the news that the four members of the Hustons had been found. They promised to run the full story in tomorrow's paper on the front page. Teagan and Candy knew the whole population was waiting for Dr. Bridger to finish his autopsy, to make sure how many of the Hustons were found. Now the results were in and they were happy that now all four would be peacefully laid to rest at the same time. None of them were taken away to be devoured in some other place and time by the ghoul and werewolf creatures. The *Gazette* was going to be a busy office today and tonight to get the issue out on time. People would be pleasantly surprised by the news once the paper was delivered in the morning.

Teagan and Candy went home for supper while the printing press ran the paper through the machines. Hunger had set in earlier, but the work needed to be finished before a break was taken. Newspaper people lived by getting the news out to the whole town for reading to make money. The *Gazette's* owners were no different in their approach to making a living, except the paper was the best it could possibly be. Russell Pagan started the local paper in the mid-eighteen hundreds, and his traditional ways of publishing and reporting had not really changed since then. The only change was Teagan and Candy bringing in a new printing press, a paper machine, and a folder to assist in getting the paper done up right.

The Wellands went home for their supper break and some hot tea as was the custom for both of them for many years. They never ate huge, complicated meals, as there were only two of them. However, meal times allowed them to be alone away from the noise and the trying times at the office. Just being at home gave Teagan and Candy a lot of peace and quiet every time. Once finished with their supper, they went back to the *Gazette's* office to check up on the newspaper's progress. It would soon be done and finished, and they waited in the main office room. Once the paper had finished the entire run, they shut down the equipment and went home for the night. The pair then could come back and wrap the papers for delivery in the morning. This was the couple's procedure after an evening of running the paper. Tonight was going to be the same way; as sleep was required after a hard day's work on the stories and items in their newspaper.

Marcasite was a good place to live tonight, as the sky was clear, the stars were out, and the moon was crescent-shaped, shining in the sky. Good news for everyone who was out in the parks and in the backyards sky watching. A meteor shower was going to take place that was going to be the best one of the year. No one thought of any ghoul and werewolf creatures hitching rides on the back of the space junk hurtling through space. A peaceful feeling had sunk into Marcasite lately and everyone knew the same thing. Maybe, finally, the past was going to be behind the residents for good. The only idea on the minds of the whole population was the meteorite shower coming soon overhead, after the sun went down under the horizon.

The End

www.ingramcontent.com/pod-product-compliance
Lightning Source LLC
Chambersburg PA
CBHW070740120726
47910CB00001B/131